What people are saying about …

Wat

"I love stories about strong, capable young women—and I love stories set in other countries. Mix in a little time travel and some colorful characters, and Lisa Bergren has stirred up an exciting and memorable tale that teen readers should thoroughly enjoy!"

Melody Carlson, author of the Diary of a Teenage Girl and TrueColors series

"*Waterfall* will whisk you away to the world of medieval Italy and have you wishing for a dashing young prince of your own. A captivating love story, the adventure of seventeen-year-old Gabi will have you eagerly flipping pages and longing for more. This book should be a movie!"

Shannon Primicerio, author of *The Divine Dance, God Called a Girl,* and the TrueLife Bible Studies series

"As the mother of two teens and two preteens, I found *Waterfall* to be a gutsy but clean foray into the young adult genre for Lisa T. Bergren, who handles it with a grace and style all her own. Gabriella Betarrini yanked me out of my time and into a harrowing adventure as she battled knights—and love! I heartily enjoyed Gabriella's travel back into time, and I heartily look forward to *Cascade,* River of Time #2!"

"I loved every minute of this adventure that took me out of our time and into the fourteenth century, and I marveled at how true to life teenage Gabi remained when facing extraordinary circumstances. Under Bergren's guidance, I look forward to time traveling again in the next book of the River of Time series."

Donita K. Paul, best-selling author
of the DragonKeeper Chronicles
and the Chiril Chronicles

"Diving into *Waterfall* reminded me why Lisa T. Bergren is one of my favorite authors. Unfolding adventures, fascinating characters, and exciting plot twists make this a stellar read. I loved it! Highly recommended!"

Tricia Goyer, award-winning author of twenty-five books, including *The Swiss Courier*

"With more sword fights than *The Princess Bride*, more swoon-worthy heroes than Twilight, and adventure and intrigue in abundance, Lisa Tawn Bergren has penned a fabulous story in *Waterfall*."

Rel Mollet, TitleTrakk.com

WATERFALL

WATERFALL

The River of Time Series

LISA T. BERGREN

WATERFALL
Published by David C Cook
4050 Lee Vance View
Colorado Springs, CO 80918 U.S.A.

David C Cook Distribution Canada
55 Woodslee Avenue, Paris, Ontario, Canada N3L 3E5

David C Cook U.K., Kingsway Communications
Eastbourne, East Sussex BN23 6NT, England

LCCN 2010940549
ISBN 978-1-4347-6433-1
eISBN 978-1-4347-0329-3

The author is represented by Steve Laube.

The Team: Don Pape, Traci DePree, Amy Kiechlin,
Sarah Schultz, Caitlyn York, Karen Athen
Cover Design: Gearbox Studios, David Carlson
Cover Image: Photoshoot and iStockphoto, royalty-free

Printed in the United States of America
First Edition 2011

2 3 4 5 6 7 8 9 10

091611

For Liv and Emma:

I love you. Yesterday, today, and tomorrow.

–Mama

Taking a new step,
uttering a new word,
is what people fear most.
–Dostoevsky

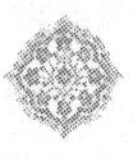

PROLOGUE

We paused on our hike, panting and wiping our upper lips as our guide—the old Italian farmer who owned this land—chopped down a small sapling, clearing the overgrown trail. "*Ecco, vedi,*" he said, pointing at the ground. *See, here.*

"See that?" my mom cried, pushing the tree branch back farther, squatting beside a slightly sculpted limestone paver. Not really expecting a response, she spoke more to herself—or was it Dad's ghost she addressed?—than to us. But the hairs on the back of my neck prickled with echoed excitement.

"Here, too," she said, her blue eyes wide, pointing at another. She followed our guide, tossing her Danish blonde braid over her shoulder, ignoring the brambles scratching at her lean, tanned legs. She never noticed much of anything in such situations. I could fall and break my leg, but it would take a fair amount of screaming for her to turn around and tune in.

My sister, Lia, rolled her blue eyes—so much like Mom's—as if to say, *Oh brother, here we go again.*

We'd seen it before. My mother, Dr. Adri Betarrini, was on the trail of more Etruscans, the mysterious people who predated the Romans in this region of Italy. Most considered her and my dad to be the preeminent Etruscan scholars in the world. When he died, archeologists from around the world showed up to pay their respects at the funeral.

Sighing, I followed my mom up the trail. If we didn't stay right behind her, this crazy path was likely to spring closed, and the woods would swallow her and the guide up like fairies in the forest. Finding these ruins had become like an obsession to her, some crazy connection to my dad.

"C'mon, Lia," I grumbled over my shoulder. My sister liked these hikes less than I did and tended to fall behind, examining a flower or particular branch, always planning another sketch in her mind. If I let her, she'd sit down right where she was and draw, as lost and absorbed as our mother became in a dig.

"Wait up, Gabi."

Frowning at her slow pace, I looked back then forward again. I had a moment of panic as the trees closed in around me. In most parts of Tuscany, the trees were farther apart and older; grand old oaks and pines dominated more space. Here the saplings were young, fighting one another and the underbrush for their place in the sun. But then my mom popped into view, climbing a large boulder behind the goatlike farmer.

We paused beneath them and looked up.

The old man looked back at Mom with a mixture of curiosity and triumph in his eyes. "It is good, no?" he said.

My mother seemed to find her voice. "Good," she said with a cough. "Very good." I could tell by her voice she was really excited but trying to guard her reaction. She knew better than to let her enthusiasm show in the midst of bargaining for land to excavate.

"What is it?" I asked, a bit put out to not be in on the discovery.

"What'd they find, Gabi?" Lia asked.

"I don't know."

Mom wasn't listening to us, so I picked my way through the remaining brush and then climbed the rock.

The old, sturdy farmer reached down to help me, and then my sister, up. My mother was already making her way forward through the bramble. The forest thinned here, and bigger trees dotted a field before us. But I knew that was not what had captured my mom's attention—it was the rounded burial mounds, covered in thousands of years of soil and grass, nearly swallowed forever.

As we battled our way forward, I glimpsed the remains of an old medieval castle on the next hill, undoubtedly the domain of a lost lord of Toscana, now barely more than a few standing walls and the slight curve of one tower.

My mother ignored it. She had eyes only for her guide and these ancient curved *tumuli*—like none we'd seen other than a site south of Roma. He led her to the nearest mound and beckoned me and Lia forward. As we got closer, we could see that the top had been opened, like a wax seal on a clay jar.

Hurriedly, my mother shrugged off her day pack, her eyes shining in the sun. I did the same, studying her intense expression as her long, elegant fingers found her flashlight and she moved out, leaving her backpack open. Clearly, she thought we'd found the elusive colony.

The one Dad had been looking for when he died.

I fished for a bottle of water as she gingerly moved forward. These old tombs were inexplicably strong, given that most of them were over a couple thousand years old. But that didn't mean they weren't just as likely to collapse as stand.

"Gabriella, come help me," Mom said over her shoulder, her eyes focusing on me, really focusing, for the first time. I surged into action, just steps behind her.

Mom crawled up and over the arc of the structure, which was little more than thigh-high, it was so buried, and then reached back to pull the flashlight from her waistband. I took hold of her belt as she leaned over and then into the hole, her head and torso disappearing as she hung halfway into the old tomb.

"Mom," I warned, anxious that it wasn't safe.

"It's okay, Gabs," she called, her voice all muffled and echoing.

I held my breath as her body shifted left, but still, the old tomb held.

"Okay, pull me up!"

We knew as soon as she straightened and we saw her face, but still she announced it. "Fourth century!" she cried, grinning and falling into my arms, reaching out to include Lia. I hadn't felt that much joy from her in months. I didn't want the hug to end.

Fourth century. She meant BC. As in, Before Christ. Seriously old.

She'd found it. The lost city of the Etruscans.

She moved out to take a closer look at the other eleven mounds, and I sat down on a rock beside Lia. Gradually, I felt my smile fade. I looked around and over my shoulder.

I wanted to be happy for her. I did. It was her dream, this. But it also meant that my entire summer was now claimed.

By this place.

The middle of nowhere.

Where the nearest unattached boy appeared to be about seventy years old.

CHAPTER 1

Okay, fast forward. Over the next few weeks, my mom settled in, finding us a lame apartment—probably built in the 1970s, judging by the burnt-orange and avocado decor. It was outside Radda in Chianti, which, trust me, was not a happenin' town, and still a thirty-minute drive down stomach-bending roads and a hike into the archeological site. Did I mention she made me and Lia get up at 5:00 a.m. every morning to come with her? The only good thing about that was that we gladly hit the pillow early each night, and I was able to dream of better places for a teen to spend her summer.

Things progressed on the tumuli "campus," as my mom called it, as expected, with two of the old tombs already largely free of the five feet of soil that once surrounded them, and all trees and brush cut down and pulled away from the remaining tombs. The rest would be unearthed by volunteers trucked in from Roma and Firenze, as well as American university campuses, in the coming weeks. But my mother had been all excited about getting inside these first two—the one the farmer had broken into—"Tomb Two"—and the other, the one she referred to as "the mother ship."

She wouldn't let us near them. Sure, as usual, she was happy enough to hand us a shovel and pail and tell us to get within six inches of the structure. But inside? No. She and my dad had always been like that at a dig. Worried we'd "compromise" a site. You practically needed a doctoral degree to enter, until everything was documented from top to bottom, sketched, photographed, videotaped, logged on paper. Then, a couple weeks later, they'd let "the kids" in.

Basically, I was sick of it. I was seventeen. I felt ignored. Used. Just how much damage could Lia and I do to the place? And I was curious. Had this site really been worth my dad's *life*?

So I was a little bit grumpy when we drove up that morning and tiredly blinked in the pink, early-morning light. The new dirt road was blocked by two uniformed guards and a jeep with the words *Societa Archeologico dell' Italia* emblazoned on the side. Whenever these guys showed up, it inevitably meant delays and trouble for my parents.

A man stepped out of the back of the jeep, wearing khaki slacks and a starched white shirt that was rolled at the sleeves, as well as expensive leather shoes. He looked like the slick, rival archeologist in the first Indiana Jones movie—yeah, my parents loved those old flicks—and my mom reacted the same way Indy had, muttering the man's name like a curse word.

"Manero."

I knew if she could she'd bang her head against the steering wheel. I glanced over at Lia, in the back seat, and raised my brows. We hadn't run across Dr. Manero for more than a year, but the last time…well, it wasn't pretty. Dad almost decked him, he was so mad.

Could Manero shut her down for good this time? The upshot would be we'd have to go home to Boulder—or at least to Roma or Firenze for a time—but Mom would be seriously bummed.

"Doctor Betarrini," Dr. Manero said in a thick Italian accent, as my mom rolled down the window.

"Doctor," Mom returned with a nod, her voice even, polite.

"I've reviewed your documentation in the Commune"—by Commune, he meant Siena—"and discovered you haven't filed forms 201B or D for this dig," he said, crossing his arms.

"Imagine you, digging around in our paperwork," Mom muttered. She still had a habit of referring to projects as *ours,* the result of two decades of working alongside my dad. I wondered how long that would last. I'd kinda miss it when she stopped.

"What was that you said?" Manero asked, leaning down toward her window opening.

"I can't imagine we didn't file the right paperwork," Mom amended. "We filed over fifty documents."

"It seems a common problem for you," he said with a thin-lipped smile. "Always one or two missing, it seems."

"And you appear to have appointed yourself as our personal guard dog," my mom said, losing patience.

"This isn't about you," Manero said, standing erect again. He gestured behind himself. "I guard Italia's treasures. That is my only goal."

My mom looked up at the ceiling of the car as if she wanted to scream.

"Please," Manero said. "I've set up a tent beside your own. Let us discuss what must happen for you to continue your work here."

"You mean, in order for you to horn in on the glory," Mom said.

"Please," Manero repeated. "Let us sit down and discuss this as fellow scholars. I have espresso in a thermos. . . ." He smiled, clearly trying to kiss up.

"Espresso?" my mom said, her tone softening.

"Si." Dr. Manero's slight smile moved across his handsome face. He reached for the door handle and opened it. "Sounds inviting on this chilly morning, does it not?"

Mom ignored his outstretched hand and climbed out on her own, slamming the door. She brushed by him. Dr. Manero hurried to catch up with her.

"C'mon, Lia, let's go see it," I said.

"See what?" she said, frowning as if in a fog.

"The tomb," I said, eyes wide. "We won't get another chance for, what—another month or two? While they debate it, let's go see what the fuss is all about."

Lia paused on the other side of the car, door still open, and frowned at me. "I dunno. . . ."

"C'mon," I said, irritated by her hesitation. What was the risk? If we were going to spend our summer here, we might as well know what the sacrifice was for. I, for one, was going to see it, with her or not.

I trudged past the new guards that had arrived with Manero, pretending like I was following my mom, and after a bit, glanced back to see that Lia was coming after me. I smiled smugly to myself. I could always get her to do anything—especially if she felt like she was getting left behind.

My mind whirled with memories of my parents' hushed, excited conversations, shared in an intimate tone. It had always been an affair of the mind between them, as well as the heart. They'd been connected like no other couple I had ever known.

I'd loved it. And hated it.

Sure. I was glad that my parents loved each other, but we always felt left out. It was like Mom and Dad were always in the same orbit, Lia and me in some constellation around them, never quite intersecting. I wanted to know what it was like, to share the same airspace, even for a moment. And since Dad died…well, it was like Mom wasn't even in our galaxy at all.

So I trudged forward, ignoring the questioning glances of a couple of students heading in the opposite direction. The sun was gaining now, cresting the trees in the east, casting long, dusty streams of light across the field, illuminating the tops of wild lavender, spiraling upward, and the domes of the tumuli.

I ignored my suddenly speeding heartbeat and went directly to the nearest tomb, as if my mother had sent me there on a mission. Lia was right behind. Pausing for a moment at the entrance of the tunnel, I took a deep breath, bent down, and crawled through, glad I had my jeans on. I hoped Mom had left an electric lantern ahead, as she often did on site. In a moment, I bumped into it, and eagerly fumbled for the switch.

I was inside Tomb Two. I swung my legs around as the halogen bulb caught and flickered on, casting blue light all around.

I gaped at the artwork inside. Mom had gone on and on about it, but her voice had become like a buzzing bee, and I'd tuned her out. The colors were magnificent, some of the best we'd seen. Bright. And so many of them.... Men and women, black stick figures depicted feasts, hunts, battles.

I lifted the lantern and cruised along one wall and then another, mouth agape, as my sister came through the tunnel.

"Gabi, we really shouldn't be here," she said, standing there as if she hadn't already made the decision to join me.

"We're here. Aren't you the least bit curious?"

"Yes, but you know how Mom is." She brushed her hands against her jeans. "They—*she* likes to choose when to invite us in."

"So we'll act surprised," I said. "Check it out. If this is Tomb Two, what is Tomb One like?" I raised the lantern so that we could both better see a family dining at a table, a large, roasted bird on a platter before them. "It looks like it's Thanksgiving."

"In China. That's a goose."

"Nah, not big enough. Probably a pheasant. Or a quail."

"If that's a quail, they grew them big, back in Etruscan times."

I smiled. "Okay, a pheasant."

I moved on down the wall as Lia studied images I'd already taken in.

A sound at the tunnel entrance made us both draw in our breath for a moment, but whatever it was moved on, and so did we.

I stared at the portrait of a fierce warrior with sword in hand. Dad and I had sparred from time to time. He'd been trained in the art of fencing and made me learn too. I didn't mind much—it'd been one way we could spend time together. And now that he was gone,

I kinda missed it. But this guy on the wall hefted a much heavier, broader sword than I'd ever picked up.

To the right of the warrior, there was a moon, a sun, and two handprints. "Lia, check this out," I said.

She moved over to me and stared. "Ever seen anything like it?"

I glanced at her, and she shook her head. "Have you?"

"No." I handed her the lantern and then lifted my hand to the print. It seemed familiar, somehow. Like I'd seen it before, even though I knew I hadn't. I heard my sister's sudden intake of breath—Mom would kill me if she found out I was touching anything in here—but it was like I couldn't stop. I was drawn to it.

"Mom will ground you for weeks for touching that," Lia hissed as I put my hand on the fresco again. The oils from our skin and ancient paintings were never to meet; it was a cardinal rule in the Betarrini workplace. I knew this. Lia knew this. But still, I couldn't resist.

"It's a perfect match! Look!" I said, nodding toward the handprint. "And what's weirder…it's warm, Lia. *Warm*."

Her angry blue eyes moved from me to the wall in confusion. Stone wasn't warm. It was never warm.

"Maybe there's a hot spring on the other side."

"Thought of that. But I don't smell any sulfur, do you?" We both took a big whiff of the air. No, just your standard Etruscan tomb—with odors of water evaporated on old stone. "And it's just the handprint that's warm. This handprint that fits mine." I stepped back and looked again to the pair of prints on the wall. The left fit my hand, but the right was smaller—and was the normal-temperature cool stone I'd come to expect in places like this. "Lia, here. Come here." I wrapped my right arm around her so she could edge in closer, directly beside me. "The left print fits my hand, but the right is too small." I glanced from the print to my sister. "You try it."

Lia glanced at me and then toward the tomb entrance, down a long corridor to my right. We were both thinking about our mother arguing with Manero in Italian. I doubted the espresso was helping.

"They're not coming anytime soon. Go on, try it. It's so weird, touching a handprint from someone who's been dead for a couple of thousand years."

I knew before Lia's fingers were settled within the lines that it would fit as surely as the other print had fit mine.

"I thought you said this one was cold," Lia said.

"I did."

"It's—it's warm," she said in wonder.

"Yours too?" I frowned. "Really?" I leaned in and put my hand on the left again. "When I touched it—"

My voice broke off because something odd was happening. The room was spinning, slowly, the paintings on the wall stretching as if I was looking at them through fun-house glasses. And the wall was getting warmer. I tried to pull my hand away, but couldn't.

"Gabi!" Lia cried. I tried to focus on her, the only thing in the room that seemed static. Her wide blue eyes flashed terror. "It's hot!"

I looked up, to the tomb raiders' hole. Up top, I could see trees, which comforted me for a moment, but then I blinked and looked again. Hundred-year-old oaks were shrinking, rising, shrinking, rising like one of those time-lapse cameras…set to record a thousand years.

There was no sound. I couldn't even hear Lia any longer.

My mind raced. Handprints that fit our own. Heat where there should be cold. A room spinning, faster and faster about us. A tomb built three or four hundred years before Christ came to earth. Were we…

I screamed, but it came out as a mere breath, come and gone as if it had never happened. I glanced up again. The trees outside were rising, shrinking, rising, faster than ever before. We had to stop it. Had to pull our hands from the wall. It was so hot my skin felt fused to it, as if it might tear the flesh from my palm if I dared to move. But we had to. Had to!

I looked again into my sister's eyes, silently telling her to get ready, since we couldn't speak. I had to put my foot on the wall and yank, so surely was my hand now one with the print. As I wrenched it away—so hard it was like breaking a powerful magnetic connection—I wrapped both arms around my sister and fell to the ground behind us, like a football player sacking the quarterback. Except backward. But as my shoulder met the travertine floor, I knew I didn't have her, after all. My arms were empty.

It was dark.

I groaned, taking stock, wondering if I'd hit my head. But it felt okay. Even my hand had immediately ceased burning. I blinked in confusion, hoping my vision would clear. "Lia?" I ventured.

As soon as I said it, I knew I was alone. My voice echoed around the chamber with nothing but inanimate objects to absorb the sound. Mom's lantern was long gone. Up top, there was no daylight. Had I passed out? Was it now night?

Mom's gonna be so mad…

But I detected other sounds, odd, muffled sounds, the sounds of men crying out, and alarming sounds like horses, metal clanging, men screaming. Had Manero brought in reinforcements?

"Mom?" I cried. "Lia!"

I had to have hit my head, forgotten. I looked up—willing my eyes to see stars, moonlight, anything—but was met with only darkness.

"Hey!" I yelled upward. "Hey, I'm in here!" All I could think was that the *Societa Archeologico* guys had ordered the tomb resealed, replacing the stone and covering the hole. My mom had lost her temporary jurisdiction over the site and somehow had not noticed that my sister and I were inside—or at least I was—before it was resealed. As for the warm handprint, my sister's disappearance, the time-lapse forest…I had no idea what that was all about.

I had to have fainted or something. Or picked up some weird bug and was running a fever. Maybe, in opening up these tombs, we'd awakened some odd virus. That'd be uncool. I reached up to feel my forehead, fully expecting a raging fever. But it didn't feel like it.

"Don't panic," I said to myself, feeling my heart race. "Gabriella, get a grip." I'd spent far too many years in and out of Etruscan tombs to be creeped out. And I knew where the entrance was. I knew the way out.

I got to my feet and felt my way toward the corridor. "Sorry, Mom," I muttered, knowing that I was now spreading oil from my skin all along the wall. I used my right hand; my shoulder ached from my fall to the ground. I brushed up against a smooth shape and winced as I felt it give way, then crash to the floor. I'd seen the urns on the way in—seventh-century Magna Graecia, Mom said.

Four matched urns, now three, miraculously surviving three centuries before they were put in this tomb. Somehow, the tomb raiders had left them behind. The urns had thrown my mom into an excited frenzy, because she couldn't connect the style of the frescoes with the dating on the urns.

"Oh, she's *really* gonna kill me," I said, heartsick, thinking of the coming wrath of my mom when she discovered what I'd done. Never before had I so damaged a site or artifact, even as a little kid.

But I'd gladly face her fury rather than be stuck in here.

The urn at least helped me know where I was, for sure. At the end of the passageway was the curved stone that marked the entrance. I could see the outline of daylight around it as I neared. Only problem: It was plugged with the entrance stone again. And the entrance stones were heavy, maybe three, four hundred pounds. I knelt and ran my fingers around the edge, considering options for removing it, remembering how my dad would pry them away with a crowbar. But always from the outside.

I leaned my shoulder against it and pushed. My height—and fencing—made me stronger than most girls. But the stone barely moved.

I paused. There were odd sounds coming from the other side. Men shouting, grunting. The clang of metal again as if…I shoved the thought aside. Impossible. And the main thing I had to focus on right now was escape. "Hey! Help! I'm in here! Help!" I shouted, so loudly it made my throat hurt.

I could hear the pause in whatever metalwork was happening. "Mom? Lia! Help! Help me!" I screamed again. But then the sounds resumed.

"Oh, brother," I muttered. I maneuvered in the tunnel until my back and shoulders were against one side, and at an angle, I could press my feet against the stone. I pushed, pushed so hard that my butt lifted from the ground. I grunted, willing that stupid rock to move, to move, move...and then it did, scraping, groaning, then falling away to the dirt outside with a big thump.

My eyes narrowed, and I cautiously peered outward.

There appeared to be some sort of Renaissance faire battle-scene reenactment going on. How'd all these men get here? And why here? Perhaps some protest by the local Sienese, bent on reclaiming this land? Manero's doing? It figured...now that they knew it held the treasures it did.

But then I saw a man block another man's sword strike with his own, then plunge a dagger into him with his other hand. I gasped, too surprised to scream. The injured man fell to his knees, clutching the hilt of the knife, his mouth agape. Blood spread across his white shirt in a slowly seeping circle. No Renaissance faire I'd seen had had special effects like that. With growing horror, I glanced to my right, where another man was writhing on the ground, groaning. My hand came to my mouth. His belly had been split open, and some of his intestines were bulging out. Blood spread across the ground in a wide pool.

It was real.

I was in the middle of a real battle. Suddenly I could smell the stink of sweat and coppery blood, all around me. Men were wounded or dying. Others seemed dead set on bringing the rest to the end of their lives. I glanced left and saw that one wasn't battling any longer; instead, he stared at me as if I were a female Lazarus, emerging from the tomb in my grave clothes.

I wanted to look away from him, but I couldn't. He was the most handsome guy I'd ever seen, with a model's physique and a face to match. Big, chocolate-brown eyes, square jaw, aristocratic nose, pronounced cheekbones...a serious hottie.

I'd never encountered such Italian hotness outside of Roma.

And he was certainly the first man I'd seen holding a real sword and in full-on knight gear—tunic, tights, breastplate, the whole enchilada. Somehow, he made the look work—

It was then that I noticed the young man behind him, equal in height but a little narrower at the shoulders. His eyes were hard, shifting from me to the man before him. He raised his sword as if to strike. "Look out!" I screamed.

The first man frowned and then, as if remembering where he was, turned, pulling his heavy sword from the ground and heaving it in an arc around to parry the other man's strike. My mind immediately moved from the silly explanation I had come to—that this was some sort of Renaissance faire battle reenactment—to again attempt to absorb the truth.

These men were fighting to the death. Why? Just what was going on?

The question died in my mind as I caught sight of that castle in the distance, the one on the next hill that had been such a disaster when I'd first sighted it. It was no longer in ruins. The walls were erect, the tower intact. Crimson red flags waved from the battlements, in designs that matched the second knight's coat of arms, visible on his shield as he raised it to deflect the first knight's repeated blows.

My eyes went back to the castle. It was as if I'd traveled back in time. Impossible. I was dreaming. I had to wake up.

Wake up, Gabi! Wake up!

I pinched myself and shook my head, slapped my cheeks, but the two small armies were still before me and that castle hadn't changed a bit. Those two guys—princes from the castle or what?—fighting for what reason? My hand went to my head as I struggled to remember what little I knew of medieval history. We'd covered a bit last year in school, and my parents had always tried to plant kernels in our minds, hoping they'd somehow grow up into some harvest of historical knowledge, but what I really knew was Etruscan history, culture. Anything in the last couple of thousand years was still pretty fuzzy in my head.

The crimson knight whistled and shouted at two men nearby, gesturing toward me. The hot knight glanced over his shoulder and frowned, then shouted at his own men.

Suddenly six knights were in a dead run, all heading in my direction. But when they met, they began to fight one another. My heart pounded, and I turned, intending to escape into the forest behind me. But there was another knight—by the color of his tunic I could tell he was from the scarlet-flagged castle—steadily approaching me. He must have sneaked around the tomb, intending to surprise me. He rose from his crouch and smiled, as if this were some game, capturing me. I could hear the fighting continue behind me, a shout, a cry, as if another had been wounded.

The knight was coming closer. I retreated until my back hit up against the curved wall. I fought for an idea, an escape route out of this terrible nightmare. Madly, I thought about dashing back into the tomb, but he'd be on me in a second.

This was no dream; my attacker was real, leering, scanning my body as if he had never seen a girl in pants. I paused. Maybe he hadn't. Suddenly I was aware of my skinny jeans and my cami top, barely covered by a thin cardigan that reached my elbows.

He laughed, lowly, and was now close enough for me to see he had green eyes. And really bad teeth. He lifted his sword tip, studying me as it reached my throat. There was no rounded nub, as with the fencing swords my father and I used. This was broad and so sharp I feared he would actually cut me. I stayed as still as possible. But it was hard. I was shaking pretty badly.

He asked me something in Italian, but in a dialect that made me pause for a moment. Slowly, my mind translated. "Are you a witch?"

"A…a witch?" I returned in Italian, frowning.

"A witch," he repeated. "I saw you. Saw you come out of there. And your clothing…" He moved forward, changing the sword from tip to side at my throat in order to keep me in place, and allow him closer. He reached a hand up to my hair. "Your hair. No one allows their womenfolk to parade around as such. Are you a witch or are you a Norman?" He spit out *Norman* as if it were a foul word, referring to the French to the north.

"I am no witch. I am from—" I clamped my lips shut. He wouldn't believe me if I told him. "Look, you big jerk," I said in English, finding strength in my frustration. "You don't *want* to know where I've come from. It'd freak you out. It's freakin' me out!"

He leaned back, as if surprised by my anger and confused by my odd language. But then he turned, sensing the man stealthily approaching him from behind. I'd tried to distract him—had been moderately successful—but these men were trained soldiers. That was clear enough. He met the knight's heavy strike, barely deflecting it from slicing his head like a melon.

I had to get out of here.

A hand clenched my forearm, and I let out a yelp, but then quickly swallowed it. It was the first knight in gold that I had seen. Even more handsome up close. But his eyes were no longer soft in wonder. They were hard, staring down at me in consternation. "*Venga*," he said gruffly in Italian. *Come*.

I looked across the field and saw the crimson knight, wounded, his arms draped around two of his men. He glared at me and the knight beside me, then shouted. The man, my attacker, immediately broke from the other golden knight and retreated to join his comrades. My protector's knights let him pass, unhindered, other than sending him verbal taunts. The battle was over, for some reason. The others mounted their horses, all draped in scarlet, gave us long looks, and then rode away.

I looked to the men who now surrounded me, staring at me. Suddenly I felt weak-kneed. I was now under the protection—or was I the prisoner?—of the dudes from the gold castle.

"I hope you're the good guys," I muttered.

CHAPTER 2

"Where are you taking me?" I cried in Italian, wrenching my elbow from the young man's firm grasp as we walked away. "And why are you all dressed like someone out of a Shakespearean play?"

The leader turned and eyed me, his handsome face a mass of confusion. "What is Shakespearean?"

What is Shakespearean? Who doesn't know Shakespeare?

"I could ask the same of you," he continued, hands on his hips. "Why are you out in such curious underclothes? Is this how the Normans send out their womenfolk?"

Normans? I glanced over to the two young men behind their leader. They were all in their late teens, early twenties. They'd been in battle—not mock medieval battle, but real, hand-to-hand, I-want-to-kill-you battle. And the dialect of Italian…the same as that emerging from my own mouth…Dante. They—*I*—sounded like Dante's *Divine Comedy*. My parents had made us read and recite portions of *The Inferno* last summer, in Italian. Apparently their efforts paid off, because I could now suddenly *speak* in Dante's dialect, the first unified Italian the country had ever known, but a bit different from the modern version.

I looked to my left, through a gap in the trees that allowed me to see out into the thickly wooded valley. My hand came slowly to my mouth as my eyes scanned the slant of the hills again and again, trying to make sense of it, make sure I knew where I was looking. Because there in the distance, edging out of the trees, were the refined, perfect stones of another massive fortress wall. The tip of a waving golden flag dangled above it, visible one moment, retreating the next. That castle—the one we'd passed every day en route to the site, the one that Lia and I had tramped through one day, bored out of our minds—it had been nothing but a pile of rubble. It looked as if it had just been built, just like the one we could see from the tumuli campus. Impossible. *Impossible!*

I dragged my eyes to meet the young man's. "You don't know Shakespeare. Do you know Dante?"

He laughed, a scoff that didn't even move his handsome features. Such dark, piercing eyes, as if he could see through me. Laced with wide lashes. He had a man's chin, even though he couldn't be much older than me. His voice was low, rumbly, curiously warm despite his cold tone. "Who among the aristocracy has not heard of Dante? My father was privileged to host him in our home shortly before his death."

I tried to swallow but my mouth was dry. Dante had been dead for six—no, seven hundred years.

My captor grabbed my arm again, wrenching me forward.

"What are you going to do with her, Marcello?" asked a man behind me, to my left.

"I do not know."

"How will you explain her to your father?"

"I do not know." The guy named Marcello glanced at me again. "You *are* from Normandy, yes?"

Again, with the Normandy business. The people of the north, sometimes allies, sometimes enemies. It might be dangerous to answer this. But how else to explain my curious arrival? "You have guessed well," I said, pulling back my shoulders, lifting my chin. There was only one way to play this. The superior, don't-mess-with-me route. "I am Lady Gabriella Betarrini. I am in search of my mother, and now, my sister, too."

"Lady Betarrini," Marcello said, his face softening a bit at my false title. "How is it that you have become separated from your kin?"

I paused, my mind fumbling through several believable explanations. "My sister and I came here searching for our mother. She had traveled here on business, but has not responded to our correspondence"—never mind that she couldn't if she tried—"and we feared something terrible had befallen her."

Befallen? When did I ever say *befallen?* Maybe I had some sort of illness that messed with the language part of my brain as well.

He helped me over a fallen tree, and I silently congratulated myself for my fast thinking. This way, if Lia or my mom showed up, we'd have a story. And he might even help me find them. Across a clearing, I spotted eight horses.

"She traveled alone?"

I hesitated. I could tell by his tone that that wouldn't have been very likely in his time. "With an escort, of course."

He frowned. "Her men were trustworthy?"

"Very much so."

The lighter-haired knight, apparently Marcello's right-hand man, gestured for the others to go ahead to their mounts, leaving the three of us alone. I heard Marcello call him Luca.

"And your own men?" Marcello pressed. "What became of them?"

I thought fast. "Disappeared in the night, with all our possessions."

"Your horses, too?" Luca asked.

"Gone," I said. *Like they'd never existed.*

"Blackguards," Marcello said. "If we come across them in Toscana, rest assured they will pay for their crimes."

I nodded, holding back a smile. But he was still on a roll. "What is your mother's name? Perhaps my father and I can assist you in finding her. And you said you've now become separated from your sister?"

I frowned. Where was Lia? She had been there in the tomb with me; had she made it through this time warp too? And if so, why hadn't she been there in the tomb? "We…we became separated. Lost in the woods, I found shelter last night in the tomb. I must've fallen asleep…the sounds of your battle woke me."

"A tomb of the ancients is an odd place to shelter," Luca said, eyes filled with confusion.

"It was dark," I returned. "I didn't know it to be a tomb."

"Good thing you didn't," said Luca, with a mischievous look in his eye. "Or you might not have slept a wink. The ghosts might have kept you company all night." He lifted his eyebrow and grinned.

I wasn't quite sure what to make of the guy. Was he trying to scare me? Or be my friend?

"In any case, these woods are hardly the place for a gentlewoman to be roaming about," Marcello said. "Had you fallen into the hands of our enemies…" He inhaled and looked at me sharply. "The Paratores are hardly kind to strangers."

His voice dropped, and he glanced away as if remembering some other, tragic soul. A shiver ran down my back. He returned his warm, chocolate eyes to me, and, somehow, I gained comfort.

"Forgive me, m'lady. I've forgotten proper introductions. I am Sir Marcello Forelli," he said with a slight bow and gesture of hand.

"Future lord of Castello Forelli," said his friend, gesturing with his chin at the castle with the golden flag.

"Do not listen to Luca," Marcello said, shaking his head. "My elder brother is destined to inherit the title."

We'd caught up to the others. Judging from their faces, the men behind him clearly doubted this statement, but I ignored them. There would be time enough to find out what they meant. For now, my eyes were on Marcello, and he was turning toward his men. "These are my most trusted men. My cousin and captain, Luca Forelli," he said, gesturing toward the sandy-haired one with laugh wrinkles about his eyes. "Giovanni Cantadino," he waved toward a dark-haired, pudgy guy, "and Pietro di Alberto." This last one was the biggest of the bunch, nearly as big as the guy who almost nabbed me back at the tomb.

Marcello paused, put a boot on a large stone, and then let his eyes look me over from head to toe. I struggled not to try to hide myself, as if I were suddenly naked. "We cannot bring her home in such clothes. The servants would talk about it endlessly."

"I could go ahead, borrow a dress from Celeste." Giovanni looked me over too, but his eyes seemed more like those of a tailor, merely sizing me up. Not quite so…warm. "She's about the same across the shoulders, but the skirt's bound to be a bit short. I've never seen a woman so tall."

I clamped my lips shut. I didn't appreciate these four, staring at me like I was a cut of beef from the butcher. I could feel the fourth, behind me.

Luca leaned forward with an impish grin. "If I fetch you a gown, will you do me the honor of supping with me this evening, Lady Betarrini?"

I hesitated, wondering what to do with his attention.

"That's enough, Luca," Marcello barked. Did he sound a little protective? "Such forward talk is the way of the Paratores, not the house of Forelli."

"M'lord," Luca said, immediately bowing his head, his smile fading. It was clear who the alpha male was in this group. But despite the no-nonsense tone, I could tell they all respected him; there wasn't some odd power-hungry thing going on like with the guys at home.

"Please, Giovanni, do as you suggested and borrow a dress from Celeste, suitable of a lady of some station. Tell her I'll order her two more in Siena in the coming week, in return for the favor. We'll wait for you here."

"I shall see it done, m'lord."

Eager to avoid any more of his questions or probing looks, I wandered a bit away from Marcello as he and his men talked of the battle.

Apparently the land where the tumuli sat was disputed, claimed and won repeatedly by the Paratores and then the Forellis again.

Even with several fat oaks between us, I could feel the young Forelli lord's warm, curious gaze. I turned away and stared at the castle in the distance, willing myself to wake from this crazy dream or figure out how in the heck I was going to find my way out and back to my own time.

If it was a dream, perhaps I just had to ride it out. I glanced back at Marcello. Fantasizing about an Italian hottie was far better than my normal dreams. I'd heard that if you dreamed you went to sleep in your dream, you'd immediately awaken. So, I figured I might as well embrace this crazy time-traveling nonsense and hope that when I woke, it would be to reality. In the meantime, maybe Marcello would hold my hand or even kiss me before the day was done and I had to say *ciao, bello—see ya, handsome.*

So that's what I was thinking when I heard Giovanni coming through the woods and returning to the clearing. *Make the most of it, Gabi. It'll be over soon.* Giovanni handed me a dress, folded into a neat square, with some sort of hair net and pins on top in a wooden box that slid open.

"I'll make certain you have the utmost privacy, m'lady," Marcello said, with a gallant bow.

"Thank you," I said, turning away. I moved deeper into the trees, farther away this time, somehow knowing I could take him at his word. I pulled off my light cardigan and jeans, then unfolded the dress. A light underdress fluttered to the ground. I grimaced and shook it out, trying to brush off the needles and leaves that clung to the skirt. But when I did, my hand left a streak of dirt. Sighing, I threw it over my head and looked down. Giovanni had been right. It only reached my lower calf. "That won't do," I muttered, already imagining a castle full of old women shaking their heads at me. I pulled back my shoulders. "It is what it is, Gabi," I said, repeating my dad's favorite phrase when he was trying to cope.

The outer dress was a bit more puzzling. There were five buttons, with loops that wrapped around each of them. I pulled it on, and after folding my top and tucking it under my arm, walked back to the clearing.

Marcello and the men covered their mouths with their hands, their eyes alive with merriment.

"What?" I asked.

"They do not wear such dresses in Normandy?" Marcello asked, not bothering now to hide his grin over straight, white teeth.

"What is wrong?"

"You have it on backward."

"Well, how am I to button it, then?"

He nodded to the trees. "Go back and turn it around. Return, and I'll aid you."

I sighed and did as I was told, returning with it closed behind me in a clenched fist. Although it was not nearly long enough, at least it was big enough around. I turned my back to him, as if I couldn't care less who was going to button me up. But even as his big hands swiftly moved over the buttons, a shiver ran down my neck. *Get a hold of yourself, Gabi.*

"Now your hair," he said, bending to retrieve the box. "Quickly tend to your hair, and we shall be off."

I opened the box and stared at the five pins that appeared to have been carved from ivory. Quickly I pulled my hair together, trying desperately to smooth and then wind it into a coil. I secured it, as best I could, to my scalp. He offered me the wide band of cloth and hairnet, then crumpled it in his hand. "Never mind," he muttered, staring at me like I was the most freakily weird chick he'd ever met.

I had clearly done it wrong. The bulk of my hair was supposed to hang below, at the nape of my neck, and be covered by the net. It was coming back to me, now, engravings and illustrations of women from this era. Not a particularly attractive look, but apparently one I was supposed to have mastered. "Do you think—" I began to say.

"Nay. You look fetching, m'lady." But his words, while complimentary, seemed gruff. I could feel tendrils of my hair already escaping, falling to my temple and neck. "Come," he said, gesturing toward the horses. "Giovanni brought along a mount for you."

We moved over to the tan gelding, and I waited for him to make a stirrup with his hands—the way we did as kids to give another kid a leg up. But instead, he took my waist in his hands and lifted me upward. Now I'm no featherweight, but he didn't grunt and moan at the effort. I would've wondered over that for a moment, reveled in it, gloried in it, but my mind was immediately on another issue at hand—he'd placed me on a sidesaddle. How was I supposed to sit on the thing without falling off?

"Is everything all right, m'lady?" he asked, studying my face.

I nodded, unable to come up with any reasonable excuse. This was an era before carriages. Ladies and peasant women alike would've ridden horses if they wanted to get anywhere. And they were all under the assumption that I'd ridden here to Tuscany from France....

I took hold of the reins with one hand and shifted a little, trying to feel a bit less precarious. "Uh, Lord Forelli."

"Yes?" Marcello said, looking back at me over his shoulder as he mounted.

"I…uh, I am accustomed to my groomsman leading me. Usually he ties my reins to his own mount. Perhaps it is done differently here in Toscana?" I arched a brow, hoping I looked a bit haughty.

"Of course, m'lady," he said, easing his horse over to mine. He took the reins from me, and I took a deeper breath. At least now I had two hands with which to grip the horse's mane and saddle. Perhaps I could make it to the castle.

We moved out, and I was sweating like a pig by the time we reached the gate a half hour later. How on earth did women do this for any sort of distance? At the time, I would've given all my college savings for the freedom to throw one leg over the gelding and get a decent grip.

Two guards looked down over the wall, one with his thumbs hooked in a broad, leather belt studded with metal. "Your spoils of war, m'lord?" he called down.

Marcello smiled and glanced back at me, then upward again. "Enough, Alanzo. Open the gate. The Paratores are at home, attending their wounded."

"As I've heard, m'lord. Well done. Well done! Those dogs will soon rue the day they divided from the house of Forelli and ran to the Fiorentini." He turned without further word, and slowly, the gate cranked open. I could hear the clank of thick metal chains. The door itself was of massive, hand-hewn timbers, bound together with a wide, rusting iron band. I could see the divots of a hammer, as if it had been smoothed by hand on an anvil. Which it had, of course. How long was it going to take to absorb where—or rather *when*—I was? It didn't matter…all I had to do was grab a nap in this dreamscape, and it would all come to an end. But I had to admit I was just a tad too fascinated to leave just yet.

As soon as we entered the clearing in the middle of the three-walled courtyard, people streamed from the inner castle. At the front of the pack was a richly dressed, gray-haired lord and a petite brunette in a glorious dress of deep green, followed closely behind by two girls, whom I assumed were ladies-in-waiting or whatever they were called.

The brunette glanced at me with narrowed eyes but immediately rushed to Marcello's side and reached up to take his hand. "M'lord, I am so relieved to see you return unharmed." She clutched her hand to her breast. *Oh, please,* I thought, *that's a trampy way to get him to pay attention to you.*

Then she said, "When the others returned, one so gravely wounded, I feared the worst. I don't know what I'd do, Marcello, if anything happened to you."

"You shall need to learn how to not fret so over me, m'lady. As you know, a lord's work often entails such danger. Especially in these harrowing times." He dismounted, then reached out a hand to the larger man beyond her. "Father," he said, taking his hand briefly, before returning his attention to the girl.

She looked up at him, dragging her eyelashes upward in such a slow, seductive fashion I almost groaned aloud. "Well then," she said lowly, "I am blessed by God that you are more than gifted with the sword and shield. I shall have to train my heart to trust in your talent."

Didn't he see how she was playing him? Maybe boys back in this time were as idiotic as boys in my own. *If only Lia were here,* I thought. No, it was good she wasn't. We'd be giggling ourselves off our horses.

"And who is this?" the girl said, taking his arm and turning toward me. Closer now, I could see she was about my age, and very pretty. Straight nose, wide, greenish brown eyes, full lips. Marcello's girlfriend, most likely. Behind them, her posse frowned in my direction, but this one was now all sweetness and light, portraying nothing but confidence and hospitality. All an act for Marcello, I was sure. I could see it in her eyes. She didn't want me here.

Luca came over and lifted me down off the saddle as easily as Marcello had placed me in it. Did these guys have a weight room where they worked out or something? I shifted, struggling with the pain in my backside, already a bit saddle sore.

"Father, Lady Rossi," Marcello said, turning to me, "allow me to introduce Lady Gabriella Betarrini of Normandy."

"Lady Betarrini," the girl said, with a princess sort of nod. Had her eyes cooled a bit at the mention of Normandy? Was that going to be a bigger issue for me than the fact that I was from another time altogether? *Problems with your story already, Gabs.*

"Are you on a journey? Mayhap en route to Siena?" Her condescending eyes flicked so quickly from my hair—looking pretty disastrous by this point, by the feel of it—to my short hem, that I was certain no one else had seen it. *This girl's a sly one.*

"Mayhap," I said, picking up on her word for *perhaps*. "I am in search of my mother, whom we have not heard from in some time."

"We?" she asked, looking over my shoulder, as if innocently expecting someone to appear. Man, I was glad women didn't have to play dumb in the twenty-first century. Most of the time, anyway.

Marcello cleared his throat. "She and her sister became separated and lost in the woods. She awakened to find herself in the midst of our battle and was nearly captured by a Paratore knight."

"How frightful," Lady Rossi said, bringing a hand to her throat.

"Quite," I said with a little nod.

"We will, of course," the older man, Lord Forelli, said, "aid you in any way possible to reunite you with your family." His mouth and eye drooped a bit on the left side, as if he had once suffered a stroke. My grandpa had had a stroke when I was little, and I remembered that aftereffect. Lord Forelli's voice and eyes were so kind, I did a double take.

"Thank you," I said. I frowned, embarrassed by my sudden tears. Was it the man's fatherly tone? *Oh, Dad,* I thought, longing for my father.

More had gathered around us by this time. "Poor dear," said a portly, middle-aged woman, whom I took to be a servant. "No doubt you'd like a good bath and a decent meal. You must be famished."

I straightened, shaking off my tears, when my stomach rumbled as if in response to the woman's offer. I'm sure they all heard it. A couple of them turned away, but not before I saw their smiles. Lord Forelli, the servant, Lady Rossi, and Marcello kept straight faces.

"Come then, m'lady," the woman said, turning me around and ushering me across the clearing. "I'll get you settled into a room for the night. All I have at this hour is a bit of bread and wine. But it'll hold you until supper."

"Thank you." I hesitated. Had she said her name?

"My name's Maria Mariani, but most call me Cook here in the castle."

"You cook for all?" I said. There had to have been more than fifty people milling about.

She looked at me strangely for a moment, as if she didn't quite understand me, then quickly regained her expression of deference. "I oversee all aspects of keeping the castle in order, and feeding everyone within its walls, with the help of others. Perhaps it is different in Normandy?"

"At times," I mumbled.

We walked by an open doorway that led to one of the castle's turrets, and I glimpsed a tall, thin man in a long, brown overcoat, staring at me. He said nothing, and Cook ignored him. I did too. But his unblinking eyes gave me the creeps. Thoughts of the Paratore knight asking me if I was a witch returned, and I grimaced at the memory of a research paper I'd written on the Salem Witch Trials. What did they do to supposed witches in the fourteenth century? When did the Inquisition happen? *Yeah, I need to grab that nap and get the heck outta here....*

The round woman led me down a long, narrow, stone hallway, lit by a torch at the end. Even though it was the middle of day, the place was as dark as the inside of an Etruscan tomb. We reached the end of the corridor, and Cook pulled a ring of keys from her waistband and slid one into the lock. "Good for you to have a locking door, m'lady, to protect your valuables." She looked beyond me, as if expecting to see two footmen carrying my trunks, and then seemed to remember herself. "Oh, dear. You've arrived with naught but the clothes on your back?"

"I'm afraid so," I said, "and this is good for little else than traveling. Might you know of a tall lady from whom I might borrow a gown or two?" Their antiquated method of speech was coming easier now, like a language I'd forgotten, but had always known. Like when I'd read a Shakespearean play and have a hard time at first trying to understand it, but then, after a while, I'd be into it and get it.

She studied me, and it was like she was considering a giant. An Amazon. *I know, lady, I know. I'm tall.* "Mayhap," I said, trying to curb my irritation before I lost it, "someone my size up here?" I said, gesturing to my shoulders. "But with a longer skirt? You know, until we find my trunks." *Which will be, like, never.* But she didn't need to know that.

"There's nothing for it," she said briskly. "The tallest lady in court is still a hand shorter than you." She gave me a gentle smile. "You have the stance of a warrior queen, m'lady."

A warrior queen? Well, that was something to cling to. I stood up a little straighter. "Anything you could do to aid me would be most appreciated."

"Of course. At the very least, I'll send a seamstress over and add a length of cloth to the underdress you have on."

Two maids arrived, carrying heavy, sloshing buckets of water. A footman arrived behind them with a curved wooden tub bound together like a wine cask. He set it down, and the maids dumped their water inside, pulling them up, so the water arced gracefully into the basin below. Another arrived with a length of rough cloth—was that what they expected me to use for a towel?—and what appeared to be a cake of soap, and set it on my bed.

For the first time, I glanced around. I was in a corner room, so there were two windows high above, covered with iron grates. They allowed fresh air and light into the room. The walls appeared to be covered in a thick, white plaster. The only decoration was a simple carved crucifix above the narrow bed.

"When you've finished your bath, come back to the courtyard," said Cook, the only one left in the room aside from me. "I'll see you and escort you to the family. But take your leisure, m'lady. Supper's not for hours yet."

"Thank you," I said. I crossed the room and put a hand on the edge of the heavy door.

"It'll be all right, m'lady," she said, looking up at me with compassion in her eyes. She gestured for me to turn and swiftly unhooked the buttons that Marcello had pulled together only a short while ago. "Mayhap it's the Lord's intention that you be here with us."

"Mayhap," I mumbled, turning and forcing a smile to my face. I shut the door, set the latch, and then shed the dress, which was suddenly suffocating me, itchy and raw against my skin. I pulled off my cami and settled into the steaming water. I had to fold my long legs up close to my body, but at least it was deep enough to come almost to my shoulders. I took a breath and sank beneath the surface.

Maybe when I come up, I'll be back. Back at the apartment. Or back on site with Mom and Lia. Maybe this will be over.

As interesting as the new place was, I wasn't eager to stay. I wanted to be home. With people I loved. And who loved me.

I rose up from the water and slowly willed my eyes to open.

But all I saw was the big wooden door that separated me from a world of danger. I glanced over at the cross. "Was Cook right?" I whispered. "Did You summon me here?"

Spending as much time in Italy as I had, I couldn't escape the Man and the cross. He was everywhere. I had a hard time translating the lifeless figure on the cross as a deity capable of such madness. But then, I'd always thought the crucifixion itself was a severe form of insanity. I mean, God becoming man, dying to save man, returning to God resurrected? It was a leap of faith for sure.

But then, I would've never believed that this, me being here, in another time, was possible. If God was crazy enough to die for His people, wasn't it feasible that He was crazy enough to send a girl back in time for some reason? Was I supposed to change the course of history? Save the people? What?

I wasn't the faithful sort, by any means. My family went to church strictly on Christmas and Easter, and my parents treated it as more of a nod to culture and tradition than any personal profession of faith. My gramma had been big into the religion thing, when she was alive. She'd given me and Lia children's Bibles, back when we were little.

I closed my eyes, feeling pretty desperate. *So, Big Guy. If You brought me here, how am I supposed to figure out what You want from me? Are You going to give me a sign? Speak to me from a burning bush or something? Because it's gotta be big, Lord. Big. Clear, like a text. Got that?*

I blinked my eyes open.

No burning bush.

No booming voice or even a still, small voice.

No vibrating cell phone.

Nothing at all, except me, naked in a tub older than my great-great-great-great-grandmother.

CHAPTER 3

The seamstress came and retrieved my underdress, frowning at my jeans and cami but saying nothing. In twenty minutes, she returned, a new six-inch band of lace sewn to the bottom of the underdress. I stared at it a moment, in awe, as it dangled above my feet, which were now properly in slippers of tapestry just big enough to cover my long toes. "This was hand-done, right?"

She looked at me like I'd lost it, and I clamped my mouth shut. *Stupid, Gabi.* This was an age far before machinery intricate enough to generate lace on a loom. They'd only been doing that for, like, a hundred years.

The woman seemed to gather herself. "Let me help you with your hair, m'lady."

Obediently, I sat on the corner of the bed as she wound it into what felt like a pretzel shape at the bottom of my scalp and swept a net over it, fastening it with pins to the small fabric piece just past the crown of my head.

She stood back and gave me a curt nod of satisfaction. "The

lord and other nobles will be gathering shortly in the dining hall. Would you like me to escort you, m'lady?"

"Not yet," I said. "I...um...need a moment."

"Of course, m'lady." She bowed a little and exited, as if half-hating to leave and half-eager to do so. *Crazy woman, she's probably thinking. She's gone bonkers. Lost her marbles.* I paced the floor, suddenly feeling on the border of insanity. *Marbles? Did they have marbles yet? What games did they have?* I again wished I had my phone with me. If I hadn't left it in the car, there might have been some way to call home, even across time. Some weird portal. Or at the very least, games to play on it. *Not that I'd have anywhere to plug it in once it died....*

Over and over I glanced at the small windows high on my wall, well aware when golden clouds gave way to peach skies. It had to be seven or after.

A gentle knock at my door made me jump. "Lady Betarrini?"

Marcello. My hand went to my throat like that silly twit's had. Maybe it wasn't her fault. Maybe this guy inspired weak-kneed reactions in every girl.

"Yes?" I said, forcing confidence into my voice.

"It's time to sup. Won't you join us? I'll escort you."

There was no way out of it. Cook, the seamstress, and now Marcello all seemed bent on my heading to dinner. I moved to the door, flipped the latch, and opened it. He stood there, a slight smile on his full lips, and glanced down at my dress. "They've fixed your gown, I see," he said. "But they can't quite tame your hair, can they?" A gentle, teasing smile touched his lips.

I reached up and felt coils of my hair escaping the seamstress's careful knot. *Curse these curls!* If only I had Lia's silky, long, blonde, straight hair. "Oh," I said in dismay.

"No," he said, looking suddenly remorseful. "I only meant to say…" He clamped his lips shut a moment, then, "It reminds me of how you looked when I found you. A nymph of the woods entrapped in a tomb, just waiting to be set free."

I tried to swallow but found it difficult under his warm, searching gaze. The guy was clearly intrigued. With me? Or just my weird story?

"Shall we?" he asked.

I stared back at him. "Shall we what? Oh. Head to dinner. Supper," I corrected myself in a rush. "The meal. Food." *Shut up, Gabi! Stop!* The less I said, the better.

But he grinned and offered his arm. "Cook's bread didn't stave off your hunger?'

"Nay, not quite," I said, wrapping my hand around the crook of his elbow like some high school dance date.

He smiled, more gently this time, and took my hand from his arm. "Here in Toscana, we proceed in this manner." He put out his right arm, hand somewhat extended, then placed my left atop his forearm and wrist. "This way, we must walk in tandem. It's far more elegant."

"Far more," I said. Seriously. Who had time for such things? I'd have to really watch and try and get a grip on such things before he had to teach me anything else.

We moved down the corridor, and he dropped my hand, softly, at the doorway, then after I came through to the courtyard, offered his arm again. With the long dress, my hair in a net, towers all around, and a couple of guards checking us out, I almost freaked out again, very aware of how far away home really was. But I managed to keep it together. Mostly.

"You are the tallest woman I've met."

"I think I'm going to get that a lot."

"Get that?"

"Hear that."

"Yes, well, I rather like it. It's far easier to hold your arm than Lady Rossi's." He said her name in a mumble, as if realizing too late, that his compliment to me was a dig at his girl.

We entered the Great Hall. There was a long table on a slightly elevated dais at the front of the room where Lord Forelli, Marcello's knights, Lady Rossi, her peeps, that tall, thin man, and a few others were already seated. All the men rose to their feet, looking in my direction. Some sort of old-fashioned chivalry? I could feel the heat of a blush climb my neck and cheeks, as well as the piercing cold of Lady Rossi's stare—along with the stares of girls who surrounded her, despite their genteel smiles. Below them, two tables stretched outward, each easily seating twenty. All the men at these tables also rose and looked my way.

I'd never seen such a dining room, except for at my cousin's wedding, where she insisted on doing the whole nine yards in a sixteenth-century theme. She and her husband had met as actors in an annual Renaissance faire in California. My parents loved it, of course, even though it was the cheesiest of historical honors. My sister and I thought they were whacked, and spent the evening making fun of them from behind our fat turkey drumsticks.

But there I was, living what could only be my cousin's biggest fantasy, as Marcello led me to the front of the room. Fat yellow candles adorned the tables in hand-carved candelabras. On the walls were candleholders with more candles, spaced evenly between massive tapestries like those I'd seen in a Venetian museum, imported from Denmark. Above us, wider candles cast light from a wrought-iron ring hanging from a chain that was wound down from the corner of the room on a winch. Food sat on wide wooden platters—something I heard Luca refer to as a "trencher"—in the middle of each group of six or so. A couple of roasted hens; grilled apples; a bowl of what looked like oatmeal; round, brown loaves of bread. Goblets held red wine, and judging by the boisterous talk behind us, I wondered how long these people had been drinking as they'd waited on my arrival.

Lady Rossi looked up at me sweetly as I took a seat across from her. "Lady Betarrini, I trust you are refreshed?" She glanced left and right, all wide-eyed and innocent. *Innocent as a streetwalker.* "We feared you had taken sick when you did not appear to sup." Her glance moved to Marcello, who was watching the exchange with interest, and held there. *Yeah, right. You mean you hoped I'd gotten sick enough to die. You're not fooling me.* Marcello had left my side and walked around the table, then stood behind his chair.

"I am quite refreshed," I said. "Forgive my tardiness."

Lord Forelli rose and gave me a smile. "Fret not over it, Lady Betarrini. You are here now." The women all remained seated, and so I did too.

Then the older Forelli bowed his head, and the rest did the same. "Lord God," the old man said, "please bless this food. Thank You for Your provision and protection over our men this day. May Your will be forever done. Amen."

"Amen," repeated the men, loud enough to make me jump a little in my seat. I hoped everyone else had their eyes closed and missed it.

She hadn't, of course. Lady Rossi looked down, but her little smile didn't escape me. She shared a little sideways glance with the girl to her right and I focused on my goblet. Nothing but wine to drink. No water. No milk. I'd have to be careful. Mom and Dad had let me taste some before, but I'd never had a whole glass. The last thing I needed was to get wasted and start yammering about modern medicine and space travel.

I took a tentative sip, thinking about the girl across from me. I knew her. I mean, I didn't *know* her–know her, but I *knew* her. She wasn't the overtly mean girl, the pretty cheerleader with the aging cheerleader mom living her youth again through her kid. She was the smarter, more dastardly popular girl who was always nice to your face and ripped you apart in the shadows. She was the one who planned terrible Facebook assassination campaigns, but no one could ever pin them on her. The one who managed to steal your boyfriend before you even realized she was a threat.

It was good that Lia wasn't here. This kind of girl routinely destroyed my naive, artsy, trusting sis. But me? I'd dealt with it, seen it before. Of course, I didn't want to take her on. There was no need. I'd be out of here soon enough. But if she thought she had me figured out, she had another thought coming. "So…Lady Rossi. Please, tell me about yourself. Where did you obtain such a fine, amazing gown?"

Her friend smiled, obviously pleased by my compliments, and I sensed a bit of a thaw, but I didn't get the same vibe from

Miss Fancypants. She answered my question as Marcello carved a slice of chicken for each of us. But while words were emanating from her rosebud lips, her murky brown eyes were fastened on me, considering me, considering her next move. Like chess players. I suddenly had the desire to take her on at a chess table. Knights and queens and horses on a table before me while I was surrounded by real knights and princes and horses. How many people could say that?

But as much as I had to keep an eye on the cat with her claws barely concealed across from me, I was drawn into the banter of Luca and Giovanni to my left, and across from them, Lord Forelli and a sickly looking young man to his left. The young man, whom I guessed to be about twenty, looked at me and gave me a small smile and a nod. Had we been introduced? He seemed so familiar, and yet not. I could have sworn he hadn't been there when I arrived.

Marcello saw the direction I was looking and stood. "Lady Betarrini, may I present my elder brother, the future lord of Castello Forelli, Fortino."

I nodded, not at all certain what the man's title should be.

"Lady Betarrini, welcome," he said tiredly, but there was kindness and warmth in his eyes. He looked remarkably like Marcello, just far more…gaunt.

I felt Lady Rossi and her girls bristle across from me. *Oh, I get it.* They didn't want me to hook up with either of the Forelli boys. If Fortino managed to survive whatever illness he suffered from, that'd rob them of the prize—future lordship of the castello; if he didn't, Marcello was next in line. I hid a smile. If I could figure out how to help Fortino, it would burn them worse than stealing Marcello's heart. Sure, she probably really had feelings for Marcello. Who wouldn't? But she was obviously out for more. And judging from Marcello's reaction to Luca's comment in the woods, he'd rather Fortino returned to health and claimed his rightful position.

That was…if I was staying. I mean, there probably wasn't time for such things. I had my hands full just figuring out the means for getting out of here and back to the tomb. Maybe Lia was there waiting for me. Or maybe she wasn't. Maybe she hadn't made the jump, and was back—or forward, whatever—where she was *supposed* to be, telling Mom that I was somewhere, lost in time. Marcello made other introductions, to Lady Rossi's ladies-in-waiting, the other knights, to Lord Foraboschi, the tall, thin man I'd seen earlier. Gradually, I learned that he was Lady Rossi's father's trusted man, here to escort his charge and watch over her. Was it my imagination, or did the man look at me like I was the worst sort of nuisance?

"Lady Betarrini, tell us of your sister," Lord Forelli said, interrupting my thoughts. "Mayhap one of our knights or ladies has come across her today."

"Your knights were rather occupied, Father," Marcello said. Was there an edge to his voice? I glanced between him, his brother, and his father, trying to figure out the dynamics there.

"Yes, and you saw it through in fine fashion, Marcello," he said, like he really couldn't care less. He turned his droopy eye upon me. "Lady Betarrini, your sister? Describe her for us."

I thought back. She'd been wearing jeans and a leopard-print shirt. Best to steer clear of the clothing.… "She's quite a bit shorter than I and—"

"Thank the heavens," Lady Rossi said, giggling. "How might we clothe two women so tall?"

I sent a fake smile in her direction and went on. "She has long, blonde hair—"

"Blonde?" Marcello repeated, clearly surprised. I'd inherited my father's overtly Italian looks while my sis was all my mom, a Dane. No one would've guessed we were siblings.

"Gold. The color of straw, long and straight. She has blue eyes and is quite pretty."

Luca and Pietro rose. "Permission to go in immediate search of this young maiden, sir," said the first.

The other knights erupted in laughter.

Marcello smiled but then waved them down. "She was not there when we found her sister. You know that as well as I."

"Unless the Paratores somehow spirited her off," said Pietro lowly.

I looked down the table at him, alarm gathering in my chest. He was in his mid-twenties, classically Italian in looks, short, broad, with the deep shadow of an evening beard. He was not joking.

Marcello met my eyes and shook his head slightly. "She was not there. I swear it upon my grave."

I took a deep breath and let it out slowly. She wasn't back at the tomb, I told myself. I didn't leave her behind. There was no doubt in Marcello's mind.

Still, doubt lingered. "Might we…could we go in the morning? To be certain? I mean, we became separated. Mayhap she took another path, and even now, is there, trying to find shelter for the night."

"With castles within view? Why not beg shelter from us or even the Paratores?" Lady Rossi said, her voice ringing with the echo of judgment. "Assuming she knows nothing of them, of course," she quickly amended.

"This is a new land for us, far from home," I said. "We were so lost, we became fearful of trusting anyone."

"Logical," Marcello said, stabbing his chicken with his knife and placing it in his mouth.

I stared at him for a moment and then looked down to my own utensils. Only a knife. *Well, this'll be tricky.... The Pre-Fork Era.*

"Tell us, Lady Betarrini," Lord Forelli said. "Where do your family's loyalties lie here in Toscana?"

Several people nearby leaned in, studying me.

I stared at him, blankly. What was he asking? Images from the battlefield filtered through my mind. This was clearly a loaded question. As in...declare-yourself-wrongly-and-you-will-die kind of loaded. We were in the fourteenth century, a time when Siena was a major power. But so was Florence. I remembered that much after all my summers in and around the two cities.

"Come now, m'lady," the man said. The entire table was silent. Only the men ate. "'Tis a simple question. Where do your loyalties lie? Be you Guelph or Ghibelline?"

"Is this truly necessary?" Marcello interceded for me.

"Indeed," said his father.

Guelph? Ghibelline? Dim recollections of lessons on Tuscan associations—or disassociations—with the Papacy cascaded through my mind. But I could not remember which was which, let alone guess who the Forellis might favor. Time to play the Dumb Girl t all Jane Austen on him. Totally the wrong era, but it was ....

"I confess," I said, fluttering lashes like my counterpart across the table, "I pay no attention to the politics of men."

Lord Forelli lifted his chin, studying me as if he knew I was trying to get out of answering his question. I ignored the heat of Marcello's gaze. Was he buying it? Why did it bother me to think that he did? "But your family, surely they—"

"Enough," Marcello said. "Father, she is our guest."

"A guest we know precious little about. Might she not be as easily a spy for Fiorentini as well as a friend to the Sienese?"

I'm sure my face showed my surprise. They thought I was a spy? And he was trying to trick me…this household had Siena written all over it. In the corner there was a fresco of a she-wolf suckling Remus and Romulus—Siena's legendary symbol.

"I fear my sister is in grave danger," I said delicately, bringing a hand to the base of my throat—*Oh, well done, Gabi!*—"If the Paratores are as dangerous as it seems, if they have fallen to Fiorentini sympathies, I need to redouble my efforts to make certain she hasn't fallen captive to them."

Lady Rossi coughed. Did I imagine that she muttered something about wishing we had *both* gone to the Paratores?

"Lord Forelli, I beg for your aid," I said, setting down my knife, no longer hungry. "Might your men help me search for Evangelia, come morning? I won't be able to sleep, my concern is so great." I was getting seriously good at talking their lingo.

The tall, thin Lord Foraboschi leaned forward, weaving his fingers together and studying me with clever eyes. "What of your mother, Lady Betarrini? Why such care for your sister, when it was your mother the two of you came to our country seeking?"

I hesitated. I thought of Mom, so far away, and tears came easily. "I fear she is lost to me for good," I said, in little more than a whisper. The tears welled so deep that Marcello and Luca half rose from their chairs. What was such action? Guys in my time didn't freak out at the sight of tears.

Lady Rossi wiped her mouth on the tablecloth—something I'd seen them all do—and leaned back, catlike eyes upon me. She was on to me. As was Lord Foraboschi—I could tell by the lines on his forehead. But I was on a roll.

I rose and looked to Lord Forelli. "I beg your pardon, m'lord. I fear the day has taxed me and I must retire." Where did I get such phrasing? It surprised me that it came so easily. I turned in a rush and swept between the two long tables toward the exit, all eyes on me.

"Lady Betarrini," boomed the elder lord, his voice echoing around the chamber.

I paused, collected myself, and then turned to face him. Marcello and Luca still stood, staring after me, but I consciously turned my eyes to Lord Forelli.

"We shall aid you in your quest. Take your rest. Come sunup, our men will set out and report to you come evening. They are most thorough."

"It is as you say," I said, keeping my voice level. "They are most thorough. If they were not, I would not have escaped with my life this day. But I confess that I cannot rest while Lia—Evangelia—is missing. I beg you to allow me to join them in searching for my sister."

The lord's face twisted in astonishment at my request. Then, after a breath, Fortino leaned over and whispered in his father's ear. Lord Forelli straightened and looked hard at me. "I grant you permission, m'lady, even though I believe it foolhardy. Be advised that while Marcello and his men won the day, it was but one battle in a long war with our neighbors. I can promise no rescue if you are captured. Or, indeed, if your sister is already in their foul hands."

"I understand." I bobbed in a quick curtsy, as I'd seen others do. "Thank you, m'lord."

He waved me off, and I turned and fled the room. As I shut the heavy door, I heard conversation erupt around all three tables. It mattered not that they were rife with gossip about me—rife? who said a word like *rife*? What was happening to me?—the important part was that we'd set off tomorrow, in search of Lia. That was, if I didn't wake up from this dream before then. And if I didn't find her, perhaps I could slip back to the tomb and try my hand atop the print.… Maybe it was coincidence that the time shift had only happened when we'd both placed our hands on the prints. Maybe it just had been the right moment, the right time of day.… Maybe Lia hadn't leaped through time at all.

I was nearly across the courtyard when he took my arm and whirled me around. I gasped and then honestly brought my hand to my chest, nearly scared out of my mind. "Marcello. I mean, er, Lord Marcello. What is it? You're hurting me."

He grimaced as if sorry, instantly dropping his hand. "*Sir* is my title. There is no lord here but my father."

But I'd heard the others refer to him as m'lord. It was all very confusing.…

"What do you think you are doing? To enter those woods again is foolhardy. My father does not jest when he speaks of the danger from the Paratores."

"And I relieved him—and you—of any responsibility. I fully comprehend your warning."

I resumed walking, leaving him behind me, but he hurried ahead and faced me, halting me again. He was even more frightfully handsome in the deep shadows, torchlight upon one side of his face. "Mayhap it's different among the Normans. These people, the Paratores"—he spit out the name like it burned his mouth with poison—"are unscrupulous."

"Again, I understand your warning. It is my life, m'lord. Allow me to live it as I see fit."

"But that is just it! I endeavor to aid you in *living* it."

I studied him for a long moment. He ran his hand through his curly hair, hair that was pulled back with a leather band but came loose as my own so often did. Who died and made him my guardian? *Sheesh,* I was all for the chivalrous knight thing, but this was getting to be a bit much....

"Lady Gabriella, we will make far better time without you," he said carefully, dragging his eyes to meet mine.

So it was my lousy sidesaddle technique that made him hesitate. I almost laughed aloud. "I'll fare better tomorrow—"

"Tomorrow?" he asked blankly.

"Yes, tomorrow." I frowned. "As in...the day after tonight?"

"Ahh, we say, 'on the morrow.'"

"On the morrow, then," I amended in irritation. "You will send a maid to awaken me?"

"I cannot promise that," he said with a small shake of his head. It wasn't that he didn't think he could find anyone up to the task, I decided. He intended to use my weariness against me.

"Fine. I will be in the courtyard at sunrise," I said, stepping forward to tap him on the chest. "With or without your aid."

With that, I turned and rushed the remaining steps across the courtyard and through the door. I let it slam behind me, then hurried down the dark corridor, the thick candle at the end now sputtering, melted down, and through the door to my room. I set the latch and slid a bar through two hoops—their form of a dead bolt, I guessed.

It was then that I looked behind me. A maid had been there, had turned down my bed—little more than a straw mattress with woolen blankets—and lit a candle. I was grateful. This room would've been really lonely and more than a little scary without it.

I hurried over to the bed and climbed in, pulling the covers up to my chin and staring at the flickering candle that waved in the slight breeze coming through my tiny, high windows. There was no pillow, so I bunched together a portion of the blanket and laid my head down on it, still staring at the golden flame glowing in bright blue at its center.

I wanted to forget Marcello's lingering gaze, the dagger glances of Lady Rossi, and the curious looks of everyone else. I wanted to be home. Now.

I glanced up to the crucifix above me, then back to the flame. "I know I've never been a praying sort of person, God," I whispered. "But I'm hoping You can hear me, lost in this time warp. Please, please, please take me home. Let me wake up in the apartment, with the avocado-green carpet and seventies fridge. Let me hear Lia talking in her sleep. Let me find Mom making eggs at the stove, demanding that I eat just a bite. That's all I want, Lord. To be home. Take me home."

I hesitated. "Not home home," I clarified, hoping He didn't misunderstand me and think *heaven*. "I mean home." I sighed. "You know what I mean. Right?"

I sighed again, suddenly bone weary. And with that, somehow, when I thought it was going to be impossible, I was asleep.

CHAPTER 4

I was dreaming that I lived on a farm. It was not yet light, but the animals were stirring. A rooster heralded the morning for the third time, and my heart skipped a beat. It all came rushing back. I hoped to open my eyes to my own day—literally. Had it happened? Had it all been a terrible, crazy dream?

The rooster crowed again, and yet I couldn't get the gumption to open my eyes. Fingers splayed, I ran my hands across the covers and groaned.

The rough woolen weave of my blankets from last night.

I threw back the blanket and sat up rubbing my face. Slowly, I allowed my eyes to blink open.

I was still there. Or *then*. I was still in the past. Lost in time. I shook my head, hands on my mouth, and looked up at the crucifix, then over to the window, where the sky was stained with the deep purple of dawn. If only it had been my mom who had been taken back in time. She would be delirious with joy. She spent half her days lost in a bygone era anyway—why not lose her entire self into this curious time vortex? Only she would have been whining about not landing in the time of the Etruscans....

Someone knocked at my door, and I jumped, my hands immediately running through my hair. Was it Marcello, here to wake me up for the search? I went to the door and opened it a crack. A maid arrived with a pitcher of water in a basin. "For your morning washing, m'lady," she said, lifting them when she saw my hesitation.

So he isn't as bent on leaving me behind as he pretended.

I opened the door wider. She introduced herself—Giacinta—and set down the basin, lifted the pitcher nestled inside, and poured the cool water for me to wash. Then she went to the hallway and retrieved two dresses, shaking them out and then laying them across the bed. They were gorgeous—elegant gowns, one with seed pearls embroidered into the bodice. "Lord Marcello asked me to bring these to you, as well as these underclothes," she said. "They're a tad outdated for a noblewoman. They once belonged to Lady Forelli. She, too, was uncommonly tall."

Marcello's mother. I paused, wondering if it was wise to ask, then, "If you please, what happened to Lady Forelli?"

Giacinta groaned and shook her head. "Ach, she died of the fevers three, no, four years ago now." She made the sign of the cross as if warding off evil spirits in mentioning the dead. "Tragic, really. Lord Forelli has never been the same. Then he suffered his spell a year past...." She stopped, seeming to recognize she was sharing too much.

I let the subject go, then turned to getting ready for the day. Giacinta helped me into my dress and did her best to put up my hair. She stepped back and studied me, cocking her head and then widening her eyes. "Take care, m'lady. You are far more beautiful than Lady Rossi and already you draw Lord Marcello's eye. His intended is a viper."

Like I didn't totally get that. But there was no explaining that I was soon outta here, so, like, no worries and all.... "*Grazie,*" I said instead. Mom always said that a simple *thank you* covered a lot of bases.

Another maid came in, carrying a ceramic plate with a round loaf and small wedge of cheese atop it. "From Cook," Giacinta said. "If you truly intend to join the men today, you need to make haste and break your fast."

It struck me then. Could Marcello be going through the motions, just looking for a way to leave me behind with an excuse? *Hey, I tried....*

I tore the small loaf in half and eagerly bit into it. "Grazie," I mumbled again, mouth half-full of the delicious, yeasty bread. It felt odd having the girl wait on me. She was nearly my age. Lia's age anyway. *Lia*. Maybe we'd find her today, and I wouldn't be alone in this madness. I grabbed the other half of the bread, stuffed the wedge of cheese into it and strode out the door.

"M'lady, it isn't safe, what you are doing," cautioned Giacinta, behind me. But I ignored her. I wasn't about to miss this. The chance to find my sister. Or even find my way out of this nightmare.

The men were filing out of the Great Hall, led by the senior Lord Forelli, whose frown said he clearly disapproved of my presence, even though he had given me permission to join them.

I caught sight of Lady Rossi then, trailing after Marcello, a lady-in-waiting at her side. Apparently she wanted her man to be thinking of her as he left the castle.

She paused when she saw me, then hurried over to me. "Surely you don't truly intend to ride with the men. You shall slow them down."

"And then, so I shall," I said brusquely. It was too early in the morning to think about what the perfect response would be.

"It is not good for a lady's reputation," she said lowly, turning to face me and keeping her voice down. She touched my arm. "To travel alone, with a company of men. I beg of you to take care."

I looked down at her at an angle and tried to don an expression that said I cared, at least a little bit. "Come with us, then, m'lady, if you care to guard my reputation."

Her eyebrows lifted in surprise, and she actually took a partial step away from me, as if I were suddenly hot like a stove burner. "No," the girl sniffed. "I think not. I enjoy a ride now and then. But anything that smells of danger—nay, I shall leave that to my intended."

I smiled and couldn't resist waggling my eyebrows. "Then, that is where you and I are different. I enjoy a bit of adventure. Good day, Lady Rossi."

I strode away from her, barely able to control my grin. If only I had been in jeans, I would've seriously *strutted* away. I tried to do my best, considering I had the gown on and all. It was *so* much easier for guys. Then and now.

I moved across the courtyard, and Marcello caught sight of me, hesitated, then said, "Lady Betarrini, I ask you again…please, remain here today."

I took several steps past him and then looked back over my shoulder. "Where's my mount?"

He shook his head and strode ahead, clearly irritated. But after a few steps, he waved to the groomsmen, and the gelding I had ridden yesterday—could a girl say *yesterday* when it was almost seven centuries in the past?—was brought forward.

Marcello was ready for me; he just had hoped I wouldn't show up. *Yeah, well, you can give up on that idea,* I thought, looking down at him as he lifted me to the cursed sidesaddle. *You haven't ever met a girl like me. In fact, you're never going to meet a girl like me again.*

He stared up at me then, his eyes searching mine as if reading my thoughts, and my heart skipped a beat. I took a deep breath, trying to steady it. *Of all the cursed luck. I finally meet a potential man of my dreams, and he's almost seven hundred years old. Literally.* I lifted my head and gestured forward. "Shall we?"

"Indeed," he said, tucking his chin, ever the gallant one. I glanced over at Lady Rossi, and she looked away, as if she wasn't watching it all play out.

I took the reins more firmly in hand and tried to find the proper seating in the saddle. I felt like I was going to slide out of it at any moment. The gates opened. The six men circled their mounts and headed out, three ahead of me, three behind.

Lia, I thought. *We're coming. Please be okay. Please, please be okay. Please be here. I can't do this alone....*

Two hours later, I pulled off the trail in a small clearing, beside a boulder, and allowed the three men behind me to thunder past. I slid down off the horrible saddle and turned back to the horse. I heard the men shout, come to a halt, and then turn back.

"M'lady," Marcello said, "we mustn't tarry here. This hill is Paratore territory. At the moment."

"Yeah, well, I only need a moment," I muttered. I grabbed hold of the leather strap, unhooked the first buckle, then the second, and slid the saddle from the horse.

"What are you doing?"

"I'm going to show you," I said, heaving the saddle behind the boulder and covering it with a huge, fallen branch, "how we ride in Normandy."

"You can't do that—"

"I'm holding you back, right?" I said, moving toward his horse, my mount's reins still in hand. "Admit it. I'm holding you back."

He returned my glance, and a coil of his gorgeous brown, curly hair flipped down over one brow. His horse danced beneath him. "Yes, you are holding us back. As I told you you would."

"Well, I can fix that," I said, turning away from him. "You'd best look away," I said.

"Why?"

"Because you're going to be totally freaked out by what I'm about to do next," I muttered, slipping back into English.

He didn't turn away. Instead he stared at me intently as if he understood neither my words nor my intentions. Which made sense. Both were from another time, another place.

I tore two strips of cloth from my under skirt and bent to tie my gown into a form of pants, lashing each segment of the gown around my knees. Now, at least, I could ride. Bareback was better than that stupid sidesaddle. As soon as I stood up, I could see the blush on his cheeks. He looked to the side, as if he had come across me naked, or something. I supposed that, given the era, it had about the same effect.

I ignored him and climbed onto the rock and then flung myself across the broad back of my gelding, settling the reins again. I trotted forward and looked at Marcello until he met my gaze. "Now, we can *ride*," I said, unable to hide my smile. Was that a tiny smile on his face? I squeezed the horse's flanks with my heels, and we leaped forward.

I allowed my grin to spread as I passed the other men, their mouths agape. This was how my father had taught me and Lia to ride—without a saddle at all—as he had been taught on a farm in Italia. It felt familiar, comfortable. Like a hug from him.

My hair was already half-unpinned. I reached up and flung the three remaining pins in my hair to the side of the path, holding back a shout of pleasure. *Yeah, you boys have never seen anyone like me. You know it. I know it. Wait until you get a load of my sis.*

After a few minutes I heard the churning sounds of galloping hooves, the squeak of leather, the mechanical breath of a lathered horse, behind me. I bent lower and urged my horse faster, along the winding path, ducking to avoid branches, bracing to jump small obstacles.

"M'lady, stop!" Marcello called.

But I wasn't stopping. I was on my way to find Lia. My sister, possibly lost in the woods overnight—

"Please, m'lady," he said, panting. "I beg of you."

I hesitated. Surely a word like *beg* hardly ever left a man's lips in this day and age. Couldn't I give him a sec? Maybe one of his men had spotted something. A clue. I pulled up on the reins, suddenly realizing I was as winded as my panting horse.

My move apparently surprised Marcello. He passed me and then turned around, pulling to a halt in front of me. His arms crossed casually in front of him, regarding me with new, curious eyes. "So that is how Norman ladies ride?"

"Better than that silly saddle," I said, jutting out my chin.

The other men arrived then, surrounding us, averting their eyes from the edge of my thin bloomer-like thingies and bare calves. "M'lord, we must make haste, back to the border," Luca said, gesturing over his shoulder.

Oh no. I had led them onto the wrong path! I glanced around. If we were on Paratore land, it looked just like the Forellis'. Silly borders and battles. All I wanted was my sister!

"Are we near the tombs?" I pressed. "The Etruscan tombs? Where you found me?"

"They are over there," Marcello said, nodding to his left.

I realized that I was turned around. I would've expected him to gesture behind him and to the right. We'd gone past the tombs and deeper into Paratore land.

"You truly think we shall find Lady Evangelia among the tombs, as we found you?" he asked.

I shrugged. "It's as good a guess as any, right?"

He remained where he was, still staring at me. Oh my gosh, could he be a little less hot? He belonged in some teen-girl magazine. Movies. Book covers. Ads for Abercrombie & Fitch.

"Well, come along then," he said, wheeling his horse around. He moved off down the path, rejoined by two men. I took my original place, in front of the other three. We surged ahead at a far faster pace than the morning's, then abruptly swerved right on another narrow road.

We hadn't gone a quarter mile when all of a sudden he pulled up. The three men behind him divided and surged past, then turned around and headed toward me. I frowned in confusion. What were they doing? Now wasn't the time to turn back—

It was then that I saw them. Eight knights, in partial armor like Marcello and his men, swords raised. Crimson lined the cloths beneath their saddles, as well as the shirts beneath their chainmail. Paratore men. They shrieked a war cry and bent lower, seemingly moving in slow motion. Marcello paused beside me as his men took off, in flight. Dimly, I understood the men behind me had already turned.

"Gabriella, you must ride hard," he said urgently, dark eyebrows lowered in urgency. "Faster than ever before."

I nodded and wheeled my horse around, to his other side. "Throw me a sword!" I cried.

He glanced over at me as if he was confused about what I'd said.

"Toss me your extra sword! I'm unarmed!"

"I will shield you," he ground out, facing the road again. "Go!"

He allowed me to head out before him when the road narrowed, keeping himself between me and our pursuers. Where had the others gone? Where were Marcello's men?

Just as I finished that thought, we raced past a line of four men, two pulling bowstrings tight, two behind them, swords raised, shields at the ready.

I glanced over my shoulder at Marcello and glimpsed a trace of a smile on his lips.

Thirty paces farther, when we met the final two men, he pulled ahead of me, then reached over to grab my reins. He handed them to one of the men, then raced back.

The man quickly pulled me off the horse and hid me behind a massive limestone boulder, then returned to his mount. I heard the throb of hoofbeats approaching, the thrum of two bowstrings, arrows launched. The cry of one man, the guttural groan of another.

One of the men near me said, "Now it's at least even."

"Do you have an extra sword?" I said.

He gaped at me. "Nay, m'lady. Only my own."

"Do you?" I cried, rushing toward the other, hearing the clash of swords, the roaring grunts of men in heated battle.

The thinner, younger man studied me for a moment, then, spying a couple men edge closer, turned to his saddle and pulled a spare sword from its sheath. He handed it to me absently, staring beyond me, to the road. I took hold of it and groaned at its weight.

Not that Soldier Boy noticed. He shared a low word with his companion, and they took up their positions on either side of the narrow road.

"M'lady," hissed the other one. "Get back! Back past those boulders. We'll protect you."

I turned and hurried over to the rocks, playing with the broadsword in my hands, shifting it in an idle figure eight.

My father had trained me to fence. But this thing, this crude piece of forged steel, weighed a ton. It was at least thirty pounds heavier than any blade I'd ever carried before. This was why they were all so dang strong—they worked out every day with *these*.

I was used to the light, springy steel, the hospital whites of proper fencing uniforms. Blades tipped in baubles that kept them from drawing blood.

What was coming toward us was anything but that.

I raised the sword before me and focused on the road beyond it, catching sight of the first two Paratore soldiers. They were chasing after Marcello and Luca, with two other soldiers in crimson behind them.

Whether I liked my weapon or not, I was glad to have it. I flipped my hair over my shoulder and settled my slippered feet in the dirt at an angle, my sword set like a baseball bat, high, as I waved it slightly in a circle, waiting for just the right ball. All sound seemed to cease as the surging horses raced toward us like animals in a silent horror film.

But curiously, I felt no fear. Only an eagerness to see it done. If I died here, would I awaken in my own time? Or would I be dead, regardless of the year?

In slow motion the men before me took the first man down. But the second escaped between them, his eyes widening in surprise at the sight of a woman, then narrowing upon me like a hunter with his prey suddenly in view.

He was coming for me.

Stand your ground, I told myself. *Gabi, you stand your ground!*

CHAPTER 5

I studied his approach, his speed, bracing myself for the impact, thinking through how I might parry his strike.

And that was when someone tackled me from the side.

It so surprised me that when I hit the ground, him atop me, it knocked the wind out of me.

A moment later a horse thundered past. Out of the corner of my eye, I had seen a man—Marcello?—deflect a swooping sword aimed right at where I had once stood.

I wanted to rise, to turn, to do anything, but all I could do was focus on making my body take a breath. *Contract, lungs! Fill!* I tried not to panic, but I was losing the fight. Tears streamed from my eyes.

I heard the sounds of battle, not five feet from me, and I rolled over to see. Something about that action allowed me my first breath, and I rapidly took several. Marcello was fighting a man—the man I'd seen yesterday at the tombs. It had to be the Paratore lord. Marcello's counterpart. Had Marcello taken me out just so he could fight the man himself? Of all the stupid, pig-headed—

Marcello glanced back at me, alarm again in his eyes. But he wasn't staring at the man he battled, but at something down the path. "M'lady, take cover!"

Cover? Cover! I'd show him.... I rose, half-crouched, and took another breath, trying to steady my suddenly shaking hands. A huge man on a massive horse was thundering toward me, a sneer on his lips, his eyes on me.

There was no way I could take on Goliath. I mean, a girl's gotta know her limits. I turned and ran to the rock just as he swept by, his fingertips brushing past my shoulder. My two guardians closed ranks in front of me.

"Bringing women to fight your battles now, Forelli?" the Paratore knight taunted, swinging his sword at Marcello, narrowly missing his chest.

"And you, as always, are low enough to attack one," Marcello said, through gritted teeth.

"Missed her yesterday," Paratore said. He tossed a leering glance in my direction. "She appears eager to lift her skirts. It'd please me to take her from you this day."

I clamped my lips together, chagrined. So that's what they thought of me banding my skirt to my legs? That I was into sleeping around or something? *Oh, brother.* I was glad I lived in my own era. There was enough to deal with, then. The massive soldier finally brought his horse to a stop and turned to come back toward us. But his eyes were now on his master. Paratore glanced at him, and in that moment, Marcello's blade tipped his forearm.

He gasped and took a halting step back. "That's the second time you've dared to strike me in two days, Forelli!"

The Incredible Hulk jumped to the ground and came lumbering over to Marcello. He did not attack him, nor did Marcello raise his sword. Instead, his weapon was at his side. What was this?

"What do you expect? We cannot continue our swordplay and not sustain damage to our persons!" Marcello returned.

Paratore clamped his lips shut, seething. Then, "What are you doing on our land? Are you begging for an all-out war?"

Wasn't that what we were in?

"We were out for a ride when Lady Betarrini became disoriented and took the wrong trail. We will be off of your land within the hour."

"See that you are. And try and keep your womenfolk where they belong."

Marcello strode forward and past his men, staring at me as if I'd done a thousand wrongs. What? Was I the reason for all of this? No, this was a war long fought, a family feud like the Montagues and Capulets, or the Hatfields and McCoys. He wasn't pinning this on me.

He took my arm and gruffly pulled me along to my horse.

I wrenched my arm from his grip. "I'm perfectly capable of walking on my own. I get it. You're ticked off. But this cannot all be my fault."

He frowned down at me, trying to make sense of my words. They came out in a mishmash of Italian and English.

I sighed, looked down at the ground, then back up at Marcello. "Why'd he stop? Why'd he let us go? You guys took down at least two of their men."

"It is understood," he said in a hiss.

"What is understood?"

"When an heir is wounded, the battle comes to an end. Anything further and our cities might be drawn into a far greater war."

Cities. Siena and Florence. These two castles were not just vying for a portion of property; they represented much greater forces.

"But you fight as if you'd like to kill him."

"As he would like to kill me. We've traded wounds on any number of occasions," he said, cocking his head, a hint of a smile on his lips. So he was enjoying this. At least a little bit.

I shook my head in confusion, trying to sort out their crazy politics, as he led me to his horse. Then I was seriously confused; where was my horse? But then he bent and lifted me to sit behind his saddle and gently untied the strips from my dress. He raised one eyebrow in warning. "You've already caught Paratore's eye. Let's not give him any other fodder for his dreams, shall we?"

My mouth fell open a little at that. I wanted to protest. Claim my own mount. But he seemed to not only be saying that Paratore thought I was attractive…but that he considered me Dream Material too. The maid's words of warning that morning echoed through my mind. "Take care, m'lady. *You already draw Lord Marcello's eye….*"

Or was he simply referring to the fact that the man apparently had his mind in the gutter? I sighed and turned toward his broad back as he mounted, trying to find a secure seat on the horse's rump by bringing my right leg slightly up beneath the skirt and tentatively wrapping my arms around his torso.

I tightened my grip as he grabbed the reins and turned his horse around. He was strong, with not an ounce of fat on him. I could feel muscle beneath his tunic. He smelled of wood fire and leather and earth and sweat. All…*man.* I shoved down a sudden, silly, stupid, insufferable *shiver,* of all things, and focused on the men in front of him, again atop their own steeds, my horse tied to the back of Luca's. They openly gaped at me, behind Marcello.

Paratore's men had receded into the wood, fifty feet off, watching us. Making sure we were leaving as promised, I guessed.

Luca frowned at Marcello. "M'lord, unless you wish for tongues to wag, mayhap it's best she ride with me."

"Nay. She rides with me. At least until we are out of these woods."

Luca's face eased, and I steeled myself as Marcello moved his horse into a light trot. I glanced back at Paratore, searching his face. He was hurting, curious, but that was all I could read in his eyes. If he had Lia, would he not have said something? Taunted us with it?

In twenty minutes, we were out of the woods and at a crossroads, presumably leading to either Siena and Firenze—the Italians' name for Florence. Marcello dismounted and then raised his hands to my waist, lifting me down. I kept my eyes averted, for some reason feeling suddenly shy. Maybe it was because his men stared at us.

"We're out of Paratore territory," he explained as he took my hand and led me to my own horse. I saw that one of his men, riding behind us, had retrieved the cursed sidesaddle from its stash in the forest and had once again firmly settled it atop my gelding.

Marcello gave me a small smile and handed me a leather band. "At least bind your hair behind you," he said lowly. "It won't do for the women of the castello to see you riding through the gates, hair loose as a maid's on her wedding day. You'll never find a moment's peace. Nor shall I."

I looked up into his warm eyes, searching for a glimpse of judgment. There was none. Only warning. And a tinge of…admiration.

I took the band from his fingers. He lifted me to the stupid sidesaddle and helped me lodge my feet—now totally filthy, I saw with a grimace—into the hidden stirrups. He handed me the reins with one more lingering look. Our fingers touched briefly, and heat seared my cheeks. He smiled ever so slightly—okay, now what was *that* about?—and then returned to his own horse.

I shook my head a little, staring at the hoofprints in the sandy soil. *I finally meet a guy who's interesting, and who seems to have a half-interest in me, and it is TOTALLY the wrong time and place.* I glanced up at the sky. *If You're out there, God, this is COMPLETELY unfair.*

The men were falling back into line, preparing to set off, and I did the same. But my eyes kept crawling back to Marcello. *Do not fall for him, Gabi. It is impossible. Impossible! Wrong, on so many levels.*

I could see my friend Keisha back home in the States giving me the oh-no-you-didn't finger wave and shaking her frizzy head. I always tried to do it, but could never pull it off in quite the same way.

Keisha. Hannah. Steph. Images of my friends' faces from home flashed through my mind, making me take a sharp intake of breath. I had to get back. To my own time. To my family. To my friends.

But first I had to find Lia. Make sure she wasn't trapped here too. We had to return home…together.

I cleared my throat. "Sir Marcello?"

He glanced back at me.

"Were we to stop in town? Inquire to see if anyone has seen my sister? Or my mother?"

He looked at me for a long moment, his eyebrows lowering, and then his eyes quickly scanned his men whose expressions said I'd stepped out of bounds. Apparently people didn't ask a young lord his plans. Ridiculous! I was merely asking a logical question.

"We will inquire on the morrow, Lady Betarrini. I believe we've done enough searching for one day."

"But—"

He raised an imperious hand toward me and frowned.

I frowned too, clamping my mouth shut.

So. I guess This Conversation Is Over.

He turned and took off for home, not looking back.

Well, fine, then. I guess there isn't anything between us after all. Never mind! I thought, shooting arrowed glances at his broad back.

We rode into the courtyard late that afternoon, weary, dirty, defeated. I knew the men left thinking they might be bringing home another contender for Belle of the Courtyard, and coming home empty was just, well…lame. They looked at me as if I might be making the whole story up of some blonde, beautiful sister lost in the woods. By and large, these men were far more civilized than boys back at home at Boulder High. They had the courtesy to avert their gazes—but not before I caught enough of a glimpse to figure it out.

I took a sponge bath in my room, pulled on a fresh gown of Lady Forelli's—with the aid of Giacinta—and then made it through supper, speaking to no one.

Conversation went on all about me. Boisterous tales, low-toned jokes, whispered secrets. But no one spoke to me.

Was it because of my actions today? I felt the echoes of shame, regret, but then shoved them away as fast as I shoved meat and porridge into my mouth, then waited for a passably polite moment to excuse myself. I had done what I had to do. *You made the best choice you could at the time,* my mother said to me in my head. It was something she always said. Not that charging on ahead, without the boys, had been my best idea.

I wished she were here. Here to tell me how to act, what to say. She was always so good at negotiating tough, new situations. She waded in as I longed to do, waist-deep, figuring it out as she went. How did she do that?

I leaned back from the table, envisioning my mother, her hair as straight and blonde as my sister's, nose to nose with the Italian archeology officials. She never backed down. Never. She always knew where she was going, and how she was going to get there. How did she know that?

For the first time, I fully wondered what it would be like to be my mother, a Dane in an Italian's world. When she met my father, she barely even spoke the language. They had conversed in Latin. *That's love,* they liked to say, sharing a secret glance. My sister and I always stared wide-eyed at each other when they did that, with a look that said *Serious Geek Alert.*

I smiled at the memory.

"Happy thought, m'lady?" asked Luca, leaning toward me for the first time, regarding me as he popped a piece of bread into his mouth.

"Indeed," I returned. "I was thinking of my family." I forced a smile, but I'm certain that he saw the flash of sorrow in my eyes. I blinked rapidly. Was I tearing up again? "Excuse me," I said, rising. I had to get out of there.

Awkwardly, all the men at the table rose with me.

I paused and looked around, then back to my half-eaten meal. "Forgive me. I am quite exhausted. I must…retire." My eyes met Marcello's. His brow knit together.

"M'lady," he said with a slight nod of dismissal, opening the door for my escape.

Everyone else echoed his farewell.

I dared not look at any of them.

I practically ran across the courtyard, gasping for breath and giving in to the tears only when I had reached the safety of my room. I lifted a hand to my forehead, lost in thought. What if I couldn't get back? What if Lia hadn't come through with me? What if I was alone here, forever, on my own to find my way?

I sank down, my back against the door, sobbing like a little kid.

Seriously. I hadn't cried that hard in a long time.

When I finally looked up, my sleeves were wet from wiping my eyes and nose. I wasn't one of those pretty criers, the type that gets a little pink in the cheeks, and their eyes all wide and bright. No, I got the swelling, bloodshot eyes, the dripping nose that made me a candidate for a Nyquil commercial. That was me. *Puurty.*

Lia was a pretty crier. I always half-teased her, saying I hated her for it. Was that what she'd remember of me? Saying mean things? Did she miss me, too? Did she even know I was gone?

I clenched my temples between the palms of my hands, pressing as if I might be able to squeeze in some clear thinking. What was I to do? What?

I glanced at the crucifix, sighed, and then rose. No, this was up to me. I'd gotten myself into this. I had to get myself out.

The tombs.

My portal.

It was the only way out. Back to Lia. Back to my mom. Back to reality.

Even if I had to get there alone.

CHAPTER 6

I thought about writing the Forellis a note, explaining my disappearance into the night and thanking them for their assistance, but in the end, the idea of hunting down quill and ink and some sort of paper just made it seem like a much too time-consuming task. Best to get to the tombs, make the jump back in time, and let them forget about me.

There was only one thing I had to do before I made my escape. I had to secure a weapon. There was no way I was going out into those woods without a sword to defend myself.

In the Great Hall, where the castle dined, an armory stood to one side. If I remembered right, it wasn't locked. But getting through the courtyard, in and out of the hall, avoiding one of the bazillion knights that might be loitering about—that would take some doing. Oh, and then I had to find my way out of an impenetrable fortress. Perfect.

I shook my head.

It didn't matter. I just needed to try. I could only try.

So I set out, quietly shutting the door behind me. At the end of the corridor, on a peg beside the stairwell that ran up one turret, was a coil of rope. It extended upward, to a hook, where the servants could raise and lower a platform that held a few more candles to light the corridor. I wondered if it was long enough to reach partway down the wall. A plan hatched in my mind.

My heart was hammering away in my chest as I came out into the courtyard. My fear and guilt made me angry. I intended only to gain my freedom, be on my way! So what did I have to feel guilty about? The Forellis were far better off without me complicating their lives. They'd probably be relieved to not have to figure me or my future out. I knew at least one person would certainly be happy to discover I'd disappeared as fast as I had shown up—Lady Rossi.

I passed two knights who appeared to be on guard duty. They nodded at me but said nothing. I eased open the Great Hall door and looked around, seeing nothing but empty chairs and the soft, flickering light from a few candles left lit in the center of each table. The trenchers and food and goblets and tablecloths had all been cleared, leaving the tables bare.

I grabbed a candle and tiptoed over to the armory, wincing when the door creaked on its hinge. Slowly, I dared to look over my shoulder, expecting to see men charging over to me, demanding to know what I was up to. But no one appeared in the deeply shadowed hall.

I lifted my candle up. Here, there were indeed many weapons. Swords of varying lengths; longbows and arrows; axes; and horrible, spiky balls-on-chain thingies. I shivered at the thought of Paratore's hulking knight coming after me with one of those. Shoving away my fear, I hurried to a wall and pulled the shortest sword down. It was ten pounds lighter than the one I hefted earlier, and I moved it about with ease. This, *this* I might be able to actually use. I moved over to a shelf and pulled out a double sheath on a long, leather strap. It was perfect. In a bit I had it wrapped across my chest and buckled at the waist. In the front pocket sheathed a dagger with a seven-inch blade. In the back stowed my broadsword.

As soon as I felt the weight of the weapons, my heart began to slow its frantic pace. I felt stronger, safer. I reached back, practicing my pull a couple times to get a sense of how long it would take to bring it forward, to ward off an attack. I looked down and saw that the dagger could be positioned the opposite way, too. I switched it around, and now I could simultaneously pull the dagger out with my left hand and the sword with my right.

Oh yeah, I thought with a grin and a nod. *You don't wanna take me on, Paratore. Don't get between me and my way home. I don't care if you're a prince. Don't mess with me!*

I pulled a cape over my shoulders and had just picked up the candle when Luca appeared in the doorway.

His eyes widened in surprise. "Lady Betarrini?"

"Oh, Luca!" I said, tightening my fist around the edges of my cape in front of me. "You frightened me." I tried to give him my most charming smile.

"Wh-what are you doing in there?"

"I think I'm a bit turned around," I confessed. "I was in search of the kitchen, hoping to get a…drink."

"A drink? Why not send a servant?"

"It's late. I didn't wish to be a bother. Might you show me where to go?" I opened my eyes wide, hoping they said innocence and not liar, liar, pants on fire.

He seemed to buy it. "Of course. It's this way, in back." He offered his arm, and I took it.

"Have you taken a chill, m'lady?"

"A chill?" I asked blankly.

"Yes, you've donned a cape, on one of the warmest evenings of the summer."

I kept my eyes straight ahead. This was Marcello's right-hand man. No idiot.

"Mayhap I'm coming down with the chills," I said, lifting my hand from his arm and to my head.

That seemed to stop his conjecture. "Oh, I hope not. Let's fetch you a cup of mulled wine and get you straight to bed. Most likely you're overwrought. You've endured much today."

"You're probably right," I said.

We moved down through a wide hall and into a massive kitchen, still full of the odors of cooling meat and fresh-baked bread. Cook looked up in surprise at us as she wiped her hands on a cloth. "Can I be of aid, m'lady, m'lord?"

"The lady is in need of something warm to drink," Luca said.

"Right away, right away," she murmured. She took a crockery mug with no handles from a shelf, then went to the wide stone oven where a fire still crackled and embers glowed. She dipped a ladle into a kettle at the edge and poured the steaming liquid into a cup, then waddled back over to us.

"Do you have need of anything else, m'lady? You hardly touched your supper. Mayhap some bread? There's some left from the meal."

It would be wise to take a little food on the road with me, I realized. It might take hours to find the tombs in the dark, if I didn't discover just the right path. "Some bread would be wonderful, Cook."

She smiled, pleased to have guessed at my need, and went to wrap a small, brown loaf in a cloth. "Anything else?"

"No. Thank you. For everything."

I saw her frown a little at that, and realized I sounded as if I were saying farewell. I lifted the cup. Maybe that would explain the *everything.*

"Sleep well, m'lady."

"Thank you."

Luca walked with me back through the Great Hall.

"Well," I said. "I believe I can make it back to my room and not get lost again."

"I'll see you across the courtyard," he said, his eyes slightly troubled. He was taking in the bead of sweat on my brow. Probably worrying that I really was ill. But that blasted kitchen had been sweltering. I longed to ditch the cape, but couldn't, for obvious reasons. If he saw my weapons…

We moved across the cobblestones and reached the corridor hallway. "All right," I said with a grin. "I *know* I can make it from here."

"Are you certain, m'lady?" he asked, his worry turning to teasing.

"Quite. Good night, Sir Luca."

"Good night, m'lady," he said. "I hope that morning finds you feeling much better."

"As do I." I eased through the doorway and ignored his curious expression. He knew something was up. "Good night," I said again, closing the door, like a girl on her first date with a boy who didn't want to leave without a kiss. I put my back to it and closed my eyes, feeling the length of the broadsword down my spine.

I listened, and after a moment, heard his soft leather boots take the first few steps away. I let out a big breath of relief and looked to the candle and rope. On closer inspection, it wasn't nearly long enough to scale down a castle wall. But then I saw another, on the other end. Its candle simply wasn't lit.

I hurriedly fetched both lengths of rope, leaving the candle platforms neatly to one side of the corridor—hoping it looked as if a servant were merely servicing them—then tied the ends together. Mom had grown up sailing and delighted in teaching us the ten knots she remembered. *Over and under and through, bippety, boppety, boo,* I remembered her chanting to us as little girls.

The knot worked now as it had then. I pulled on either end. It would hold.

I'm on my way, Mom. I'm comin' home.

I wrapped the long lengths of rope into a figure eight and pulled it over one arm. Then I ducked through the hallway door and climbed the turret staircase that led to the top of the wall where the windows were located. On the last step, I listened and then peeked out. The guard was at the other end, peering over the edge as if he'd seen something. I eased out and quickly moved to the opposite side, where I was partially blocked by the top portion of the tower. Another guard was moving away from me at a leisurely pace. I had about ninety seconds before he would turn and come back in my direction. *Ninety, eighty-nine.*

I bent and pushed the end of the rope out one slot in the wall—arrow slots, if I remembered it right—then reached to grab it and pull it back through the next slot, counting off the seconds as I worked. *Seventy-two, seventy-one.* In quick order, after glancing around the tower to be sure the first guard hadn't caught sight of me, I let the length of rope drop over the edge. It dangled six feet from the ground. Close enough. *Sixty-five, sixty-four.*

I hurriedly wrapped my hands in strips of cloth to avoid the rope burn to come, pulled the rope up and made a loop, preparing to rappel.

"So that's why you had need of a sword this night," said a droll voice a few feet away.

I gasped and jumped, nearly losing my balance on the edge of the wall.

Luca was leaning against the wall, looking down on my intended escape route. "It's a long drop, m'lady. Why not go through the gate?" he asked, as if he always came across women trying to climb down the castle wall. *Fifty-three, fifty-two…*

I shook my head, in no mood for his humor at this moment. "I can't go through the gate," I whispered, hoping to convince him to just let me go before the guard returned. "They will not allow it at such an hour."

"Indeed they will not." He nodded out to the dark woods. "You mean to return to the tumuli?"

I nodded, begging with my eyes.

"That is no place for a lady at night. Do you not remember our encounter this afternoon and the Paratores' hatred of the Forellis?"

"I am not a Forelli."

"You may as well be. A night spent in the Forelli household makes you a member."

"Please, Luca. I must be off. I must look for my sister. My mother." I took another nervous glance toward the guard. He was nearing the end of the wall.

"In the dark of night? You will find no one except yourself, lost. But you *are* likely to be discovered by a Paratore patrol. Or worse."

"Worse? Who is worse?" I looked to the guards on either end, still unaware of us. The last thing I needed was for them to come running on over here too.

Luca sighed heavily. "M'lady, the Paratores are not the Forellis' only enemy. Surely you know that. Wander ten miles north or south of here, and you'll find a castle or village who are firmly set for the Fiorentini. A Norman such as yourself cannot assume to know where it is safe to go. If you need to go, allow me to go as your guard. In the morning, out the gate."

"Nay. I must be away. I cannot sleep, knowing Evangelia might be out there. . . ."

Luca glanced over the side and raised a brow. "Then I shall go with you now, through the gates."

"Marcello will not allow you to go."

"Marcello slumbers. Come, we'll take a look, if we must. Then we can get back for a few winks before daylight is upon us."

"If we go through the gates, ten guards will be ringing the bells."

"So you truly intend to climb the wall?" he asked incredulously. "You'll fall and break your neck. Then what will Marcello do to me?"

"I will not fall," I said with a grin, putting my feet over and finding a small ledge. "I wish I had some carabiners and straps, but this will do." I gave the rope a quick tug then leaned outward. *Thirty-two, thirty-one*...the guards were probably turning by now, heading back in my direction. Quickly, I rappelled a foot down.

"M'lady!"

"I am fine, Luca," I hissed, not wanting him to draw attention. "Quit worrying over me like Cook." I went another foot and smiled up at him. The poor guy was in total shock. "Look away, Luca. Then you can say you never saw me leave, only that I disappeared in the dark." I eased down quickly then, sliding as fast as I dared, half-expecting Luca to sound an alarm.

But as I dropped, panting, to the soft peat below, I saw that as the silhouette of the guard returned, my rope was already gone, pulled in from above.

I turned and ran, stumbling a couple of times over branches. I heard a shout from the castle but ignored it. Soon I was deep in the forest, on the narrow horse path that led to the creek. There was just enough of a moon out to see it. If I stayed on it, I should be able to find the Etruscan hill.

It took me about ten minutes to realize I wasn't alone.

I stopped abruptly and turned, easing my dagger out of its sheath, but keeping it hidden in the folds of my cape.

Then I exhaled a breath as I realized it was Marcello. I could make out his curly hair, his strong, wide shoulders. Luca was right behind him.

I put a hand to my head when they came close. "You scared me to death," I scolded.

"Mayhap you are dead. Luca says you scale walls like a wraith." He moved to my side and looked down at me, then grabbed my wrist, slowly bringing the dagger to the soft, ivory light of night. His eyes met mine. "Are you a spy as my father feared, Lady Betarrini?"

"Nay!" Those words kept popping out of me, but they felt more natural now, not quite so weird. "I simply am in search of my family. And you will not let me go look for them, so I had to find another way."

He looked down at the dagger and then back to me.

"I did not know it was you two, behind me in the woods," I sputtered. "You think me daft enough to come out in the night, unarmed?" I shook off his hand and slid the dagger back into the front sheath. "I told Luca I wished to do this alone."

"And I told you," Luca said, no trace of humor in his voice, "that I could not allow it."

"Why are you so certain that you will find your sister at the tombs?" Marcello grit out.

"I'm not. I simply…have to know. I cannot sleep another night, thinking she might be out here, lost, looking for me.… What if the Paratores get hold of her?" I shuddered.

"He doesn't have her, m'lady," Marcello said, his tone placating again. "He would've used her as bait…or demanded a ransom once he connected her to you."

"Well, that is good for us, then," I said. "That makes it more likely that Lia is still at the tombs. I'll either find her there…or I will not. At least on foot, we can approach without detection."

Marcello sighed and trudged past me. "If we're to do this foolish thing, let's get it done. I'd still like to get some sleep this night."

I hurried after him, struggling to keep up with his fast, irritated pace. Luca followed behind me. It was good to not be alone. I was far less creeped out.

But how was I to enter the tomb with them hovering about?

Marcello stomped forward, never looking back. I paused to let him go ahead and put my hands to my knees, gasping for breath. Apparently, I needed a bit more cardio in my workout routine.

He disappeared into the dark, but Luca stayed behind me. "He's angry."

Ya think? I was breathing too hard to speak.

Luca took a step closer, dropping his tone. "Mayhap it's different in Normandy. Here, few dare to question m'lord's decisions. Frankly, I'm surprised he didn't drag you back to the castello."

"You didn't have to tell him," I gasped.

"Yes, I did."

"He didn't ever…have to know…I was gone," I insisted.

"He did. The protection of Castello Forelli is his responsibility."

I gaped at him. "You thought me a spy too?"

"I didn't know what to think, m'lady. I—we've—never met a woman like you."

There's a good reason for that.… I stood up straight. "Listen, simply get me to those tombs. I'm certain that I will find something there that will give me hope in finding Lia, or…cease fretting over it."

He nodded and took the path before me. We caught up with Marcello a few minutes later. He said nothing, just took the rear guard position when we passed.

And then we were there. I could see the curves of the tomb roofs, stretching out before us, the wide, flat plain on which they had been built. "Lia," I said in a stage whisper, aware of the Paratore castle, no more than a half-mile away. If the wind was right, could they hear us? I wasn't taking any chances.

"Evangelia?" I tried again, edging around a second tomb, hunched over like the men. None of us wished to be seen by a Paratore patrol in the pale moonlight. "Lia?"

I held my breath, hoping against hope that she'd emerge, jump into my arms. That I wouldn't be alone.

But the only response, after a pause, was the crickets, resuming their song.

She wasn't here. She hadn't made it through the leap in time. Did that mean she was back in our time? Or lost somewhere in between?

"Mayhap she is inside, sleeping as I did," I said to Marcello. "Let me crawl in, have a quick look."

"I will go."

"Nay," I said, grabbing his forearm, then quickly releasing it. "You will frighten her, if she's in there. She might scream."

He considered me a moment, then gestured inside. "Make haste."

I bent at once and crawled, as best I could in the cursed skirts, through the tunnel, standing to my full height when I knew I must be beneath the large, rounded dome. "Lia," I whispered, still hoping. But the echo of her name wrapped around the room and disappeared out the entrance as if it had never left my lips.

I sighed. She really hadn't made it. How was that possible?

I stepped in the shards of the pot I had broken and let out a yelp.

"M'lady," Marcello whispered.

I jumped a bit, thinking he had entered, but he was merely at the entrance. There was no time to hesitate any longer.

I squinted hard, trying to make out the frescoes by the dim light that entered through the narrow passage, looking for the two handprints. It was too dark. I closed my eyes, thinking back, pacing out where I thought the prints had been, feeling for the place of warmth....

I glanced to the tomb entrance, thought, *Good-bye, Marcello,* then blew out my cheeks and placed my hand on the spot.

I had to be right over them. Or at least within inches. But the entire wall was cold. No warmth anywhere. Quickly I switched hands, wondering if I had remembered it wrong, that I had actually used the other hand...but only cold stone met my left too.

"Lady Betarrini..."

"I'll be right out," I whispered back, stalling him. My heart was thundering. I put both hands on the wall, shifting them about, wondering if I was just missing the prints, if it had to be exact...

I leaned my head against the stone wall, trying to absorb its cold message.

There was no gateway home.

I was trapped.

CHAPTER 7

He scared me so badly I jumped.

It was only Marcello, but I'd been so lost in my swirling thoughts about the future, about Mom and Lia, that I totally missed his crawling through the entrance. I jumped away and tried to put my head in gear. What had he asked?

"Lady Betarrini," he said, and I realized that he'd been saying it repeatedly. "Are you quite all right?"

"I—I am. Forgive me. It is only that…I was certain Evangelia would be here, asleep in a corner. I had so hoped…"

I sensed more than saw him take a step forward in the dark. "You have been through a great deal. Please. Luca and I shall escort you back to the safety of the castello. In the light of day, it will feel far less overwhelming."

"I do not think so," I said, shaking my head. "Somehow, I think it will feel far more difficult."

"You could do far worse than come under the protection of Castello Forelli."

I could almost see him tensing, lifting his chin, pulling back his shoulders.

"Yes, of course," I said. "But—please try to understand…I am most grateful for your family's friendship. But Evangelia…she might be the only member of my family within reach. If she is still here at all." My voice cracked, saying that last bit.

"I do understand," he said, his voice gentling. "If it were Fortino who was lost, I'd do anything I could. I know it is difficult, but we will not accomplish anything more here, this night. And Evangelia—she'd want you to be safe, would she not? You've seen for yourself what transpires on these lands. Let us return to the castello and pursue a new search for your sister come morn."

"Yes," I said, sniffling, trying to hold back full-fledged sobs. That was all the guy needed…me, a total mess. I had to hold it together. At least until I was back in my room.

"Please," he said, stepping aside, apparently waiting for me to exit first. He probably wondered if I was flippin' insane, coming in here, hanging out like it was my best friend's living room. It was a tomb, I reminded myself as I crawled out, yanking on my skirts in agitation when they got in the way. A tomb. Place of the dead. As familiar as these places were to me, they probably creeped the guys out in a big way.

If I was to return, I'd have to find a way to do it on my own. But there was really no point now that I knew the prints wouldn't get me home. So what was I to do? Was there a way home at all?

I could see Luca, about fifteen feet away. He spotted us and pushed off his perch on a tall boulder.

"It's terribly dark, m'lady," Marcello said, so close a shiver ran down my neck. "Please, take my arm."

"Yes, of course," I said, as if I did it all the time. I was digging the gallantry of medieval men, even if it did make them chauvinistic at times. Even in modern times, the Italian guys seemed to echo their ancestors.

We'd just taken a step toward the path when Luca paused in front of us and held up a hand. A half second later, he waved it and dived to the left, between two trees. Marcello grabbed my hand and yanked me to the right.

"In there," he whispered, motioning toward a low cave. I could hear it then. Hoofbeats approaching. A Paratore patrol.

Crouched, I hurried inward and then turned. Marcello drew his sword, crouched, and came in too, turning to face the entrance. Our quarters were so cramped, he was right in front of me. To keep from tipping over, I laid a hand on his back, taking comfort in the steady rise and fall of his breath, even as four horses walked by. The guards were talking, distracted, obviously not entirely on task. But were they to discover us, Marcello and Luca would be outnumbered. But only by one. I had my broadsword too.

Happily, they kept moving, and when we could no longer hear them, Marcello glanced over his shoulder and whispered, "Come." We crawled out of the cave and brushed ourselves off.

They didn't have to say what I knew—it would've been very bad for me if the Paratore patrol had come across me at the tomb. We resumed our walk back to the castle.

"M'lady, what of your kin in Normandy? Your father?"

"My father died six months ago," I said dully. No matter how many times I said it, it never seemed quite real.

"God rest his soul," Marcello said. The news didn't seem to throw him like it did most other people. But then, most other people didn't live in the fourteenth century, where the life expectancy probably topped out at about forty. "And the others? Uncles? Cousins?"

"Nay, there is no one else. Only my mother and sister and me, now."

"I see. And what brought your mother to Toscana?"

I hesitated. I couldn't tell him she was an archeologist. "She… she has a business selling Etruscan artifacts."

"Etruscan?" Marcello said. I could almost see his big eyelashes blinking in surprise. But it was only my imagination.

"The Normans…they apparently will buy anything," Luca said over his shoulder.

"Mayhap I should aid you in searching those other tombs," Marcello said, his voice thick with laughter. "I might earn enough to fund our next assault on the Paratores."

"Etruscan art is of no value here?" I asked, irked at their teasing.

"Very little," Marcello returned. His tone softened. "But most of what we find are potsherds. Who cares for broken vessels?"

"More than you might believe," I muttered. I thought of my parents, working in sanitized conditions, humidity levels carefully set, piecing together potsherds, rebuilding vessels. I thought of their elation when they discovered unbroken pots, and the one I had destroyed.

"Her business…she makes enough to keep you and your sister in your home, with ample food?"

"With that and what remains of my father's estate." That was pretty true. Archeology was never the big moneymaker. Mom and Dad had earned their living with the occasional summer university gig, writing books on the Etruscans and picking up some speaking engagements and articles. But it was Dad's life-insurance money that was keeping us afloat now. There was no way Mom could afford rent and food and airline tickets to and from Roma without it. Not if she wanted to keep the house in Boulder, which Lia and I pushed her to do. It was one thing to spend summers here, another to give up on American life entirely.

"Then you are three uncommon women," Marcello said softly, looking my way. "It is difficult for the fairer sex, without a protector."

I tensed, then forced myself to relax. I needed him and his family. And he was right. In this day and age, especially, it was better for women if there was a man by their side. It just was the plain truth. "My father taught us well," I said, pushing my shoulders back. "We three Betarrini women will be all right."

I thought I saw a flash of a smile. "I believe you."

I'd pleaded a headache, needing time and space to sort out my thoughts, but even spending all day in my room had left me with nothing more than a real one. Headaches were no fun in modern times, but at least at home, I could pop a couple of Advil and feel loads better. People in these times relied on herbs and tonics. I wondered what they were treating poor, sickly Fortino with. Did they believe that leeches were a viable treatment in this era? I shivered at the thought. *Best not to really get sick here, now.* I tried to think back; Mom had been studying natural remedies the last few years, interested to know how the Etruscans might've once healed their own. She'd subjected me and Lia to long lectures on the subject, as well as a few tries at field medicine. But I didn't remember anything in regard to headaches.

I moved over to the basin of water and splashed my face, again and again, then dried it off with the rough cloth. I picked up a wide-toothed comb—carved out of what looked like ivory—and shivered at the thought of some walrus somewhere giving up his life for the tusk it came from. I ran its short spokes through the tangles of my hair anyway, then retied it with the leather band Marcello had given me, wound it into a crude knot, then pinned it with one pin. I felt it, testing it to see if it might stay for half a minute. Then, blowing my cheeks out, I decided it was good enough. It was soon dark. No one was out at this hour, most having retired after supper. That appeared to be the castle's routine: to bed with the sun, and up with it too.

It was crazy. Who back home would ever willingly adopt that schedule?

Sunset was well past us, judging from the bit of sky I could see in my window. I edged open my door and peeked down the hallway, half expecting Marcello to have posted a sentry at my door, given my behavior the night before. But no one was there. Only the flickering, dancing torchlight moved.

I edged out the door and closed it softly behind me. I'd heard others moving in and out of rooms down this hall, but not in the last day or so. Was I alone now? I moved down the corridor on tiptoes, past the door that led to the courtyard, to one of the turrets that climbed up to the allure, the wall walk at the top. Cautiously, I eased open the wooden door, pleased to see that it was not locked.

The stairs, carved out of the stone tower, circled upward on the edge, like the coil of a DNA double helix I'd seen in my biology textbook. I placed a foot on the bottom step and stared upward, wishing I could see better in the deep shadows. Would they take issue with my being up there again? Surely, Marcello had warned them all by now to watch out for his mad houseguest, willing to scale the castle walls to escape.

What did it matter? I moved upward, gaining confidence as I did so, barely hesitating at the top. I ducked and pushed through a short door suitable for a hobbit and emerged atop the allure of the castle.

Nobody was in front of me, the guard having turned the corner, so I took a deep breath, appreciating the cool of the evening breeze on my hot face. *Oh, Toscana,* I thought, closing my eyes and breathing in the familiar scents of spicy sage and sweet forest loam and warm, dusty oak. *How can you smell so right, so much like home, and yet be so wrong?*

I blinked my eyes open, fearful that I might have company, but still found myself alone. Where were the guards? Simply in different areas of the castle? I strode forward, able to fully appreciate the view from here for the first time. I was at level with most of the forest canopy, able to see for miles, to the parapets of the Paratore castle, flying her crimson flag, and beyond her, the hills that I knew led to Siena. Might Lia have traveled through time and gone *there*, looking for me?

I thought of our favorite spot in the city—the fountain in the central plaza, Il Campo—and wondered if she might have managed to make it there. It would have been a logical meeting place. Every time we visited a new town, ever since we were kids, Mom and Dad had drilled it into us: *If you're lost, find a policeman and tell him you're to meet your family at the fountain.* In Rome, it had been the Trevi, in Siena, the Fonte Gaia, and so on.

Lia and I loved the Fonte Gaia above all others. It had nothing on the Trevi for sure. That one was grandiose, overwhelming. But the Fonte Gaia of Siena, a simple rectangle, ornately carved of marble, did not demand undue attention. It allowed the public square itself to sing, like a box seat in the best part of a stadium. Siena's piazza was one of the best in all of Italia—a grand shell, with nine rays in the brick cobblestones that represented "the Nine," the name for the dudes that ran Siena—and all the little towns that reported to her. Grand palazzos lined the plaza's rim, forming a kind of castle wall, and on the bottom edge, the public building and her pristine tower, the *campanile,* rose like a flag of declaration.

I was glad that Castello Forelli stood for the Sienese. It seemed wrong, vaguely menacing, that Castello Paratore stood so close to her, no more than a couple miles to the north.

My hair was pulling loose from its lone pin, a heavy coil falling to either side of my face. I touched it and could feel the leather band giving way. Looking right and then left and seeing no one, I untied the string and let my hair fall around my shoulders. I leaned forward, elbows on the wall, massaging my scalp, trying to ease away the tension there. Again, I picked up the scents of oak and sage, but now I could smell ripening grain. It was no wonder that Fortino, Marcello's older brother, suffered so from "lung ailments," as Cook called them—the air was thick with life here. Why had I never noticed it in my own time?

After a moment, I sensed I wasn't alone. I slowly opened my eyes and saw Marcello, five feet away from me, hands on the castle wall, staring outward as I was. I straightened and touched my hair.

"Nay, do not," he said kindly, lifting a hand in my direction. "It suits you," he said, studying me with those warm, penetrating eyes. "Your hair about your shoulders. Is that how you wear it in Normandy?"

"If it is not in a braid," I said. "Or pulled back."

"Ahh." He looked at me from the corners of his eyes until I felt the heat of a flush climb my neck and jaw.

I hurriedly looked back to the forest, hoping he couldn't see my blush in the waning light. What was it about him that made me feel more…*awake*, somehow? Alive? I'd never felt anything like it.

"M-m'lord," I said, deciding to focus on the practical rather than some mad, romantic fantasy. "I wondered if I might borrow a horse tomorrow, er, on the morrow, and visit Siena."

"Siena?" asked a feminine voice.

I turned, knowing who was behind me already. Lady Rossi paraded down the allure, one of her ladies-in-waiting following behind.

"Goodness, Lady Betarrini, your hair does battle any semblance of rule, does it not?" she asked with a giggle. "Of course, this summer wind does nothing to aid any of us," she added.

That's right, I thought. *Soften that dig. Neither of us missed it, did we?*

"I, too, am eager to be off for Siena." Lady Rossi sniffed. She glanced up at Marcello, searching his face for some reaction, but he merely nodded, almost imperceptibly. "It's been weeks since I've been home, and I simply must get back to see to the details of our wedding ceremony."

I smiled, wanting to appear conciliatory, hoping to set her at ease a little so maybe she'd stop constantly trying to provoke me. Life was tough enough without any unnecessary enemies. "I can only imagine," I said. "How much longer until your nuptials?"

"The fifteenth of September. Generations of my family have married on that day, and all have been blessed by good fortune and many children."

"Sounds like the right day, for certain," I said.

"Why are you eager to get to Siena?" Marcello said, eyeing me suspiciously.

"I wonder if perhaps my mother and sister might be there. It is the next, closest city. . . ."

"I will send a messenger on the morrow, Lady Betarrini," Marcello said. "There is no need for you to further endanger yourself."

"Marcello," Lady Rossi said, setting a small, delicate hand on his forearm, "you know the pull of family ties for a woman. You must allow Lady Betarrini her search. What if she misses her reunion by a day or two? That would be tragic."

Tragic in that I wouldn't be out of your way for good. Whatever. Don't worry. I'll be gone before you know it.

"Unfortunately," Marcello said, "word reached me this evening that there are renegade armies all about us. Mercenaries. Until the Nine vote next week on whether or not to open their banks again to Firenze, I'm afraid we are in a state of unrest. I cannot allow anyone to leave."

"M'lord, I am neither a member of this household nor bound to your care," I said carefully, pulling my shoulders back and lifting my head. "I am most grateful for your aid, but I remain free to choose when and where I go."

His mouth dropped open a bit, and then he clamped it shut. "Be that as it may," he said, waving a dismissive hand through the air, "you are an unaccompanied female, and it is my duty to look after you."

I couldn't help but smile. *What a wacky thing this chivalry deal was....* There would be no arguing with him. I could see it in his face. I'd seen it in person, last night. Best just to disappear when I decided the time was right. This time without my shadows.

My eagerness to leave seemed to soften Lady Rossi a bit. She studied me a moment and then said, "Won't you come and join us, Lady Betarrini, for the evening reading?"

Evening reading? Maybe this place didn't roll up with the daylight as I thought. But listening to medieval poetry or whatever they read wasn't my idea of kickin' back and relaxing. "I thank you for your kind invitation, m'lady, but I am still attempting to dislodge this headache. Mayhap I could join you at the next?"

"As you wish," she said coolly, turning and then pausing at the turret doorway. "Will you be so kind as to accompany me, m'lord?" she said to Marcello.

He pulled his warm, brown eyes from me and turned to follow her. Mollified, she disappeared, her lady-in-waiting behind her, but Marcello hovered in the doorway. "There are no coils of rope hidden among your skirts this night," he said lowly.

I let a smile spread across my face and gave a little shake of my head. "Not this night."

"I have your word? You shall not step outside the castle?"

A guard came around the tower then. Caught, obviously delinquent in his duties, he mumbled a "m'lord" at Marcello with a tucked head and hurried past me. Where'd he been? Sneaking a snack out of the kitchen or something?

"This is not a night to be lackadaisical in our duties," Marcello called after him. But his eyes remained on me, waiting.

Man, he was stubborn. "Not before sunup," I said.

With that, he turned and followed his bride-to-be.

CHAPTER 8

I awakened, not to the sound of a rooster, but to men preparing for battle. Horses whinnying, leather creaking, metal clanking together.

I threw back my covers and bent to retrieve my overdress laying across the bottom of my bed. I wanted to curse the buttons and loops, but then she was there, my miraculous maid Giacinta, who seemed to sense when I was rising. Perhaps she was pacing the hall, eager for me to get up, so we could get to the courtyard and see what the fuss was all about.

"G'day, m'lady," she said, edging around me and rapidly tending to my buttons.

I sat down on the edge of the bed, and she combed my hair. "Let's see if we might have the best of this hair today, shall we?" she muttered.

I smiled. *Good luck with that.*

She braided it for a few rows, then wrapped it in a coil. She shoved eight pins into the knot, scraping my scalp, but I resisted complaint. The faster she was done with it, the faster we could be outside. "What's happening?" I asked. "Who is preparing to ride?"

"Our knights. For once it's not the Paratores, but some other band of ne'er-do-wells. They took a small manor under the protection of the Forellis, not far from here."

I frowned. That didn't sound good. Who were these guys, some sort of gang, making the most of this latest Fiorentini-Sienese conflict? I sighed and blew out my cheeks. No matter the era, there were always guys ready to swoop in and take advantage of a situation....

"There you are," she said, finishing with the hair net around my massive bun, and stepping away.

"Thank you," I said. "It feels much more secure today."

She bobbed a curtsy, and I moved past her and down the corridor with her right on my heels. "Giacinta," I said, speaking to her over my shoulder, "tell me about the Forellis' ongoing battle with the Paratores. Is it really their loyalties to Siena and Firenze that keep them in conflict?"

"Ach, it's gone on for years," she said, slightly out of breath. "And sure, the Forellis' loyalty to Siena and the Paratores' loyalty to Firenze keeps a constant tension between us. But there is a tract of land that has been forever in dispute. More than twenty men have died in trying to capture it. One week it is in the Paratores' hands, the next, the Forellis'. This week it is ours. The Paratores are set on reclaiming it, of course. Lady Forelli—God rest her soul—begged Lord Forelli to give it to them. She was done with the death, the heartache. But you know men and their infernal pride. Both houses claim ownership. Neither house can bear to let it go."

We arrived in the courtyard just as the men had mounted up. Marcello was leaning down, accepting a flower from Lady Rossi, then he straightened to bark orders at his men as she backed away.

The horses, excited by the scent of battle on the wind, circled endlessly, fighting their masters. Marcello wheeled his gelding around and caught my eye, held it for a moment as if silently asking, *You'll stay here, right?*

I gave him the barest of nods. The last thing he needed right now was to be worrying over me.

Marcello returned his attention to the men. He raised his arm, fist closed, and the men came into formation. Two by two, all eighteen of them galloped out the gates, and I felt the ground beneath my feet rumble.

Two guards closed the mammoth doors, sliding a massive metal beam across to lock it. Above them, two other guards had their backs to us, obviously watching as the men disappeared down the road. Were they sorry they had been left behind? Or secretly relieved?

I turned and hurried back to my wing's corridor and the tower stairs that led to the allure. I wanted to be up top, watching the men go, all fired up on testosterone. Wasn't this what boys in my own time longed to do? Go off to protect the land, the women, stand up for right? I wanted to see real men in action. It…*stirred* me.

So I rushed up the stairs and came through the little door, and practically ran into a guard—one I hadn't seen before—who headed in the opposite direction. My presence obviously shocked him; he took a half step back and stared at me with wide eyes. "M'lady, this is no place for a woman!"

"B-but," I stammered, hating my sudden high-schoolish response, but unable to stop it. "I was here last night!"

"The day has brought us different circumstances," he said, rising to his full height, nose to nose with me. "You must get back to the safety of the keep, where no archer might maim one of our birds."

He wasn't going to back down. So I turned and walked away, wondering if I should be offended by the whole "bird" reference, and then shrugged it off as a fourteenth-century version of "chick." I glanced back, considering an attempt at sneaking past the other guard, but he was staring right at me, arms crossed in front of him, and he shook his head as if reading my mind.

"All right, all right," I muttered, ducking back through the short turret door. And swept down the stairs, wondering what the day might hold for me. Without a search for Lia in Siena, without a chance to stare out across the forest, what? Hang out with the dreaded Lady Rossi?

Not if I could help it.

I reached the bottom of the stairs, glanced down to where my bedroom door was, and quickly decided I couldn't spend another day cooped up in there. I walked in the opposite direction, deciding to explore a little, get an understanding of what was where around the castle. I tentatively knocked on a few doors, but it was as I suspected. This wing of the castle was empty save for me. "What?" I muttered. "Do I have the plague or something?"

I was actually glad for the privacy. The last thing I needed was Lady Rossi hanging out with me, jumping on the bed like we were going to have a sleepover or something, asking me what I thought of her boyfriend. No, that wouldn't be good. When I reached the turret, I came into the courtyard, entered the next door, and continued on down the next segment of the corridor. The castle was laid out like a pentagon, with a tall, crenellated tower at each corner. Each corridor had a fortified door. Luca had informed me it was for defensibility. One wing might fall to attackers, but chances were, the castle's defenders could hold them off somewhere. I ran my hand across the pockmarked limestone bricks, wondering how long ago the castello had been built. It was no wonder she was important to Siena; she was like a tight little ship on the far edge of the sea.

What had left her dismantled, totally leveled, by the time Lia and I explored her ruins? And when? Other medieval buildings survived. What had happened here?

I moved into the next segment and immediately saw and heard more action. Here, maids were at work, and I could see massive trunks and many dresses across the two large beds in the first, big room, with tapestries on the wall and a small fire crackling in a corner hearth. It was nothing like my own austere room, suitable for a nun.

I heard Lady Rossi giggling. I shivered and kept moving. Of course it was a room decorated for a lady; it was for the future Lady Forelli. The other rooms in this wing were probably for her ladies-in-waiting.

I couldn't get through the hallway fast enough. I raced to the door, relieved when I unlatched it and escaped. I ducked into the next corridor, expecting another row of rooms. But it was a massive, dimly lit room.

In the corner, a fire smoldered in the hearth, having chased away the morning's brief chill. Two big windows let the morning light in. I had stepped into the inviting room before I spotted him, lounging on a large horsehair settee, staring back at me with mild interest.

"Oh! M'lord!" I said, horrified to be discovered snooping. Fortino's sickroom.

"No, no," he said, gesturing at me as if to say *calm down*. "It is quite all right, Lady Betarrini." He lowered his book to his lap, and when he smiled, I realized just how down he looked. I wondered if he was thinking about Marcello, galloping off to a battle that should have been his own, if it wasn't for his sickness. He may as well have been a patient in the cancer wing of a hospital, simply biding his time.

I forced a smile and shoved away a shiver of fear. He was obviously a sweet guy, and not much older than me. "I will leave you to your reading." I started to back away.

"I would much prefer your sitting with me for a moment. Please." He gestured to a chair beside his.

I met his gaze and realized that despite his frail appearance, he had the bearing of a young lord. There would be no arguing with him.

I moved to the chair and folded my hands in my lap, staring at him as boldly as he was staring at me.

"You wonder why I don't ride with my brother?" he said, each word a sigh of long-held frustration.

"Nay. I mean…you are plainly sick—ailing."

"Indeed I am." Even in those few words, I could hear the wheeze in his breath. He was far worse than he had been, even a couple days ago.

"May I ask…what is it that plagues you?"

"Are you educated in the art of medicine?"

Yeah, the art of Walgreens and Urgent Care. "A bit," I hedged.

"Lung trouble. The doctors say that I am full of water. My humours are off balance. But they cannot right them again."

"Ahh," I said, as if I understood what the heck he was talking about. Humours. Dim recollections of a medieval museum and a diagram of a body segmented into four segments called *humours* flitted through my mind. They thought that if the body was off-kilter in one area, it set you off in the others. There was probably some logic in the midst of it that actually made sense. They hadn't been total idiots. But they had some pretty wild remedies, too.

"If you don't consider it prying, m'lord, can you tell me what your symptoms are?"

He smiled and laid his book on a small table beside him. "Surely a lady as comely as yourself wouldn't want to speak of such things."

"Try me."

He stared at me, confusion lowering his brow.

"Nay, m'lord," I translated. "I am most interested to know. Mayhap I might find some small way to aid you."

He looked at me hard then and shook his head a little. "I am not seeking a bride."

He thought I was after him? For what, his money? I raised my brows. "That is of great relief to me since I am not seeking a husband." Dad always joked that I had to wait until I was twenty-one to date.... Was this guy even twenty-one himself? I had pegged Marcello as about nineteen, a couple years older than me. I was guessing Fortino was a couple years older than that, but his thin, bony structure made him appear younger.

His brows lifted, and he smiled a little, as if he had never heard such a thing from an unattached female. Perhaps he hadn't. Not seeking a husband? What else did the girls have going for them?

No studies, no working. A girl's total worth was in whom she could marry and how many boys she could birth. It made me feel a little sorry for Lady Rossi. *Maybe I should cut her some slack....*

"I awaken in the morning, barely able to breathe," he labored to tell me, staring back at the fire again, "and my servant has to thump my back, break up the mucous, at which point I cough so hard that I confess I wish for death. At times, in the middle of the night, I labor so that I fear I've reached the end."

Hmm. Sounds a bit like the asthma I had as a kid. I remembered well the horrific feeling of suffocation.... I shook my head at the memory, glad that I'd outgrown it years before.

He leaned back and returned his gaze to me, as if that might be enough to make me take my skirts in hand and run from him. But I simply stared back.

"As the morning goes on," he finally went on, "the coughing eases, but this dreaded wheeze stays with me, reminding me of my illness with every breath of every day."

"Does your nose run? Do your eyes water?"

He nodded, clearly puzzled by my questions. His eyes were ringed with deep purple, testimony to his nightly battles to breathe—and possibly to allergies that set him off in the first place. Or it might have been caused by his sleep being so disrupted....

"Do you run a fever? Are you hot?"

He shook his head, then shrugged one shoulder. "I perspire, when I cough so violently. But it is not a fever."

"And your appetite? Do you want to eat?"

"At times, but my breathing makes it a chore." He lifted an arm and studied it, as if seeing for the first time how bony he had become.

"What have the doctors told you to do?"

He glanced to the fire. "Precious little. Though they are more than happy to take my father's gold florins for every visit."

"Does steam help at all?" I thought of my mom, tenting our heads with a towel and making us sit over a bowl of boiling water when we were all stopped up. It was uncomfortable, but it did get things moving again. And in dry country, like Toscana tended to be in the mid- to late-summer, it helped with things like allergies, too.

"Steam?"

"Yes, breathing in the vapors from scalding-hot water?"

"Nay," he said, studying me with an edge of crazy hope in his eyes. "They never suggested such a thing."

I eyed the chair on which he lounged. "How often are you on that settee each day, m'lord?"

He raised one brow. "Most of every day, I'd wager."

"Do your symptoms change depending on where you are? Do they get worse when you come in here from your bedchamber?"

He pulled a handkerchief from his breast pocket as he thought my questions over. "My nose and eyes tend to run. But I assumed it was from the smoke."

I glanced at the fire. "That is possible. Or you might be allergic to horses. And lounges covered in horsehair," I said with a small smile.

He glanced down at the settee with some understanding. "Allergic?"

Hmm, maybe that word isn't in use.... "It simply means that being near horses or couches made with their skins might interfere with your...humours."

His eyes opened wider with understanding.

"One can be allergic to horses, or hay, or cats, or pollen."

"Pollen?"

"Mm, that fine dust from the trees that is so thick this time of year. Even grass or weeds. Mayhap in Toscana, your doctors have not yet heard of this. It is quite common in Normandy." I was lying through my teeth, of course, but I wanted him to give my words some weight in case I could actually help him.

I rose and went to the small bookshelf, running my hand over the thick, odd goat-leather bindings and trying to remember enough Latin to read the titles. It had been a pet peeve of Dad's, that most kids never learned any Latin. He'd insisted we learned the basics. You can imagine what that did for my rep at Boulder High. [illegible] Geek Alert, when you have to meet your Latin teache[illegible]n Saturdays—

"Do you read, Lady Betarrini?" he asked, interrupting my reverie.

"Well, yes," I said, before I thought it through. I dragged my eyes toward him. Being schooled enough to read in this era was probably rare, even for the guys.

But he was smiling in delighted surprise. "Books are my constant companion. Father has little use for them. Marcello can read only a few pages before he falls asleep each night. He tolerates a reading in the Great Hall each eve, but his mind is clearly elsewhere. Tell me, have you read the poet?"

The poet, the poet, I thought, wracking my brain. "Dante. Of course." That's what all Italians called their most famous writer.

"Wonderful," he said in approval. "We shall have to discuss *The Divine Comedy* at your earliest convenience."

Everywhere I go, I can't seem to escape that thing…but if it turns your crank—

He regarded me and then took a slow, wheezy breath. "Pray tell, Lady Betarrini, how does one avoid daily things such as horses when one lives in a castle? Or dust from the trees?"

I smiled at him. "It is difficult. But I think I know of some measures that might bring you some relief. Might I hope that you would try one or two of them?"

"I don't see why not."

"Great!" I said, then seeing that my exuberant response shocked him a little. "I mean, very well. We shall begin on the morrow."

"Why not now?"

I blinked in surprise. "Well, all right. Please, m'lord, summon a servant." *We're gonna need a little help in here.*

He reached behind himself and pulled a rope. My eyes followed it to the ceiling, where it disappeared through a small hole. In a few moments, a footman appeared.

"Enzo, Lady Betarrini is of the mind to aid me this day."

The servant did not react. Perhaps that was what they strived for—no reaction, just obedience.

"Be at ease, Lady Betarrini. Tell him what to do."

I tapped my lips, thinking. "Is this where you like to spend your days? Is there another room with more air? More windows?"

"Nay, I'm afraid this is the best. And I confess, my favorite."

"All right, then. I'll need you to do exactly as I say for a week, no matter how mad it sounds. Are you willing to give me that much time?"

He gave me a lopsided grin. "I might be dead on the morrow, m'lady. But what time I have left is yours."

I returned his subtly flirtatious smile. We weren't serious about it, of course. It was just fun. "Good. Then Enzo here better fetch some help. I need this room cleared out, from top to bottom, and then the maids will need to come and wash every inch of it, from top to bottom, with hot, hot water, and some sort of cleanser.... What do you use to disinfect?"

Both men stared at me blankly. "I mean when there's been something foul, what do the maids use to clean, make it safe again?"

"Ah, lye is what you're after. And vinegar."

"Excellent!" I said, remembering. Lye was still the main ingredient in a lot of soaps. "Yes, hot, hot water, vinegar and lye. The same for your bedroom, m'lord. I beg you to empty it, and bring back only the barest of essentials." I began to pace. "The horsehair settee has to go, for example. You'll need to find a hardwood chair for the week."

"Be this a treatment or a punishment?"

I smiled. "I'm attempting to help you. Remember that. Please do not bring any of these woolens back in. Let's remove the tapestries, just for the week," I added quickly. "I saw women working upon a loom in the courtyard. Bring that new blanket in, fresh from the loom." I leaned closer to him. "Our doctors believe that things like dust get lodged in linens, and therefore, if that is what irritates your lungs, you are beneath one, huge irritant."

He nodded as if he understood me, but I could see a little of the This Chick's Crazy look in his eyes. *Whatever.*

"And me, m'lady. All this is well and good for the room, but I thought your aim was to aid me." He looked at me from the corner of his eye, that flash of flirtation and humor there again. In that moment, I could see the resemblance to Marcello, the glimpse of the young man he was supposed to be. I paced, thinking about Mom poking around the sites, pointing out herbs used in remedies for centuries.

"Peppermint," I told the servant. "More hot water. The finest, thinnest cloth you can obtain." I turned to Fortino. "In the meantime, I need you to bathe, head to toe, and wear a dressing gown, again, of the finest possible cloth."

He flashed me a grin. "Will you be seeing to my bath yourself, m'lady?"

"Nay," I said, lifting my eyebrows and smiling back. "I believe that Enzo is more than capable of seeing you through that." I liked the color our game brought to his cheeks, even if we both knew it was futile. When he said he might be dead by tomorrow, he wasn't joking. His skin was so ashen, his bones poking at his flesh that he looked like he belonged in hospice. But in the meantime, I could give him some hope.

Fortino disappeared on the arm of Enzo, moving slowly, and I assumed it was to see to his bath. I dared not ask; I didn't want him to think I was truly flirting. He needed to see me more as nurse than Potential Girlfriend Material. More servants were brought in, and the room was quickly emptied. Tapestries were rolled up and removed. Furniture was carried out. The books, the precious books, so rare in these times—priceless, were they to survive until my own—were lovingly wrapped in linens and placed in trunks.

"Saints in heaven, what is going on here?"

I turned to see Cook enter the room, and smiled at her rounded eyes and pink cheeks. "Hello, Cook." I moved over to the older woman and said, "I learned a bit of doctoring in Normandy, so Lord Fortino has asked me to do what I can for him."

"Ach, you watch that one, now," she said lowly, waving a finger. "He was quite the randy one before the illness got the best of him."

Randy? Did she mean he was a player or something? He felt far from any kind of Romeo to me. I mean, if he wasn't on the verge of death, it might be different....

But I nodded in understanding. "I'll take care. May I ask you for something for him?" Her brow furrowed. "I wonder if we might give him good soups in a clear broth for the next week. Chicken would be best. Lots of vegetables and meat. Do you think you can manage that?"

"Certainly," she said, as if offended. "I could do that in my sleep."

"Wonderful. The more simple and hearty, the better. Let's feed him five times a day."

"Five times a day?" she blustered. "He barely eats once!"

"Yes, well, I will see an end to that." No one could get better on such rations. And Mom always said that chicken soup had healing properties...if I could get him to even eat a cup of it every few hours, it'd give his body the energy to fight whatever was slowly killing him.

"If that's what the master has asked for..."

"Yes," I said simply, speaking for him.

Five maids arrived, steaming buckets of water in each hand. I looked about the empty room. "First, let's sweep it out and put out that fire. Can you fetch some brooms? I will aid you."

They glanced at each other, and I knew I'd crossed a weird line. "Fine, fine," I said in irritation. "Do it yourselves. We must hurry, though. I want the water to stay hot."

Two scurried out and returned in short order. In minutes they'd swept the room with their crude straw brooms, piling the dust and then carrying it outside. Another poured water on the fire and cleaned the embers from the fireplace and carried it out. I gazed around. "All right, now. Let's start up high. Like this." I picked up a bucket and threw the water in a massive arc, so it went to the top of the ten-foot walls, even reaching a portion of the ceiling. The maids twittered and giggled, but I ignored them. They were just nervous. "Like that. Every wall. Then the floor."

They went about their business. In half an hour, lye had been spread, more buckets of water had been splashed, and all of it had been sopped up and carried out. I returned from the hallway and surveyed their work, hands on hips. "Nice work, ladies!" I crooned.

They looked at me, wide-eyed.

"Grazie, grazie," I said. "This is perfect. Now I need those wooden chairs for Lord Fortino, and a bucket of boiling water and clean, clean cloth. Can you fetch that for me, please?"

"Yes, m'lady," they all said, bobbing and moving out like a line of housekeeping soldiers. I was beginning to like this Lady business. I paused to enjoy the wonder of it. Where else might I have enjoyed such power as a typical seventeen-year-old? I could get used to this, I thought, crossing my arms, watching the women do as I bid.

The furniture returned, two simple wooden chairs, a table, and a more elaborate wooden settee. They hardly looked comfortable for reclining, but there was no way around it. If we were after a non-allergic room, this was it. They brought back the tapestries and crates of books, but I held up my hand. "Forgive me," I said, choosing my words carefully. "But, for a week, could you put those in another room?"

Eyes wide with confusion, the servants turned and left, speaking in hushed Italian to those behind them, passing on the word. "Sorry, Fortino," I muttered. "It's hardly a cozy den without them, but you wanted my help.…"

Fortino himself returned then, looking more pale than before. He was in a thin white dressing gown, shivering, even though it was a good seventy degrees. It was going to be a hot one today, but he, obviously, was not yet feeling it. I went to the opposite side of him and helped his servant get him to the chair.

"What have you done with my possessions?" he asked.

"It's all in your own quarters for now. Remember, you gave me a week. I'll fetch any book you wish, but we need to be careful what we add to this room. The goal, of course, is to make you feel better."

"Goal?"

Seriously? He didn't know that word? "Uh, desired outcome."

He nodded. Cook arrived with the first of his soup, and I explained to him my hope—that he would try to eat constantly through the day, at least a cup of it, five times. He began the task gamely, but after a few bites, sat back, looking at me as if he might throw up.

"All right, all right. Next time," I said, looking to Cook, "let's just do the broth." She nodded and departed, and another servant arrived, with a fresh bucket of boiling water, a dancing coil of steam rising from the sloshing top.

"Right here." I gestured toward Fortino's feet. She set it down and handed me a yard of clean, gauzelike silk cloth. "Do you have access to more of this? A lot of it? It's perfect for the master, unlikely to disrupt his health." We could use it to pad the wooden settee. He was already shifting uncomfortably, probably because he had so little fat or muscle. And I could use more to block off the windows, allowing air in but hopefully keeping some of the pollen out.

She bobbed a curtsy and set off to do as I bid, but I walked over to the table and the basket of supplies they'd brought me from the kitchen. I cut a lemon in half and selected some peppermint from a basket of herbs. Fortino regarded me with suspicious, worried eyes, as did his servant.

"Cease your fretting," I said. "I do not aim to harm you."

"Nay, just remove any comfort I have left."

"My desire," I said with scolding eyes, a little irked with him, "is to see you to better health. Try to remember that, all right?"

"I'll remember…with every creak of this bench," he said, waving at me tiredly.

I squeezed the lemon into the water and then let the rind float atop it. I tore the oblong mint into the steaming water, watching the pieces drift across the surface for a moment until the water at last stilled. I had no idea if these would do anything more than make it smell good. Was I remembering it right? That mint had calming properties? *Whatever. At least it's something.*

I looked up at him. "Do you still feel sick to your stomach?"

He shook his head weakly.

"Here," I said, waving him forward. "You must sit with your head above the steam, so you feel it upon your face. Breathe it in as much as you can. I'm going to use this," I said, reaching for the yard of cloth, "to stretch across your head, making a form of tent, which will keep the steam coming your way. All right?"

The servant looked at me with distrustful eyes and then around the room, as if catching himself. I ignored him and placed a hand on Fortino's back. "How do you fare, m'lord?"

He nodded in response.

"If it gets too much, if you're feeling faint, please sit back and take in some fresh air, all right?"

He nodded again.

He was so terribly weak. If we were in my time, he'd definitely be in the hospital. He probably needed a transfusion or something. An IV, for sure. I needed to get as much liquid into him as I could. Water. Tea. Broth. That would go a long way in making him feel better. And hopefully my weak attempt at a breathing treatment would help him too. *If only I had access to a nebulizer and inhalers, I could fix you right up....*

He sat back, the cloth about his head and shoulders, panting, but within fifteen minutes the steam had brought some color to his cheeks. "Good, good," I soothed. "You're doing well."

"It makes my nose run faster, but I think it aids my lungs."

"Yes," I said with a smile, encouraged. "That's what we want. To loosen the phlegm inside your lungs so you can breathe better." I considered him for a moment. "M'lord, in your library, do you have a book by the nun named Hildegard? She is from Bingen, a place far from here, but she is known for her healing, her fame spreading to even my country. She might have some recipes to aid you."

He shook his head, and I sighed in disappointment. Maybe the woman hadn't even been born yet.

"How many more times will we do this?"

"As much as we can; all day if that's what it takes," I said. "Then, if you improve, less. But it's worth a try, yes?"

He nodded again, so tired, and then bent forward over the bucket, determined to keep at it.

What would it be like to be twenty-one and think you could die any day?

The thunder of hoofbeats and the muffled shouts of men told us that Marcello and his men were back.

I hesitated, but Fortino said, looking out from beneath his tented cloth, "Go. But kindly return and tell me of their victory." His words held none of the question in his eyes.

"Indeed." I moved out of the room and out the corridor door to the courtyard. The men swirled, like leaves caught in a whirlwind, still hollering about their victory as if they'd won the World Cup or something. I quickly counted. All eighteen of them were back, plus two captives.

"They put up a brief fight, then scattered like dogs," Marcello said proudly to his father as he dismounted. I struggled to hear over the noise, but I didn't want to get too close, to interfere. It wasn't my place. And Lady Rossi was already on the move, heading to her man. I wasn't going to get in the middle of that.

"We captured these two," I heard him say.

"Well done, son, well done," Lord Forelli said, patting him on the back. "Have they spoken yet of the man who would back such a nefarious venture?"

"Nothing, yet."

"Well, stake them here, in the courtyard. We shall get it out of them soon enough."

I turned to study the elder Forelli. *Stake them?* Surely I hadn't heard him correctly.

Marcello paused and then nodded. Had anyone but me seen his moment of hesitation?

Lord Forelli moved in front of the two prisoners. "I am Lord Lorenzo Forelli, master of this castle. You attacked a manor under my protection and killed a man. You shall pay for your crimes, but it will go better for you if you tell me who your master is."

Refusing to do as he bid, both men looked anywhere but at the older man.

Lord Forelli waved his arm and then leaned forward to say so lowly I barely caught it, "You will tell me of your master, sooner or later."

The knights, save for Luca, Giovanni, and Pietro, moved out and around the main building, to the back, where I assumed the stables were. Servants brought stakes and ropes, and in quick order, the three remaining knights had the prisoners staked to the ground, spread-eagled on their backs.

I took a step back, trying to cover my horror and probably not doing a very good job of it. I had heard him right, after all.

"Are you all right, m'lady?" Cook asked, coming beside me.

"What will they do with them?"

"A fair bit of torture, I'd wager, if they don't tell the master what he wants to hear."

I remained silent and Marcello came near, Lady Rossi beside him. Behind him, Giovanni kicked one of the prisoners.

"Why not throw them in the dungeon?" I said bitterly, unable to stop myself. "Push bamboo shoots beneath their fingernails? Put them on the rack?" I never was good at standing idly by when someone else was being harmed.

Everyone turned to look at me, mouths hanging open. "Mayhap it is different in Normandy," Marcello bit back. "However, I ask you to refrain from your judgment, Lady Betarrini. You clearly know nothing of how order is kept in Toscana."

"Clearly," I repeated, feeling Lady Rossi's triumphant gaze but not daring to glance at her.

"If this troubles you, m'lady, mayhap you should return to your quarters."

"Maybe I shall," I said, feeling a sense of numbness come over me.

Lord Forelli strode over to us. "Once we have their master's name, we shall get them to Siena," he said to Marcello, ignoring me and Lady Rossi. "The Nine can see them—and their master—to justice. But we must first have a name."

"It shall be done, Father."

"Siena?" I said, seizing upon the word, worried I might've just blown it. "Lord Marcello, may I go with you? I may have better fortune there, finding my family." I thought of the rectangular Fonte Gaia there again, in the piazza, Lia looking for me—

He shook his head. "The woods are rife with bands of robbers like these, capitalizing on the unrest between Siena and Firenze—to say nothing of the Paratores."

"That could go on for weeks, months!" I cried. "Please," I said, reaching out to touch his forearm, feeling the dagger glance Lady Rossi shot me, "I must try to find Lia. Please."

"Lord Marcello," Lady Rossi said, turning to flutter her eyelashes at him. "I do agree with Lady Betarrini. If I were separated from my mother and a sister for so long, not knowing if they lived or died, I'd be beside myself. And as I've expressed, I, too, would like to return to Siena. Our nuptials are not very far away, and there are many plans I must turn my attention to."

"So you wish for me to see two women to Siena?" he asked in irritation. "In the midst of the worst strife we've seen in a decade?"

We both stared at him, waiting him out. Who'd have guessed I'd ever be on the same side as Lady Rossi?

"Fine," Marcello said, throwing up his hands. "We shall leave on the morrow. But only because my father wishes us to see these men to Siena. And *only* if they give us the information we need." He turned on his heel and walked off. And I turned away, resisting the urge to see if Lady Rossi shared my feeling of victory.

Upon his invitation, and eager to be apart from the rest, I took my supper with Fortino. I spent an hour urging him to eat some more.

"Please, m'lady," he said, leaning back, eyes shutting, shoving away the wooden bowl, "will you not read me a bit of the poet?"

I picked up the volume from the table between us, fingering the parchment pages. The pages weren't smooth and uniform like modern books—they were deckled and rough on the edges. I opened it carefully, feeling as though I should have on white gloves like my parents wore when handling artifacts. But of course, that wasn't quite possible.

"What is it about the poet that you love so dearly?" I asked.

Fortino's brown eyes slowly opened. "You do not care for his work?"

"I did not say that...."

He studied me a moment. "He is very wise. When I was a boy, I remember him coming to stay, a fugitive from Firenze. The pope was very angry with him, and my father was an avid supporter. So he lived with us for several weeks. Important men came from far and wide to listen to him."

I watched him as he looked to the window, remembering.

"Did that make the pope consider your father his enemy too?" I ventured.

Fortino cocked a brow. "It certainly did not endear him. But Father did not care. The lines were already being drawn, between Firenze and Siena." He reached for the book, and I handed it to him. "Dante gives us wisdom in regard to the faith as well as politics in this work. I find new insights every time I read it...or hear it read." He opened it and turned a few pages. "Please, begin there."

It was my turn to cock a brow at him. "I will read it if you will eat another bite as I read."

He smiled. "Tyrant."

"Truly, m'lord, you will feel better, the more you eat."

"I've already eaten more today than I have all of last week."

"Which is why you feel a bit better. Please. Just half that bowl," I coaxed.

"Very well," he said, not at all pleased with my bargain. He lifted the bowl to his lips and eyed me and the book.

I began to read. "'Midway on our life's journey, I found myself in dark woods, the right road lost.'"

I paused. *Dark woods. Right road lost....* Perhaps the poet had more to say to me than I thought. But that was when I heard the men screaming. I half rose, letting the book fall. It freaked me out, hearing grown men scream like that.

"Lady Betarrini—" Fortino cautioned as I picked up the book and set it on the table again. But I was already moving toward the door. "You mustn't go out there."

"Why?" I said, looking at him over my shoulder. A man screamed again, and I faltered, as if I'd been hit.

"Because of that," he said. "It is not a lady's place to witness the base work of man."

I swallowed a snort and turned toward the door when I heard yet another cry. "I shall return in a moment."

I ignored his call, banking on the fact he was too weak to follow. But I had to know what was happening. It had to be the men who had been captured. I knew them to be mercenaries, Castello Forelli's enemies, perhaps even killers themselves, but what was happening to them? I strode out into the courtyard and pushed my way between a line of soldiers, then came up short.

The two captured men were still splayed out on the ground. The first man had an arrow in each leg, literally pinning him to the soil beneath. He writhed in pain, as did the man beside him.

I looked in horror to Lord Foraboschi, who stood over the second man, drawing his arrow back to drive a second arrow into his leg too.

"If we tell you," cried the man, writhing as if he could free himself, "we are dead already!"

"Remain still," said Lord Foraboschi, "or I might nick an artery."

"Stop!" I cried. A knight near me grabbed for my arm, but I dodged him. "Stop!" I shouted again, stepping past the first man.

Lord Foraboschi glanced at me and then back at his target, pulling the bowstring farther back. I was enraged, and before I could think more clearly about it, stepped forward and lifted his arrow just as he released it. It went flying across the courtyard, narrowly missing a servant.

"Lady Betarrini!" Marcello cried. I could hear the men behind me collectively suck in their breath, and it finally registered that perhaps I shouldn't have done that....

Lord Foraboschi turned toward me, his eyebrows knitting in hatred. "What are you?" he seethed, stepping toward me, raising his hand. "A filthy Fiorentini sympathizer? A Guelph?"

He was about to backhand me, but Marcello caught his arm midstrike. "M'lord, that is quite enough. I will see to Lady Betarrini."

Lord Foraboschi, was thinner, older, and several inches taller than Marcello, but there was no way he could overpower him. He looked at Marcello and then to me and back again, his anger clearly growing. But Marcello's men, Pietro, Giovanni, and Luca, were right behind him, waiting to aid him if a fight was to ensue.

"Bah," Lord Foraboschi spat out, wrenching his arm from Marcello's grasp.

One of the prisoners groaned, and I turned toward him. Tears were lacing down the side of his face, and he gritted his teeth, doing everything he could to keep from screaming. "Please," I muttered, forgetting the mess with Foraboschi, feeling my heart race even faster, "we must get these arrows out," I said. I knelt beside the man, thinking through how to remove the arrow, bind the wound—

And that was when I felt Marcello's hand on my arm, Luca's on the other. They lifted me and hurried me past the circle of men, back toward my quarters. My feet barely touched the ground. "Stop! We must help them! Marcello! Luca—"

We entered the hallway, and the door shut behind us. Then the men released me. "You," Marcello thundered, pointing at me, "shall not go out there again!"

"Somebody must stand for decency!" I spat back. "What kind of barbarians are you?"

"We?" he said, eyes awash in confusion. "We?" He shook his head, shared a look with Luca and paced back and forth a couple of times. "Do you *know* who those men out there represent?"

"No doubt, your *political* enemies." My tone was full of sarcasm. Big. Freakin'. Deal. Wasn't life more important? Every time?

"Those men," he spat out, "killed a good man. A man I considered a friend," he said, tapping his chest. "We were boys together. He married a fine woman two years past—someone I also considered a friend—and fathered two beautiful sons, one barely walking, one still a babe in his mother's arms." He stepped closer to me, inches from my face. "Those men," he said, nodding his head toward the courtyard, "those men you are so eager to *defend,* made my friend *watch* as they burned his family alive. Then, and only then, did they kill him."

My mouth was dry. In the last five days, I had seen men in battle, men wounded. But a woman? Two tiny children? A husband, a father, forced to watch such horror? My knees weakened, and my head swirled.

Oh, Mom. Lia. I'm so far from home. So, so far—

"M'lady!" I heard Marcello dimly grunt, as if he were far away.

But I was falling.

Blacking out…

When I awakened, I was in my room, Marcello beside me, looking miserable. Luca was standing by the door, as if on guard, trying to stare straight ahead. Failing at it.

"Forgive me, m'lady. I forgot myself," he said before I could speak.

"It's…it's all right," I said, lifting a hand to my head and staring at the ceiling, piecing together what had happened. I'd fainted. Unbelievable. Since when did I become a fainting sort of girl? I'd passed out only once before, when I was sick.

"You were overwrought," he said, standing, bringing a hand to his own head, as if it ached. "As was I."

I sighed and sat up, swinging my legs to the ground. The guy was really beating himself up over this…and I realized now that I had deserved his earlier words. I didn't have a handle on how things worked yet, here. Now.

I mean, duh. I was living in medieval times. People were monsters in this era. I had only come across a tiny piece of what was going on out there. Marcello was simply using the tools he had at hand to try to get the information he and his father needed…not that I thought Lord Foraboschi was okay. He was a major creeper.

He clearly *liked* shooting those guys. I shivered at the thought of him.

Marcello bent and touched my shoulder lightly. I shivered at his touch. "Do you have a chill?" he said. "Perhaps a blanket—"

"Nay," I said, laying my hand on his and looking into his eyes. "I am well. Truly. Please. Fret no more over me."

Our faces were overly close, and in that moment something more passed between us. I'd never felt this kind of thing with a guy—such a connection. I knew, in my head, that we were practically strangers; but this thing—whatever it was—made me feel *known*. Seen. Acknowledged and appreciated and admired.

I shivered again and dropped my hand. He pulled his back and stepped away, staring at me as if he couldn't figure out what had just happened. "I…I must see to the men," he said, gesturing with his head. "You will remain here?"

I understood his question.

"I shall not interfere again," I promised. *On any level…*

CHAPTER 9

"How do you fare, m'lord?" I asked, pausing in the doorway the next morning.

Fortino looked toward me. He had more color, despite his surly glance. "That was the most uncomfortable night I've ever spent. But I must say, I feel better than I have in weeks." He patted his chest. "Today I am able to breathe again. Truly breathe." He smiled, and I thought again about how much he looked like Marcello, just thinner. The spark in his eye made him resemble his brother even more.

"'Tis truly a miracle of sorts," he said. "I am most grateful for your ministrations, m'lady. You've done more for me in one day than all the doctors my father has ever summoned."

"That is wonderful, m'lord," I said, unable to suppress my grin. The hope on his face filled me with joy. I'd never done anything that had really helped someone like that before. It made me feel bad about what I had to tell him. So I just plunged forward with, "I am to take my leave of the castello today—"

"Leave? You cannot leave! I am just now on a mending path."

"And I am so happy that I could aid you in some small way. But I am beside myself with fear for my family. I must be off to find them. I'm certain you understand."

He clearly didn't. I could see it on his face. He looked like a pouty little boy about to be abandoned by his mother. I shoved away a pang of guilt.

"What does Marcello say of this plan?" he asked. "It was my understanding that the woods were full of bands of mercenaries."

"He says much the same, but he and your father feel it's important to report to the Nine about these mercenaries—and the man who hired them." I shuddered, remembering again the screams that picked up again after Marcello left me, then abruptly ceased in the middle of the night. I had not dared to peek my head out into the courtyard to see what had become of them.

"Who is it that set them to such a task?" Fortino asked.

"I have not yet heard," I said, shaking my head.

"But surely Marcello wouldn't subject a woman to such—"

"Do not fret over me, m'lord. Once we catch sight of Siena, we will be safe."

"Siena is six hours' ride from here."

"So we will have to ride fast enough to make it in three, faster than any mercenaries," I said, more jauntily than I felt. I didn't want him to worry. *It might send him into an asthma attack or something.* "I am fairly good with a sword," I said, walking to the only adornment to the room I'd allowed back into the room, six swords crossed in Xs on one wall. I ran my hand along one edge.

"Do not tell me that you can wield a sword as well as read."

"I can," I said, grinning at him over my shoulder.

"They raise women in Normandy quite differently than in Toscana."

"Quite. Fortino, might I borrow this one? I'd feel better, if I was armed in these woods. And anyone who dared to attack me would be as surprised as you to find my bringing a sword against them. It would give me an advantage."

"Those are uncommonly heavy," he said. "They were my grandfather's."

"Better than nothing," I pressed. After last night, I dared not try to steal into the armory and recover the short broadsword and dagger I'd worn before. "I could return it to you with Marcello."

"If you must," he said doubtfully.

I took it gingerly from its hooks and moved it in a slow arc, with both of my hands on the hilt. It was heavier than the one I had held two days earlier, but I felt instantly stronger with it in hand.

"You shall get yourself killed," said a voice from the door.

I turned, knowing already it was Marcello.

"An armed woman will be more of a target for knights on the prowl."

"And unarmed women can find themselves without defense," I said pointedly. "I shall not be that woman."

He studied me. "It is one thing to play with swords in the safety of one's castle, with servants, as your father apparently allowed you to do," he said.

"Marcello," Fortino began, interceding for me.

But Marcello held his hand up to his brother, his eyes still on me. "It is quite another to encounter a man on the battlefield."

I wanted to shudder at the memory of the giant in the employ of the Paratores. But Marcello's story of what had happened to that family yesterday was worse. I lifted my chin. "I will take my chances."

"Lady Betarrini, trust me and my men to protect you."

"You might be otherwise occupied."

"You are not prepared for what may come if you unsheathe a sword."

"Try me. Draw yours."

I felt Fortino shift in his chair, but my eyes were solely on his brother. Marcello studied me for a long moment, his gaze intense and warm, but then, so quickly I could only take half a breath, he drew his sword and was rushing across the room at me, yelling ferociously.

I barely had time to bring my sword up to block him, his sword pausing just before it hit mine, so I knew he didn't indeed plan to slice my head from my neck.

I turned and let out a cry, using the momentum of my turn to bring my sword around. Belatedly, I realized I didn't have the strength to stop it, as he had his own blow, but he blocked it, staring at me with brown eyes full of wonder. A couple of servants had entered the room, as well as a knight or two, obviously alerted by our cries, but Marcello raised one hand to them. "All is well."

He advanced upon me, choosing his steps, watching me, my hands, my eyes, casually trying to figure out my next move. At that moment, what I needed most was to convince him that I should be given a weapon before we took to the road. So again, I swung around, ending with my sword en route to his heart, confident that with his strength and size, he could again stop it.

He dodged and deflected my sword, but I quickly regained my footing and waved it before me, advancing steadily upon him as we crossed blades to one side and then the other. Out of breath, I stopped, and he let a slow smile spread across his face as he stared down at me, barely panting.

"Surprised?" I asked.

"You might say that." But he used the moment to attack again, pushing me back. I almost stumbled and fell, barely blocking each blow he now dealt me.

"All right, all right," I said, lifting a hand, hunched over, breathing harder than before.

He lowered his sword and grinned over at his companions, who teased him about defeating a woman. But then I saw the opportunity. I pulled back my sword and turned, bringing the flat of the weapon against his belly, like a bat to a ball.

His breath left him in a whoosh as his men hooted with laughter and the servants twittered in hidden giggles. He bent over, trying to regain his breath, and as he did so, I lifted my skirts slightly, put a slippered foot against his shoulder, and shoved against him.

Clearly caught unaware, he fell to the floor.

The room fell silent, and I wondered if I had crossed another line, but I didn't care. I moved toward him and set the tip of the sword on the stone beside his head. "Might I carry at least this sword, m'lord?"

"Fine," he said. He rolled to his side and then sat partially up, looking over to his brother. His face changed in that moment, to one of surprise, as he saw the color in Fortino's face.

"A healer as well as a warrior," Fortino said, in naked admiration.

"Indeed," Marcello said, glancing up at me. "With eyes the color of the most fertile ground. You, m'lady, will give the troubadours of Siena something altogether new to sing of."

I smiled and then offered a hand to help him up, but Luca and Pietro were there a half second before me, both staring at me in wonder.

I turned toward Fortino, suddenly embarrassed with all the attention. The last thing I needed was anyone whispering—or for heaven's sake, singing—of my actions. I needed to escape this place, this time, and get home before it was discovered I wasn't who I said I was. *You've gotta blend into the walls more, woman,* I berated myself. *Make 'em forget about you so you can disappear, back through the sands of time to your own.*

"Are you quite well?" he asked me as I took the chair beside him and the others filtered out.

"Quite," I said, focusing on him again. He did look far better than he had just yesterday. "I beg you to continue on with your regimen, m'lord. Work up to solid foods as soon as you can, and when weak, return to the soup. You can add blankets and other comforts and examine if they interfere at all with your breathing. If they do, remove them again. Understood?"

He nodded. "We never did get back to our reading of the poet," he said, fiddling with a splinter in the arm of his wooden settee. He was so desperately lonely. How would I feel if Lia left me each day, with nothing but books to keep me company? At least we had Internet.

"Mayhap our paths will cross again and we shall have the opportunity to read more together," I offered.

"That would be a delight," he said, his eyes meeting mine. "Go with God, Lady Betarrini."

"Um, thanks," I said. I turned and left the room, then walked down the corridor to my own. Go with God? Was this God's path, this crazy adventure in a forgotten age? And if so, what did He want me to do?

"Change the course of history? Right some wrong? What?" I muttered to the stone ceiling. No voice came to me from the sputtering torch like Moses' burning bush. No angel appeared in the light streaming from my window. "Whatever it is, just let me know so I can get it done and get home, okay?"

"M'lady?" asked a girl tentatively, and for the first time I realized I wasn't alone in my room.

"Oh! Giacinta! I didn't see you there. I was just saying I need to gather my things and hopefully get a little closer to home."

She pointed to two satchels. "I packed your other gown, and your other things, as well as a fine, new gown that Lady Forelli, God rest her soul—" she paused to cross herself again— "never had the opportunity to wear. It had been intended for Lord Fortino's nuptials."

"His nuptials? He was married?"

"He was intended for Lady Vitti of Siena. But when he took so ill, the betrothal agreement was broken. Soon afterward, Lady Forelli died of the fever, and Lord Forelli never seemed to consider it again."

I paused, thinking over that. Poor man. So much lost. So much promise, hope, joy, gone within what? A year? "Thank you for your care, Giacinta," I murmured.

"Who will see to your hair, m'lady?"

"I can only hope someone with hands as fast as yours," I said with a smile. *Maybe they have a hair dryer in Siena,* I joked to myself. *Trust me, I can manage this mop with some decent product and a roller brush.* "Thank you."

"Go with God, m'lady," she said with a bob of her head, and headed for the door.

"Go with God," I returned, wondering again at the words.

In the courtyard, Marcello and his men were bent over in a circle. Marcello was drawing with a stick in the dust. A plan, I sensed; he was making a plan. I crept closer, hoping none of them would notice me.

"The Paratores will not wish us to reach Siena. They'll know we intend to return with reinforcements, which might aid us in conquering them." He looked about at the men, eyes full of warning, and then he spotted me.

I was clearly not welcome. There was none of the delight and wonder in his eyes that had been there when we had our swordplay in Fortino's den. I turned and walked toward a servant holding a brown gelding with my stupid sidesaddle, feeling as if Marcello had slapped me across the face. *Dumb boys' club. Women's lib is obviously a long way off.*

Lady Rossi emerged from the dining hall, on the arm of the senior Lord Forelli and followed by Lord Foraboschi and her ladies-in-waiting. The girls looked a bit wan at the prospect of riding out in the midst of such danger. I turned away so Lady Rossi wouldn't see me rolling my eyes, and tried to feel compassion for her. She was a product of her environment, given few choices. What might I have been like, had I been born when she had been? Six hundred and seventy years made a world of difference to society.

Enzo arrived and lifted a sheath to me. "Courtesy of Lord Fortino," he said. He quickly strapped it to my saddle, and I slid the sword inside. "It'll be covered by your skirts, m'lady," he said, delight in his eyes. "They shall never suspect that you carry it."

"I hope not," I said.

Marcello was there then, behind him, watching us. I felt my heartbeat pick up. "Do not take undue comfort in that old sword," he said lowly. "As I said, if a knight finds you are willing to use it, you might very well become more of a target."

I looked over his shoulder at Lady Rossi, who was staring at us, then back to him. "I'd rather die than be taken."

"You might very well have the opportunity to choose," he muttered. He leaned down, and I caught his smell again—that lovely mix of pine and leather and wood. But he gripped my waist and lifted me up to the saddle. Without looking, he took my heels and slid them into the stirrups, side by side. "No bareback today, m'lady."

"I realize that," I bit back, unable to control my irritation at his I Make the Rules Here attitude. Liking the way his hands felt on the backs of my ankles made me even more irritated.

He paused and looked up at me. "I'll have enough to deal with, guarding Lady Rossi. My men are charged with the prisoners as well as Lady Rossi's ladies-in-waiting. You will ride beside Luca, right behind me. If you break formation or do anything to try my patience at all, I shall send you back here immediately and refuse to take you to Siena for a month. Understood?"

I clenched my lips and glared at him. "Could you be any more clear?"

He looked puzzled at my sarcasm.

"I understand," I finally said. He left me then, even as Luca rode up. With his sandy hair, green eyes, and quick smile, I knew this one would charm my little sister. She always went for the California surfer-dude types. Luca was about as close as Italy could offer.

He glanced over at the rest of the girls still getting settled in their saddles. "If I may ask, m'lady, where'd you learn to wield a sword?"

"My father," I said.

"Ahh," he said, sorrow shadowing his eyes for a moment. "No sons, eh?"

"My father would've taught me to wield a sword, and my sister to shoot her arrows, whether or not he had sons." I nudged the gelding's flank and moved away from him, toward the others.

"Your sister is an archer?" he asked, by my side in seconds, unperturbed by my irritation.

"She is quite accomplished," I said. *Took State, last year, in the juniors....*

"I must say, I like how they breed women in Normandy," he said, cocking a brow. "I do hope we find her in Siena with your mother so we might be properly introduced."

"Yes, well, it depends on how much you agitate me in the meantime," I tossed back at him.

He nodded and smiled, then instantly sobered when Marcello caught his eye. The young lord was all business, his brown, intelligent eyes flicking over the retinue. I shivered a little at the sheer power of him. I'd never encountered it in a guy so close to my own age.

He turned toward Lady Rossi and said lowly, "M'lady, I beg you to leave your ladies behind. They are far safer here than on the road between here and Siena."

"We have discussed it thoroughly, m'lord," she said, her tone sweet but her words unbending. "It is unseemly for me to travel without them. They are willing to take the risk."

I glanced behind us, back to the women two rows behind me. They did not appear at all willing.

Stupid, selfish girl, making them do something they don't want to do. I looked back to Marcello and Lady Rossi. It was not my place to speak. *Blend into the walls, Gabi.* I reminded myself again. *Make 'em forget about you.*

"Take close care, son," Lord Forelli said, reaching up to take his son's hand. "We will be anxiously awaiting word from you."

"I will send a message as soon as we are in the city, and another as soon as I have any news."

My eyes shifted back to a mule that was tied behind the last two guards. Cages with pigeons rested on either side of the mount. Homing pigeons. I had wondered if they were to be lunch, but messenger pigeons made far more sense.

"Mind the gates while we are gone, Father," Marcello said.

A priest came out of the Great Hall, swinging what looked like a tin lamp before him, its sweet smoke trailing in a line and then spreading along the ground. The others bowed their heads, as if in prayer, and the small man chanted in Latin, crossing the air before himself, over and over. He moved down the line, continuing his litany. When he caught my eye, I hurriedly shut mine, whispering my own prayer that he wouldn't call me out as a heretic among them. But he moved on.

His nasally prayer came to an end, and Marcello immediately set off. I glanced at Lady Rossi, who so easily kept her seat in the saddle, and shifted, hoping to find peace with my own span of cursed leather. *Maybe my rear is that much bigger than hers,* I thought. The things were probably meant for size fives, not my more…curvaceous figure.

"All is well with you, m'lady?" Luca asked, beside me.

"Well enough," I muttered. I glanced at him, but his eyes were already tracing the forest, alert to any attackers huddling there. I looked down the line and saw that the other sixteen knights did the same. A shiver ran down my back. I was glad for the sword in the sheath beneath my skirts.

Let 'em come, I thought.

But we moved on. As the hours passed and we saw no sign of any interlopers, we all relaxed a bit, enjoying the warming morning sun, the doves cooing in the dense scrub oaks. In front of me, Marcello and Lady Rossi talked, and I realized they had some semblance of an honest relationship. She smiled at something he said, and he smiled back. Maybe they were actually in love. Who was I to judge? I had no idea, really, how medieval love affairs were conducted. I thought back to the spark I'd felt the night before after I'd passed out. Had it all been my imagination, or was he a little into me? I glanced at them again. She was looking into his eyes, batting her lashes.

I shook my head. It didn't matter anyway. I was soon outta here.

About an hour or more into our ride, everyone seemed to settle down. There was something about being halfway there that made us feel like we were going to be okay. A scout that Marcello had sent ahead returned, and Marcello brought our train to a halt. The man reported a clear road, no sign of the rogue bands of mercenaries nor the Paratores.

Marcello shook his head and glanced back at Luca. "It makes no sense. The Paratores could not have missed that we are en route to Siena. They always have spies out, watching the road."

Luca returned his look, and then his green eyes widened. "Get down!"

Marcello immediately ducked, as did I, instinct taking over. I could hear the singing whistle of arrows. I glanced to my left. Luca tugged me down from the saddle, using our two horses as shields. *They are shooting at us,* I thought distantly, as if I wasn't in my own body. *Ambush.*

The men had been covered with gray cloth, blending into the granite boulders above us. But the archers were only the first volley. They were now swarming down over the rocks, like an army of Gollums with uncanny agility. Marcello frowned at them and made a sound of frustration. He looked to Luca.

"They purchased his loyalty," he said, jutting his chin toward the scout, who scurried over to the boulders.

I let out a humorless laugh. Some things never changed. For the right amount of money, one could always find a traitor.

They were getting closer.

Marcello looked back at me with alarm. "Can you keep your seat?"

"What?"

"Can you keep your seat, on your saddle?"

"Well, yes, but—"

"I need you to ride ahead with the women. Your only chance is to outride any that give you chase. I'll send two men with you, but your best chance is to ride fast."

I nodded, not feeling it, but seeing no opportunity, really, to disagree.

Luca tossed me back up to the saddle as Marcello did the same with Lady Rossi. They whipped our horses on the behind, and the animals lurched forward, nearly unseating me. I glanced back. Marcello and Luca were pressing through the knights and horses behind them, trying to get to the ladies, to free them, too. Our horses, sensing the urgency, were churning down the road, and from the side, I saw more men coming down the hill toward us, attempting to cut us off. "Ride hard!" I cried to Lady Rossi.

But she was already pulling ahead, much more adept in her saddle than I. She looked back over her shoulder and screamed toward her ladies. "Make haste! Make haste!"

I leaned down, trying to become one with my gelding and his gait and that crazy saddle, knowing speed was truly our only ally. We were more than halfway to Siena. If the forest was similar to what it was in a modern age, if it gave way to farmland outside the city gates, across rolling hills, we might reach safety sooner than I thought. Or at least someone to help us.

The last of the men on foot missed us by a mere eight feet, roaring in dismay, but then turning to wave their arms, attempting to make the other approaching horses rear so they could capture the ladies behind us. Lady Rossi pulled up on her reins at the next bend of the road. No one came into sight. "We cannot leave them," she sputtered, her horse prancing in a nervous circle around mine.

"We must get to safety! There were knights with your ladies. They will do their best to protect them."

Still, she hesitated.

"We do none of them any good by becoming captured as well!"

She chewed her lips and studied me, her wide, murky brown eyelashes fluttering prettily. The pounding of hoofbeats grew closer, then, behind us.

"M'lady," I urged.

In response, she lifted her reins and pressed her horse into action, as did I. One benefit of the sidesaddle, I discovered—it was easier to see both before and behind. I glanced back to see who it was, behind us.

One lady. One Forelli knight.

Fantastic. Hardly reinforcements. I wished it had been Marcello and Luca. Then I might have been able to breathe. But at least it was better than none. Perhaps Marcello and Luca were fast approaching too.

We turned around another bend in the road, and I sensed Lady Rossi pulling up before I saw them. Another group of men, six of them. Two on the road, hands on their hips, two on either side. Just waiting for us. Lady Rossi's mare again circled mine. "Come with me," she said lowly, then pushed into the woods.

I groaned. She had disappeared through an impossibly small gap in the trees. Bending as low as I could, well aware that men were charging up the road, toward us, I followed her, as did the lady and knight behind us.

One of my feet caught on a tree trunk, which bent it back painfully, but I kept my seat, my eyes searching the forest for a glimpse of my leader. I ducked under one branch after another, seeing the rump of her horse, the gold of the cloth beneath her saddle.

But then, there she was, in a clearing before me, eyes wide in frustration and fear. We were in some ancient limestone canyon, blocked on three sides by twenty-foot cliffs. I looked back. The path in was filled by the lady and the knight, who looked around and groaned as soon as he saw our predicament. We could all hear the men crashing toward us.

"Climb, ladies," the lone knight said. "I'll hold them at bay. It is your only hope."

I had to hand it to her. I thought the girl far too prissy for such things, but Lady Rossi was immediately off her horse and shoving a dagger into her belt. Her lady assisted her to the top of the first boulder, and she turned to help her up. Okay, not as selfish as I thought, either.

They turned to me and frantically waved me over. "Come! Make haste!"

"Nay," I said. "I shall assist him," I said, gesturing over my shoulder to the knight. The first of our attackers was now just ten feet away from him. "He cannot do it alone, and if he breaks, you two will be caught as well. *Climb*," I growled, rushing to my saddle.

Lady Rossi turned and scrambled up another rock, and then another.

"You cannot hold us off alone!" barked a Paratore knight, showing his allegiance with his crimson colors. "Surrender or die."

"He is not alone," I said, heaving the ancient sword into the air. "You shall have to get through us both."

CHAPTER 10

The knight beside me—I thought his name was Adolfo—used the momentary surprise of the Paratore knights to lunge forward, piercing the first man in the shoulder.

I took a step back, horrified by the blood that literally spurted from the gash in the man's cloak and flesh. But then I tensed. They were attacking now, and they were seriously cranky.

I glanced back and was relieved to see the two women, on a ledge twelve feet above us, reaching for their next perch. They were nearly to safety. At least I would die for something. Marcello needed to marry the chick for some reason.

Maybe they'll name their first girl after me—

Two knights came closer to me, hands out in placating manner. "Now, this will not come to any good, m'lady," said the first. "Womenfolk should never play with the weapons of men."

"Nay, they should not play with them," I said, adopting a guilty look and pretending to agree with him. "They should learn to wield them," I said, already circling to gain the momentum I needed, "properly," I finished, ramming the sword into his. He had barely brought it up in time.

I arced it upward and used the weight of it to bring it down at him again, from the other side.

Again, he narrowly blocked my blow, eyes widening in understanding that I was no pretender. "Aww, we have a lioness here," he sputtered in a delighted but patronizing tone, beginning his attack. He was as large as Marcello, a good four inches taller than I, and far stronger. Surprise, my temporary ally, was gone.

"Lady Betarrini!" cried Lady Rossi, now atop the cliff, as if she could reach down and pull me up.

"Go!" I called back in irritation. She wasted precious seconds with the theatrics. "Go for help!"

Swords clanged behind me. Adolfo was battling two others. Two more came down the path toward us.

"A lady, eh?" the man said, using his sword to pick up the edge of my skirt and peer beneath it.

I slammed it away with my own.

"No lady I've seen has ever had her hands on the hilt of a sword," he sneered, his tone thick with innuendo.

"So I've heard." I turned and brought my sword around as hard as I could.

But he was ready for me this time, blocking every one of my attempts to bring the blade down on him. I panted, my arms as weak as noodles. It was like using a fifty-pound bat.

Noting my weariness, he surged forward, driving me back with blow after blow. I didn't see his companion until it was too late. I barely had a chance to glance behind me when I felt his leg, blocking mine. I tumbled to the ground and the hilt of my heavy sword rammed into my thigh. I dropped it, waves of pain radiating out. The thing was so dang heavy.

But then I saw him pulling up his own sword, as if intending to plunge it into my other leg. I cried out and rolled, hearing the sword slice through my skirts and into the dirt beneath. I tried to pull myself up, immediately realizing I was caught, but I couldn't budge. The fabric was too thick, the sword too wide, like a massive dragon tooth, holding me in place.

I looked up at him and saw him catch another sword from his companion. I rolled back, watching his action, preparing to dodge at just the right moment to save my other leg.

But as he plunged downward and the sword sliced through the other side of my skirts, I realized that he never intended to stab me at all. Just my gown. I was pinned, as neatly as a butterfly on a collector's cushion. Unable to fly away. Simply awaiting the inevitable.

He laughed as realization must have spread across my face. So did his companion behind me. I looked past him to see Adolfo, dead, not three yards away, then to two Paratore men swiftly climbing the boulders. In minutes they'd reach the top. How long would it be until they captured Lady Rossi and her companion? How foolish of me, to believe I might truly stave off trained knights.

Mom, Lia…I'm sorry.

One thought gave me hope. Perhaps in death, I'd find my way home.

But he was untying his trousers. He did not intend to kill me.

He had darker intentions still.

My heart picked up and anger boiled in my ears. I glanced over to my sword, just a few inches from my hand, then madly tried to think through how I could bring it up and plunge it into his creepy, black heart. But as I turned and grasped it, I could feel the rumble of the earth beneath my ear. Horses approached. Many of them. And apparently my attackers didn't know it. They seemed to be preoccupied…with me.

The rogue laughed at my move and hurried over to wrestle the weapon easily from my grasp. "Tie her hands," he said to the other man. "She has some fight left in her. We'll use her sword to secure her arms above her head."

I wrestled against the other man, but he was wiry and strong, easily capturing my hands beneath his legs, then tying my wrists together in seconds like a cowboy wrapping a calf's hoofs. He pulled the cord tight, and I cried out.

They laughed, and he tugged my arms above my head. My first attacker drove my sword into the ground just above my head. Tied as my hands were, and pinned by the sword, I was defenseless.

That was when they charged into the clearing. I closed my eyes as dust billowed up from beneath horse hooves, wondering if I might be trampled, but then men's boots landed in the dirt and swords clanged.

My attacker pulled his sword from one side, but I remained pinned by the other. I rolled, hoping to not get trampled by man or beast, and clenched my eyes shut, praying the first real prayer I had ever prayed. The first prayer I *felt*. *Please God, please God, please God…*

I had no idea how long the fight went on. But then I could hear more tearing as the second sword was pulled from my skirts, and my sword was heaved from the ground and laid at my side. I pulled my aching shoulders downward and dared to look at my rescuer.

Marcello knelt above me, mouth and eyes grim, and swiftly untied my wrists, rubbing them to urge circulation back into them. I let out a gasp of relief, and then I was weeping, crying like a five-year-old that had just been hit by a car but discovered she was all right.

"Oh, Marcello," I said through my tears, rising to my knees and throwing my arms around him. "Thank you. Thank you, thank you."

After a moment's hesitation, he reached his arms around me and patted me awkwardly. It was then that I realized how awkward this sort of action was. He wasn't a kid at school who had just fought off a bully. He was a knight. A lord. A prince, of sorts.

Betrothed to someone else.

I leaned back and hurriedly wiped my face of the embarrassing tears. "Forgive me, m'lord. I forgot myself."

He studied me for a moment, the compassion in his eyes making him all the more enticing, and then reached out a hand, tucking a strand of hair behind my ear.

"Do not give it a thought, m'lady. You have borne much." He ducked his head and sought my eyes again. "But where are Lady Rossi and her companion?"

Ahh, so he only wanted to know where his intended bride had gone. Why did that bring me a pang of jealousy? It only made sense.…

"Two men were chasing them," I said. "Over there, they climbed the rocks."

"Lady Rossi climbed?" he said incredulously.

I nodded, dragging my eyes from the bodies of the four soldiers who had been cut down by Forelli men. My attackers. And those that had pursued Lady Rossi.

"More than one woman has surprised you this day, m'lord," Luca said.

"Indeed." He looked at me, hard. "No other knights reached the top? They alone reached safety?"

"Only them," I said, nodding. "You cut down those that pursued them."

"It is unlikely any of the Paratores would've given them chase, m'lord," Luca said. "Chances are they're in the care of a shepherd's family by now."

"Go and make certain of it."

Luca moved off immediately.

Marcello stood and reached down to me. "M'lady? Can you rise?"

"Of course," I said in irritation, hurrying to my feet. But as soon as I straightened, I cried out, feeling the pain radiate from my thigh again.

"M'lady!" Marcello said. "You are injured? I saw no blood." He looked back to the dirt where I had lain, his face a mask of confusion.

I took a step, stumbled, nearly fell, but Marcello caught me and picked me up in his arms.

"Marcello—m'lord, there truly is no need."

"I will not let it rest until you tell me what has happened. Were you…were we too late?"

"No. Nay!" I cried, figuring out what he meant. And the question brought back all those terrible moments, so recently lived.

"Please, let me go," I said, squirming in his arms. "Unhand me!" It was far too intimate, and my mind and heart were a mash of jumbled emotions and thoughts.

I needed space to think.

Gently, he set me down where I could partially sit upon a boulder. "What transpired? Out with it."

I grimaced at him. "They tripped me. When I fell to my back, the hilt of my sword came ramming down into my thigh. I think I have a bruised muscle. Nothing that won't heal in a few days." *Can we stop making such a big whoppin' deal of it?*

A hint of a smile touched his lips. "I told you a sword is dangerous in the wrong hands. But I must confess I was thinking of the blade."

"Unfair!" I cried, in defense. "It's heavy!"

He lifted his hands in surrender, laughing to himself.

Yeah, yeah, yuk it up, I thought. *I sustained this injury saving* your *chick.*

I was angry for a moment, until I thought of how he and his men had arrived just in time to save me. It didn't matter, really. We were all relieved that it was over. "How many men did you lose?" I finally asked.

"Five. And Lady Rossi's other lady-in-waiting suffered a grave wound."

I groaned. "An arrow?"

He nodded. "Come. Let me get you to your steed. I am anxious to meet up with the others and gain word of my intended. Mount up," he said to his remaining two men. Luca and the others were already up the cliff.

Before I could say a word, he lifted me again in his arms and carried me to my horse. He set me down alongside the gelding, as gently as if I were made of glass. He straightened and then looked down at me.

For a crazy moment, I thought he might kiss me.

For a crazy moment, I *wanted* him to kiss me.

But he only tucked a strand of hair behind my ear again and held one side of my face in his hand. "M'lady. I am so relieved…."

That I lived? That I was okay?

"So grateful to you. If it weren't for you, Lady Rossi might not have escaped."

My breath left me in a sigh of disappointment, but I forced a smile and shook my head as if it was no big deal. I cursed myself for my stupid romantic teenage fantasies. This guy was not in my league. By six hundred years, at least. *Give it up, Gabi. Give it up! Keep your mind on getting home!*

But then he had his big hands on my waist. He bent down a little, getting ready to lift me to the saddle, just as I looked up at him. Our lips were so close, I could feel the heat of his breath on my skin.

We froze. Neither of us moving, simply staring at each other, wondering if the other was going to move first.

"You are," he whispered, "uncommonly stirring."

He closed his eyes then, as if he had to in order to break the bond between us, then lifted me to the saddle and stared at the ground as he guided my feet into the stirrups.

I wanted him to look up at me. I wanted to recapture that moment of heat, of connection again. I'd never experienced it before. But he was stronger than I. He took the reins of my horse and mounted his own, tying my reins to the back of his saddle. He led me through the tunnel of the forest. I had to duck and concentrate on keeping my seat in order to not fall to ground again. But it did not keep me from staring at his broad shoulders, shoulders that swept down to a trim waist. My eyes bore into his back, willing him to turn and look at me again. But he refused.

His reunion with his lady was like a scene from a movie. Gaining sight of her, coming up a small dirt road that led to this more major thoroughfare we were on, Marcello hurriedly handed my reins to Giovanni and broke away in a gallop, pulling up just in time to dismount and run to the side of her borrowed horse, reaching up to grasp her hands in his, kissing them. She bent down with a tender smile and put her head to his.

Whatever I had imagined behind me, it was just that. Wild imaginings. I might have "stirred" Marcello. But these two were clearly meant for each other. They had an understanding, a bond. I had no business even thinking of interfering. What was I going to do? Steal him away and fast-forward to the twenty-first century? I apparently left my brain back in modern times.

Get ahold of yourself, Gabi.

They spoke for a moment, then Marcello looked back at me, the first time he'd really looked at me since our moment in the clearing.

He looked confused at her words, but nodded.

"What happened to her lady? The one that was injured?" I mumbled toward Giovanni.

"Ah, I had a man take her to a nearby villa. They are seeing to her injuries."

I thought that over for a moment, how easily it might've been me on the edge of death, left behind with strangers. The thought left me aching with longing for my family.

When our two roads intersected, Lady Rossi came directly over to me. She reached over to grasp my hand and smiled into my eyes. "I owe you my life. My father will see to it that you are rewarded richly."

"Help me find my sister, Lady Rossi," I said. "That is all the reward I need."

"Please. Call me Romana," she said with a smile. "I will not rest until you are reunited. When my father hears that that is all that is required…be assured, men will be sent for miles, searching every corner for your loved one."

"Thank you," I said, suddenly choked up with unexpected gratitude for this girl, of all people. I felt hope, real hope for the first time. If Lia was here, perhaps this woman could find her. "M'lady, I must get immediately to the fountain in Il Campo when we reach the city. My family agreed long ago that if we were separated, if one of us was lost, we were to go to the main fountain."

She stared at me as if this was obvious. I knew Siena had been pretty big, back in the day.

"Of course," she said. "My family lives on a palazzo on Il Campo. I will place you in a room where you can look upon Il Campo, day and night, if you wish."

"You—your father is one of the Nine?" I asked. Few but Siena's ruling party owned palazzos along the edge of the shell-shaped piazza.

I remembered that much of the medieval Sienese history Mom and Dad had repeated to us.

She nodded, as if I should've known that she was so important already. No wonder it was so vital for Marcello to marry her, I thought. A union with the daughter of one of the Nine...the Forellis' connection to Siena would be golden.

She pulled her horse alongside mine, and we traveled for a time together. "Is your mother quite a successful merchant in Normandy?"

"She is quite successful at anything she turns her attention to," I said, shifting on the saddle. I didn't like to lie outright, but I'd have to continue to fudge a bit.

"Pardon me," she said, her eyes meeting Marcello's. He was waiting for her, ahead.

Beyond him, a group of men thundered down the road toward us. Soldiers of Siena, I wagered, patrolling the road. In minutes, they reached the front of our group and paused to speak with Marcello and Romana.

They were strong, men at the height of physical perfection, like our modern Navy SEALs. The leader looked beyond Marcello and caught my eye.

I stared back at him, intrigued with this breed of men who were so clearly male. Were they like this everywhere, in this time? Or was it just the ones I was running across?

Marcello followed the captain's gaze, and I saw the muscle in his cheek clench. What was that about? Protection? Jealousy? What?

"This marriage between Lord Marcello and Lady Rossi," I said lowly to Luca. "It is vital to both families, yes?"

He slowly turned to me, but I did not look away from Marcello. "Yes, m'lady," he said, looking from me to Marcello.

I didn't care that he was piecing it together. What did it matter, if he knew that I thought Marcello was All That? I needed to know the consequences of following through on my fantasies—it would help me bury them.

"It has long been arranged," he continued. "To go against his father's wishes would mean that Marcello would bring terrible consequences down on his family. You've seen for yourself that we live on the front lines of the conflict. Without the Nine's backing, I'm afraid the castello would fall."

I turned my gaze upon him. "Be at ease, Luca. I will not interfere."

He gave me a lopsided grin and cocked a brow. "I, myself, however, was not promised to a beautiful woman as a child." His grin spread. "The benefit of being born to parents with a good name, but little land, and far less wealth."

I smiled too. He was handsome, no doubt. But he didn't have any of the deep, primal pull that Marcello seemed to have for me. I sighed.

It figured that I'd manage to fall for the unavailable guy.

I glanced forward again, and my heart skipped when I discovered Marcello gesturing toward me, motioning for me to come forward. Luca and I moved to the front of the line together. As we got closer, I could more clearly see the uniforms of the patrol—dark leggings tucked into boots; long, stiff jackets with puffy sleeves and high necks. *Those would be un-fun to wear…miles on the road, in the dust.* I shivered, inwardly, at the thought.

Somehow, the captain, all handsome Italian hotness, managed to pull it off. I returned his small smile.

"Lady Betarrini," Marcello said, his tone a little sharp, like a scolding. I looked at him, and he cleared his throat. "I'd like you to meet Sir Orlando Rossi, Lady Rossi's cousin, and captain of this patrol."

"Captain," I said with a small nod.

"M'lady," he returned. His green-brown eyes—so much like Romana's—had a fun, mischievous glint to them. But then his face became more stern. "Tell me, m'lady, your attackers...were any of them *not* in the Paratore crimson?"

I frowned, thinking. "I think they were all of the house of Paratore. But it happened so quickly..." I shook my head. "I cannot be certain."

"I understand," he said, giving me another genteel nod. He looked to Marcello. "We will find them, and extract vengeance. Only the foolish dare attack a daughter of the Nine."

"Had she fallen into their hands," Marcello said gravely, "she would've been a handsome tool of leverage."

Orlando's horse danced beneath him, anxious to be on his way. "We will go and remind them that such a tactic should never be considered again."

He had just turned when Romana said, "Take care, Cousin."

"I shall." He paused and met my eye again, just for a moment, then on to Romana. "There is a ball to attend in two days' time. It is my hope that all your guests shall be in attendance."

Okay, so what was the deal? In my time, guys barely gave me the time of day. Here, I caught the eye of everyone I met. It was hardly fair. Of course, that had all been part of my father's plan—to keep me and my sister surrounded by geeks more interested in treasures in the dirt than any bounty aboveground. Still, it was a bit overwhelming. My head buzzed with all the attention. Maybe they sensed I was different somehow, and that intrigued them.

The soldiers thundered off, leaving six to serve as our rear guard, leaving no room for further attack.

"Luca," I said lowly once the captain was out of sight, "do you dance?"

"Are you asking me to accompany you, m'lady?" he brought his hand to his chest and fluttered his eyelashes.

"No," I said, stifling a smile at his messing around. "I am asking if you can teach me the proper steps of the dances of Toscana. I am certain they are far different from those of…Normandy."

A slow smile spread across his face. "Certainly. It would be my pleasure, m'lady."

"Thank you," I said, hating the blush that crawled up my neck. Would he think I had the hots for him too? "It comforts me," I rushed on. "Your friendship."

He studied me with his steady, green eyes. "And I am at your disposal."

CHAPTER 11

Traffic on the road increased as we got closer to the city—wagons on carved wooden wheels, chickens in twig cages, small boys driving tired milk cows—but it was Siena and her high, red walls that captured my attention. She looked pristine, clean, grand, and I gawked at her many towers, which I knew no longer stood six hundred years later. In this time, families with power all built towers, from which they could shoot at any intruders—even if those intruders were their own neighbors, turned against them. The closest thing we'd toured in modern times was San Gimignano, but even that city had but a fraction of the towers that stood here. There were hundreds, drastically changing the skyline of the city. Again and again I tried to connect what I remembered of Siena—my favorite of Toscana's towns—with what I was seeing now.

The new wall had recently been built—I could tell because it was another shade of red—with new buildings inside it to make room for the growing city. We rode forward, ignoring the pigs and goats that were nearly trampled in our wake, as well as their irate keepers.

The people divided before us, as if they knew that one of their nobles approached, and on we climbed, curving up the cobblestone street.

I smiled in recognition. Siena was one of the finest preserved examples of a medieval city that we still had; that meant that a lot of it felt familiar to me. My parents had spent a summer here once, when we were little, teaching Italian archeology students. They always said it was the worst summer of their lives; Lia and I remembered it as the best.

If she was here, she would be at the fountain. My heart surged with hope and excitement. It took everything in me to maintain my place in line and submit to the dull, clopping rhythm of our train. I wanted to press my horse into a full gallop and ride past the others. I closed my eyes, fighting against the pull of it.

What if she was there, now? Giving up on me? Wandering off, deciding to try somewhere else?

Stay there, Lia. If you're here, stay there. I willed her to fight against the impulse to give up, urging her to remember what our folks always said: "If you're lost, stay where you are. We will find you. If you keep moving, that will be harder to do." *The fountain, Evangelia. Stay at the fountain.*

We turned on a major street, and I smiled at the sign. Via di Banchi. The road of the banks. This would take us just one street away from the massive piazza. So close! So close!

"M'lady, are you well?" Luca asked, peering over at me.

"I am eager to get to the fountain," I confessed. "Would you kindly accompany me?"

"After we greet Lady Rossi's family," he said. "We'll be off immediately."

I looked at him in horror. "No, I don't think you understand. I am beside myself with worry over my sister. I must know right away, if she's there, awaiting me."

He studied me. "And if she's not?"

I pulled back a little. Not there? If she wasn't here, where could she be? I wasn't ready to deal with the idea that she hadn't made the jump at all. To think I was all alone here, with no one to help me figure out a way back.

I didn't answer Luca's question, but I began checking out every blonde or near-blonde I saw, knowing, just knowing that I would soon spot her. Perhaps she was on her way to the fountain even now, perhaps on this very street. I sat up straighter when I saw a girl about Lia's height, her hair tucked into a knot and net, that same wheat color....

"M'lady?" Luca asked. I ignored his worried tone.

My eyes were on the girl. She had a basket on one arm and was weaving in and out of the crowd. She was the right height, with the same figure, I was sure of it. We were getting close to the cutoff where Romana would lead us away and around the piazza and to her home—one of the grand palazzos on the piazza. Here, at this corner, I was as close to the entrance and the fountain as I was going to get. The blonde was weaving away from me now, heading to Il Campo.

"Lia!" I cried. "Evangelia Betarrini!"

Several in the crowd before me stared at me, their heavy brows furrowed at my outburst, then looked away when they decided I was just whacked.

"Lia!" I tried again. She was getting farther away. "Lia!"

I kicked my feet from the stirrups and slid to the ground, landing on my bad leg. I cried out and leaned hard against the brick wall of a shop.

"M'lady," Luca said, separated now from me by a portion of the crowd. "Wait."

"I cannot," I muttered, shaking my head. I limped after her, in a sort of lurching gallop, heading down the small street that led through a tunnel and out into the piazza. It spewed us forth like water from a hose, and I pulled up short, trying to make sense of the piazza I thought I knew so well.

In my day, the "clam" was lined with shops and restaurants, its basin filled with tourists and students licking gelato cones or sitting and staring at the beautiful Palazzo Pubblico and towering campanile.

Here, now, Torre del Mangia—the campanile, or bell tower—appeared to be half-built. Bricks had yet to be laid in the fishbone rays that represented the Nine. It was all a uniform cobblestone. The entire piazza was full of row upon row of vendors, selling vegetables, fruits, woolens. And I couldn't see the lovely white marble of the Fonte Gaia.

I spotted the blonde and moved out after her again. She was looking around, admiring the merchants' wares—so like Lia—and my heart surged with hope. I pressed on after her as she ran her hands over one length of cloth after another. "Lia!" I called. "Lia!"

I was five feet away when she turned to face me.

It wasn't her.

I pulled up short and brought a hand to my mouth, trying to make sense of it. I had been sure, *so* sure it was her.

"M'lady! Lady Betarrini!" Luca said, arriving at my side. A moment later, Marcello was beside me too, panting.

I stared hard at the girl, as if I could morph her into my sister, make her be who I wanted her to be. My eyes welled with tears as she cast me a confused look, turned, and walked hurriedly away.

"It wasn't her," I said to Marcello, my tone as empty and lost as I felt, an echo of me.

His eyebrows knit in worry. "Did you not believe you would find her here? And there has to be more than one blonde in a city as vast as Siena, yes?"

I clung to his words with the tiniest measure of hope. Luca took my arm—I guessed because Marcello wished to beg no questions in Lady Rossi's own city—while Marcello parted the crowd for us, leading us to a massive well. I tried to reconcile what I was seeing; obviously the big fountain was yet to come.

It was busy at the well. There were many there to fetch water for drinking, washing, cooking—resolved in my day by indoor plumbing. It made it hard to approach now. Might that keep Lia away? I looked around, so frenzied now that I could barely focus on each face.

I was hot, dizzy, as if suffering a fever, but I continued to turn.

"M'lady," Marcello said. "M'lady," he whispered, gripping my forearm and stilling my incessant circling.

He looked to Luca with a *help me* expression, and the other man came and took my arm. We left Marcello behind. Over and over he said *mi scusi,* edging us closer to the well. Once there, he flipped a coin to a man, and he pulled out a bucket and ladle. "Drink," Luca demanded of me, brooking no argument.

I did as I was told, suddenly very thirsty, realizing I hadn't had a thing to drink since morning. I dipped the ladle again, drinking the sweet water.

"Now, splash your face," the man demanded.

I hesitated.

"Do as I say," Luca said, no trace of humor in his voice.

I dipped my hands into the bucket, bent, and splashed my face twice, then wiped it with my palms and flicked the water again.

He ducked his head and peered at me. "Better?"

I nodded, coherent enough now to be embarrassed by my behavior. "Forgive me. I just thought…"

"It is well," Luca said, dismissing my apology. "Do you see her, m'lady? Your sister?"

I looked slowly around. "Nay."

He crossed his arms and pointed upward. "See that palazzo there?"

I followed his upward gaze and gaped at the building, three times the size of its neighbors. "The Rossi family?"

"One and the same."

When the girl had promised a room with a view, she hadn't been joking. I glanced over at Marcello and then back to Luca. "Send him ahead of us. We will follow. Reputation is important, yes?"

"Indeed," he said grimly. He moved off to speak to Marcello. Marcello gazed at me a second, as if to make sure I was all right, then turned his back and disappeared among the crowd. I took another sip of water and offered Luca the ladle. He drank from it, gave the well man another coin, and then offered his arm. "At least you know now. Take comfort, m'lady, rather than despair. You are to receive the aid of one of the most powerful families in all of Toscana. If anyone can find your family, the Rossis can."

We walked a bit. "Did I offend her, do you think? Running after that girl, when we were so near her home?"

"Nay, she has her own sisters. I imagine she has a fair measure of empathy for your situation. Does your sister truly resemble that one?"

I nodded. "In hair, stature. But she is far more beautiful than that woman we saw."

His green eyes widened with wonder. "I will assist you all the more in your quest, m'lady," he said.

"She is but fifteen," I protested.

"More than old enough to find her beloved," he returned with a grin. "Or would your family not entertain a knight with no money?"

I considered my response with a grin. "I think you would find my mother the understanding sort."

Dad would've been a different story. A pang of pain poked at me. I stared at the cobblestones disappearing beneath my slippers. This last Etruscan find promised to put an end to our ever-present need for more cash, for living expenses, to fund the next dig. If Manero didn't succeed in blocking her path, finding the fabled settlement and its riches would put my mother on the map; land her book contracts, speaking gigs, funding—from the Italians as well as Americans.

But at what price? The disappearance of one or both daughters?

I needed to get back to the tomb with Lia. It was our only logical way back home. But my two encounters in the woods that bordered the castello told me I couldn't get there alone, sword or not. I needed an escort. And that would take some serious finagling.

I picked up my head as we reached the horses. The rest had moved off, but a knight held our two mounts, waiting on us. Luca lifted me to the saddle and helped me slide my feet into the stirrups. "We'll find her, m'lady," he said. "I promise."

I gazed down into his earnest face and longed to believe him. But at that moment, every part of my reality seemed so far from reach that I seriously doubted he could deliver.

We arrived at the palazzo and were immediately shown upstairs, to the grand salon that took up the entire length of the building on this level. Marcello and Romana were beside a small, gray-haired man who sat in a thronelike chair, apparently regaling him with tales of our journey. He frowned in fear and then clapped in glory when he heard of his daughter's climb to safety. Romana looked up then, and caught sight of me.

"And this, this, Father, is the heroic woman who came to my aid." She rushed over to me and dragged me to him. I felt like a giraffe next to her, being inspected by a new zookeeper. "She pulled a sword from her saddle and wielded it like some fierce Viking queen."

He studied me, then rose and took my hand. He looked up at me. "Lady Betarrini, I am indebted to you," he said. He bent and kissed my hand, then held it in both of his. He was nowhere near as tall as my father, coming only to my shoulder, but his movements were familiar in their fatherly nature. It brought sudden tears to my eyes, just as being with Lord Forelli had. "My daughter tells me you have become separated from your family," he said. "In gratitude to you, my sole goal will be to see you reunited."

There was no way we'd be reunited. Not all four of us, ever. But maybe, Lia and me. Somehow, with Mom, in time. "Thank you," I managed, tears spilling down my cheeks. I wiped them away, embarrassed, but unable to keep them back. It was too much. It was all too much.

He patted my hand. "You are exhausted. The day has clearly taxed you. Someone shall see you to your room, and we will speak more of it this evening, or if you prefer, on the morrow. Good?"

"Thank you," I repeated. Why did the man give me such hope? Maybe it was just the sight of a man with his daughter that moved me. Lady Rossi bent to speak in a servant's ear, and the woman came over to me. "Come, m'lady. I shall see you to your quarters."

I followed behind her, so tired I could barely force myself up the stairs. At the top, the woman pulled a ring of keys from her belt and unlocked the first along the hallway. I peered down it—there appeared to be about eleven more. She opened it and gestured inward. "Please."

I walked forward and went directly to the window of the narrow room. There was little more than a double-sized bed, a chair, a table, and this, the window, overlooking the piazza. I pushed open the shutter and looked down on the well. People swirled about it, but no blondes among them.

"Do you have need of anything, m'lady?" She fiddled with her ring of keys. "I will send a girl up with fresh water, or would you favor a hot bath?"

I could feel the grime of the road on every inch of me but knew that if I sank into a hot tub, I might never emerge again. And I needed to stay alert. "On the morrow, a bath would be grand. But this day…I fear I do not feel my best. Perhaps a bit of bread and cheese along with a pitcher of water? Then in the morning, the bath, along with the sun?"

"I'll see it done, m'lady," she said, nodding toward me. Quietly, she disappeared out the door. I dragged a chair over to the window and sank into it, absently rubbing my aching thigh. I leaned my head on the edge of the sill and stared down at the well, watching people come and go for hours. I had given water little thought in my own day; when I turned on the faucet, it came out. What would it be like to fetch every ounce I needed and more?

I studied the well and the statues that dotted the piazza—long gone, in my day—until my eyelids grew too heavy to fight. Even though there was still daylight, I allowed them to droop, pushing them upright once, then giving in. I awakened to moonlight streaming through my window, into the room. I rose fast, alarmed, trying to place where I was and *when* I was, and dizzy. I slumped against the wall before the tall, thin window.

The three-quarter moon reflected in the still waters of a pail at the window's edge. Two men walked past the Palazzo Pubblico at the bottom of the piazza, deep in conversation. No one else appeared, a stark contrast to the afternoon's activity. I sank back to my chair and rested my chin on my hands, staring out at the plaza beneath me, a constant stream pouring into it at one side, sending ripples through the moon's reflection.

No Lia.

Evangelia, where are you?

I looked out across the plaza, across the skyline, so foreign with all her towers. Siena was vast, with thousands inside her walls, many more outside. Why had I thought that if I just came here, I'd find my sister? What was I thinking?

I rubbed my head, massaging my scalp, trying to ease away the tension. That was when I felt it—the thick coils that had fallen from Giacinta's careful arrangement that morning. Had I really met the head of the Rossi family, one of the Nine—one of the most powerful men in all of Tuscany—looking like I'd just rolled out of bed?

I groaned. It was testimony to his character that he had come to me and looked at me with nothing but admiration. *He must really love his daughter.*

"Testimony to you, too, Romana," I said, flicking fingers off my brow in silent salute. Two more points for her.

Staring at the water below made me realize how badly I had to go to the bathroom. I'd avoided it as much as I could at Castello Forelli, but there, as here, I could do nothing other than what the rest did—go in the pot. I rose and winced—half from the pain in my thigh and half from worrying that I'd never find Lia. Then, raising my skirts, I squatted over the bucket and did my business, dragging a piece of wood across the top when I was done to contain the smell. "My kingdom for a flush toilet," I muttered. For all our whining, Lia and I really had no idea how good we had it, even in an apartment decorated in seventies favorites.

I glanced at the wooden chair by the window, and then the bed, so inviting with its mound of down-filled covers, and immediately abandoned my post. I was so tired…and Lia was not likely to show in the dark of night.…

I awakened to maids arriving, carrying a deep tub between them. Four others followed behind, and in the deep shadows of morning, I could hear them pour their steaming liquid into the tub. Two others arrived, adding four more buckets. One moved to the corner and picked up my chamber pot—oh my gosh, it was so embarrassing, like she was changing my diaper or something—and paused at my bedside. "Is there anything else, m'lady?"

"Nay," I mumbled, wanting to pull the covers over my head. I wanted it all to go away. To wake up in my time, my place.

Then the maids disappeared, quietly closing the door behind them, and I got up and bent over the bath. It was hot, too hot to sink into yet. But the rising steam reminded me of Fortino, and I wondered how his regimen was going, if he was still faring better. How good it felt, to *do* some good, here and there. Perhaps this was what it meant to be an adult. To grab the opportunity at hand, make the most of the day, regardless of what it looked like.

I sighed and stared out the window, at the cityscape becoming as rosy in hue as the sun that climbed in the sky. I was sitting in the middle of one of the most famous medieval towns of all. *What will you do with the opportunity?* I heard my father ask.

Every summer he asked us the same. "What will you do with this? Do you know how few get this opportunity? To be in Italy, of all places, for the summer? You don't have to dig with us. The summer is your own. Make it yours. Seize the day, my girl. Seize it."

For the first time, his words took hold for me, moving out of the monotone, wordless litany of a parent's diatribe to true wisdom.

Seize the day. What could I do, to make the most of this day, whether I was in my own day, or this one? What amazing history was I seeing firsthand? Would I embrace it, instead of crying and whining? Was it in me to be grateful for my situation? Truly in me?

I pulled off my clothes and tentatively sank into the hot water, wincing at first at its heat, then melting into the edge of it, staring out at a corner of sky covering a plaza that would be marveled at for centuries. *Here I am. Now.* What would my parents do? What would God have me do? It had to be God who'd done this. Or allowed it. *I am here for a reason. This is no haphazard mistake. What good can I do with what I have?*

These were big thoughts. Grown-up thoughts. I sank beneath the surface, and felt the water close above my head. I stayed under there as long as I could, liking that my lungs burst with longing for air, confirmation that I was truly alive, living this, not merely dreaming it. *You want me to seize the day—Mom, Dad, God, whoever. I will.*

I broke the surface and gasped for air, feeling the cool of the morning breeze against my hot, wet skin. I reached for the square bar of soap and rolled it in my hands, watching as strands of dried purple lavender broke free of it. There was some sort of fat in it—it was immediately more soothing than the soap they had at Castello Forelli. Maybe it wouldn't destroy my skin like that had.

I lathered it into my hair, then ducked beneath the surface, driving it out with my fingers. I was suddenly eager to see what the day held. And if Lia might be in it.

I finished with my task, lounging in the warm waters for a precious minute longer, then rose in the cool air to reach for the cloth that served as a towel. *I could make a fortune discovering Egyptian cotton,* I thought. Was that how I was to seize the day? To become the killer importer maven, rich beyond my wildest dreams, because I knew what people wanted next? "Nah," I muttered, rubbing my head as best I could. There was something more for me here, something bigger.

I dried the rest of my body and then flipped open my first valise, expecting to see my extra gown.

I sat back, gaping at what I saw. Wrapping the towel more tightly around my body, I tucked the edge and then bent and pulled out what I could only equate with a wedding gown. Except it was a vibrant, russet red. I kept pulling it out of the small case, and it kept coming, yards and yards of fabric. With the same colored beads sewed to the bodice. I spread it across the bed and then stood back to marvel at it. It was the finest silk I had ever touched, an explosion of softness. It had a square neckline, wide and low. Its waist was so narrow I wondered if I might actually get into it. This was Marcello's mother's?

Dimly, I remembered Giacinta saying something about how it had been meant for Fortino's nuptials. A wedding forgotten. I doubted Marcello's father complained when she took it from their dressing room. It represented promises lost. Hope turning into sorrow. Celebration becoming mourning.

Could I really wear it? Truly? Would Marcello remember it? Remember its true purpose? Turn away from me with sorrow in his eyes?

It didn't matter, I thought, running my hands over it. I knew it was the perfect color for my eyes. And what else was I to wear to a ball? It was probably outdated. But it was so gorgeous, no one would dare to remark on it. "Now, to work in the ten-mile run that will allow me to sweat off enough weight to wear it tomorrow."

I eyed the narrow hourglass of a bodice and shuddered. I wasn't going to be able to breathe all night, let alone dance. Suddenly, I wished Marcello's mother had been a large matron instead, given to tent dresses rather than tight-fitting gowns designed to draw the eye of every man in the room. I shook my head in wonder. "You must've been amazing, Mrs. Forelli. Wish I'd known you."

A knock sounded at my door, and I hurried over to the other valise. "Just a moment!" I called, shaking out the second, known dress I'd worn at the castello, then the underdress. Hurriedly, I pulled it over my head and across my still-wet, sticky skin, then moved to the door. "Yes?"

"It's the maid, m'lady. I'm here to aid you with your hair."

I lifted my brows and opened the door a crack. "That is a good thing. My hair is a…leviathan," I said, coming up with the most ancient form of monster I could. And indeed, without conditioner, it was. *What a mess,* I thought, feeling up to the mass on top of my head.

"It's of no concern," the girl said, checking me out. "I've dealt with far worse."

I raised my eyebrows and then sat where she indicated. "Actually, do you mind if I sit by the window as you work?"

"Nay," she said, gesturing toward the window.

I moved over to the chair, and sank into it, staring to the well below. "Tell me, do you know everyone who visits the well below?"

She looked over my shoulder. "Most by sight, at least. All but the visitors, anyway."

"Have you seen a blonde stranger, a visitor, in the last few days?" I inquired.

"Blonde?" she asked, as if unfamiliar with the word.

"Si, the color of straw in the high noon light," I said, letting my chin sink to my crossed arms again.

"I'm sorry, m'lady, there are few with hair the color like that. Is that the sister you seek?"

"Indeed."

She paused and then resumed her work, detangling my long tresses. "I might ask my papa. He is a vendor below, selling vegetables. He will know if the woman you seek passes by."

"Thank you," I said, sighing heavily. It was a long shot.

That she was here. In Siena.

Now. With me. Hanging out beside an old well, when Fonte Gaia was not even designed yet, apparently.

I shook my head, knowing how impossible it was.

"M'lady," complained the maid.

"I'm s—forgive me," I said. I remained still, my eyes trained on the square below, watching as the pace increased, as the sun grew higher in the sky. The noise echoed from beneath us. Dudes selling fish, calling out to shoppers, trying to sell their smelly wares, days old. A man selling vegetables, far more enticing. Others selling meat, pushing fly-infested beef and lamb that made me shudder, glad to not know exactly where my last meal had come from.

Hundreds entered the lineup to reach the well. But none of them was my sister.

"The master shall find her," said the maid in confidence.

"And if he doesn't?"

"What the master sets out to do, he does," she said. "Cast your mind to Lady Rossi's betrothal to Lord Forelli."

I caught my breath but gave her a tiny nod, hoping she'd go on. My mind was suddenly focused on little else.

"The lady, given her uncommon beauty, might have had her pick of any," she said proudly. "But she set her sights, early on, on Lord Forelli. The two houses formed an alliance, one that has benefitted both, for many years, before Lord Forelli and m'lady came of age."

I remained silent, hoping she'd go on.

"But it has been the master's work, his desire from the beginning, to strengthen this line against Firenze, and Castello Forelli is key. She is one of five outposts, vital to our holding the line."

One of five outposts? What if but one of them fell? What would become of Siena and Castello Forelli? I thought back, to the Civil War in the States. What if Fort Sumter had not fallen? Or others along the North-South boundary line?

I tried my best to remember my Italian history, lamenting not listening when my mom tried to tell me of significant events in Toscana's history.

Those who do not remember history are doomed to repeat it, my parents drilled into us, quoting someone else.

Why, oh why, could I not summon this in my memory? What happened to Siena in the fourteenth century? What happened that turned the course of time? My mind flicked to the devastated castle in my time, the overturned stones of Castello Forelli that we'd walked through in the twenty-first century.

I knew that Florence, Firenze, ultimately reigned victorious. Why was that? Because of the plague? Politics? War?

I shook my head, and the maid cried out in alarm as I pulled strands from her elaborate updo. "Sorry," I muttered, chin on hands, staring below again.

The day passed, after my giving a detailed description of my sister and—against all odds—my mother, taken by messenger to the other Eight of the Nine, and presumably, to many more.

"Rest assured, Lady Betarrini," Lord Rossi said to me, "If any of your kin are within reach, we shall hear of them by the morrow."

I took comfort in his confidence, his bravado, his fatherly tone. I had done what I could. All I could do now was wait for an answer. To busy myself, I eagerly accepted Romana's kind invitation to join her and her sisters in their version of hanging out with a couple of friends, but in truth, I could not wait to get back to the house and my perch over the piazza. I took my supper in my room again, unwilling to leave my post.

A knock sounded on my bedroom door as the sun was sinking lower in the sky. I turned from my chair at the window and wearily went to answer it.

Luca stood there, a crooked grin on his lips. "You've sat at your window far too long."

I glanced back at it, wondering if he might have seen me there, then realizing he assumed it.

"Come," he said, lifting his hand. "You can see the well from where I'll take you. Let me teach you the dances of Toscana."

I lifted my brows, knowing I had asked this of him, but now wondering at the wisdom of it.

"Come, come," he said, flicking his fingers, sensing my hesitation. "I have found someplace private where we can practice."

I studied him a moment and then agreed. It was far better to suffer embarrassment with him, someplace private, rather than in the middle of a ballroom floor. He cocked a grin and offered me his arm. "M'lady."

"M'lord," I returned.

"Nay," he said, leading me down the corridor on his arm. "Such a title is reserved for Marcello or Lord Forelli. Take care with it. Sir is title enough for me."

"Understood, Sir Luca," I said, with a curt nod. He wasn't chastising me, I realized, he was attempting to help me.

We climbed a narrow stair, then another, and still another, until we emerged on the rooftop of the palazzo. I turned, full-circle, in wonder at the view. Past the towers and the city wall, I could see miles of green rolling hills. "It is marvelous," I said.

"Indeed," he grinned. He closed the door and then turned to stare at me, crossing his arms. "So, tell me of what you know about formal dance."

I sucked in my breath and gave him a sorrowful glance. "I am afraid it is not popular in my own land. I know little." There was no way I was going to pretend I knew anything. Not here. Now.

"Hmm. Very well." Luca stepped forward, all man. I felt a pang, wishing I felt something more than a let's-be-friends thing with this guy. He raised his hands and waited for me to place mine in them. "The first is an *estampie.* Step forward, step left, step backward, then pause, and then forward again…." He repeated it, counting, as if in time to some unheard song.

A four-square sort of step. I nodded and moved into his arms. We made it through the first three counts, and then I missed the pause. He released me and then looked at me, his eyes slightly narrowed, as if exasperated, as if we had gone through it a hundred times.

Oh, come on. "Give me a chance!" I cried. "That was once! How many times were you taught that square?"

He cocked a brow, apparently reluctant to give me room to fail. He flicked his fingers forward. "Let's give it another try," he said tiredly, acting as though we'd been at it all night. "This time, close your eyes. Think only of the rhythm."

I sighed, trying to get above my frustration. I closed my eyes and listened to the beat of the dance, along with his counting, feeling the shifts, the pause at the end, then resuming. "Good, good," he encouraged.

On and on he went. "Ahh, yes. That is it. Perfecto," he said.

I gloried in his praise, melting into the feel of his hand at my waist, the other at my shoulder. "I'm going to release you for a moment, but you keep your count, as if another man is taking my place, as they will in the dance on the morrow."

His hands left me, but then slid back in place, at my waist, but wrapping a bit more behind my back this time, as if a tiny bit more possessive.

My eyes fluttered open. And encountered Marcello.

I stopped, glancing at Luca, his profile aglow in the setting sun. He shrugged. "What m'lord asks, he receives."

I looked up to Marcello and stared hard into his eyes. "And what the lord wishes is to dance with a sword-carrying girl with a penchant for running off?" I asked.

"Tonight that is my wish," he said, his voice strangely husky, his eyes unwavering. He began to count off the dance again, and I, apparently devoid of will, followed it.

"Now, has Luca taught you this one?" he asked, raising both hands to me, palm up.

I frowned and shook my head, then glanced toward Luca. He was gone. I sighed. I was alone with Marcello, receiving a dance lesson. This was fraught with disaster, as my grandmother would say. I could do nothing but place my hands in his.

"This is an eight-count dance," he said, staring down at me with all earnestness.

He dropped my hands and counted it out, as if I were in his arms, closing his eyes, turning at the fifth count, and again at the seventh.

"Tricky," I said, raising a brow.

"The key is following your partner's lead," he said, a teasing glint in his eyes. He cocked his head. "Tell me, Lady Betarrini, can a woman who can wield a sword find her place on the dance floor?"

"I believe them to be quite similar," I said, moving toward him, placing my hands in his. "Don't you agree? Swordplay is a dance of sorts, an understanding of the logical, most sophisticated next step. Except that in a fight, one must take the unexpected step. In dance it is all about taking the right, expected step."

He stared down at me, clearly wondering at my odd words, but letting them slide.

He began counting the dance, turning me at count five and seven. I moved with him, without hesitation, and the eighth count found my left hand in his, at chest level, and my right hand above my head, facing him. Our mouths were inches away from each other. "I believe you have this mastered, m'lady," he said, still not releasing me, still staring into my eyes.

"I believe you have taught me well, m'lord," I returned, staring steadily back at him. *Oh my gosh*, I thought. I *so* wanted him to take me into his arms and kiss me for all I was worth. I had never been kissed like that. And in that moment, I was clear on who I wanted to be the first.

I turned away when *no matter the cost* cascaded through my mind.

It could cost a great deal. For me. For him.

"Lady Betarrini?" he asked. "Gabriella," he said, dropping his tone, in such an enticing manner, I nearly turned.

"You need to go, Marcello," I said. "Depart." *Vamoose*, I added, in my thoughts. *Hasta la vista, baby.* "I only represent danger for you. Loss. All you need is below us, in this house."

"How can you be so certain? Might there be a new path for me? One my parents might never have foreseen?"

He was speaking of me. I drew in a shaky breath. What could I promise him? A wife who disappeared into the future? No, it wasn't fair....

I looked back to give him a pretty speech, some small comfort, but he was already gone through the gaping door, taking my hesitation as answer enough.

I stared for a long time at that empty doorway, recognizing that I had killed any chance to be with the hottest guy I had ever run across. But it was for a good reason, a solid reason. I was being responsible.

I tried to swallow the regret that filled my throat, tried to feel assured, courageous. But I couldn't even manage that.

My mouth was dry.

And my heart was empty.

CHAPTER 12

In my dreams that night, I did all the steps the men had taught me. And no, they weren't cool, romantic dreams, all about Marcello and his warm hands and strong arms, holding me. No, they were all the nerdy counting thing, freaking out when I missed a step.

Call me a perfectionist.

Whatever.

I just knew I was about to mess this up. The coming dance drew us all in, the house abuzz.

I had a sense of destiny about it all.

I also had a distinct sense of disaster about it too.

The combination wasn't pretty.

I paced the room for hours before it began, already in the deep, wine-colored gown. My carefully coiffed hairdo began to pull and curl—*What I'd do for a little product,* I lamented again—and yet not able to summon up the strength to stop walking.

Tonight, tonight, Lord Rossi would share with all his friends and acquaintances my plight—sending out word to every corner of the kingdom that a girl was here, longing for her mother, her sister.

In days I would know if one or both of them were here…or if I was all alone.

I managed to make it down the steps without catching a toe in my skirts and tumbling all the way to the bottom. I thought that was a major plus. Luca was waiting for me. He put a hand over his heart as if it was about to burst out of his chest. "Truly a vision, m'lady."

I smiled and looked ahead, catching a glimpse of Marcello's curly hair and Lady Rossi's golden gown. Gold? That was a little much, I thought. She might as well be wearing an "I Belong to Marcello" T-shirt. I sighed. I was just jealous, jealous over a guy I couldn't have anyway.

"I thought I might be of service as an escort," Luca whispered. "If you'll have me. Otherwise, I'll never get a chance to dance with you, once the men of the city catch a glimpse of you."

"I'd be most grateful," I said, looking up at him. The last thing I wanted was to go solo to this party. He offered his arm, and I rested mine on top of his. Although I knew the palazzo had a private door onto the piazza, it was likely down in the kitchen. So we left through the front entrance. As we, the household of Rossi, paraded down the street, I realized that half this deal was like any high school dance at home. The point was to see and be seen.

We moved down Via di Banchi and then through the tunnel that led to Il Campo. The piazza was more as I remembered it from my time, with no vendors and stalls, but rather groups of regulars, standing about to gawk at the rich and powerful in their brightly colored gowns and elaborate jackets. I tried to ignore the pain in my thigh—now a massive, purple-green bruise—and focused on not tripping. As a part of the Rossi party, I somehow represented them. I didn't want anything to get in the way of their aiding me in my search. Like falling flat on my face in the middle of the plaza. That would not be good.

It was like we were on a virtual red carpet or something. I briefly imagined *Entertainment Tonight*'s pretty-boy host stopping us, microphone in hand, asking us who designed our clothes, where we got the diamonds—not that I was wearing any—and who our hopefuls were for the Oscars tonight.

At the bottom of the piazza, we entered the small courtyard of the Palazzo Pubblico, then through the doors to the grand salon on the main floor. In my time, the place had been made into a museum, with carefully restored, famous medieval frescoes on the wall. Now I was staring at those same works, but it was like the paint had just barely dried, the colors as rich and vibrant as the silk the women wore about the room. *Mom would totally pee her pants.*

It was in this building that the Nine and their buddies met to discuss political matters, making military plans to protect the city from her enemies, negotiating issues that arose among the guilds—basically the workers' unions of the day. It was with some surprise that I remembered all that from the charmless museum guide who droned on and on, and who Lia had become quite adept at impersonating, making us both dissolve into giggles. Now I was seeing his boring stories explode into a 3D movie. Men were shaking hands and laughing, others with chin in hand, listening earnestly.

I couldn't see Marcello at the moment—there were hundreds of people in the big room—but I caught sight of Lord Rossi, and when he pointed in my direction and the man with him regarded me, I turned to Luca. "Might you be able to find a cup of water for me? I'm feeling just a bit faint."

"Of course, m'lady," he said, looking concerned. Of course he was nervous; he'd seen me pass out cold before. He took my elbow and led me to a chair at one of the long tables and then set off on my quest. The tables were covered in a rich, light sage-green cloth, the color of Siena's hills in late summer, and in the center of each were massive platters of fruit—apples, oranges, pears, pomegranates, grapes—so enticing and gorgeous that if Lia had been there, she would've whipped out her sketch book to capture the image. It was almost too bad they would be eaten.

I finally saw the place cards among the hand-blown, red crystal goblets, in a delicate, artistic script, and I realized that was how Luca knew where to park me. Mine said *N. Rossi* at the top, *Lady Gabriella Betarrini* at the bottom. *N for Nine?* I wondered idly, searching the crowd for my escort, suddenly desperately thirsty. Parched.

I still didn't see Marcello, and I berated myself for looking for him. Perhaps he and Romana were in the other wing, around the corner. Scanning the cards, it appeared that the Rossi household was split up a bit; every other couple had a different "N" name at the top. Perhaps a plan to force some mixing.

With this many people, there was a slight chance I wouldn't see him all night. Perhaps that was Lady Rossi's grand scheme. To keep him all to herself.

As it should be, Gabi.

I knew that upstairs was another grand salon—I remembered it from the tour. Might that be where we would dance after we ate? I cast aside my concerns over remembering the dances when I saw Luca, with my water, as well as Lord Rossi and a nobleman approaching me. I hurriedly took a sip before the men arrived, then set the glass down on the table before rising to greet them. Introductions were made. A description of Lia was shared. The man had reach, across hundreds of miles, to the east of Siena, he said, and he promised to tell everyone he knew to be looking for la familia Betarrini.

"Tell me of your mother," he said. "She is a merchant? In what, specifically?"

My mind spun. What was logical to say? I decided to stick with my story. "Artifacts. Especially Etruscan artifacts." It would hardly do, telling him she was an archeologist. Not that it mattered. It was highly unlikely that she was here. My goal was to find my sister.

The stranger seemed intrigued. "There are many who believe we should be students of the past, that we have forgotten much of what our ancestors knew, learned. But why Etrusca? Why not Romana? Were the Romans not far more powerful?"

"Only because the Etruscans came before them," I said. "The Etruscan cities, their ports, gave the Romans an unprecedented base of operations from which to expand, but eventually they wiped out the remnants of Etrusca itself. They were a fine and mighty society. My mother has found a good trade in their wares."

The man raised an eyebrow and then gave me a thin-lipped smile. I'd said too much. "You feel passionately about it."

"Forgive me, m'lord. I have heard my mother defend her chosen profession all my life. Mayhap it is because I miss her so that I feel… defensive."

"Pay my words no heed, m'lady," the man said. "Your overbearing nature is already forgotten."

I stomped down my irritation at his high-and-mighty manner, knowing that I needed this man on my side if I was going to find Lia.

"Tell me, m'lady, does your mother resemble you?"

"Nay, my sister favors our Danish mother, with long, blonde hair and blue eyes. I take after my father. His grandfather came from Italia."

"I believe," he said, leaning in toward me, "that you inherited the best traits of both. The room is abuzz about your beauty, m'lady. With hair the color of the river at night, and such expressive eyes…." He leaned back, chin in hand. "If you should decide to stay with the Sienese instead of returning to Normandy, I have no doubt you could find a suitable husband. You may miss your family sorely, but are you not of an age to begin your own?"

I leaned back. How to answer that? *Why no, you creepy old man, looking at me like I'm a sweet little sow ready to be bred. I'm only seventeen! I have my whole life ahead of me!*

Luca coughed and leaned in. "We are doing our best to convince her, of course, m'lord."

I faked a flirty smile as the men laughed and patted Luca on the back. More men joined us. Soon I had met seven of the Nine. Two were young men, in their late twenties. The rest were in their fifties or sixties, kinda old in this era. Unless you were rich, most died of disease or of things as silly as an infected cut or an impacted tooth. Mom always said that infection was the number one killer of people through the ages, more than war, even. Maybe that's why I was so obsessed with scrapes and cuts—I was always certain they'd become infected and become gangrenous or something....

Sometimes death came hunting and there was no way to cut it off at the pass. I shivered. I really had to take care of myself here. If I landed in their version of a hospital, I was as good as dead.

A stately servant called out that dinner was to be served, and conversation moved to the long lines of tables as we all took our seats. I saw Marcello and Romana then. They were hard to miss, seated directly across the twelve-foot-long table from me. I looked everywhere but at Marcello, and he carefully did the same.

Red wine was poured into the goblets, and I was thankful I had sent Luca in search of some water. I needed to keep my wits about me, especially with the dance still ahead of us. People reached for fruit as servants brought in small plates of hard salami and tiny wedges of pecorino cheese, as well as thick slices of crusty bread. Bowls of coarse sea salt were passed, and I sprinkled some across my fruit, as the man to my right did, and Luca did after me. No one baked bread like the Italians, I thought, relishing my first bite.

After that, small Cornish-like hens were distributed, a whole one on each plate, covered in a thick, brown sauce full of dried fruits. I sighed with relief that I saw forks here at each place setting. *Ahh, a tiny bit of civilization.* Maybe the city dwellers were early adopters. I tried not to gloat as I picked mine up and used it with ease in tandem with my knife, ignoring the admiration of those about me. Finally, something that was not foreign.

Plates of gnocchi were passed, but I only took one. I'd never been fond of the little dumplings. They always got stuck on the roof my mouth. After that, people took more fruit and sat back, enjoying their wine and conversation. That was the first time I glanced Marcello's way and found him looking at me. Our eyes met, held, and then we both broke away. His intended was to his right. Her sister was to his left. I couldn't risk looking his way again; but then, wasn't that obvious in itself?

I looked to Romana. "M'lady," I said. "I am so grateful to your father for his aid in searching for my sister."

She wiped her mouth with the edge of the tablecloth and smiled at me. "It is his good pleasure."

I understood her more in that moment. She wanted to help me; she truly was grateful. But I saw then that if she could reunite me with my beloved family, I would disappear from her life. Her worst nightmare was that I would decide to remain at Castello Forelli. *Don't worry, girl. I'll be out of your territory soon.*

But the thought of it sent a pang of grief through me. Everything in me wanted to look at Marcello in that moment, but I knew I could not. I might look at him and never look away.

I took in a deep breath and let it out slowly in relief when the music began upstairs and people began dispersing from the tables. As much as I wasn't really excited about hitting the dance floor, it was bound to be less excruciating than sitting here, across the table from him. Lord Rossi still had more nobles to introduce me to, which might mean I could just do a few dances but spend most of my time talking. That was far safer.

Luca rose and pulled out my chair. Together, we took to the wide staircase that led up to the next level. Windows had been cast wide, letting the evening breeze flow through, perhaps so the music could flow out as well, to the locals below, eager to catch an echo of their nobles' fine party. I drifted over to one and looked up to the top of the piazza, but saw no blonde women.

I turned as Lord Rossi approached, introducing me to a stern, tall gentleman, who checked me out like he didn't trust me. Perhaps we were moving from friendliest to meanest in the crowd.

"Take care with this one," Luca whispered in my ear, then reached for a goblet of wine from a passing servant and grinned at the new arrival, another tall, distinguished man with quick eyes. I had the immediate impression that he missed nothing. That he could take in a room and name everyone in it from memory. He looked me over like he was going to paint my portrait later, slowly moving over every inch of my face. My skin pricked, and goose bumps ran down my back. Why, exactly, had Luca warned me about this one?

Lord Rossi made the introductions, as he had with all the rest, but his tone was much more cool and aloof. Civil, but barely. What had this man, Lord Vannucci, done? I only became more alarmed when Marcello appeared, wine goblet in hand, to stand on my other side. He'd avoided me all evening. So was I in some physical danger with this Vannucci guy?

But the man merely listened to our story, told by Lord Rossi, and studied me the whole time. As if my face might portray some nuance that would give him insight. I fought the desire to squirm under his intense gaze.

"*Normandie,*" he said in French. How could a look be so… probing? It was as if he was slicing open my head and had access to all that was inside, like a computer programmer popping open a unit and sliding out the data panels. "*Où habitez-vous exactement en Normandie?*" *Where is your home in Normandy?*

I hesitated. It had been a month or so since my last French class, and it was the first time that someone called me out on my whole I'm-from-France story.

"Near Dordogne," I said in a rush, hoping my accent was somewhat believable.

His lips thinned in a wise smile. "*Je connais bien la Dordogne,*" he said.

My heart skipped a beat. Just my luck. The dude knew it well.

"*Où est votre maison située?*"

He wanted to know where my home was, specifically. I cast back through my memories of a brief trip through the region. "*Un manoir près de la rivière.*" *Near the river.*

"Ahh," he said approvingly. "*Un endroit charmant.*"

I don't think I took a full breath until he finally nodded and disappeared into the crowd. Had he bought it? I didn't think so. Not really. Lord Rossi took a deep breath, made his excuses and departed, and Marcello turned to the window. I did as well. "So, I assume you should have warned me of that one."

"Indeed," Marcello said.

"Why?"

"Many suspect him of spying for the Fiorentini," he said lowly. "He oft argues on their behalf, urging peace, citing ways our city might gain if we worked with them, instead of against them."

I raised an eyebrow. "Forgive me, but isn't that a possibility? Might the Sienese not gain from peace shared?"

Marcello frowned at me, as if I had just uttered heresy. "Our ongoing war is their doing, not ours. If peace is to come to Toscana, they shall have to repair many years of damages done to us."

Fine, fine, whatever, I thought, backing off. I wasn't going to win that argument, with him all hot and bothered. But how did a known sympathizer of the Fiorentini remain in the upper crust of Sienese society when emotions ran so hot? The guy had to be buying his way in, somehow. Wasn't that how it was done, regardless of the era?

"Come, Lady Gabriella," Luca said. "Marcello needs to escort his bride-to-be to the dance floor, and I am eager to see if my fine lessons have remained in that pretty head of yours."

The floor erupted in polite applause as the previous song ended. Some moved from the lines, others moved into them, as Luca and I did. I refrained from looking for Marcello and Romana, and focused only on Luca, determined to get the steps right.

"Smile, Gabriella," he coaxed. "This is not a punishment. It is joy in movement."

I gave him a fake smile, though when he lifted his eyebrow in doubt I had to grin in earnest. The music—performed by a small orchestra of lutes, flutes, and violins—began again. We moved in time to it, and I gasped at the glory of everyone doing the same move at the same time. It was as if I was a part of society in a whole new way, connected to them all, in this shared experience. How I wished we would dance like this in my own time! It was refined, flirtatious, fun. None of the bumping and grinding that the kids did at my high school. This was a celebration of men and women, of life, of the draw between us all. I clapped in perfect time and turned, smiling back at Luca.

"Perfecto," he whispered, nodding at me in admiration.

"I had a decent tutor," I whispered back. But then my smile faded as I thought of Marcello, holding me in his arms, then later disappearing through the door, leaving us both quaking with disappointment. I doubted he'd try and dance with me this night. No, Romana would likely keep him by her side the whole evening. I was surprised that he had escaped to come and stand by me when Lord Vannucci neared.

Romana's cousin, Captain Orlando Rossi, approached, and Luca reluctantly released me into his care. I danced with him next, then two others.

Seriously. If the guys were this hot in Siena in 1342, their great-great-great-grandsons had to be there in the twenty-first century. I had to get my mom to leave the ruins and get us to the city. At least once in a while. It would make my summer so much more fun.

But then Lord Vannucci came near, and the hair on the back of my neck stuck up again.

"Forgive me, m'lord." Luca tried to intervene, again at my side. "But I believe Lady Betarrini had promised the next dance to me."

"I will wait," he said, bowing his head a little, still staring at me. Was that a tiny smile on his lips? My heart skipped a beat. There was no way I could have an extended conversation with the man. My French petered out at level two.

We moved off, and I fumbled through the steps this time, too aware that Lord Vannucci was boring two holes into me with his hot stare. "Do I have to dance with him?" I whispered, as Luca came by me again in our group's circle.

"Just once," he said, sorrowfully. "Make it through, and you can feign a headache. I'll escort you out."

"All right," I said.

I clapped with little enthusiasm for the end of the song, and then he was there, in front of me, offering one hand, palm up. He was over six feet tall, about forty. And he never released me with his dark eyes.

I took a misstep, and he began to count with me in a low, whispered French. "That's it, Gabriella, that's it," he said, as if soothing a lost kitten. As far as I knew, few dared to speak to a relative stranger using their first name. It was reserved for people who really knew you. People who'd earned it.

This guy, using my first name? Major Creeporama.

I concentrated on my count and steps, looking over his shoulder, refusing to meet his gaze. I was proud of myself for not messing up again, then got all irritated at the thought of his believing it was because he counted for me, like a patient instructor. We were on the last round. I took his hand again and then couldn't resist staring back into his eyes. He was handing me a slip of paper. There was the tiny smile again. A smile of victory, like he had me already.

The dance ended, and I slipped the note into my waistband and clapped, side by side with the tall man. He smiled and leaned over to me, as if to thank me for the dance, but instead he whispered, "Make your excuses and meet me alone, out in the courtyard, in the far corner. *En toute hâte, s'il vous plait.*" *In all haste, please. Hurry*. He smiled and then nodded cordially before sauntering off, as if he was your average dance partner, off to catch a cup of punch or something.

Luca arrived. "Are you all right?" he whispered, taking my elbow. "You look ill. What did he say?"

"Nothing, nothing," I muttered.

"Do you want to take your leave?"

"Nay. Not yet." I had to shake him, if I was to read the note in privacy. "Listen, Luca, would you kindly find another glass of water?"

"There's wine—"

"Nay. I'm afraid that will only make me feel worse. Please. Water?"

He studied me a moment and then left.

I moved around a pillar and down a small hallway. Finding a door unlocked, I slipped inside and moved over to the window, where the moon was just barely bright enough for me to read the note.

Votre recherche se termine avec moi. Je sais où est votre sœur.

Your search ends with me. I know where your sister is.

CHAPTER 13

I slipped down the staircase, knowing that Luca was probably already where he left me, glass of water in hand. I had to hurry.

I moved through the dining hall, where servants were clearing the tables, and out into the courtyard, surrounded by three levels of arched colonnades. The moon was climbing higher in the sky, casting deep, spooky shadows. A couple moved through, whispering to each other, then, spotting me, hurried off.

I swallowed hard, wishing I had that glass of wine now. I'd down it in one gulp. Maybe it'd give me the courage I needed to face the weirdo. I lifted my chin and pulled back my shoulders, refusing to appear afraid, even if I was terrified inside. He knew where Lia was.

I moved down through the ground-floor colonnade, looking left and then right, wondering if I had misunderstood him. But then I saw his silhouette in the far corner, leaning against a wall, casually waiting on me.

I stopped, a few feet off, and looked back. We were alone for the moment. "You know where my sister is?" I whispered in French.

"I do." He pushed off the wall and walked around me. "You may drop your faulty French now, Gabriella. I know you are not who you pretend to be."

I made myself stand still, to bear his stare. He didn't touch me. But it was like he had.

"You resemble her."

"Nay, I do not. You are playing with me. You have not seen her." I turned to leave.

He reached out and touched my arm, deceptively gentle. "I have. She is with the Paratores."

I froze, hands on my skirts. The Paratores. Impossible. Right? Or most probable of all.… I had convinced myself we would've gotten to her before they had the chance.

Slowly, I turned to face him.

"Come closer, Gabriella," he said. "What I have to tell you is for you to know alone."

I moved closer, and he offered his hand. Reluctantly, I reached up to take it, and he pulled me into the corner, until my back was against the wall. He traced my cheek with the back of his knuckle, down to my jaw, then down my neck, studying me. There, he let his hand drop. "You did not let me finish. Evangelia resembles you, not in eye or hair color, but in the fine bone structure of your face. It is unmistakable. And she has drawn you, your portrait. I knew you as soon as I saw you."

He did know Lia. How else would he know such things?

He stepped back, letting me absorb his words.

Two sets of boots came running into the courtyard.

Vannucci pressed a hand against my mouth and pushed me into the wall. "Stay…still," he hissed.

It was Luca and Marcello, hands on the hilts of their swords, looking about madly. But they barely paused to peruse the shadows before they were off to the piazza. They thought I had gone out…to Il Campo, perhaps home to the palazzo.

Slowly, he moved away from me, the sick expression on his face telling me that he liked being close to me.

"What do you want from me? Why not take me immediately to her?"

He let out a humorless laugh. "There are a hundred different reasons, silly girl. The Paratores are Fiorentini. That presents certain… challenges."

"But you were with them. You saw Evangelia."

"I did."

"Then you can get me to her too."

"I could…if I chose to."

I stared at him. What did he want?

He leaned in, his hand against the wall above me, to my right. With his left hand, he gently touched my temple, as if trying to coax a solution out of me. "Think, Gabriella. What would I want from you?"

Did the guy think I would…? My face twisted in revulsion. He laughed softly, as if he could read my thoughts. "Nay, I have plenty of women to warm my bed. I need something more from you."

I cast about for what he was after, bewildered.

He leaned in, and his breath warmed my ear. "I want…Castello Forelli."

I pushed him back and took a step away, unable to tolerate his proximity for a moment longer. He wanted me to sell out the people who had rescued me, fed me, sheltered me? The people who had done nothing but show me kindness?

He laughed again, circling me like a wolf about to devour a trembling, lone lamb. I ignored him, trying to figure out a solution, something else I might give him in exchange for my sister. "Is she a prisoner? Or a guest?"

"A guest, for now. Lord Paratore finds her fascinating. He says she showed up among the tombs two days past, the same tombs where he first saw you. She hit her head in her struggle with Paratore's knights, and ever since, she has been speaking of a time ahead, that she 'traveled through time.' And," he added, his eyes narrowing, "she remembers nothing of your 'home' in Dordogne."

I stared at him, hard, glad that he seemed to think her demented. But she'd arrived only two days ago? When I'd been here a full week. "She…she must be terribly injured. I must see to her. At once."

"And so you shall. The price of your reunion is but this one task: You must find a weakness in the castello that my allies can utilize."

"You intend to hand over the castello to the Fiorentini?" I said incredulously.

He grabbed my arm, sending shards of pain to my shoulder. "Keep your voice down," he hissed. He looked out to the courtyard and then back to me. "If you want to be with your sister again, you will help us gain access."

"Every man in Castello Forelli will die defending her."

"Nay," he said dismissively. "No one's ideals are as high as they believe. Life is too precious. They shall surrender."

I shook my head. "You do not know the Forellis or their knights very well."

"And you do not understand the intricacies of Toscana politics. Go, Gabriella. Fetch your sister and return to Normandy, if that is where you are truly from. Simply be on your way and never look back. Leave Toscana to us."

I considered his words. Maybe it was best, for me to leave, fast, before I could mess it all up further. I'd done enough damage to Marcello and Romana's coming marriage. Maybe I could somehow warn Marcello in time, after I had Lia…somehow, some way, we had to find our way out again. Without selling out the good guys.

At least, all the way. "How will I get word to you?"

A smile spread across his face and for the first time, I saw his white teeth, gleaming in the moonlight. "That's a good girl. That's a very good girl." He leaned forward and pinched my right cheek between his thumb and forefinger. "I'll come to you at Castello Forelli. They do not yet have just cause to decline me a measure of hospitality. Be certain you have what I need when I arrive." He leaned closer, dropped his hand, brushed his lips swiftly across each of my cheeks, and then strode off, his dark cape fluttering behind him.

I wiped my cheeks with my hands—as if I could wash off his kisses—and shuddered.

The good news was that my sister was alive and within reach.

The bad news was I had just made a pact with the devil.

I hurried across the piazza, staying near the side in case I needed to pause and hide in the shadows. Marcello and Luca would freak if

they knew I was out at night, unescorted. They were still looking for me. When they found I wasn't in the palazzo, they'd probably return to the dance, certain they'd just missed me in the crowd.

I saw them then, moving through the tunnel, toward me. I ducked into a stone doorway and froze, listening to their muffled voices echo across Il Campo but unable to tell what they were saying.

I had to leave, return to Castello Forelli on my own, and figure out a way to get to Castello Paratore and free Lia before Lord Vannucci got there himself. Otherwise, I was doomed to play spy for them…and I couldn't live with myself if I sold the Forellis out.

I thought through my plan to reach Castello Forelli. I could hide in the woods if I came across any rogue bands of mercenaries or soldiers. It was my only chance. In the light of day, I'd never make it.

The men disappeared into the Palazzo Pubblico and I rushed up and through the tunnel, then down Via di Banchi to the Rossis' home. Hurriedly, I knocked at the door, and a wide-eyed servant allowed me access. "Lady Betarrini! Lord Forelli was just here, looking for you."

"Yes," I said, feigning confusion. "Somehow we got separated in the crowd at the dance and then I was outside, all alone." I brought a hand to my chest as if even the memory brought me breathless with fear. "I am so frightfully weary. I believe I might be taking ill."

"Oh, my poor, dear, lady." She drew me in and shut the door, locking it behind me. I eyed the keys on her waistband, knowing I would need them to get into the stables and get a horse. There was no way I could walk all those miles in the stupid tapestry slippers. My feet would be a mass of broken blisters by the time I arrived. Lady Forelli had been my height, but clearly, her feet had been a half-size smaller.

She tucked her arm in mine and led me upstairs. "I'll help you out of your gown and you can go right to sleep. You'll see. You're probably just overwrought with excitement over the ball and all those dashing young men."

"I'm certain you are right," I muttered, faking my agreement.

She unlocked the door and entered the room in front of me. Before she could hook the ring back on her waistband, I turned to her and presented the back of my gown. "Oh, please, dear lady. Suddenly I feel faint. I must be out of this dress in an instant!"

I forced back a small smile when I heard her drop her keys to the table as she immediately set about her task. I had seen enough of her to know she was kindhearted but a bit forgetful. *Forgive me, friend,* I thought, as I carefully placed my lace handkerchief over the keys.

"Would you like me to brush out your hair, m'lady?" she said once I had shed the russet gown.

"Nay, nay," I said turning to her. "I can see to it myself. But I might want to take a turn on the rooftop, gain some air, if my stomach doesn't settle. You know how it is. Can you help me into this other dress?"

I lifted my regular gown out of a trunk at the foot of my bed and handed it to her. She held it up as I put my arms in, then turned to allow her to button it up the back. "I know how you feel, m'lady. If I dare to eat onion, my stomach gives me fits all night."

I hustled her to the door, and she paused there a moment, looking befuddled. She put her hands in her pockets as if looking for something. I held my breath. "Oh, dear. I have the strangest sensation I'm forgetting something."

I bodily turned her and gently urged her outward again. "If you remember what it is, come back at once. It's late, and no doubt you're as weary as I."

"Yes, yes," she muttered, walking, not at all convinced, but obedient, above all things, just as a good servant ought to be.

I closed the door and leaned against it for a moment, then hurried to shove my other things in my two valises. I wrapped the bread in a cloth, and stuffed it in too. I took the round bottle of wine, emptied it in the chamber pot, and then filled it with water from a pitcher, popping the cork back in.

Then I rushed to the door and quietly pulled it open.

He nearly gave me a heart attack.

Marcello stood there in the doorway, left hand on the casing above, right thumb tucked into his waistband. Luca was across the hall, arms crossed, leaning back against the wall.

"Where are you going, Gabriella?" Marcello asked me.

"I have no time to explain," I said, pushing past him.

He caught my arm and whirled me about. "You shall explain. It may be different in Normandy, but here in Toscana, only certain sorts of women scurry about unescorted in the night."

I wrenched my arm from his grip and resumed my flight down the stairs, Marcello right behind me. I had no time for this. With trembling hands, I searched for the right key for the door that led to the stables.

"Nay," Marcello growled, pulling the keys from me. They clattered to the ground. "You are not leaving!"

Luca came down the stairs slowly, and glanced back up, as if wondering if our voices would draw a servant.

But Marcello only continued to stare furiously at me.

"Marcello, I need to go," I said urgently. "It is for the best. For you. For me. Please, please let me go."

"Where are you going? You've only just been introduced to the men who might aid you in your—"

"Back to Castello Forelli," I said, feeling as if I might cry. "If your father and brother will have me. Only for a few days, until I figure out where I will go next."

He frowned at me in confusion. "Did something frighten you?"

"Nay," I said, pacing a bit. He had to stay here—if he showed up, back home, Lord Vannucci might take Lia away, back out of the deal. I looked back up at Marcello and chewed my lip, considering what I could tell him. "I think Lia is back there, near your home. I want to get back. I fear I might miss her, and that we shall never be reunited."

"You asked to come *here*."

"And now that I see she isn't *here*, I must move on."

He took a deep breath and held it. "We will see you to safety. You can leave when you choose. I only intend that you not come to harm."

"You cannot accompany me. What would Lady Romana think? You are betrothed to her, remember?"

He stepped back, as if my mentioning her name had splashed cold water on his face.

"I will escort you, then," Luca said, stepping forward.

"Nay, nay. I will draw far less attention if I travel alone."

"Untrue! Do you not remember what became of you the last time we traveled that road?" Marcello said.

"Exactly my point. We were part of a train full of soldiers. You are like magnets, pulling your enemy forces in. They will ignore a single rider."

"Marcello…" Luca said. He held up a piece of paper.

The note. It must've fallen from my waistband when I disrobed, and Luca had nabbed it from my room. Marcello looked at me out of the corner of his eye and then reached for the paper. He unfolded it and scanned it.

I closed my eyes, bracing for what was to come.

"What does it say?" He leaned toward me. "Gabriella, what does it say?"

"He knows who has my sister," I translated softly.

"Who? Who knows?" Marcello said. "Where is she? It was Lord Vannucci, wasn't it? He was the one who gave you this note."

I shook my head, my eyes still closed, and then let out a gasp when he took hold of my shoulders and shook me.

"Who has her?" he ground out, suspicion making his eyes cold, studying me. "There is only one family that would make you keep her whereabouts a secret."

I nodded, looking to the stones at my feet. It was going to look bad, any which way I cut it. "The Paratores," I whispered. I looked up at him, misery washing through me.

"What do they want? What is their demand, for you to be reunited with your sister?"

The quickest way out of a mess is to face the truth, Dad always said.

I steeled myself and made myself look at him as I said it. "They want Castello Forelli."

Marcello released me, almost shoving me in his frustration. He lifted his hands, and they shook with rage as he paced away from me, then clenched them into fists.

"I wasn't going to give them what they asked," I pleaded, stepping toward him. At least, I wasn't going to *totally* sell them out. "I was going to figure out a way. Make them think I was giving them access, but allow you to know the truth in time. I could not…I would not…Marcello."

He glanced at me, his face a mask of fury. Over and over he shook his head. His eyes moved back and forth as if he was thinking, trying to come to a solution.

I looked to Luca, hoping he might help me out a little. See what we could not.

He walked down the remaining steps slowly, gripping the balustrade pillar. "If you think about it, Marcello, it could be quite perfect."

His master looked to him as if he might be going crazy.

Luca held up a hand. "No, think on it a moment. The Paratores believe they finally may have access to the castello. Their intent will be annihilation. All previous treaties will be null and void as soon as their men enter. We would be free to kill every last one of them. Be done with them. Storm their castle and claim it for the Sienese, making our outpost nearly invincible. Consider it, m'lord. We can arrange it all, while here."

I shuddered at the thought of men dying.

But my feelings were clearly the only twenty-first-century ones in the room.

Marcello ceased his pacing and stood before me. "Can you maintain the charade? Truly, see it all the way through?" His tone was calmer now, as if his fear for me returned. "If the Paratores—or Lord Vannucci—discover that you intend to double-cross them, they will not hesitate to slit your throat. Or your sister's." He shook his head. "There will be no second chance, Gabriella."

I stared back at him. "It is a great risk. But I am prepared to do anything—anything—to get my sister back. So please, let me be off. They'll be far more apt to believe I could sneak away from Castello Forelli and to them if you and your men are here in Siena."

"But why would they believe that we let you return, alone?"

"I will say I escaped, in the dark of night, while you all were still at the ball."

"We've seen firsthand how good she is with a rope," Luca said.

"But wouldn't they expect me to come after you? Or at least send some men?"

"Not if you want her gone," Luca said softly. "She is coming between you and Lady Romana. You are unaccountably drawn to each other. And you cannot let anything break this union with the house of Rossi."

I held my breath and kept my eyes on Marcello. Luca spoke nothing but the truth. We both knew it.

"Scorned, her heart broken, Gabriella is willing to sell out the Forellis. Her only goal is to regain her sister and flee," Luca finished gently.

Marcello's eyes were warm again, searching mine. He seemed to struggle to swallow, then he gently took my hands in his. "It is an enormous, grave risk."

I let a smile spread across my cheeks. "I'm becoming accustomed to it."

He reached up and touched my face, and Luca turned away.

"Gabriella," Marcello whispered, shaking his head. "I've never known a woman like you. If we had met before—"

"When? Your betrothal to Romana has been in motion for too long for us to stop it," I said, turning away. But he held me fast and stared at me until I dared to look back into his eyes.

"I shall never forget you."

"Nor I, you," I whispered back.

His handsome face a mask of anguish, he leaned down, closer, as if he intended to kiss me.

But then we all heard it.

Luca turned toward the door. Marcello straightened and released me.

People, laughing, talking, shouting. Returning.

He grabbed the keys from the ground, swiftly cycled through them, and shoved the right one in the lock. He pushed me through, but grabbed my hand and whispered, "Send me word through Cook. Trust no one else. I shall be nearby in three days. Tell Paratore to attack in four."

I nodded, even as he shut the door in my face and turned the lock. I stayed still, feeling foolish for my irritation at him for shutting the door in my face, knowing it was impossible to do anything but that, listening to the men making fumbled excuses, feigning drunkenness as the rest of the household passed. "We were considering a moonlit ride," Luca said, his words slurred. "But then we thought we might be apt to fall on our backside if we were to attempt it."

"Lord Marcello, I am surprised to find you indisposed," Romana said, when the rest of the footsteps receded. "I didn't see you imbibe all evening."

"I confess it was me and my wretched debauchery," Luca said. "I drew my lord in, celebrating our victory over those Fiorentini scoundrels on the road. We quite forgot ourselves."

"Quite," she said icily. "You forgot yourselves so thoroughly you left me behind at the ball. It was…a horror."

"Forgive me, beloved," Marcello said lowly. "It shall never happen again."

Nay, I thought. *It shall not.* I would see to it myself. No more interference with the man's hopes, his family's dreams of security. I would free my sister, and we would be away.

More people came in then, but Marcello and Lady Rossi seemed to hover. I could not bear to break away from my eavesdropping. And until the household turned in for the night, it was not safe for me to ride off down the road anyway. I would run a serious risk of interception.

"Marcello," she said lowly, almost too quiet to hear. "Did you accompany Lady Betarrini home?"

"She was here when we arrived. A servant told us she was complaining of stomach ailments and had gone to bed."

"Poor girl." But her tone was more of relief than any genuine empathy.

"Romana, I've asked Lady Betarrini to depart before sunup."

"Oh? Where is she going?" It sounded as if they had paused halfway up the stairs. I leaned closer, pressing my ear to the crack in the door.

"To Castello Forelli. She confessed certain…feelings toward me. I made it clear that my heart could only belong to you."

I knew he was only taking up the story we had agreed on,

soothing her fears, just as I wanted him to do, but it still stung, hearing him say it.

It was quiet then. Were they kissing? Or had they just moved too far away for me to hear any more?

I sighed sadly. *Well, that was over before it even got started. Gabi's stellar love life resumes its amazing run!*

I was dragging a crate over to my horse, preparing to mount, when Luca showed up, dressed to ride. "What are you doing?" I said. "I thought we agreed it best that I go alone."

"You thought it best. Lord Marcello and I thought it foolish." He put a hand up, palm facing me. "With just the two of us, we'll still not be as likely to draw attention. And if stopped, we can claim to be man and wife, traveling through the night."

"I don't—"

"Gabriella, they won't let you out the city gates without me. And Marcello has charged me with the task of devising the battle plan with you."

I hadn't thought of the city gates. "Well then, be quick about it," I said in irritation, knowing he had me.

He grinned and helped me mount. "Do you have your sword?"

I patted my shoulder strap. I preferred the back sheath to the one on the saddle and had found a couple of them here, on a peg. It gave me faster access and was reasonably hidden.

He had his horse saddled in quick order and led the gelding to the front of the stables, eased opened the double doors, peeked out, and waited for me to come through too. Then he closed them behind me, and we were off.

I had to admit that even riding through the streets of Siena at night, I was glad I had a companion. It warmed me that Marcello could not bear to see me off alone.

He had sent his most trusted man to watch over me.

Or was it to watch me?

Maybe both.

We encountered no one on the way home to the castello. It was almost eerie how well my plan worked. No Sienese soldiers were on patrol, nor were the bands of rogue knights or Paratores. And the road was visible enough for us in the moonlight to make good time.

"You should always travel by moonlight," I said to Luca. "It seems far safer than what we encountered en route to Siena."

"Some days are better than others." He pretended to sigh, as if referring to our battles as the good day.

Boys and their bravado. I had to admit, it made me laugh. And I needed a laugh about then. But my giggles were swallowed when Castello Paratore came into view with the morning light. Luca pulled up on his reins. "This is where you're on your own. If you don't show up by sundown, I'm coming for you and your sister."

"Nay," I insisted again. "Give me until sundown tomorrow."

"Nay," he said. "It will either work or it will not. If it works, they'll believe you to be an ally and allow you to leave. If they don't, you will be their prisoner. Why languish a day in their dungeon?"

"But if you're going to defeat them, don't I need to learn as much about their weaknesses as they wish to know about yours? That might take some time."

He nodded, lips clenched. "Take care, m'lady. You enter the lions' den. May the Lord shut their hungry mouths."

I smiled, remembering the old Bible storybook our grandmother gave us. If only I might have the courage Daniel had shown....

"I'll be at Castello Forelli, waiting. Please, don't make me fret over you."

I grinned. "I'll do my best." I wheeled my horse around, and we crossed the shallow creek that formed the border between the Paratore and Forelli lands, the border each family was forever trying to push forward.

I wound around it and eventually met up with the road that led to Castello Paratore and Firenze. It was well maintained, and I climbed the curves at a good clip, until two knights came trotting down the road toward me, Paratore crimson clearly displayed. Two other knights emerged on the road behind me. I pulled back on my gelding's reins. He circled, agitated by the four new horses, but I made him stop, facing the castle.

"State your name and business," said the man closest to me.

"Lady Gabriella Betarrini. Lord Vannucci sent me to speak to your master."

The two knights shared a look. "Lord Vannucci, you said." His eyes flicked toward my saddle, atop Forelli gold.

"Lord Vannucci," I confirmed.

"You are alone?" His eyes moved down the road.

"I am now. But I am expected back at Castello Forelli by sundown."

He stared at me a moment longer. "Come ahead, then."

We rode up to the castle gates, a far steeper entry than Castello Forelli's. But she did not boast as many towers as Marcello's family's home. Only two were visible from this side, but they looked formidable.

Heavy gates were cranked open, and we moved inside.

Lord Paratore was immediately striding toward me, a hulking knight and three others right behind him. I recognized them from the tombs and our battle the following day. "Ah, the lovely Lady Betarrini has at last seen the error of her ways and has come to seek shelter in a castle of real men."

Yeah, I came because I thought you were so hot.

I stared at his green eyes, which were his best feature, avoiding his mouth, full of decaying teeth. I allowed him to reach up and assist me down, and I even managed to thank him.

"Lord Vannucci sent you?" he asked, as two of his men grabbed my arms.

"What—what are you doing?" I asked, struggling against them. But I could not free myself.

He stepped closer and slowly untied my cape, pulling it from my shoulders and dropping it to the stones at his feet. With wise eyes, he stared at my sheath a moment, then reached down to unbuckle it, sliding it from my shoulders and handing it to The Hulk. "My men returned with tales of a female Forelli warrior brandishing a sword. It appears they were telling the truth," he said, lifting a delighted brow.

He was pretty decent looking, except for his teeth. But the way he talked to me made me feel sticky with sweat. *Ugh. This guy grosses me out.*

I was already longing for the comforting weight of the sword on my back. It had been a long shot, hoping I could get in armed. But I still had—

"Check her legs."

Inwardly, I groaned.

A knight guffawed over his good luck and bent to run his hands up my left leg and then down my right. When he reached my right calf, he paused and grinned up at me.

I stared straight ahead as he lifted the edge of my skirt and unhooked the other dagger sheath, strapped there. He was lingering, taking too long.

"Enough," I said, putting my left foot to his shoulder and kicking him.

He tumbled to his rear, making the others hoot with laughter. He leaped to his feet, looking as if he wanted to slap me, but Lord Paratore held up his hand to halt him.

"You have my weapons," I said. "Keep them. I'm here for one reason."

Paratore smiled then, and I again concentrated on looking at his eyes instead of his wretched teeth. "You are beautiful, m'lady," he said, tucking a knuckle under my chin, "but I must say I fished the fairest Betarrini from those Etruscan tombs. I have a special weakness for women with blonde hair."

He *did* have Lia. My heart sped up, and I glanced around, as if I might spot Lia wandering the ramparts. "Where is she?"

"Resting," he said. "Come, m'lady. We have much to discuss. If you give me what I seek, you shall see your sister this day."

He offered his arm and the guards dropped their hold on me.

After a moment's hesitation, I laid my hand on top of his and allowed myself to be ushered inside. As the doors closed behind me, I stifled the desire to scream. Why did I feel as if I had just made a fatal error in judgment? That I should have broken away and done my best to escape?

The other men floated away down two hallways, leaving us alone in a den. Maps of Firenze and Paratore land dominated one wall, the border clearly marked by the new path of the creek. I turned away from it to face him.

"Please, m'lady, sit." He gestured to a generous settee and waited until I obeyed, then he took a chair with a high back directly across from it. He folded his hands. "You and I were not properly introduced. You have to understand that I thought you some sort of…loose woman, out in such odd clothing that day at the tombs. Our women wear nothing like it. I would've never attacked a noblewoman."

My skinny jeans and top. There was no sense in arguing with him. He was trying to make amends.

"I see the Forellis have put you in proper clothing, as I've done for your sister."

Lia. Just the thought of being with her again made my heart speed up.

"May I see her?"

"In time, in time. As I'm certain Lord Vannucci explained to you, there is only one thing I will trade you in exchange for your sister. Access to Castello Forelli."

"And I will not even consider such a betrayal, until I know for certain that you have my sister and she is well."

He smiled. "Oh, she is very well. I think you will find her quite content here." He leaned forward. "We are not the monsters the Forellis make us out to be."

"It is unfortunate when neighbors find themselves on opposites sides of a dividing line," I said, trying to sound understanding, like he might win me over. "It is bound to cause much strife."

"Much," he said. He steepled his fingers in front of his face and peered at me.

I waited him out, determined to say nothing until I knew she was okay.

"I see that you are uncommonly resilient. Far more stubborn than your sister. She's rather…" He played with the horsehair on his chair's arm—"dovelike."

Apparently, he didn't know my sister that well yet. Still, I waited. *If you have harmed even a hair on her head, I swear I'll—*

He rose and offered me a hand. "Come. I will show you the dungeon where your sister is kept."

Dungeon? I rose, ready to attack, but he laughed, and I caught the glint of teasing in his green eyes. "Come along," he said over his shoulder.

We moved to a grand staircase that curved up one side of the grand salon and then down a hallway to the last room. The floor had thick Persian carpets and Danish tapestries lined the walls, much as they did at Castello Forelli.

He knocked at a massive, ornately carved door. Was this a game? I held my breath.

"Yes?" came a feminine voice from the other side. *Lia.*

"M'lady, it is Lord Paratore. I have a visitor with me whom I think you would like to greet."

She opened the door, then, and her blue eyes went wide with excitement when she saw me. Was she real? Or was I dreaming? I pulled her into my arms, never more happy to see my sister than I was in that moment.

She was here. With me.

Which was both good and bad news.

"Might we…might we have a moment, m'lord?"

"Please," he said, gesturing into the room. "But come and speak with me in an hour, will you?" He gave me a look that told me not to argue.

"An hour," I confirmed.

He closed the door behind us, and I drew Lia deeper into the room. She enjoyed far more sumptuous quarters than I had been given, but then, Lord Paratore apparently did not have a potential bride in one wing. At least, that I knew of…

"Where have you been?" Lia asked me.

"I could ask the same of you!" I said in a hushed whisper. "I arrived a week ago. Yet I heard that you arrived only two days ago?"

"Right. I landed in that tomb, but you were nowhere around. I wandered over here to the castle.…" She gave me a *sorry* look. "It took me a bit to put it together. I claimed that I'd had a bump on my head."

Hearing English again was like a hug from home. A step closer to being there! "You told them…you were from the future?"

She nodded, looking embarrassed at her foolishness. "Lord

Paratore told me he'd seen you, but you'd been taken away by those terrible Forellis."

"Terrible? No, they're wonderful. I—"

"But Gabi, how did you get here so far ahead of me?" she asked, shaking her head in confusion. "We were together, our hands on those prints, and then you were gone a second ahead of me. It was as if you became dust before my eyes. And then when I arrived and you weren't with me—I thought I'd lost you for sure."

I shook my head, remembering that moment. "I think it has to do with when we pulled our hands from the prints. My split-second ahead of you was the equivalent of days, almost a week, here." I grasped her hand. "We need to get back to the tomb, Lia. I think we both need to be there. If we put our hands on the prints again, maybe we'll fast forward, back to our own time."

"Or...will we go deeper? Into history." She shivered and crossed her arms. "I don't know about you, but this is about as deep as I want to go."

I smiled. "Can you imagine Mom here? Dad, had he gotten the chance?"

"Oh, they'd go crazy," she said.

I nodded and my smile faded. "We have to try, Lia. To get back to Mom."

She nodded too. "You're right, of course."

"So how can we get you out of here?"

She frowned. "Get me out? Let's just tell Lord Paratore we are heading out on a stroll, and make our way down to the tombs."

"I...don't think it's going to be that easy. He's made you feel a guest in his home. But he is using you as a pawn, Lia. He wants me to betray the Forellis in exchange for your freedom."

She frowned. "Then we must escape. Right away." She rose and looked back at me.

I nodded, but couldn't seem to move.

It took all of two seconds for her to figure out my reason for hesitating. "Oh," she said, grabbing my hand and sitting again. "You met someone."

"No. Yes." I looked at her. "Not anyone I can have, on a hundred different levels."

"The unattainable. Always the most attractive. He is a knight at Castello Forelli?"

"He is likely to become Lord Forelli in time," I said miserably.

She sucked in her breath, bringing her fingers to her mouth. "You really gotta stop aiming so high, girl."

"It doesn't matter. It's over."

"But it began?"

"Before it began." I didn't want to talk about it anymore. It made me feel sad and weepy, to finally come so close to finding someone I might fall in love with, and then to have to let him go—

"How did you talk him into letting you come here, to his enemy?"

I gave her a sad smile. "You're my sister. He has a brother. He understood."

"Oh, I'm sorry, Gabs. If I hadn't come, maybe you would've lived happily ever after with him."

"No, no." I pretended to whack her across the shoulder. "Stop with the schmaltzy romancy stuff," I said. "You know I never go in for that."

"You didn't," she pressed, staring at me. "But there's something different about you, Gabi. Something's changed."

"Yeah, we jumped through some time continuum," I deflected. "It's gotta change us somehow."

She lifted her chin, and for the first time, I saw how her cheekbones and jawline were very much like mine—exactly as Lord Vannucci had said. I always thought we were so different, her as blonde as I was brunette. Her straight hair to my curls. I had four inches on her. But we did share the same facial structure.

"You have a lot more connecting you here than I do," she said. "I'll gather my things, and we'll be off. I'd like to meet your lord, anyway, before we leave him behind forever. It will help me spot the right kind of guy for you in our real time."

I stared at her. "Lia, you still don't get it. We are in the middle of some of the toughest Sienese-Fiorentini relations in history. Do you remember what year Siena fell?"

She shook her head. "I never really listened during those tours. I was too interested in the art."

"Me neither," I said, rising to pace. "But I'm worried it's soon. I think Firenze was fully in power when the Renaissance happened, which is around the corner too. Do you remember the year that started?"

She shook her head. "What about the plague? Has the plague happened?"

I felt woozy and quickly took my seat again. The plague. The Bubonic Plague. I shook my head. More than a third of Siena and Firenze had died in those years—I remembered that much.

"No, I haven't heard of anything like it happening. Fevers, but nothing widespread. Just your typical medieval maladies. So it must still be coming."

"We have to get out of here, Gabi," she said, wringing her hands. "It's one thing to play at this lords and ladies thing, another to take on the plague."

"I have a plan, but it means you're going to have to lay low till I come for you. Lord Forelli and his men are going to break you out."

Her eyes widened in disbelief. Then she strode over to a wall and ran her delicate fingers over two swords and a bow. "I dunno," she said. "Find me some arrows, and methinks I could fight my way out."

I smiled at her lame medieval-speak. "I've had to do much the same this past week."

Her blue eyes widened. "You've used a sword? In battle?"

"Twice. Tried to bring it with me in here, but they caught me. As soon as you can, secure some arrows to go with that. Tell Lord Paratore you wish to practice. Pretend you're a beginner, so he has no idea how good you are. Appeal to his sense of pride and generosity. Flirt with him if you have to."

She shivered. "Ugh. No way."

"Lia, look at me. You have to do what you must. We are in a fight for our lives, whether you feel it yet or not."

"I think you're exaggerating."

"No, seriously. Trust me. I've seen guys *die*."

She clamped her pretty lips shut and stared at me. "They will try to kill us?"

"As soon as they realize we have double-crossed them," I whispered.

"Really? Lord Paratore has been nothing but kind to me. Giving me more food than I want, this room, art supplies—"

"It's all a ruse. He'd kill you in front of me if he knew it'd make me give him what he wanted."

She paled, and I regretted my frank words. But she had to know. Had to know what we were up against. Had to be ready. "And…and you're sure there is no other way out?" she asked.

"Not that I've seen yet," I said.

"Okay, then," she said, patting her knees and rising. "Hurry, Gabs. The faster you go, the faster you can return to me."

I pulled her into my arms and hugged her. "Be ready, Lia. Day or night, be ready. All right?"

She nodded.

I turned from her then, before I gave in to the impulse to take her hand and try and run out of this place together now. I moved down the hall, down the stairs, and back into the den, where Lord Paratore waited for me. He must have heard me coming, but he did not turn from his place in front of the map of Paratore land.

"You will deliver what has been asked of you?"

"I—I don't know. Is there no other way, m'lord? Nothing else I might give you in exchange for my sister's life?"

He looked down at the table before him for a long moment, then turned to face me. "There is nothing else, m'lady."

I wrung my hands. If I showed no hesitation, he might doubt me. In truth, it wasn't difficult to work up. He looked from my hands, up to my face.

"You and your sister are obviously fine, noble women, and that is unfortunate. But there is no way around it. I must use the tools I have at hand."

"Women are hardly tools."

"They are at times. A man will live and die for the right woman." He moved forward, circling me as Lord Vannucci had. "Sir Forelli…I wager you have caught his eye, have you not?"

"He is promised to Lady Rossi."

"Lady Rossi represents nothing but an alliance for his family." He shook his head and rubbed his chin. "Nay, you must have caught his eye."

"I know no such thing."

"Don't play with me, Lady Betarrini. I know men. And I've known my share of women. And you aren't as innocent as your younger sister—I can tell that much."

I stared straight ahead for a moment, then looked to the ground. "I may have caught his eye."

"Good, good," he crooned. "Then he will be blinded by love, never suspecting that I have found a hole in the corner of his chicken coop. Keep leading him on. Use his weakness for our strength."

I nodded, feigning misery.

He again put a knuckle beneath my chin and lifted it, forcing my eyes to his. "Ahh, he has spun his web around you as well. You are in love with him?" His eyes hardened with suspicion.

"In truth, I fancied myself in love," I said. I pulled away from his hand and went to the picture window, with its view of the courtyard. "But he sent me away. He said that I was interfering with his alliance with Lady Rossi's family. There was no other way than for me to leave. The timing, however, was providential. He had no idea I would be coming straight to you."

He moved over and placed his big hands on my shoulders. "I am sorry for your pain." Slowly he turned me around, his hands still on my shoulders. I dared to look him in the eye. Was he trying to comfort me?

No, he was testing me, trying to sort out what was truth, what was lie. But I could see he wanted to believe me.

"You shall use your pain," he said, a sick smile twisting on his lips. "Turn it into anger, vengeance, Lady Betarrini. And you shall get your reward. Not only your sister, but horses, and a chest full of gold to see you safely on your way. I'll even send four guards with you, as far as Firenze. But we shall wait until Marcello returns home. I want him there to witness it, when I breach his defenses at last. He is the last of the line of Forellis. With him gone, no other can stand in my way."

I looked back at him, as if considering his words. Then after the right amount of time, I simply said, "Agreed."

Now let go of me.

Instead, he moved his hands to my neck, caressing it, but the threat was clear enough. He rubbed his thumbs, back and forth across my jugular vein. "M'lady, you do understand that if you double-cross me, I shall hunt you down and kill you. But not before you see your sister suffer in ways that you have never imagined. Evangelia is quite...*untried*, yes?"

If I'd had a sword I would've run the man through right then. But I controlled myself. "You dare to lay a hand on her—"

"You are hardly in the position to make threats, m'lady. Do you understand me? Are you ready to serve me as your lord?"

I nodded, unable to speak. For a moment, I considered charging upstairs and trying Lia's lame plan for escape by fighting our way out. Better to die fighting than to die via torture. But I knew Marcello, too. I knew I could trust him and that he would do everything in his power to get her out of this place. And we'd have a far better chance with the Forelli men beside us.

But he was then ushering me to the door. "Thank you for your visit, m'lady. Return to me with the information I seek, or your sister will be ushered out of her quarters and into a far less appealing room, one with chains and all sorts of unsavory tools."

I turned toward him, but he shut the door in my face, a smile on his lips. Did he half hope I proved to be his enemy so he could take it out on Lia? I shook my head, trembling at the thought. The hulking knight led my gelding forward and watched me come near. I felt numb, lost in a stupor.

He lifted me into the saddle, tucked my feet into the stirrups, and slapped the horse on the rump. Two more knights opened the gates before me, and I plodded out, glancing back over my shoulder to Lia's narrow window. She was there, watching me.

I raised my hand to wave, but then they were shutting the gates.

Shutting me out.

Shutting her in.

CHAPTER 14

The elder Lord Forelli was outrageously angry when word reached him about what had happened in Siena, that I'd been sent away because Marcello deemed me a threat to his union with Romana. He summoned me to the solarium the next day and paced back and forth, sputtering, trying to be gracious in his word choice but too angry to be very successful at it. Fortino stared at me in misery from a corner chair. I believed it was only because of him that I wasn't immediately shown to the castle gates.

"I have no choice, m'lady," said the older man. "You must be on your way, as soon as possible. You cannot be here when my son returns. I'm certain you understand. There is simply too much at stake. Far too much at stake."

The man had no idea.

He wanted to secure his relations with Siena.

I wanted to save my sister.

"I intend to be on my way as soon as possible, m'lord," I soothed. "It is why I left Siena immediately. I have no desire to interfere with Lord Marcello's plans nor his coming nuptials."

He opened his mouth to say something else, but then clamped it shut. "Forgive me, my dear." He reached up a bent, age-spotted hand to rub his temple. "These are such trying times. Were they not, I would allow love to flourish where it may." He cast me a sorrowful glance. "You are an uncommon woman, as brave as you are beautiful. Your courage clearly helped save Lady Rossi, and your ministrations have surely rallied Fortino. For both of those things, I shall be eternally in your debt."

I shared a smile with Fortino. He rose, then, looking shaky, but reveling in newfound strength. "It is little surprise you caught Marcello's attention. You captured us all."

"Please," I said, lifting a hand to stop him. "Truly, I cannot bear to speak of it any longer. All I await is word of my sister, and I shall be on my way."

Lord Forelli nodded, appearing more as a broken old man than lord of the castle. "I shall have our priest pray for nothing else. Now if you'll forgive me, I must go and rest." He reached for a servant's arm and tottered out of the room.

Luca peeked in. "M'lord," he said to Fortino, "with your permission—"

"Come, come," Fortino said wearily, waving him in and sinking back to his chair.

I took a seat beside him, and Luca sat across from us, arms on knees. "Was it truly awful?" Luca asked me conspiratorially.

"About as we suspected," I said.

Luca and I'd clued in Fortino as to what had transpired in Siena, and of Paratore's plans. Luca had told me that Marcello's brother was once one of the most brilliant strategists in Toscana, before he took ill years before. We needed his expertise. And it was his place, as eldest of the Forelli sons.

"Father's anger and fear are dissipating a bit," Fortino said. "He believes that you intend to leave, Gabriella. But he'll be beside himself if Marcello returns and you are still here." He looked at me with regret.

Luca nodded, considering his words. "Marcello will be five miles out, on the morrow. That was our agreement."

"And Gabriella can go to Lord Paratore on the morrow with her final plan."

"What plan?" I said, hating the squeak in my voice. "We still don't have an entry point to suggest to Lord Paratore, right?"

They shook their heads. Fortino rose on trembling legs and went to the fireplace, stirring the cold ashes and then dividing them into mounds. Luca cast me a wise eye and waited—Marcello's brother was thinking it through.

"Lord Paratore knows you are adept with a sword," Fortino said, looking at me from the corner of his eye. "He knows you are daring. What if you go to him and tell him the truth—that you see no weakness whatsoever in the castle. But his threats are understandably making you fear for your sister's life. Propose that you take out the two front gate guards yourself. Plunge a sword into one, toss a dagger across at the other. Swing down and open the gate before any others can reach you."

I opened my eyes wide. "Swing down. Just like that?"

He looked embarrassed to have assumed so much. "Luca said that you slid down a rope one night—"

I held up my hand. "That's quite a plan. But I am not prepared to kill Forelli men to save my sister's life."

"We feign your attack, their death," Luca said with a shrug, picking up on where Fortino was going. "In the dim, flickering torchlight, it will be easy enough."

I leaned back, considering it. "Dare he believe it would be that simple?"

He thought it through too. "Cosmo Paratore has never had a spy on the inside of Castello Forelli before. Not since his father's time has there been such unrest between us. It was he who seized that hill and redrew the property boundary. He is power hungry, willing to do whatever he can to secure his place in Fiorentini society. If Castello Forelli is breached from the front gates, so much the better. That sort of thing lives long in tales around the table. He'll glory in the plan, and never suspect that reinforcements might be nearby."

"And those inside the castle? They could withstand such an attack? Resist them until our reinforcements arrived?"

"Yes. We'd have them divide into the various corridors. Barricade the doors. Paratore's men would have to divide as well."

That put me on edge. What would happen if they broke through one of those barricades?

Fortino saw my trepidation and touched my hand comfortingly. "We can build additional barricades that will surprise them, inside the first, further slowing them down."

I shook my head. "I don't know, Fortino. It is such a grave risk. If anyone was to perish…."

"M'lady, we've lost many men in the last three years. Lord Paratore and Marcello have been saved, neither side ready to bring down the wrath of the city the opposite represents. But people continually die around them. If this could be decided, now, if we could capture Castello Paratore and claim it for Siena, it is as Marcello hoped. We become more formidable still. It is a wise risk to take, given the increased hostilities between our cities. And freeing your sister becomes an added benefit."

"And I am always amenable to rescuing damsels in distress, especially if it means they will be forever grateful to me," Luca said.

I smiled at his bravado. "So, when they attack, would a portion of our soldiers go directly to Castello Paratore? Before Lord Paratore could return from here?"

He knew what I was asking. I didn't want any chance that Paratore could fall back and get to Lia before us.

"Mark my words. If Lord Paratore dares to attack Castello Forelli, you will find him nowhere but at the front of his men, charging through those gates."

I swallowed hard, imagining the men in crimson coming in on horseback. Open battle within the courtyard. It was hard to fathom.

"Which isn't to say that your sister will not be heavily guarded," Fortino cautioned. "He knows she is significant, a powerful pawn in this game. His only hold on you."

I stared at him. "But we can get to her?"

"M'lady," Luca said, "all manner of unexpected things transpire during battle. I can promise that I will do everything in my power to get to her, to free her." He shrugged his shoulders. "That is all I can promise."

I sighed and looked around the courtyard. "Begin your preparations. Make it appear as something else. You're certain Marcello shall return on the morrow?"

"He promised. Even Lady Rossi couldn't force him to stay in Siena."

I shook my head. Lord Forelli would have a heart attack, seeing me in the same room with his younger son.

"You shall go to Lord Paratore tonight," Luca said.

"And how do I manage that?"

"Over the wall," Luca said, waggling his eyebrows. "You'll bribe a couple of guards. They'll turn a blind eye, even as they lower you down in a basket. When you return, they'll raise you back up, making it appear as nothing more than a clandestine exit and entry by a woman with a secret to keep. It will help in convincing Lord Paratore that you can manage the guards, the night of the attack. Tell him you're using a good measure of your feminine charms. He's a leech at heart."

I sighed. The plan just kept getting better and better.

"We've come this far," Luca said, cocking his head. "Do you have it in you to see it through?"

I nodded, pretending to be a hundred times more courageous than I felt.

But that was the thing about courage. Sometimes you had to fake it to feel it.

That night, I did as Fortino and Luca had instructed. They'd spoken to the guards, and all was in place. All I had to do was climb the turret stairs and they would have me over the edge in minutes. Under my skirts, I pulled on my skinny jeans. Somehow, having pants on made me feel extra protected, prepared. It seemed silly, even to me, but at that point, I was grasping at anything I had.

I was about to invite the enemy into what had become my home.

And I had to go and tell the enemy all about it. Lie with everything in me. Academy Award kind of performance. Make him believe it. If he doubted me at all, we would lose on every front. At Castello Forelli. At Castello Paratore. *Lose, lose, lose,* I chanted, running down the path.

There was no horse in the whole basket plan. Which was just as well. It was easier to steal away from Castello Forelli and toward the Paratores without being on top of a mount. But that still meant I had to jog two miles in those cursed slippers again. I wished I could have pulled on tennis shoes as well as jeans, but somewhere along the way my sneakers had been stolen or misplaced.

I looked about, trying to make out Luca's shape in the shadows of the forest. He had promised to be out here, waiting on me, following me across every acre and back again, even if I didn't see him. It was vital he was not seen with me. That the Paratore crew all thought I was alone. But it comforted me to think that he shadowed me, watched over me. It allowed me to ignore every spooky sound I heard in the forest, only chalking it up to Luca, on guard duty.

Just put one foot in front of the other, I told myself, pressing on, picking my way across the creek in bare feet, donning the cursed slippers again on the other side. I hurried now, thinking of Lia, awaiting me. A half hour later I reached the road that led to Castello Paratore. My heart beat in double time, and not just because of the jog on over there.

I reached the gates, and the guards lifted torches high, then tossed one down at my feet in order to see me better. I scattered backward, aghast that they risked setting me on fire in order to catch a better glimpse, but I maintained my stance, looking up. A man slid open a tiny view window. "Open the gates, quickly," I hissed, looking back and forth, as if I was afraid I'd be seen.

The guard shut the window and the gates creaked open, only wide enough to allow me passage in. They closed quickly behind me, and I tried to get a grip. Wordlessly, I submitted to a search for weapons, but this time, I had come unarmed. There was no reason to endure more groping than was necessary—although they did puzzle over my jeans.

"It's the Norman way," I said. To which they furrowed their brows and shrugged.

I was then ushered inside the living quarters, through torch-lit halls to the grand salon where I'd first met with Lord Paratore. I steeled myself for the moment when I'd see him again.

The guards brought me into the room, then slowly closed the doors behind me. I stared at the figure by the fireplace, frowning. He didn't look quite right. But it was dark in the room. Only three candles in the massive space.

And then he turned. *Lord Vannucci.* He gave me his thin-lipped smile and turned to eye Lord Paratore, in the far corner, gazing out the window. My head whipped to face the other man. With both in the room, that whole fight-or-flight thing kicked into high gear. And I had a serious impulse to fly.

"Lord Vannucci," I managed. "I am glad you made a safe return."

"And I am glad to see you. Although a bit surprised." He came over to me and circled me. "I thought it was understood that I would come to you at Castello Forelli. Imagine my surprise in finding you had already been here."

"I could not wait," I said, shaking my head, "knowing Evangelia was so close. I had to see her, talk to Lord Paratore myself. And I've made progress," I said eagerly, cursing myself for sounding more like a guilty schoolgirl, eager to make things right, than a trustworthy confidant.

"I'm interested to hear of it," he said, pausing before me, taking my hand in his and covering it with the other. "You have a plan?"

"I believe so."

Lord Paratore moved to speak with the guards outside, and then quietly shut the door again. He went to a small table and poured me a glass of wine. I accepted it, cursing my trembling hand.

My heart was pounding like crazy. *Get it together, Gabi. Academy Award, Academy Award…*

"Please, sit. Tell us what you've discovered." Paratore sat across from me. Lord Vannucci sat nearby, staring hard at me. Why? To see if I'd crack?

Quickly, I began to spit out the plan, lamenting the impenetrable nature of the castle and the audacious attack that would be required to take her.

"I've been inside Castello Forelli," Lord Vannucci said, leaning toward me. "What is to keep the people from merely barricading themselves in the corridors?"

"Castello Forelli has not sustained a breach in her gates or walls in decades," I agreed. "The people sleep with the doors closed, but they are unlocked. I've seen servants enter every corridor, late at night, and early in the morning. And I assume that even you, Lord Paratore, would not attack them during the light of day."

He nodded at me, as if I'd just tossed him a serious compliment.

I smiled at him as if I wasn't thinking *jerk* in silent reply.

He looked to Lord Vannucci, and they consulted, turning their backs to me so I couldn't hear as they considered my plan.

A quiet knock sounded at the door. Lord Paratore rose and went to open it, swinging both sides wide.

"Lia," I breathed. She was a vision, dressed in the palest blue silk, as if she were a princess at a ball.

"Forgive me," Lord Paratore said, touching Lia's bare shoulder lightly, "but I find this necessary to make clear my position to you both."

I frowned. What was he talking about?

Lord Vannucci put a hand on my lower back and propelled me over to the others. At first, I went along willingly, but then I saw Paratore wrap his meaty hand around the back of Lia's neck. My sister blanched.

Vannucci's hand moved to my forearm and gripped it tightly. They dragged us into the hall and to the end, then down a narrow, stone staircase.

"M'lord, what are you doing?" Lia asked, voice quavering.

"Ensuring that our plan goes as your sister has laid it out."

No. No, no, no!

"Fear not," Lord Vannucci said to Lia, but his eyes were on me. "I'm certain this will be soon over. In a day, perhaps two at the most."

Dread surged through me. Lord Paratore reached for a torch and went first, pulling Lia behind him. We descended more stairs, curving down into the depths below the castle. It was immediately twenty degrees colder, and I shivered, wanting to rub the chill from my bare arms.

"Ahh, here we are," he said proudly, as if he were about to show us his most glorious quarters. He went about the room and lit the other three torches, placing his own on the fourth wall. "It gets so dark down here without a little torchlight. Those shall last a good four or five hours," he said.

He pulled Lia to the far wall and wrenched her hands together, wrapping a leather band around them and tying it tight.

I cried out to her, but Lord Vannucci held me fast, wrapping an arm around my shoulders, pressing my back against him, keeping me in place.

"Please," I said, tears dripping down my face. Lia did not cry. She merely looked utterly surprised, still unsure this was really unfolding. As if Lord Paratore was joking around, about to let her go and escort her to the ball he had dressed her for.

But I knew. I *knew*. This was all about me. And making me remember how much was at stake.

I closed my eyes, unable to bear watching Lord Paratore attach a hook to Lia's bindings and the hook to a chain. He reached over and cranked the chain until she had to stand on her tiptoes.

"Lord Paratore," she gasped, wide blue eyes upon him.

But his gaze was on me. He moved to a contraption in the corner and lovingly ran his fingers across it. "Do you know what this is, Lady Betarrini?"

"I can guess," I said.

"You attach a prisoner's feet here." He pointed to the bottom. "His hands here, and then you crank, crank until you hear his vertebrae begin to crack and pop. Sometimes it's his shoulders or knees. I'd wager it would work for a woman as well."

Now Lia was crying. "Stop it," I spit out. "Cease! I understand." *You're the biggest jerk ever. A bully. And I have to do what you say.*

"Do you? There's another alternative." He walked over to a cage in the corner. "She's a pretty thing. Birdlike. Mayhap I'll put her up in the corner of the courtyard. Give the men something fine to play with and admire."

I shook my head, speechless at his evil taunting.

"So let's go through the plan again, Lady Betarrini," he said. "We shall not have time for a protracted siege. Sienese forces would arrive within hours, and then we'd lose the advantage."

"Cut off their messengers. Make certain no word reaches Siena," I said, remembering what Fortino had told me to say when this came up.

He lifted his chin, considering my words.

"But the length of the siege is not up to me; it is up to you. Our deal"—I pried Lord Vannucci's arm away and turned to face him—"and *our* deal," I said, whipping my head around to face Lord Paratore, "was that I help you gain entrance—*entrance*, that was *all*. And then you were to give me my sister."

The two men shared a long look, then glanced back to me.

"Gain us entrance as you promised, and in two days' time, you will be away with your sister, under the protection of my own men," Lord Paratore said. "You will reach Firenze as day breaks, your load of gold behind you." He stepped forward and stared down at me. "Go now, Lady Betarrini, back to the Forellis," he said slowly, "before you are missed."

I looked to Lia. "I'll be back for you," I promised. She nodded, trying to be brave, but there were still tears running down her cheeks. Taking a deep breath, I turned to go, but Lord Vannucci put an arm in front of the doorway. I looked up at him. What now?

"Know this, m'lady," he said in a whisper, leaning toward my ear, "if we run into a trap, your sister will bear the full cost of your betrayal. She will die, and not before she begs for it."

CHAPTER 15

I was walking with Luca the next morning, telling him of Castello Paratore's dungeon and the route inward, shivering at the thought of Lia still suffering, listening to details of Fortino's plan, when the guards called down to open the gates.

Fortino wanted Paratore to believe that he could have the castello—so that Marcello, in turn, could attack Castello Paratore and claim due provocation. If war came, they were ready for that, too. Years of having to hold back, of not being able to invite full-on war, was about to end. Fury and greed could have their full sway.

And it all hinged on the Betarrini girls' arrival from the twenty-first century. *Super.*

We paused and watched as an old, hunched-over man came limping into the castello courtyard, pulling a mule, which in turn pulled a cart loaded with hay. Two guards moved in on the old man to search his robes.

But as soon as the gates screeched to a close behind him, he lifted his hood and straightened. The guards took a step back and laughed.

It took a sec, but then I knew.

It was Marcello in disguise.

He grinned at the knights and his brother, who rushed over to meet him.

Luca patted my hand, grinning like a kid who was just given permission to open his first Christmas present, and went off to greet Marcello.

Lord Forelli and Fortino entered the courtyard from the Great Hall.

I turned on my heel and fled.

I thought I was ready to see Marcello. I wasn't.

And Lord Forelli would totally freak if we didn't stay as far apart as possible. Fortino had tried to tell him of what was to come, of a potential attack, of reinforcements…that it was all due to me, really, that they could even consider vanquishing Castello Paratore, once and for all, but it seemed to send the old man over the edge. He had become more shaky and distant, having trouble focusing and even forming words.

I wondered if he had had another stroke. Because of me?

I heard Marcello call out my name, but I continued my escape. I would see him later. When I got myself together. When he'd had a chance to say hello to Luca and Fortino. When Lord Forelli wasn't staring at me with those old, watery eyes like I was about to bring disaster on them all.

Or maybe I wouldn't have to. Maybe I'd do my part, Marcello'd do his, and Lia and I could just get to the tomb and get the heck out of Dodge.

"M'lady," he called, sounding exasperated, still coming after me.

I paused and slowly turned.

We were alone in the corridor.

And I *so* wanted to race into his arms. Looking at him again, after a few days apart, made me weak in the knees. Seriously. I felt like an idiot. Maybe it was because I needed a man's embrace right then. Anyone's hug. Comfort. Encouragement.

He ran a hand through his curly hair, and it flopped right back into place, in a deep wave across one eye that I thought was especially hot. His hand fidgeted with the hilt of his sword as he moved toward me, unsure of himself—had I ever seen him unsure of himself?

"All is well, m'lord?" I asked, cursing myself for not outlasting him in the silence game.

"All is well," he said eagerly, taking my words as welcome, still approaching. "A false rumor of an attack to the south has been circulated. Sienese soldiers moved out this morning. Paratore will think it's Providence, God's sign that this is the night to attack. He'll think Siena's soldiers—including my own—are distracted, not waiting but a half hour's ride to come to our aid."

I really wasn't concentrating on what he was saying. All I could think about was him, *here,* so close. In his enthusiasm and excitement, he had moved but a foot from me. I continued to retreat until my back bumped up against the end wall. I looked back in surprise and then to my door, then to him. He stared down at me, as if recognizing, for the first time, how he affected me.

"Marcello, Paratore will have spies out, in all directions. If he catches wind that there are reinforcements…" *Evangelia!*

"Nay," he said soothingly, face alight. "Paratore will only hear what I wish him to hear."

"If he intercepts your messenger…" I swallowed hard. "Marcello, he has Lia. Down in his dungeon. He threatened to do unspeakable things to her."

The muscles in his jaw tensed, and all trace of anticipated glory disappeared in his concern over my sister.

I couldn't look into his warm eyes any longer. They were covering me, pulling me in. "They threatened to torture her—" My voice cracked then, and I looked down. I felt the heat of a deep blush climb my neck.

Marcello reached out and took my face in the curve of his warm hand. He waited until I looked back up to him. "So the warrior is not made of stone."

Stone? *Stone?* He thought me made of stone?

He put his left hand on the other side of my face and leaned down to look into my eyes. "You are courageous, Gabriella. And clever. And strong. Remember that, in the thick of battle. You can utilize all three. And I will see to it that neither Lord Paratore nor Vannucci ever has the opportunity to harm either you or your sister."

They were brave words. But only words.

And yet I wanted to believe them then. I had to believe them.

But we were much too…close.

"All right," I said. "Thank you."

Hands off me, Bucko. Remember, your heart belongs to someone else. And my heart is apparently…stone.

I was starting to squirm out of his magnetic pull when he moved an arm around me and tugged me closer. "Gabriella," he said lowly, tracing my temple and cheek with the back of his right hand. He stilled, staring at me. So tender. So warm. I melted. "There is something I must know," he said, "something I've wondered about for days."

He leaned down then and kissed me, softly at first, then deeper, searching. I knew I should stop him, push him away, but I didn't have the strength. All I wanted was more of him, more of his warmth, his comfort. When he stepped back he looked as dazed as I felt. He rubbed his lower lip with the pad of his thumb, still staring at me intently, as if reliving our kiss. And then his eyes sharpened again with a glimmer of victory. He nodded at me. "I was correct."

I put a hand to my forehead and shook my head, frowning more as his smile grew. "No, Marcello. This, *this* can't happen."

"Yes, yes, it can," he said, grinning, pacing in his excitement. He stopped and put both hands on my face, and, God help me, I wanted him to kiss me *again.* I knew I was a total weak-willed loser. But I couldn't help it. He was just so totally amazing. And completely into me. I'd never had a man into me like that. I usually only got my share of the dorks and weirdoes. Those guys loved me with a passion.

"Marcello—"

"Nay, we will speak of it on the morrow. When we conquer Castello Paratore and free your sister. You'll see, all will be well."

"But what of Lady Rossi?"

"Lady Rossi has a hundred prospects. I am appealing, convenient, expected. We are friends, but there is no passion, no love between us. She will understand."

When he said *no passion, no love between us,* he looked at me like he totally saw the opposite end of the spectrum between us. Love?

This can't be happening. Not here. Not now. He couldn't break up with Lady Rossi. For me. Just when I was about to disappear. He would be crushed when I went home.

"So Lady Rossi will recover. But what of the alliance? Castello Forelli is vulnerable out here, on the border. You *need* Siena behind you, Marcello. Remember?" I shook my head. This was crazy. He'd gotten totally off track because of…me?

He shook his head too, slowly. "We shall find another way to strengthen our ties to Siena. Capturing Castello Paratore will do much to soothe the Nine's ruffled feathers."

I blew out my cheeks. He'd really thought this through. And he was making this so much harder…"Marcello, there is a great deal to come. Let us see if we both *live,* and then we can speak of whether it is wise—"

"Wise?" he asked, taking a coil of my hair in his hand and running his fingers down it. Could it not stay in place? For once? "Nay, this is most definitely unwise," he said, leaning in until my back was against the wall again. He hovered, waiting, until I gave in, lifting my chin to offer him my lips. He kissed me again, not touching me with his hands, just tilting his head one way and then the other. He tasted of cinnamon and wood smoke. My arms, like they had a mind of their own, came up and wrapped around him, inviting him closer. But then he was pulling away, a teasing smile on his face. "Nay, this is not wise at all. But sometimes the heart tells us to venture where the mind fears to tread." He leaned down and kissed me on the forehead. "I shall see you in an hour. I must go speak to my brother and the men. Unless you care to join me."

I shuddered, thinking of Lord Forelli. "Nay," I said, shaking my head. "I don't believe your father can tolerate seeing us together. I'll stay here."

He nodded, waiting for me to look at him fully in the eye. "My father will come to see this as I do, Gabriella."

"You don't understand," I said miserably. "This is all happening so fast...."

He smiled and kissed me again, then was off, striding down the hall. "It is happening at just the *right* time. All of it," he said, lifting out his arms in exuberance. "You shall see, m'lady. You shall see!"

He lifted the latch and pushed the door outward, letting in a brief burst of sunshine before it banged shut behind him, leaving me in the relative darkness.

"Great," I muttered to myself. "Just great, Gabi." I leaned against the wall, trying to get my head around what had just happened.

How had everything been in order a half hour before?

Because right now, my grand scheme seemed to be in shambles.

I was at my bedroom door, trying to focus enough to open it and lie down for a few minutes, when the courtyard door banged open and Marcello appeared at the end of the hall. "Gabriella! Gabriella, come quickly!"

I frowned and rushed down the hall.

"It's Fortino," he said grimly. "He's collapsed."

We entered the courtyard together. Three Forelli knights were carrying Fortino toward us. He was in the midst of a full-scale asthma attack, each breath a horrific seal-like bark. "Take him to his sitting room," I said.

I looked around for servants, then instructed, "Boiling water, buckets of it. Fresh, lightweight cloth, never used. Lemon, mint, caraway, fistfuls of it. As fast as you can!"

I glanced at Lord Forelli, who definitely looked like he was going to have a heart attack now. I reached out to Marcello. "Your father—get him to his quarters and encourage him to rest, will you? Tell him we'll send him word."

Marcello followed my gaze, nodded once, and was off to do my bidding. I raced to follow the men. As soon as they had Fortino laid out on the wooden settee, I asked them to take off his shirt. The muscles between his ribs contracted with each breath. The poor man was working as hard as he could just to inhale one more time.

I took his right hand with my left, and leaned down so he could see my face. "We will aid you, Fortino. Hold on. Just concentrate on each breath. Do not give in to the fear. Slow it down. Slow it down." I took a breath with him, staring into his eyes, willing him to match my pace. "You can do this. One breath at a time. In… and out…"

I felt more than saw Marcello move into the room. I took comfort in his presence. But I continued to concentrate on Fortino. "Do not give up, Fortino. You have come so far. You simply overtaxed yourself. It will be all right, I promise. One breath at a time. There you go."

I turned to see the three knights, staring at me with wide eyes, and others in the doorway. "Find out where that water is!" I cried. "We need the boiling water and cloth now!"

The three closest scurried to do as I bid, breaking up the crowd in the hallway. But then the servants were there with the water.

"Tell me what I can do," Marcello said lowly, at Fortino's head, trying not to interrupt our process. There was fear in his eyes, the first I'd ever seen in him.

"Boiling water, two buckets on each side of him. Use the cloth to make a tent above us. Try and seal us in, as best you can. And have them fetch more boiling water. We need steam. Constant steam."

Marcello rose and barked orders.

A maid arrived with the herbs I'd asked for.

"Quick as you can—everyone tear all that into piles."

Fortino was mouthing words, trying to tell me something. I shook my head furiously. "No. It can wait. Do not try to speak right now. Do you hear me? You breathe, and that's it. In…and out." I was about as tender as a drill sergeant. But he was seriously freaking me out. People still died of asthma attacks in the twenty-first century. How much harder was it to keep them alive in the fourteenth?

In two minutes, Marcello had the cloth spread above us and water inside. It didn't take long for sweat to drip down my scalp and back, but I wasn't leaving Fortino. Not that I could. The man gripped my hand, so hard it scared me all the more. As weak as he was, if he held me like that, he was afraid, deathly—literally—afraid.

Marcello was there, on the other side of our makeshift tent. "The herbs are torn, Gabriella. Now what?"

"Mix them with olive oil, into a thick paste. Quickly." I watched in horror as Fortino's eyes began to roll back. "Fortino!"

They slowly rolled back to focus on me.

"Stay with me, Fortino. Stay with me."

His eyes remained locked on mine.

Marcello came under the tent, staring at my flushed, sweaty face, then at his brother's, which was almost blue from lack of oxygen. New buckets of water were slid under the tent, the cooling water removed.

"Go over there," I said to Marcello, nodding to the other side.

I looked back at Fortino. "Marcello is here. I need to pack your chest. He shall hold your hand."

Marcello gently took his older brother's hand from mine, moving it to his side. There was such care in his movements, such love, that I thought I might burst into tears. Fortino's eyes shifted to his brother, as hungry for encouragement from him as he was from me.

None of us wanted to be alone when we died. A chill ran down my back at the thought, even though it was hotter than Hades in there.

"Fortino," I said, slapping a bunch of the herbal slop—heavy with mint, caraway and lemon—over his chest. "You breathe, man. Breathe!" What was I doing? I was guessing at an old recipe of my mother's, hoping I remembered it right. Hadn't Lia had a major allergy attack? And hadn't she put such things on her?

I studied him as I placed handful after handful of the stuff on his skin.

I might finish him off if he's allergic to any of this stuff.

But I was desperate. There was nothing left for me to do. I couldn't just sit there and watch him die.

"We must pray," Marcello said, glancing from his brother to me.

I stared back at him. Pray?

If praying would save the man, I was up for it. God had never seemed to pay much attention to my pleas, but maybe he'd listen to Marcello.

The man closed his eyes and began to speak in Latin. My mind raced, trying to keep up with his words. I knew just enough Latin—on my parents' insistence—to totally massacre any attempt at speaking it. But I could understand it well enough.

"Mighty God in heaven," he began, a little awkwardly, "reach down and touch this man. Heal him. Save him. Grant him breath. God on high, You are all-powerful. We beg that You spare Fortino now. Amen."

"Amen," I whispered. I glanced at him, but he was looking only at his brother. It wasn't his words that struck me. It was that he appeared to believe in them.

His face relaxed, as did Fortino's. Marcello reached up to wipe away the sweat from his brother's face with a cloth, and smiled his encouragement.

"Gabriella, you look as if you are about to faint," Marcello said, his eyes suddenly on me. "Take your ease a moment outside the tent and get some cooler air. I will stay with him."

I nodded and put the back of my hand up to wipe my forehead and upper lip of sweat. I was feeling a little dizzy. I moved from under the edge of the cloth and looked about the room, to a sea of waiting faces. "He still struggles," I said, sinking to a chair. "Please, fetch more boiling water. We must keep it coming, constantly." Three set off to do as I asked. Another brought me a ladle of cold water, and I gulped it down. Then when I felt more myself I returned under the edge of the tent.

"God has heard our prayers. He's breathing a bit easier," Marcello said.

I studied the side of Fortino's ribs, where herbs and oil streamed down, and watched the muscles. Just a tiny bit less desperate and lurching. He still sounded like a sick seal, gasping for every bit of air he could take in, but any improvement was a small victory.

I rose and looked into Fortino's eyes. He didn't look quite so close to giving up, but he was still working so hard…and he was again trying to form words. He looked at Marcello this time.

Marcello rose and placed his ear next to his brother's mouth, closing his eyes as if to concentrate on deciphering what Fortino was trying to say.

"Marcello," I complained in a whisper, "he shouldn't try to speak."

Marcello held up his hand to shush me. After a moment, he went back to kneeling beside his brother. After several long minutes, he said something back and lifted his face.

"What'd he say?" I asked.

"He said to carry on with the attack. To leave him with a sword in hand, in case they breach this corridor."

The knights in the room, clearly hearing Marcello's words, all cheered.

I put a hand to my forehead. How could I leave Fortino struggling like this?

"There is no choice," Marcello said, reading the question in my eyes. "The plan is already in motion. Your own Evangelia is counting on us to rescue her in the wee hours of morning."

I dragged miserable eyes to his brother and back to Marcello again.

We might save Lia—how I hoped we would save her—but if the Paratores breached this corridor, we would most assuredly lose Fortino.

CHAPTER 16

Marcello made his "return" the next morning with golden flag flapping in the wind beside the flag bearer's horse and all of his trusted men riding behind him. Hours later, I still paced back and forth. We'd gone through the plan with all the knights, then again with the servants, ten times. It had to appear natural. Nothing could smell of a trap. They had to confine the battle within the courtyard, so that the Paratore knights remained engaged there, until the reinforcements arrived and could capture and kill them all—and so that they would not give chase to those who were attempting to breach the Castello Paratore wall and save my sister.

Marcello had thought of a few things to give our side an edge. He put fifteen knights into common clothing, and they took the quarters at the front of the castle, while the servants sheltered in the rear quarters, which were more defensible. Five brave servants agreed to make a run from two separate corridors, and into another, making it appear as if the castle had truly been surprised and all servants were where they usually were, in the hall across the courtyard from mine. They practiced it, like actors on a Hollywood movie set, timing it, men on horseback charging about, so it was all perfectly choreographed. The idea was that at first, Paratore men would think they'd breached the castle doors just as they had planned, surprising all inside.

Ten men were positioned along the walls, hidden under woven tarps, with bows and countless arrows. After twenty minutes of siege, they would be allowed to rise and take aim at the interlopers. But not before then. Marcello wanted to be certain that his reinforcements would arrive in time to capture any that tried to escape. "If you stay down, they'll concentrate on breaching the corridor entry points," Marcello said. He smiled. "And then the secondary barriers."

All afternoon, men had been busy erecting heavy, new interior doors within four of the corridors, where the castello's unarmed would hole up. The other corridors would be locked up tight, but if they were breached, the interlopers would find them empty. Indeed, at the twenty-minute mark, the knights had permission to openly attack any Paratores they came upon.

"They'll think us cowards," they grumbled, irritated that Marcello would not allow them to defend the castle upon the enemy's entry.

"They'll be dead come morning, and you shall be alive," Marcello snapped back. "Do as my brother has planned. Nothing different. It's a brilliant plan. And an honor to him to see it done."

They clammed up then, unable to argue with the whole Dying Brother card.

I did fear that Fortino was dying. That he wouldn't make it until daybreak. He still labored to breathe, and his poor heart couldn't sustain many more hours of such suffering. Marcello had had to drag me out of his room.

In the hall, he had taken my face in his hands, his own features full of heavy misery. "I know. I *know.* But we can do nothing that the servants can't do. Right?"

I stared at him for a long moment, tears slipping down my face. "Right," I said at last. "And your father?"

He dropped his hands and turned away. "Dim and chatting on and on about my mother. He keeps trying to send servants to fetch her."

"It could be that he's suffered another…spell," I said. I moved toward him and after a moment's hesitation, put a hand on his back. "Marcello, the stress of what is to come…there is a good chance that neither your brother nor father will survive the night. Perhaps you should remain here, with them."

He turned to me then. "Fortino wants us to do this, and were my father in his right mind, he would suffer no halt to the plan. I honor them best by seeing it through and looking to the castello's future, Siena's future." His eyes sought mine. "And ours."

I shook my head and broke away from his light hold on my hips. "I've been thinking about that, Marcello. You belong here, defending what you love."

He gave me a gentle smile and tucked a loose strand of hair behind my ear. "I belong where I can defend *all* that I love. I will be here at the beginning, engage in a skirmish or two, then retreat, barricading myself into the first corridor across the way. An empty corridor, of course. Once I see the flags of the Sienese reinforcements, I'll come and find you."

My eyes widened with alarm. "Except the Paratore men will be circling the castle, making certain no one escapes."

He cocked his head. "And we shall fight our way through."

"You and Luca," I said.

He nodded. "You didn't think we'd expect you to rescue your sister on your own, did you?"

"I didn't know what to think." I rubbed my temple. "This plan, Marcello…it could go wrong in a hundred different ways."

"Or perfectly right." He took my hand in his now, bringing me back to the present. "Are you ready, my sweet warrior?" He slowly kissed my knuckles, his eyes solely on me. I knew the entire castello watched us, but I could look nowhere but at him. We stood at the first corridor entrance, where I was to climb and pretend to murder the two front guards.

"Do not die this night, m'lord."

He gave me a pained smile. "So on the morrow or the next is all right, just not *this* night?"

"No," I said, laying my other hand on his chest and willing him to promise me what he could not. "Ever."

His smile faded. "Only if you promise to do the same." He kissed my knuckles once more. "Luca and I will catch up with you before you reach Castello Paratore. I promise you that. Gabriella, the battle ahead will be fierce. You must *fight.* Fight with everything in you, beloved."

Taking a deep breath, I ripped my hand from his, turned and entered the hallway, then the turret, my mind screaming at me to stop, to turn around, to take cover alongside Fortino, or better yet, in a corridor with the rest of the weak and completely freaked out. I didn't feel strong. I felt coldly afraid, even though I hurried up the stairs as if I hungered for nothing but the battle ahead. At the tiny door at the top, I stopped, my hand on the latch.

"*Fortes fortuna adiuvat,*" Marcello had said to his men. *Fortune favors the brave, the bold.*

That was all well and good. But it was remembering my dad talking to me about bravery in life that pushed me onward. We'd been on a rare father-daughter walk, and I had shared my fears about something. He'd said, "I read once that courage is not the absence of fear, but the decision that something is more important than that fear."

I pushed through, walking hunched over, as if trying to avoid being seen by those inside the castle but close to the edge, so that those who watched me from the outside could clearly see my progress. I raced to catch up with the guard, Giovanni, who was walking away from me, as was our plan. "Coming on your left," I whispered to him, raising my short broadsword high in the air where it could catch the gleam of torchlight. "Three, two, one," I counted lowly, still mirroring his steps. He pretended to not hear a word from me. I turned the sword and plunged it between his shoulders, where it caught a hidden wooden plate and slid downward. We went down between the edges of the wall—where no one could see us—and I rolled off of him. "Nicely done," I said. "How does it suit you, being dead?"

"Feels mostly the same," he said in a whisper, grinning at me as he rolled over.

"Well, prepare for a second death," I said, rising and making a great show of stabbing him once more. This time, I knew only I would be visible from the Paratores' vantage point, so I plunged downward—waited for Giovanni to give it a quick wash of cow's blood—then wrenched my sword up as if it had been stuck in a body. I raced forward, shoving the bloody sword into the sheath at my back.

"Go with God, m'lady," I heard the knight whisper behind me.

And with you, I thought, surprising myself. All the God talk was rubbing off on me. I hoped the Big Guy was listening.

At the end of the wall, I rose and looked into the center of the enclosed courtyard where Marcello stood, alongside Luca, watching me. I stared at him overly long, wondering if it might be the last time I would see him alive. But then he pointed at the other guard, approaching me from the other side, reminding me of my task.

I crouched down and moved into position. The other guard, Pietro, feigned surprise when he saw me. He moved his hand to his sword as if to draw it. I pulled the dagger from my front sheath and pulled back, my eyes on the center of his sternum.

"Aim true, m'lady," he whispered a second late, since the dagger already flew across the space between us.

His timing was as perfect as my aim. As the blade plunged into the leather and padding that made him appear as portly as Giovanni, he wavered, then reached for it, pretending to try to pluck it out. Just as I was silently urging him not to milk it, he crumpled with an anguished groan to the ground.

I hurriedly tied off my rope and rappelled down the inside of the castello wall, shaking in fear when I heard the massive numbers of horses rumbling toward the gates.

"Go, Gabriella," Marcello mouthed.

I turned to the massive, rusted metal beam and unlocked it, then, pushing with everything in me, slid it back in its track.

They didn't wait for me to open it all the way. The giant door barely missed me as I leaped aside. They burst through with a roar, fifty men on foot, with twenty on horses behind them.

Knights, dressed as servants, ran for the corridors that had two barricades. Our twenty minutes were now counting down. "Knights to arms!" one cried. "The castle is breached!" Ten knights joined Marcello and Luca. Women ran screaming to the corridors farther back, just as they had practiced. The first sounds of iron meeting iron sounded in the yard.

Lord Paratore came through the gates on his horse and pulled up on the reins when he reached my side. "Off with you, then," he said, gesturing with his chin over his shoulder. "You have done well. Go and claim your prize."

I nodded and smiled. I turned and scurried out, straight through the third line of men who stood there, swords drawn, ready to enter at their master's call, to the Paratore knight on his horse. "I need a mount," I said to him.

"You can walk," he sneered.

I stared hard at him. "I need a mount. I've done all that your lord asked me," I spit out. "The castle is yours. Now *give* me what should be mine. Lord Paratore promised a horse."

He looked down at me, plainly irritated that I was even talking to him. But I stubbornly refused to look away. After a moment, he grimaced and glanced behind him. "Bring the wench a gelding."

As soon as the horse was within reach, I took the reins, put my foot in the stirrup, and swung across the saddle, ignoring their lecherous glances at my legs. I was already turning, kicking the horse's flanks, leaning down, racing across the path that was clearly visible in the moonlight.

I'm coming, Lia. I'm coming.

CHAPTER 17

From the corner of my eye, I'd seen a patrol of Paratore men, riding around the edge of the castello, just as I thought they would—just as Marcello believed they would too.

Dear God, please bring Marcello to help me! Keep him safe! Keep us all safe!

I bent lower and raced down the path, far faster than was wise. But adrenaline and hope combined to make me feel strong, as if I could see in the dark. Again and again, I urged my horse to leap stones and logs, making me believe it was true.

That was right before I turned the corner and a low-lying branch caught me across my chest.

Pride goeth before the fall, and all that. Yeah, yeah, I knew. I was foolish.

But it didn't register with me, of course, until I lay on my back, staring up through the trees at the bits and pieces of the moon, partially covered by leaves, fighting for breath.

This is what it feels like to be Fortino.

Mentally I cataloged my body, trying each limb as I waited for my breath to return. I was looking at my fingers, flexing before my face, trying not to panic, when I felt the rumble of horse hooves on the path.

Horses, coming my way.

I surged over to my right, rolling once, twice, until I was under a low-hanging bush as two men on horseback raced past me. They pulled up ahead and turned back. I groaned inwardly, just taking my third breath. They'd seen me. I forced myself to rise and draw my sword, still willing my breathing to return to normal. Again, I thought of Fortino and found myself whispering a prayer to God that he might be breathing still.

The men came into view down the path, and I pressed back among the trees.

"Gabriella?" the first said, and I frowned.

I edged out. "Marcello?"

He rode closer then. "Are you running to Castello Paratore?"

"Do not ask," I said, sheathing my sword again. He surged forward, reaching for my arm and using the momentum to swing me up behind him. I looked over my shoulder at Luca and grinned. I wrapped my arms around Marcello, so glad he was alive, so glad I wasn't alone.

How had they managed to escape and get to me so quickly? Were the Sienese already surrounding Castello Forelli, capturing the Paratore forces? I hoped so; but I was most glad they were there, with me. Ready to help me find my sister.

Marcello tensed and looked back at Luca. Luca stayed deadly still and then nodded once. I heard it then too.

More riders were coming. And they weren't ours.

We rode hard, then suddenly veered off on a narrow path I was fairly certain didn't lead to Castello Paratore. We came out on a sandbar, farther up the creek than the normal crossing, and waited in the thick brush that lined the banks. Six knights on horses crossed a ways down, their mounts sending water flying into the air—a thousand droplets catching the moonlight. It was almost beautiful, terrifying and gorgeous at the same time. And surreal. Because they were obviously hunting, chasing us.

Luca looked over at Marcello. "No one saw us escape. I'm certain of it."

Marcello tensed. I could feel his torso contract, his breathing hesitate. "Then they're after Gabriella."

"Me?"

"Yes," he said simply. "Paratore has sent them to fetch you because you double-crossed him." Memories of Paratore and Vannucci's threats rang in my mind.

"We cannot let them reach the castle," Luca said lowly. "If they do, they shall warn the guards, and Gabriella shall never free her sister, only find herself captured."

Marcello twisted in his saddle so fast, lifting me to the ground, I didn't have time to react. Thick creek pebbles met my feet, and I stumbled a bit backward, against a scrub oak. "Hide, Gabriella. We'll be back for you as fast as we can."

Without waiting for my response, he pressed his mount into action, and he and Luca were off.

I bit back my indignation, the desire to call out his name, insist he return for me. Luca was right, of course. Our only hope was that they could overtake the men, surprise them and somehow kill or capture all six. And they couldn't do that with the weight of two people on one mount.

Two against six. *Fortes fortuna adiuvat. They're probably reveling in those odds,* I thought, pacing back and forth. *Idiots. Brave, wonderful, idiots.*

They considered me more a liability than an ally, which was probably right. But they didn't know that, for sure. They didn't *know* it.

I picked up my skirts, pulled off my slippers and moved across the creek bed, wincing as the rocks bit into my feet. On the other side, I dried my feet with my skirt and pulled on the slippers again, then set off running, moving to the main path, knowing it was upon that one that my men would engage their enemies. I settled into a steady jog, not wanting to become too winded. But that was hard with the sword on my back. Carrying an extra thirty-pound sword was like weighing thirty more pounds yourself. I felt like I'd been sitting around all summer, watching TV, eating Twinkies. And I was dying now that I had decided to go out for cross-country.

Not that I'd ever gone out for cross-country. I liked to hike. Not run for miles until I was in pain. But still I pressed on. Perhaps I could sneak in, take one man down, help Marcello and Luca before they even knew I was there. I had to do something. Hide, he had said. Hide! This was not a night for hiding. It was a night to scream, "Bring it on!" to the entire valley and then prepare for the onslaught.

Yeah, a part of me really wanted to hide. But I ignored it.

I caught my breath as I eased down a hill and when I rounded the corner, I could hear men calling out and swords clashing. I doubled my pace, then pulled up short, studying the battlefield. Three men were on the ground already, obviously dead, one with his head at a grotesque angle. Two were advancing upon Marcello. Luca and the third knight moved toward me, their swords clanging again and again. Slowly, I drew my dagger out.

They still hadn't seen me. Luca was tiring; I could see it in the speed of his sword as it rose to meet the enemy's. The man's sword sliced through the air three times in quick succession, and Luca spun away from the last a second too late. The sword tip lanced his upper arm, and he cried out. The man did not break from his attack, whirling, preparing to bring the full weight of his sword into Luca's neck or torso.

I didn't think. I bent and lunged, dagger in hand, exactly at the moment his belly was most exposed.

He crumpled to his side, clutching the dagger and gasping.

Luca stepped forward and ended his misery, eyed me a moment, then turned toward Marcello.

I ran behind him, drawing my sword from my back sheath. We saw Marcello, then, wrestling on the ground, barely holding off a knight's dagger, an inch from his throat as another knight hovered, waiting to strike. The second turned when he heard our approach. Luca climbed a small boulder and leaped toward him, a bloodcurdling cry bursting from his throat.

I cried out too, as the dagger touched Marcello's skin and blood glimmered in the moonlight. I swung my broadsword in an arc, missing cutting off the man's head, but managing to nick his neck.

He screamed and rolled off of Marcello, clutching his neck in shock, but it was clearly no use. Blood spurted everywhere. He'd be dead in moments.

Dimly, I realized that Luca was nearing us, no sounds of pursuit behind him.

Marcello rose, clutching his side. "Gabriella," he said, grabbing my shoulder and studying my face as if he was trying to read my thoughts in the moonlight. "Are you all right?"

But I could only stare at the other man, now choking on his own blood. Had I done that? Really? Me? My head swirled in a sickening mix of horror and fury.

"Turn away, Gabriella," Marcello said, moving between me and my victim when I did not obey. He pressed my head to his chest as we heard the man emit a horrible gurgling sound and fall, face-first, to the ground.

Luca stepped up beside us and laid a hand on my back. "The She-Wolf of Siena," he said proudly. "Saved my neck too."

Marcello laughed lowly and then lifted my chin. "I told you to stay behind. It would've been far safer." He lifted one brow. "But Luca and I might've died without you. You must keep yourself together, She-Wolf. Think of Evangelia." His voice hardened. "There is certain to be more bloodshed ahead. Are you prepared?"

"Yes," I mumbled.

He shook me, trying to break me from my stupor.

"I like having her behind us," Luca quipped. "No one expects one so beautiful to be a wolf on the attack."

"They know of her strength, those ahead of us," Marcello said. "Do not think you can surprise them, Gabriella. You must go in poised to kill. Understand me?"

I swallowed hard. I'd just killed two men, two men who were someone's sons, someone's husbands, someone's brothers—

"I will leave you here," he said gruffly, almost shouting at me while trying to keep his voice down. "God help me, I will tie you up here, if you don't show me you can tolerate this. Must I do that?"

We stood nose to nose, glaring at each other.

"No," I managed.

He released me, still clearly angry, but I knew it was the kind of fury that grew from fear. He was afraid for me. Women didn't go to war, in this time. Joan of Arc probably hadn't been born yet in France. And yet here I was…and suddenly, I was regretting it. If only I hadn't put my hand on that terrible print. If only Lia hadn't done the same.…

Water splashed over my face, and I sputtered and blinked.

Luca took a swig from his water spleen and smiled at me. He cocked his head, and his eyes narrowed, as if remembering something. "It's a shock, that first time, to kill a man. But keep in mind, they were about to kill me. And Marcello."

I looked to Marcello, who was binding a cloth around his bleeding neck. Blood spread across the sleeve of Luca's upper arm. And then I remembered.

This was war. It was us versus them. To live or die.

They would not show me mercy.

And neither could I.

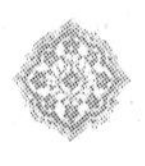

CHAPTER 18

We found four of the Paratore knights' horses, munching on scrub oak, seemingly unperturbed that their masters had all been slain. The Forelli horses were long gone and would probably return to the castello stables on their own.

"M'lord, God has smiled upon us," Luca said to Marcello, grinning over at him.

Marcello returned his smile and immediately retrieved the nearest mount. Luca and I did the same, leading them back to the clearing. The men handed the reins to me, and although the horses shied and shifted, not liking the smell of blood, I held them fast. Marcello and Luca moved quickly, stripping the dead men of their crimson vests and pulling them over their shoulders.

"Can't say I ever thought I'd see you in red," Luca taunted Marcello.

"It chafes, even through my shirt," Marcello joked. He bent to grab a man's heels and dragged him into the brush. Luca followed suit, and in short order, all the dead Paratore men were hidden from sight.

Marcello turned and took the reins of his horse from me. I handed Luca his and then mounted my mare, ignoring Marcello's approach to assist me. He looked at my bare ankle and calf and flashed me a wolfish smile with cocked brow. I shook my head. Showing these guys the skin exposed in summer capris got the same reaction as walking around in a bikini at home.

I laughed under my breath and kicked my horse in the flanks, knowing the men could easily catch up with me. Besides, we had to hurry. If we weren't inside the castle gates before word reached them that the Paratore forces had been overrun by Sienese, we'd never get in. We'd lost precious minutes, battling the six soldiers.

Soon we were on the cobblestone entry road. As agreed, we paused so that the men could get situated, posing as wounded soldiers. It helped that there was blood upon both of them. Luca went as far as to lie across the saddle, arms dangling. Marcello hunched forward, as if barely holding on. I pressed on as fast as I dared and paused before the massive castle gates.

"Allow me entry at once!" I cried, looking over my shoulder as if I were being pursued. "I am Lady Gabriella Betarrini. Lord Paratore has sent me to retrieve my sister!"

Four knights stared down at me from the wall above. The little peephole window slid open, and a man peered out at us.

"Do not tarry," I said. "We narrowly escaped a Sienese patrol. Let us in!"

The man's small eyes shifted to the crimson on Marcello's shoulder and then to Luca. "I do not know those men."

Marcello groaned and shifted.

"They said that they are mercenaries, hired by Lord Paratore," I said hurriedly. "But they are no account to me. I simply believed you may wish to take in your own wounded."

Still, the man paused.

"Leave them here if need be," I bit out, "but allow me entrance immediately. You try my patience." I lifted my chin and clamped my lips together. "Lord Paratore will certainly be hearing—"

The man groaned and slid the tiny door shut. Perhaps he was a henpecked husband, and he'd decided to risk Lord Paratore's wrath rather than my whining.

I heard the bolt lock *clang,* and the beam begin to slide. I allowed the corner of my lip to curl in victory, but then bit the side of my cheek, regaining my angry edge. I needed to stay in character. I moved forward into the courtyard as if I intended to drop the soldiers' reins into the gateman's hands.

It was then I saw four knights, hands on the hilts of their swords, advancing, two from either side. "No!" I cried, digging my heels into the sides of my horse cruelly hard. "You are spooking my mare!" I pulled hard on the reins, and as she reared, I leaned hard, forward, determined to keep my seat. The men paused, surprised, confused, and when the horse came down on all four hooves, I pressed her forward, as if she was out of my control, trotting away, dragging the two mounts behind me. We were quickly on the other side of the courtyard. "Now," I said lowly.

Marcello and Luca sprang from their horses, each drawing their weapons as I ran to the door and opened it. Marcello and Luca entered. I slammed and barricaded it behind us, just as the men rammed up against it in pursuit.

"This way," I said, grabbing my skirts and whirling, running down the hall to the door that led to the dungeon.

"Luca, I need to find a way to keep those gates open, or our hope of escape dies," Marcello said.

Luca nodded once. "I will go with Gabriella."

The men gripped hands briefly, and Marcello turned toward me and nudged my chin. "Do as he says, She-Wolf. I shall see you when this is all at an end."

I nodded, half wanting to cry out at the thought of his leaving me. Didn't we need to stay together? Weren't we a team? But I knew what gaining this castle meant, to him and many more.

"Do you know of another way out of here?" he asked.

I thought back to my last visit. Did I remember someone leaving from the side, toward the back? When I looked back to see Lia in the window?

"There might be a passageway, back there and to the left." I pointed.

I watched, still a little stunned as he turned on his heel and ran to the back of the building, in search of my alternative exit.

You had to go and fall for a guy who goes all-in for a cause....

"Come," Luca said, easing through the door. We crept down the stairs, taking a sputtering torch with us. At the bottom, Luca lit another torch, which he handed to me as we moved forward.

They hadn't even bothered to lock the dungeon. A shiver of fear rolled down my back. What if they had moved her? What if she wasn't here? What if she was? What if her hands were paralyzed after spending a night hanging from them?

Luca stepped into the room at the bottom of the stairs and then stood stock-still. I peeked around the corner. Of course, it had to be him. Of all of the Paratore knights…

The hulking knight came to his feet and drew his sword. Another movement caught my eye. It was Lord Vannucci. He, too, rose.

"Now, see here," I said, edging past Luca. "I am here to retrieve my sister. Lord Paratore promised me her release." I blinked, relieved to see her not still dangling from the chain. She was in a cell behind the Hulk, sitting up at the sound of my voice. But seeing her, clearly miserable, helped me find my anger and push back my fear. I strode over to Lord Vannucci. "Release her. Now. And send us off with the promised gold as well. We must be away."

Lord Vannucci didn't move. He just stared at me so steadily, so coldly, I again imagined he was seeing right through me. "Who is he?" he asked, flicking his eyes toward Luca.

"It matters not," I said, edging a bit between Luca and him. If he recognized him as Marcello's captain…

"It matters to me," he said, eyes narrowing.

"We are in love," Luca said, stepping forward and slipping a hand around my waist. I struggled to keep my expression in order, lifting my chin as if I was verifying his words as truth. "Once we are safely in Firenze, we shall exchange our vows."

Lia was now at the front of the cell, hands wrapped around the bars. I took in a little breath and cast her an encouraging smile.

Lord Vannucci stepped over to me and said lowly, "I thought it was Sir Forelli who had lost his heart to you."

"Indeed, he did," I said, letting a wicked smile turn up the corners of my mouth. "He was so lovesick, he never saw that my heart had been claimed by another. It aided me in opening the gates this night." I stopped in front of him and looked up into his face. "I have done what you and Lord Paratore asked of me. Now honor our bargain."

He whipped out his hand so fast I didn't even realize it was his hand until I felt it pressing cruelly into the sides of my throat. I heard the slide of Luca's sword, as well as the massive knight's, but my eyes remained locked on Lord Vannucci's. "You think me a fool," he ground out. "You are lying."

Lia cried out as he turned me around and rushed me to the stone wall, knocking me against it. I could see Luca doing his best to battle the massive Paratore knight, but he was not faring very well.

"What deception is going on here? Tell me now, and you may just survive this night."

He released the pressure on my throat a little, and I hunched over, gasping for breath. I eased one hand under my cape, as if holding my chest, still trying to recover, but as I did so, I unsheathed my knife and then sprang away, raising the dagger between us.

"You little deceiver," he snarled, advancing upon me as if he wasn't scared at all.

"You are the deceiver, pretending friendship, alliance with the Sienese, supping with them, and then betraying them to the Fiorentini." I pulled my sword from the back sheath, even as I dodged a swipe from the Paratore knight, who was aiming for Luca.

I heard Lia gasp, but my eyes remained on my most lethal enemy as he moved to pull an ax from the wall. My eyes widened.

"'Tis a pity, slicing such a delectable creature to bits," he said, moving toward me again. "But at least I'll have her sister for myself."

His words stopped me cold. I stood my ground and let him approach, timing his footsteps, calculating how fast that ax might come, probably gaining speed as it arced downward—

He whirled and brought the ax around, full force. I pulled back just enough, sucking in my breath, feeling it slice through my cape, as Lia screamed.

But as Lord Vannucci pulled up on the ax, intent on bringing it down on my head this time, I made my own strike, slicing through the leather of his pants and cutting his thigh.

He glanced down at his leg and his face became a mask of fury. "You little witch," he bit out, raising his ax with powerful arms and bringing it down so fast that I felt the wind across my forehead and nose. He didn't let up then. He continued his attack, bringing it past me, beside me, over me again and again, never letting up, never giving me an opportunity to strike again, as I barely found time to take my next defensive stance.

I bumped into a stool, bent, threw my blade at him and then pulled the stool around to toss it at him. I was getting weaker and more desperate. I was shocked when he ducked in the wrong direction, perhaps thrown off by the fact that his ax was again whirling around in an arc, and the stool slammed into his nose. He let the ax sink to the ground and stumbled backward, holding his blood-spurting nose.

"Gabi!" Lia cried.

I glanced over to her and then to Luca, who was up against the wall, his leg pushing against the hulking knight who was trying to shove his sword into Luca's throat. Luca's leg trembled; sweat rolled down his flushed face. The knight's face was red and sweaty too, determined.

I grabbed another ax off the wall, whirled, and slammed the beastly, heavy thing between the shoulder blades of Luca's attacker.

He recoiled, tottered backward, and fell to the ground, the ax still lodged in his back.

I looked up at Lia, who had her face in her hands, staring at me with wide eyes. And in that moment, I felt torn between two worlds. My sister was gazing at me as if she wondered who had taken control of my body, and I was looking at my hands, dirty, blood spattered, as if they might belong to someone else, indeed. What was I doing? How on earth had I come to killing three men?

"Gabriella!" Luca cried, wrenching me to one side, just as Lord Vannucci swung his ax past me.

I fell against the cell door and looked back to see Luca charge against the man, pushing him across the floor, his long ax of no use in such close proximity. He rammed him into the wall and then punched him across the face. Lord Vannucci was instantly unconscious. He sagged to the floor.

With trembling fingers I pulled the ring of keys from the giant's belt, afraid that he might not be dead, the ax still lodged in his back, like in some freaky horror movie.

Luca, panting, wiped the back of his hand across his mouth and then stumbled over to the stairwell. He held his breath for a second, listening.

"Anyone coming?" I whispered.

"Nay," he whispered back. "But we best be up top as soon as possible. I doubt the Paratore guards are feigning their own demise, assisting Marcello to open the gates." He smiled, teasing me.

"Hey!" I cried. "I did my part. 'Twasn't as easy as it appeared."

He continued to grin. "I'm certain of it." His eyes shifted from me to Lia as I finally found the right key, shoved it in and turned it.

Lia came through the door and drew me into a fierce hug.

I hugged her back, then turned to Luca.

"Saints in heaven," he said, crossing himself even as he shook his head. "We might fight our way out of here, but then Marcello and I will spend the rest of our lives defending the gates, with two ladies as lovely as you behind them."

I rolled my eyes and shook my head. Ever the charmer, this one. "Sir Luca Forelli, I present my sister, Lady Evangelia Betarrini."

He crossed the room as if he had all the time in the world, took her hand, looked into her eyes, and then bent to kiss her knuckles, his eyes never leaving hers.

I sighed when I heard Lia's breath catch. It was enough that I was torn, with my feelings for Marcello. I didn't need Lia all messed up too.

"Luca," I said, more sharply than I intended. I paused, eased my tone a bit. "We need to get up to the courtyard, right?"

His eyes sharpened, and the dreamy haze disappeared. My knight was back. He turned, hurried over to the wall of weapons, and began shoving daggers into his belt. I did the same. "Are you decent with a sword too, m'lady?" he asked over his shoulder to Lia.

"Me? Nay," Lia said.

"She's an archer, remember?" I said, wrapping a dagger sheath around my calf and tying it off.

"Ahh, right," he said, eyebrow cocked. "Most excellent."

"Yeah, yeah, Romeo," I muttered, grabbing the leather quiver of arrows from him and handing them to Lia. She already had the bow in her hands and was looking at it like it was some museum artifact—which, of course, it could've been. "Come on."

My mind was on Marcello again. We ran up the stairs and out the building from the side, edging around it.

Guards at the top of the castle parapet were charging forward, to the front gates, when we first heard it. The sound was loud enough that it reverberated in our chests, a tremendous pounding. They were here, the Sienese, attempting to storm the gates, to break them with a massive battering ram. The sound became rhythmic within a minute's time, a tremendous pounding, a battle between trees.

Luca curved an eye around the corner, and it was all I could do to keep myself from throwing him aside and looking for myself.

"*Gabs,*" Lia hissed, and I immediately flattened myself against the wall again.

A knight ran by, not ten feet above us on the wall. I was sure all three sets of our eyeballs followed his every move. But his attention was outward, not inward.

"Gabriella!" Luca said over his shoulder. He was moving out.

"Stay behind me," I said to Lia.

But there was little need to urge her. She was like a shadow, so closely did she follow me. I smiled a little smile. We were not going to be separated again.

Luca, hunched over, scurried to an outbuilding twenty feet away, and after a second's hesitation, we followed suit. But halfway across, I spotted him.

Marcello was under attack.

And in grave danger.

"Lia," I mumbled.

She straightened, beside me, and her long fingers wrapped around my upper arm. "Is that him?"

"That's him," I said. But I couldn't move. I was paralyzed by fear.

Marcello was trying to keep three knights at bay, and two men were drawing arrows on him from up above.

I was about to watch Marcello die.

"*Lia...*"

But she was already moving forward, calmly crossing the courtyard like she owned it, ignoring Luca's harsh whispers. Her attention was on the first knight, pulling back his bowstring, taking aim. She paused, sensed the wind, and revised her aim, then let her arrow fly.

I watched it, as if in slow motion, as it shot across the space and split through the first knight's throat.

But Lia was not done. She was already on one knee, squinting and taking aim at the second as he turned, spotting us. She let the next arrow fly, and the arrow struck him in the chest, driving him backward, over the parapet wall.

"Saints in heaven, I believe I'm in love," Luca growled, running past me, sword drawn, to go to Marcello's aid. He glanced from my sister to me with a wink.

Lia was drawing a third arrow, as if she was calmly taking another target in practice, not eliminating the enemy, and Luca's momentum spurred me on too. I drew my sword and ran after him, shouting, trying to draw the attention of those bent on bringing Marcello down.

Marcello tripped and fell to his back and stilled, watching his opponent as the man drew back his spiked ball.

I stumbled, watching him, and almost went to the dirt myself. But then I saw him dodge the pounding swing and leap to his feet from his back. He smiled and whirled, bringing his sword around, again at play, not yet beaten.

His smile allowed me to take what seemed like my first breath since I spotted him, surrounded. Hope surged through me. *We just might get out,* I thought. *We all might live. Please, God, let us live.*

And as I ran forward, as the foreign sound of a warrior's cry rose in my throat, as I clashed with the first knight and felt the jarring clang of our swords that made me shudder like I'd just taken a jolt from a loose electric wire, as Marcello caught sight of me and mouthed my name—the din too loud to make out the syllables—as Lia took down two more knights from the walls with her arrows, as Luca narrowly saved Marcello from a death blow, leaving me breathless, I knew we were gaining.

Impossibly, we were gaining.

CHAPTER 19

"Look out!" Marcello cried, his voice breaking through the dull sounds that seemed to fill my ears, as if I were underwater, looking at me with wide, frantic eyes. But I couldn't move out of the way fast enough. The man came from behind, the coward, and I was just turning to parry his strike, but I was too late, too late, too—

The deepest I'd ever been cut before was a kitchen knife incident. And it didn't require stitches.

This was way worse.

As Luca jumped between me and my attacker and blocked his next blow, I hobbled away, unable to see anything but the blood seeping out into an ever widening pool of crimson at my side, crimson like the Paratore flag. I put my hand to my wound and pulled it away, staring at it, thinking that it was like something from a Halloween store. Fake blood. Like that much blood couldn't be real.

I lifted my fingers and blood actually dropped from them, plopping to the cobblestones at my feet, exploding, dividing, hopping into ten more.

I didn't feel any pain for a minute, maybe two. Probably shock, I assessed distantly. I turned, trying to get a better look at the gash.

Okay, huge mistake. I saw my gown, sliced open. Flesh, like a rare steak.

I turned and gasped for breath as Lia ran to me, taking a shoulder roll to dodge raining arrows, then taking aim and shooting again. Would we never reach the end of the Paratore knights? Were they not all supposed to be over at Castello Forelli?

She glanced at me, my wound, and then paled. She dropped her bow, letting it skitter to the ground—was it odd that I couldn't seem to hear it?—and ran the few remaining paces to me. She took my arm as I went to my knees, fighting the urge to vomit.

"To your back, Gabi, go to your back," she said.

I did as she said. But how was this supposed to go? I did as she said; I had always been the one to see to her scrapes and bruises, to comfort and care.

But I looked up to her as if she was more mother than sister in that moment. I was desperately afraid. And beginning to feel the searing pain in my side.

"Evangelia! The wall!" Luca screamed.

Two new archers had arrived and were running down the castle allure, alongside the outer parapet. We would be within range in seconds. Another was still shooting. We were lucky he had terrible aim.

Lia closed her eyes as if willing herself to take courage, then checked out my wound. She turned an odd shade of gray-green and looked away, gasping for breath. Then she turned to me, leaned over and took my bloodstained hand, pressing it to the wound. "You hold it there, Gabriella. Hold it!"

I pressed, but all I felt was soft, not muscle. Mushy flesh moving far too much. I could make no sense of it.

Lia was behind me, then. Lifting me by the armpits, dragging me around, behind a well. "Do not stop pressing," she demanded. "You cannot die on me here, Gabs."

And then she was gone. To bring down more archers? To help open the gates? I didn't know. And truthfully, I had a hard time caring, one way or another. The sky was still a dark purple dotted by stars, and I could feel the drumming beat of the battering ram at the front gate of Castello Paratore, as if it were keeping time with my heartbeat, which seemed to be weakening, slowing, along with my ability to process what was happening around me.

I looked up to the stars, so familiar to me from my summers in Toscana. Clytemnestra, Orion. They all began to spin, above me, as if I were watching a time-lapse video of the constellations in motion. Here and there, the dark shadows of those fighting entered my field of vision, but I found them irritating, a distraction. All I wanted to do was watch this swirling pool of starlight above me, a dance that transcended this trifling world of humanity, an homage to God Himself.

God? God? Am I going home now? I want to go home now, I think....

I was descending—or was it ascending?—when one thought abruptly stopped the skies from swirling.

Lia. I couldn't leave without her.

And then a second thought.

Marcello.

I don't remember much from those first days. Flashes of light. Screaming. Tears slipping down my face. And the blessed abyss…White light. Calming. Beckoning. Calling me.

Come…

Marcello's hands covered my left. I knew him by his smell of wood smoke and cinnamon. But I couldn't seem to open my eyes. He was praying for me, in Latin. Begging God to save me, to bring me back to him.

But wasn't it easier if I just left now?

Returned to my own time or…disappeared altogether?

"No, Gabriella," she was saying.

Lia.

"No. You come back to me now," she whispered in my ear fiercely. "I cannot do this alone. And Gabi, I can't get back without you," she said, her tone rising several notes. "I've tried." Was she crying? "God help me, I went back to the tomb, put my hand on the print. I was so scared, Gabs, so scared. But it's cold, Gabi. Cold. We need to do it together. I don't want you to die, Gabriella. I don't want to grow old without a sister. But Gabi, Gabi! If you leave me now, I'll be stuck here forever! I can't get back to Mom! Gabs, Gabi...please. Please wake up. *Please....*"

It was time. Choose a path.

Succumb to the light and its entrancing pull, filled with peace, joy, completion.

Or drag myself back to fighting my way out, living my life until I glimpsed this gateway again.

It was that clear, that matter-of-fact.

Now? Or later, Gabriella?

Was that God speaking to me? Asking me? Was life and how I lived it—if I lived it—up to me?

Free choice, Dad always said. *We all have freedom of choice. Over and over again, minute by minute. How will you live your life? For yourself? Or for others? For something good? For love?*

Love.

Evangelia. There was no one I loved more. My sister, so different from me, and yet one with me.

But it wasn't her beside me now.

Marcello was by my side. I smelled him again. Felt his hands covering mine. So warm. So warm. Hot. Almost like the cave wall.

My eyes flew open, wondering if I was about to transport back to my own time. Away from him.

And in that moment, I knew I didn't want to.

My vision, as if I was waking from a deep and long dream, was fuzzy. But bit by bit, from the outside in, each inch of what I could see was clarified. And there he was. Marcello.

His big, brown eyes grew watery, and he cradled my face in his hands and shook his head. "Gabriella. Gabriella?"

I tried to say his name, but my voice was garbled, weak.

Eagerly, he went for a cup of water and then gently eased it to my lips. I felt the water on my tongue, my cheeks. Knew enough to be embarrassed when most of it slipped down my face and neck.

But his eyes were alight, as if I were a miracle on earth.

I pushed what I hoped was some semblance of a smile onto my face, but I could feel my lips cracking as I did it.

Still, he looked at me, not like I was some monster of the desert, bleeding, pale, rising before him as a ghost…but rather like an angel coming to him across the far, green hills.

His lush lips parted in awe as my eyes flicked open. And he blinked with heavy, dark lashes, as if he might be dreaming.

Was I?

Could a guy—a guy like *this* be that anxious to see me to health, to wellness?

"Gabriella," he said, winding his warm hands more firmly around mine, so wretchedly cold. "Gabriella," he whispered, leaning forward and kissing my temple, my forehead, my nose, my eyes. "*Gabriella.*"

He spoke my name in the same way he might say *beautiful* or *wondrous* or *amazing* and really mean it.

"Marcello," I croaked, wincing that it came out in a froggy voice in comparison to his princely tone.

But he smiled as if he had heard it as I had meant it.

Marcello. *Dedicated. Strong. Mine.*

CHAPTER 20

It was Lia who had sewn me up. That was enough of a shock that I almost melted back into my week of unconsciousness.

My sister, weak-kneed, slightly green at the sight of manure or moldy cheese in the fridge, had found it in herself to disinfect my wound with alcohol—thank God I had been unconscious—thread an ivory needle with sinew, and sew up my side like I was an elementary school project.

I turned and stared at my six-inch wound again, gaping at the perfect, even curves of sinew like whipstitches in a thermal blanket.

But then I looked up at her and groaned. "They'll have to come out."

"Yes," she said.

I closed my eyes and winced, thinking of the pain to come. But not yet. The trick was we had to let the flesh weave itself together again without letting the sinew become embedded within it. It might lead to infection, which miraculously, I seemed to have been spared.

That didn't mean it couldn't still get infected.

Modern-day thoughts of flesh-eating disease, MRSA, sepsis, staph, cascaded through my mind. My dad always said I was a bit of a hypochondriac, always reading up on possible ailments and feeling certain I had them. I tried to think back to what I'd read.

I could feel the whisper of air as Lia fell to her knees beside me, her skirts billowing. "Gabi, what are we going to do? They're calling us 'princess warriors.' That's all I hear. They think we're All That and more. Seriously. And that Luca dude is following me around everywhere I go." She rolled her eyes.

"Well, you saved all our lives with your arrows," I said. "I'd bet you money he's never seen a woman do that before."

She shook her head. "How are we going to get out of this?"

I closed my eyes, heaved a sigh, and then peeked at her. "I have no idea." *In so many ways…* "Lia, how is Fortino? Marcello's brother?"

"Oh, amazing," she said. "Apparently, that's just another reason to throw you a big party. They're all excited because he's back from the dead or something."

I smiled and closed my eyes. I was so afraid that I'd wake up to find Fortino gone, even buried.

Lia rose and gestured in the direction of the courtyard. "Gabi, everyone's going *crazy* out there. Now that you're back from the brink, there's no way they're going to be able to hold it off any longer."

My smile faded. "What do you mean?"

"It sounds like all of Siena is coming in for the celebration. Something about a three-day feast to celebrate our victory. And we're the guests of honor."

Victory. Castello Paratore defeated. For Siena, it would be huge.

It all seemed like a movie I'd seen. I reached out and grabbed Lia's hand. She was so tenderhearted. She had cried when she shot her first bird with a bow and arrow. I knew killing those men must've been excruciating for her. "Lia, do you want to talk about it? I mean, the battle. All those guys—"

"No." She pulled her hand from mine. "No, I don't. I want to get out of here, Gabi, and forget this all happened. It's like a nightmare." She shook her head. "We have to get back to the tomb. Try it together. I mean, to make the jump back."

I nodded, but my mind was already pulling me in two directions.

"You'll do it, then?" she said, relief flooding her face. And in that moment, I remembered how badly I wanted to return to our own time, how I longed for Mom and Lia just a week ago. But now…

Maybe it was having Lia here, with me. Maybe I was being selfish. But having her here settled me, made me feel less homesick, less vulnerable.

It wasn't just me.

It was us.

And that freed me to think more broadly about Marcello.

It was as if some bonds had been broken. Over and over, I had resisted Marcello because of Lia, because of my mom, because I needed to get back. And because he was promised to another. Another who could help him, help his family, help Siena. But now that Lia was here…

"Maybe I can get you to the tomb on my own somehow," Lia said, looking at my side again. "It'd be better if we could get you home and to the doctor."

"And how do we explain that?" I asked, pointing to my side.

"That'll be tricky," she said, pursing her lips. "Can you believe I did that? Sewed you up?"

I laughed under my breath. "No. But then you pulled through for me in so many ways, Lia." I grabbed her hand and waited until she looked at me. "We'll have to talk about it at some point, you know. I don't want you to have post-traumatic stress disorder or something. You know, like the guys who fight in wars sometimes get, coming home? I know I've been having nightmares—"

"I really don't want to talk about it," she said. Was she a shade paler?

"You had no choice, Lia. If you hadn't killed them they would have—"

"Stop!" She yanked her hand from mine again. She stepped away from me and brought a hand to her forehead. "I just wanna get back, Gabs. This is all so crazy…."

A knock sounded at the door, and a moment later, Cook peeked in. She looked at me with her kind eyes. "I thought you'd enjoy a bath, m'lady."

I winced as I tried to sit up, then lay back down. A bath sounded so good. "I would like nothing more. But my wound." I glanced at it again and shook my head. "I think it best if I not get it wet."

"Well, what if we assist you? To wash your hair, at least. Take care with the rest."

Finally I nodded my agreement. Four maids with pails of hot water and a manservant, carrying the deep wooden tub, followed her, set up a screen, dumped the water into it, and then left again. Lia looked like she wanted to follow them.

"On the morrow, these halls will be filled with Siena's finest," Cook said. She beamed over at Lia and then back to me. "They're coming to honor you two, you know. As much as the Forellis are the favored sons of Toscana, at the moment, all of Siena wishes to know about the she-warriors of Normandy."

"I don't know," I mumbled. I hadn't yet managed to rise from my bed. Part of me feared that if I moved, I'd tear out Lia's stitches. I shuddered at the thought.

But then I caught Lia's expression, which plainly said, *Yeah, you should take a look at yourself,* and thought of how nice it'd feel to be clean again. It had been over a week. And that last day had hardly been a prissy-girl experience. I leaned down and sniffed my armpit. "Uhh," I said.

Lia arched a brow and moved over to my side. "Come on. We'll help you."

I almost screamed when I sat up, and after a moment, I gritted my teeth to stand. Any movement along my side was excruciating. Sweat rolled down my face. Briefly, I considered what it would be to have Lia remove the stitches soon, and quickly cast that thought out. I'd have to bite down on a stick, down a bunch of *grappa,* or something...because that was going to *kill.*

I wrapped my right arm around the shoulders of Cook, who was much shorter than me. Lia held my left hand, more for encouragement than support. Slowly, we moved to the tub, and I sat down in a chair and leaned my head back, letting my hair fall behind me.

They moved quickly, tag-teaming the process. Cook dumped a pail of water down my head, dousing it, and Lia moved in with a bar of lavender-laced soap, scrubbing my hair into a thick lather. Then they each began with the pails of water, dumping one after another. It felt delicious, and I sighed in relief at the sensation of getting clean.

Then they brought me a basin and cloth, and together, we washed the rest of me, the best we could, without submerging. Beads of sweat lined my upper lip even as I shivered. Lia frowned at me. "You don't look so good," she whispered, when Cook left the room. "I mean, you look far better than you did, but are you feeling sick?"

I shook my head. "Just the exertion, I think." I sat up as straight as I could as Lia began the long process of combing out my tangled hair. That was another thing that definitely sucked about living in medieval times: no conditioner.

Cook returned with two servants. They each set a trunk down, on the edge of my room, and left, never looking in my direction. But Cook was grinning as she opened the trunks. "Gifts, for you and Lady Evangelia."

Lia stopped combing and leaned over to see what it could possibly be. Cook flipped the brass latch on the first trunk and opened it. She pulled from it a magnificent robin's-egg-blue gown, embroidered with what looked like silver thread. "For you, Lady Evangelia," she said, dragging it across her arms and carrying it across the room.

"Oh, Lia," I breathed, reaching out to run my hand across the finely woven silk. It was amazing. And the exact color of her eyes. "With your hair…my goodness, no one will be able to keep their eyes off of you."

"I agree, but she'll have a firm competitor in her sister," Cook said, going to the second trunk. From it she pulled a copper-colored silk gown, this one embedded with tiny seed pearls all across the bodice.

I gaped at her. "I cannot wear such a thing. It is far too beautiful."

"It is only fitting," Cook said with a dismissive snort, "for them to honor you so. Were it not for you two, Castello Paratore would not be ours."

"My side," I said, hating the whine that crept into my voice, "with my wound, I'll never be able to endure being in that gown."

"Nonsense," Cook said. "Lord Marcello has seen to every detail. He had the seamstresses cut it a couple inches wider than your other gowns, so that there will be plenty of room to bind your wound so it won't chafe."

I looked her in the eye. "This is a gift from Marcello?"

"But of course," Cook said, smiling at me quizzically as if to say *Who else?*

I shared a look with Lia. She turned to Cook. "Is my gown from Marcello as well?"

"I believe that was more of Sir Luca's doing," she said, turning back to the trunks again. Did the woman think it was odd that two men more comfortable with swords had spent the afternoon at a Sienese seamstress's shop?

She pulled several more gowns out of each trunk to show us, one for each of the days of the feast. "Your other two gowns should arrive with our guests," she said.

"Two more?"

"Indeed," she said, brows raised. "The ladies of the castle are all expected to be in their finest for the festivities. You'll find in each trunk new sets of underclothes, underdresses, and the like." And with that, she went out the door, closing it softly behind her.

Lia was again at my hair, but she wasn't paying attention. The comb caught in the tangles, and she pulled hard, ripping out some strands of hair. "*Lia*."

"Sorry," she muttered, dropping the comb to the bed. "Okay, I *so* wanna wear that gown. I've never seen anything so pretty. It's like something out of a dream." She went over to it, lifted it into her hands, and then draped it across her body.

I smiled and shook my head. "You'll look amazing in that."

"You'll be gorgeous in yours, too."

I looked at my own and then back to her, hope lifting my heart. *We don't have to go. Yet.* "So…we'll try to get to the tomb after the feast?"

She didn't answer me for a moment. "What's one or two more days? We don't have to stay for the entire feast, right? And you need a few more days to mend. Mom would freak if she saw those sinew stitches."

"Right, although it may be hard to slip away."

"Okay, but we'll go right after the feast, all right? Promise me." She laid the gown down and came over to me, kneeling beside my chair. "Promise me, Gabi."

"I promise. We'll get to the tomb." She seemed mollified by my words and went to retrieve fresh bandages to rebind my wound. What she missed was that I didn't promise the rest—to put my hand on the print, to make the leap back. Might there be a way for me to send her home, give her what she wanted, but stay, myself? But if she were gone, could I stay? Would I not be crazy with longing for my family, homesick?

It was too much to consider. I had a few days. I'd figure it out.

CHAPTER 21

A servant knocked on my door, awakening me from my nap. The bath had pretty much wiped me out.

Lia went to the door and was speaking in hushed tones, but I said, "Wait. Who is it?"

She glanced back at me with a worried expression. "Lord Fortino," she said in a low tone.

"Let him in," I said, closing my eyes.

I could feel her hesitation. She was worried about me, getting so tired.

"I'm fine, Lia. Let him in," I whispered. I willed myself to turn over and then push myself to a sitting position, turning away so Fortino couldn't see my face, riddled with pain, as I did so.

When I turned back, I saw him, halfway across the room, leaning heavily on the arm of his servant. "Lord Fortino," I said, "you shouldn't have taxed yourself so."

His eyes, beneath concerned brows, went from my torso to my face, which was covered in sweat. "Pay me no heed, dear lady. I fear it is you I tax. Shall I leave?"

"No. Come, come. Please." I glanced at the volume beneath his armpit. "You visit to share a bit of the poet with me?"

"Indeed," he said. The servant pulled a chair beside my bed, and Fortino sat down on it. I could hear the wheeze in his breathing.

"At least you fare better than when last I saw you," I said.

He gave me a rueful smile. "I bear no wound of battle, just those that God has allowed me to bear within my lungs."

I reached out and put my hand on his arm. "It is enough."

He patted my hand and looked at me fondly. "Lady Gabriella, you did so much for me, my family, Siena. We are eternally grateful to you and your fair sister." His eyes shifted to Lia, but she had turned to fiddle with the herbs and bandages on the table.

I smiled. "We only did what we could. Truth be told, we were fighting to free Evangelia more than anything. I fear Siena's future is something I have not given much thought."

He lifted his brows and nodded, understanding. "Most women do not think of such things. But fortunately for us, our intentions aligned." He raised the golden volume. "Shall we?"

I nodded, leaning my head back against the goose-feather pillow and closed my eyes. Fortino began to read, his voice surprisingly strong, and yet pausing often for him to catch his breath. We were in the midst of the *Inferno,* the part in which Dante and Virgil climbed out of the hellish underworld to find themselves on an island called *Purgatorio,* somewhere between heaven and hell. "'To get back up to the shining world from there,'" Fortino read, "'My guide and I went into that hidden tunnel; Where we came forth, and once more saw the stars.'"

My eyes sprang open. "Please. Read that last line again."

"'My guide and I went into that hidden tunnel; Where we came forth, and once more saw the stars.'" He lowered the book and stared at me. "What is it that captures you so, m'lady?"

I couldn't really tell Fortino what I was thinking. I'd had a crazy thought that maybe Dante, once here, in this very castle, had traveled through time and space himself in the tomb. The tunnel, the passage…could he not have seen much more than a distant time? Perhaps even a different space, world? Heaven? Hell?

I shivered, hoping that was not what was at the end of that tomb's tunnel.

When I remained silent, Fortino said, "It is a remarkable turn for our hero. Here, he begins his true trek toward salvation."

A cough at the door made us both turn. Marcello. He smiled at me, clearly glad to see that I was clean and changed, looking as if I felt better even if I was miserably tired. He stepped forward and took a seat at the foot of my bed. "The image is evocative because Dante has seen the depths of hell, and now he's glimpsed heaven."

I shifted uneasily, because Marcello's eyes were intently on me. Fortino was staring at him, then me, then his brother again.

"He's on his way toward Beatrice, our heroine, *and* God. In the midst of such darkness, he's seen the light. The stars."

I knew he was trying to speak to me, reach me, through the double meaning of his speech. Fortino clearly heard it too. He mumbled an excuse, bent to kiss my hand, and departed, with Lia on his heels, leaving us alone.

Marcello moved to kneel beside my bed and took my hand in both of his. "Forgive me for my absence, Gabriella." He stood, hunched over, and kissed my brow—a slightly disappointing move since it'd been a week since we kiss-kissed, but sweet. He was still treating me as if I was made of glass. "In truth, I have thought of little other than you, but there is much to attend to, with the feast upon us on the morrow. And neither my father nor Fortino is prepared for such a task. My day has been spent with cooks and bakers and vintners and falconers and dignitaries, all swirling in plans for our grand meals and festivities over the next days."

I nodded, but I lifted my eyes to meet his. "'Tis truly necessary? Could we not allow Siena their festivities…in Siena?"

He smiled and turned his head, repositioning his hands over mine. "We represent the front lines. 'Twould not do for us to do anything but celebrate this victory, and loudly."

I nodded and then looked to my thick blanket and wondered if I had the guts to ask what must come next. I plunged onward. "Marcello, what became of Lord Paratore and Lord Vannucci?" I remembered nothing more of that night, and I hadn't had the nerve to ask Lia. She clearly was in denial about that whole night.

"Both are imprisoned in Siena." His eyes flicked away, to the window. "Most likely they shall be traded at some point for one or two men we wish to free. But with tensions so high, it may be some time."

I nodded, as if happy to know of their fate, but in that instant, I knew I wished them dead and gone.

His hands gripped mine. "Gabriella, 'tis the way the Nine wished it to go."

"I understand." I raised my eyes to meet his. "But the thought of either of them, free…" I shook my head. "Given what they've seen, what they've experienced, Lia and I are as much enemy to them as you and Luca."

He blinked his heavy lashes and then nodded once. "Indeed. It is a grave danger. But I do not foresee them ever threatening you again. They shall be exiled or traded, deep into Fiorentini territory. Or put to death."

Put to death. Hanged. Dismembered. Drawn and quartered. Death was a bloody business in medieval times.

I wanted to feel a measure of compassion for them. I wanted to hope that the exile card won out, but I knew that selfishly, I was hoping they would die, never to be a concern for me and Lia again.

"Gabriella, we must speak of something else."

My eyes moved to his.

"Lady Rossi and her family are arriving on the morrow."

I studied him, waiting. Knowing I should take him off the hook, release him of responsibility, tell him I was on my way out, that it couldn't really work between the two of us.

"I shall break our pledge, make it clear to both Lady Rossi and her father that no union shall be formed between our families."

I frowned, even though my heart pounded with hope. It was not good for Marcello to end his plans with Romana. She wouldn't go down without a fight; she'd try to bring me down with her. *If I can't have him, neither can you.* We'd all suffer her wrath, her father's wrath.

Marcello was feeling strong, invincible even, after our capture of Castello Paratore, and perhaps it would afford him some protection amid Sienese politics. But didn't he need every protection possible? If Firenze was to attack, they would surely target a point such as Castello Forelli first. And Castello Forelli needed to know they could rely on reinforcements from Siena. That Siena had their back. Without a marriage between the Forellis and the Rossis, was that truly possible?

Marcello was studying me. "M'lady, do you doubt me? Doubt my fervor for you?" He stroked my forehead, cheek, and stared into my eyes with such love, it set my heart pounding. "'Tis not simply what I owe you as a man loyal to Siena. 'Tis what I owe you as a man. Gabriella," he said, looking intensely into my eyes, "you own my heart. My life, and all I have in it. You have captured me, m'lady, like no one else. My hours are spent absorbed in thoughts of you, dreams of you. I cannot imagine a life without you in it. Might I dare believe that you would leave Normandy for good? To remain here, with me?"

I stared at him, stricken. There was so much to figure out, ahead of us. "Marcello, you draw me as none other. But I am still pulled by the desire to find my mother, and Evangelia—" I sighed. "She is desperate to continue our search for our mother. I must see to my family's reunion before I can legitimately consider my future. I am certain you understand."

I appealed to his sense of honor, family. And it worked.

"Indeed. I must assist you in this endeavor, for I intend to speak to your mother."

I looked at him sharply. *What? How in the heck was that supposed to work out? "Hey, Mom, I want to meet you my Handsome Prince from 1342."*

He narrowed his eyes in my direction and lowered his forehead. "If we are to continue our courting, I must gain her approval," he whispered.

Ahh, yes. Courting. Going out, in medieval terms. Sweetly conducted with everything in order. Would Lord Forelli bless his younger son's pursuit? When there was not one whit of political gain to be found from it? Unlikely.

The only thing we had going for us was that Lord Forelli seemed pretty out of it since his last stroke. I doubted he'd even fully absorbed the victory over Castello Paratore.

But if he came to his senses, this news of Marcello breaking his pledge to Lady Rossi and pursuing me would truly send him over the edge. He'd have a full-on heart attack, keel over, and die for sure.

And it'd be on my head.

"I do not know, Marcello," I said, dragging my eyes to meet his. *Stick to the truth, Gabi.* "What is between us in unmistakable. In truth, I've never felt anything like it." I looked at him for a long moment. "But both our families look to us to sustain them, into the future. They rely upon us. Promises between us cannot yet be made."

He frowned and looked at me as if he had not heard me right. "Are you saying…Gabriella, are you saying that you do not want me to break my pledge to Romana?"

It took me a long time, but I finally found the words to say it. "No. Marcello, I want you to break your pledge. Because selfishly, I want you for myself. But I cannot ask it of you. You are a future lord of Siena. And I do not know where I belong, here or Normandy."

"Here," he said, squeezing my hands, "you belong here."

I shook my head miserably. "I do not know that. I wish I did. But I do not."

His eyes filled with sorrow. "You do not know it? How must I prove it to you?"

"Ah, Marcello. It is not up to you," I said, reaching up to cradle his cheek this time. "I understand your feelings for me. My heart echoes them. But I need to know we are doing what is right. Or not. That makes me hesitate. I need time. More time."

"I have no more time," he said in desperation. "She arrives on the morrow."

"Then you must carry on as before," I said. "For the sake of your family, for the sake of Siena." I shook my head. "I cannot break such a union. Not yet."

"Not yet?" he asked, broken hopefulness in his voice.

"Not yet," I said.

CHAPTER 22

I didn't know what I was thinking. Somehow, I thought it was the good thing, the right thing to do. I thought myself above it.

But seeing Marcello with Romana, after her being out of the picture a while, threatened to rip me to shreds. I actually had to lean a little harder on Lia's arm when I spotted them together, across the courtyard.

"Gabs," Lia said, looking over at me with a worried expression in her eyes. She followed my glance across the courtyard and then steered me into an arched doorway, hidden from view. Once I was braced against the wall, she paced before me, hands on her hips, apparently thinking it through. Then she stopped, turned, and looked into my eyes. "All right, I think I'm ready. How bad is it?"

I looked up to where the arches connected, two paths intersecting…then back to her. "Bad."

She closed her eyes as if pained, then shook her head. "No," she said, pinching the bridge of her nose. "No, I can't believe it. Gabi—"

"I'm sorry, Lia. It's bigger than I am. I don't expect you to get it—"

"Get what?" she asked, her voice ratcheted up an octave. "That you've gone and fallen for a guy you can't have?"

I glanced out at the courtyard, wondering if anyone had overheard her, and she hushed in volume, if not intensity. "We should go, now," she said, leaning toward me.

"Go?" I said, gaping at her. It was the first I'd been out of bed for more than twenty minutes. She wanted me to make the journey to the tombs, more than a mile away? And under what pretense? It sounded as if all of Siena was soon upon us. Were we to simply ride by them all, with a smile and a cheerful wave?

Hey there, how are ya? We're the She-Wolves of Normandy, just on our way back to the place we came from…don't mind us!

"I knew you had feelings for him," she said, one hand out. "But I didn't know you had *feeling*-feelings for him."

"Is there a difference?" I asked tiredly.

"I guess not," she said, bringing an arm to the stone arch and looking out to the courtyard. "I didn't know," she said, talking to herself so lowly I almost missed it. "I mean I knew, but I didn't *know*."

I leaned back and willed myself to find the strength for what was ahead. More people were already arriving. The castle would be filled, every room of it. Additional tents had been pitched outside, more than a hundred, Cook said, to house the others. I wished I could share a word with Cook right now. I needed a woman's perspective, not my sister's. But she was a tad too busy to tend to me. To say nothing of the fact that I could hardly lay it all on the line.…

"Let's go, Gabi. Before this all gets much worse. While we still can. I'll find a couple of horses, and we'll get out of here, back to Mom. She'll know what to do about your wound—"

"Nay." I looked past her, to Marcello. Romana had gone inside, but he was looking across the courtyard at us, a curious, daring look in his eye.

"'Nay?' You mean *no?*" She reached over and grabbed my shoulders. "You are from the twenty-first century. This is wrong, that we are here, Gabi. A weird hole in some space-time continuum that we fell through."

There was fear in her eyes. I was torn between the desire to ease her stress and the desire to defend myself.

"Is it wrong?" I looked at her then. Really looked at her. "Or is it, in some divine way, perfectly right?"

She gaped at me. "It's wrong. Of course it's wrong."

It was as if I'd changed somehow, in my extra week in this time. I'd adopted it more fully than Lia had.

She was all about getting back.

I was all about figuring out why I was here in the first place and what I could accomplish if I stayed.

I grabbed her hand, and she frowned at my fingers, then me.

"Lia, I need you to give this a chance. To explore it with me. Please. Don't rush me. I'm afraid to leave. Because of my wound. Because of Marcello. I'm afraid that if I leave, so much will be lost. So much."

Her blue eyes, like a stormy sea beneath her furrowed brows, stared into mine for a long time. "How long?" she asked at last.

"Through the feast," I said. "I think that by then, you can pull out my stitches, bind me in fresh cloths, and we can make it to the tombs."

"Why through the feast?" she pressed. She stepped closer. "Why not now?"

My eyes trailed from her to the courtyard again. Marcello was striding across to us, his brow now knit in consternation. "Maybe not all the way through the feast," I whispered. "I just know that today is not the day. All right?"

She hesitated. "All right," she whispered at last.

But clearly, things were not all right. When Marcello arrived, she bristled and turned, ignoring his friendly greeting.

"She thinks me a coward, unable to stand for what is true," he said, watching her stride away, then brush past Luca with an angry hand. "She thinks I toy with you, while maintaining a charade with Lady Rossi."

"Nay, that is not it at all."

He drew closer. "Come. Tell me the truth." His brown eyes searched mine.

Okay, try this on for size, Tall, Dark, and Handsome. I won't be born for almost seven hundred years. How's that strike you?

I chose a more moderate path. "Marcello, this is hardly the right time."

He shook his head and stepped away from me, hand to his temple. "I do not know if I can continue to pretend, Gabriella." He gestured to the courtyard. "She arrives, head full of details for our nuptials, and though it's been a part of my vision for as long as I can remember, I now cannot fathom standing beside her before a priest." He reached for my hand and brought it to his chest, nestled beneath his own. "It is a position that cannot be taken by anyone but you."

I wrenched my hand from his. "Marcello," I whispered harshly, "what if someone sees?" That's what came out of my mouth. But I was thinking, *Again with the marriage thing! I'm too young! You are too!*

"What if they do?" he asked, frowning. "I cannot live this way. Lord Rossi arrives this night. I cannot face him, knowing I do not love his daughter! I love you!"

I tried to swallow. Love? Surely that wasn't it.

Infatuation. Connection. Maybe a little lust. But love? I shook my head. I had to get out of here. I was going crazy. Overthinking it. Overfantasizing about it. Lia was right. It was drawing me in. Pulling me down.

"Where are you?" Marcello asked, taking my hand again. "Your body is here, but your mind is elsewhere."

You have no idea.

"Marcello, we must carry through with what we agreed upon," I said. "There is too much at stake for you. I have no choice but to continue my search for my mother."

"And I will aid you in that."

I shook my head. "Lia and I…after the feast, we must carry on. You have more than enough to care for, between your father, your brother, your responsibilities to Siena. I fear that you and I weren't ever meant to meet, Marcello."

"How can you utter such words?" he asked, holding tight to my hand as I tried to pull away. "When I believe that our meeting had to be of the hand of God Himself?"

I was finding it seriously difficult to resist him, wondering if we might share just one more kiss before I hurtled away through time.… I wrenched my hand away from his and walked to the other side of the arched colonnade, my back to him. "You must pretend, Marcello," I said, "I can make you no promises."

"Gabriella—"

"Nay," I bit out, tiredly, feeling the sweat pour down my back. "It is what it is."

Not that it should be at all.

I hid away that afternoon in my bedroom, skipping lunch, and sleeping through crazy dreams in which I was forever saving someone—or getting saved. But by evening, a good third of the guests had arrived, all "clamoring" to meet the ladies of Normandy, the warriors, the "she-wolves," Siena's "saviors," and I was roused.

People didn't seem able to tell them no. I wasn't able to tell them no. So I rose, on Lia's silent, brooding arm, and together we walked across the courtyard and into the Great Hall.

When we entered, the entire room rose. I mean, every one of them came to their feet. And the place was packed. They cheered, clapped, smiled.

And we did our best to be gracious and smile. But what I was able to fake on my own seemed triply hard beside Lia. She kept sending me angry, frustrated glances, until I feared everyone near us had figured out that something was seriously wrong between us.

I tried, best I could, to keep my eyes from straying to Marcello and Romana, but again and again, that was where they landed. She returned my look, dolefully staring my way, plainly wondering what was to become of us all now. Marcello had told her he'd sent me away because I was attracted to him and it was safer for us to be apart; and yet, now here we all were again, one big, happy family, celebrating Sienese victory.

Pleading exhaustion and weakness, not all that far from the truth, I excused myself from the table on the dais as soon as I could. Lia and I were halfway across the courtyard when Lady Rossi's voice stopped us.

My sister groaned, frozen. I paused, gathering myself, and then turned, forcing a smile to my lips. "M'lady," I said, as kindly as I could.

She reached us, with two ladies-in-waiting at her side. They were newbies. Had the others defected, refusing to endure the treacherous ride to this outpost again? She curtsied, deeply, prettily, and her ladies followed suit.

I glanced at Lia and resisted the urge to roll my eyes. "Please, m'lady," I said, embarrassed by her show of deference.

She rose slowly and dragged her pretty brown-green eyes up to meet mine. "M'lady, I am indebted to you and your sister, as is all of Siena."

I shook my head. "We did only what we could. What you yourself might have done, in the moment."

It was her turn to shake her head. "I think not," she said, raising one brow and smiling. "You and your sister are indeed uncommon."

I made the introductions then, between her and my sister. To her credit, Lia managed to hold her own, like she was playing a part in a medieval play. I then excused her, and Romana did the same with her ladies-in-waiting. Arm in arm, like two old friends strolling the park, we moved off, with me trying to act like I wasn't dying, both from the pain in my side and the pain in my heart.

"I am to leave as soon as I can, Lady Romana," I said. I dared to glance into her eyes. "I only need a few more days to heal, and then I believe I can endure the ride to Normandy."

She nodded, staring ahead, as if weighing my words, deciding if she believed them. "I know you were most severely injured."

"Yes," I said. *Most severely. My heart has been lacerated. Split open. Or is it my brain? I don't seem to be thinking clearly.*

She stopped and turned toward me, taking my hand in her two small ones. "Lady Betarrini, my father believes he has a credible witness—that your mother is known to have been in Pistoia."

I pulled my head back, hoping I didn't appear as doubtful as I felt. My mother, here? Could she have found a way to travel through the tomb? Or had she found another portal? Was it not far more likely that Romana simply wanted to get me away as soon as possible? To Florence's north, deep beyond the border? I smiled, leaping on this tidbit, a tiny path out of our sinking sand.

"Truly?" I said, squeezing her hand. "Oh, that is good news. We'd be off today if it weren't for this wound." I gestured down to my side.

"Nay," she said, "You mustn't endanger yourself. You have already suffered much. But my father has already sent four men on the journey there. They should return soon with news."

"That is more than kind," I said. I shook my head. "You don't know what it would mean, to be reunited." I stared at her, hard. "And then we can be off. Back to Normandy."

"Oh?" she said, lightly. I had to give her credit. Had our roles been reversed, I would have been offering to help her pack, pushing her out the door, promising that my father's men would meet her on the road in between.

"Oh, yes," I intoned. "As soon as we are together, we are gone from this far country. We have politics of our own to consider."

Visions of my mother arguing with the Italian archaeology authorities raced through my mind. *It's hardly the life-and-death stuff of this era, but hey, it's still politics....*

"I am certain it is as absorbing as our own," she said. Her wise eyes studied mine, and finding some sort of confidence there, she squeezed my hand again and turned. "I bid you good night, Lady Betarrini. You are undoubtedly in sore need of rest. And I must return to my betrothed, or he shall wonder where I have gone."

I forced another smile and nodded. "I must get to my quarters at once, or I fear I might collapse and sleep the night through, right here."

She smiled prettily and giggled. "Oh, that wouldn't do." She steered me back to the first corridor and waited while I went through the door.

Making sure I wasn't coming back out, I mused. "Until the morrow, Lady Romana," I said.

"Until the morrow," she repeated, a bit too bright, a bit too friendly.

I turned and walked down the corridor. Lia waited for me inside my room.

"Talk about a she-wolf," she said as I shut the door. She came over to me and, seeing the exhaustion in my face, helped me sit, then immediately began unbuttoning my gown as I pulled the tiresome pins from my hair. "That girl has her claws out. They're just hidden under gloves."

"That girl is a daughter of the Nine."

"The Nine-Nine?"

"The Nine-Nine."

She let out a long breath. "Marcello's intended, daughter of one of the Nine. You sure know how to pick 'em."

"Yes," I said in irritation, rising as she undid the last button. I reached to pull my dress over my head and then gasped at the pain brought on by my sudden, irritated movement.

She said nothing, yet she said everything with her big, blue eyes that looked anywhere but at me. She eased the dress over my head, then pulled a loose gown over my shoulders next, reaching for a brush and combing through my hair.

"She says Mom's been seen. In Pistoia."

Lia's hand stilled and after a moment, she came around to face me. "Pistoia?"

I knew she was thinking the same thing I was—Pistoia was an old city, built atop Etruscan and Roman ruins. But there was never any draw there for my parents. No real evidence of a site big enough to excavate. Why would Mom go there?

I shook my head. "She lies. Or her father does. They only want me gone, out from between her and Marcello."

Lia grunted. "Clever."

"Clever doesn't begin to cover it," I said. Gently, I eased myself down to my good side and lay down as Lia pulled the covers over me. "These people have been planning on this union between the house of Forelli and the house of Rossi since Marcello and Romana were children."

"Seriously?"

"Seriously."

She had her arms folded and was pacing, a sure sign that she was all riled up. I wished I had the energy to calm her. But she was going to want to talk. I could feel it. And I didn't know how long I could stay awake to listen.

"Gabi," she said, kneeling beside me.

"Yeah?"

"I've been thinking."

"No good can come of that," I said dismissively, closing my eyes.

"No, really. I was thinking. Well, it's not really right of me to get in the way. To demand you leave here. Leave Marcello. Not if you think this might be where your heart is leading."

"My heart is leading me home," I said, drilling my eyes into hers. I didn't need her doubt. I had enough of my own to deal with.

She sighed in relief but still looked confused. "But you said—"

"Forget what I said. Tomorrow, you pull the stitches from my side. We'll be on our way the following day."

Her eyes became as cloudy as the Caribbean on a stormy day. She shook her head. "I do not know if I can pull them out," she said forlornly.

"Then I shall get Cook or Fortino or someone else," I bit out, more sharply than I intended. I sighed heavily. "Please, can we let this go now, Lia? I'm wiped."

Really, it seemed to take everything in me to draw my next breath, and then the next. I went to sleep feeling like I didn't really care if I woke up. It was just too hard…so hard…

CHAPTER 23

I knew if I didn't do it right away, I'd never be able to endure it later. And the stitches had to be out, the bleeding mostly stopped, before we went home. There would be no explaining them, back in our own century. So as soon as Lia awakened the next morning, I said, "We need to do it now."

She rose and stared at me, brows arched. "I can't do it, Gabi. I can't. It's one thing to operate on you when you're almost dead." She shook her head once, "Another to do it when you're...well, alive."

I rolled my eyes and turned to my back. "The kitchens will be full of alcohol, with all this feasting business. Grab a jug of grappa. I'll drink until I won't feel anything, I promise. Bring Cook's sharpest knife; we'll put it in the fire. You might need to cauterize the wound."

"Cauterize?"

I groaned. "Burn me! If I start bleeding. It's the fastest way."

She blanched and shook her head.

"Lia, if you want to go home...."

"I do! But I can't do it, Gabi," she said. "I can't." I could see in her face that the idea of bringing me more pain, of touching the wound itself, was bringing back all kinds of memories she wasn't ready to deal with.

I groaned, totally exasperated. "Go. Go and fetch Fortino. And Luca, if you can find him. But not Marcello." I needed to steer clear of the man as much as possible. Being with him only made me feel… confused.

She nodded, fast, threw on a day dress, pulled her hair into a quick knot—oh for the ease of her long, straight hair!—and was out the door in minutes. I rose, went to relieve myself in the chamber pot, washed my face and hands, and then lifted my gown to see the wound.

It was still swollen and red and angry, barely knit together again, yet the skin was growing around each strand. Already, I knew the pain ahead might be enough to knock me out.

Feeling sick to my stomach, I let the gown fall back to the floor and padded over to the bed and with some effort, pulled up a blanket. A few minutes later, I saw the latch move on the door and she was inside, but she wasn't alone. Sheepishly, she looked over her shoulder and raised her eyebrows.

Marcello.

He strode in, staying on the edge of the room, far from me. "M'lady, your sister has brought me troubling news."

"Oh?" I asked lightly, shooting Lia an arrow glance.

"She says that you intend to have your bindings out this day. Might we not wait another day? I have sent for the finest of Sienese physicians, and he will see to your care."

"Nay. I believe they must come out today. To tarry a day will only bring me an extra measure of pain."

He frowned. "Are you certain?" He hesitated, running a hand through his hair and then gesturing toward me. "I've seen my share of such gashes. Might I examine your sutures?"

I glanced at Lia, then back at him. "All right," I said tiredly. "Allow my sister to situate me."

He nodded and turned his back. I pushed down the covers, and Lia brought my gown up, to my chest, leaving my side exposed. She covered my lower hip, thigh, and legs with the blanket again and then coughed. Marcello turned slowly. To his credit, he moved without hesitation to my side, looking at my wound with all the detachment of an ER doc on a TV show.

"You see?" I asked.

"It could be another day or two," he said. "Wait until after the feast. The skin is not yet fused—"

"I want them out, Marcello," I said lowly, inviting no argument. "To spend the next few days, thinking about it…" And I had to be able to move, immediately, to the tomb, if we had to. If my mom saw those things, those massive stitches, she'd freak. She'd freak enough over the wound itself.

"Let me send a messenger to tell the physician it's urgent. He can be here this night."

"Nay," I said, grabbing his hand. "Take them out yourself. Fast. You can do it. You have a steady hand."

His lush lips fell open a bit, then clamped shut. "Nay, I cannot," he whispered, kneeling beside me and touching my forehead, ignoring Lia. "I cannot do such a thing—bring you pain."

"Then bring me a knife, and I'll do it myself."

He sighed heavily as he stared at me. "Nay. You shall wait for my physician."

A maid arrived then, casting her eyes hurriedly from me, with my bare waist, and Marcello close beside me, to the table. She set a pail of steaming water, a knife and bandages there, bobbed a curtsy to Lia and fled.

I glanced up to the ceiling and sighed. "Fetch *Fortino,*" I said to Lia. She turned and left the room immediately, probably glad to escape the tension between us as much as the maid before her.

Marcello looked at me, hard, then. "He won't do this for you."

"Yes, he will. After all I've done for him, he will do this for me."

"Why must you be so stubborn?" he cried, rising fast and flinging out his hands toward me. "What is the matter with you? Why must this be done now? The feast is upon us. Where will you be? In here, in agonizing pain!"

"Trust me," I said, looking away from him. "I know it is time." *It'd be good, if I couldn't go to the feast tonight. I'd have a legitimate excuse.*

He paced, beginning to speak, thinking better of it and stopping, time and time again.

Soon, thankfully, Fortino arrived. Seeing my bare waist, his eyes moved to the wall. "M'lady?"

"Lord Fortino," I said, waiting until he dragged his eyes to meet mine, carefully hopping over my exposed skin. "I need you to remove my stitches."

He frowned. "The physician—"

"Will not arrive until the morrow. I need them out now."

He swallowed, visibly, and then looked into my eyes. "I will do as you have asked me," he said. He moved to the pail and the knife, then to our tiny fire to place the blade in the coals.

"Fortino!" Marcello barked.

But Fortino shook his head at his brother. "She knows what she needs, Marcello. Hold her hand."

Marcello paced twice more, then reached for a small flask on the table, uncorked it, and brought it over to me. "Take a long drink of this," he said, begging me with his big, brown eyes. I turned obediently and took a long swig, then another, ignoring how the liquid burned all the way down my throat and inside my gut. He took the bottle from my hand and poured a liberal amount on my wound, making me gasp for breath at the sting and burn. Then he took my hand in his, clasping it as if we were about to arm wrestle. Not that I was any match for him; I was already weak with fear.

"Clip each loop," he said to his brother. "Then move quickly, pulling the threads out. That will be the worst part."

He spoke as if he had gone through this before. I stared into his eyes. Where were his wounds? Evidence of his own stitches, long removed and healed. On his back? His thigh? Thoughts of scars, purple and healed, gave me strange comfort. If he could do it, so could I.

I winced when Fortino cut the first loop. There were about eighteen, in total. Staring into Marcello's eyes, I found strength in them. I thought of having but a minute left with him, forever, and how I'd want every second I had, regardless of the pain. He stared at me, seeming to count in his head too. It was then that Fortino paused, and I knew what was to come.

"Fast," I panted, my heart racing. "Fortino, don't stop, no matter what happens. Just get them out." I turned and eyed him. "Understood?"

He nodded once, his eyes still on the threads, now crazy white snippets rising from my side like a sad, sparse, white patch of grass.

I turned away and saw that Luca had arrived. Lia brought her fist to her mouth, staring at me. Luca reached out for her, and in spite of her hesitations, she turned into his chest, clearly wishing not to see what would come next. He wrapped a hand around her head and stared hard in my direction.

"You hold on to me," Marcello said, drawing my attention again.

"Do it," I said to Fortino, still staring at Marcello.

I was able to hold my tongue through the first two. He moved so fast, my mind barely had time to capture what was bringing me the searing pain, even though I knew what was to come. But then my brain caught up and I started to whine with the third and fourth, wail with the fifth.

By the time he reached the sixth, I was in a full-fledged scream, biting into my blanket to muffle the noise, no longer able to look into Marcello's eyes and be the strong heroine. It was about the thirteenth that I passed out instead of throwing up, giving in to the blessed, black tunnel that closed in around me.

I awakened to the smell of burning flesh. It took me a moment to feel the fresh pain in my side and realize that they had taken up my idea and cauterized the wound in a couple of places where the skin threatened to spring loose. *Thank God I was out for that,* I thought. The aftermath was pain enough to deal with.

I opened my eyes, fearful that he had gone, but he was still beside me, holding my hand, tenderly now, not in the death grip of a soldier about to lose a comrade-in-arms.

"Thank you," I mumbled. Luca and Lia and Fortino were behind him, all anxiously watching me. They seemed to take a collective breath when they heard me speak.

"Take another sip of this," he said, lifting a cup so that I could take another drink of the clear liquid. It floated down my throat, not so hot this time. Without asking, he gave me another. I felt the fog of the alcohol descend, giving me a slight reprieve. Not from the pain, but from caring about the pain.

"The castle is in an uproar," he said lowly, wiping my forehead of the beads of sweat with a cool cloth.

"They heard me screaming?"

He gave me a small nod. "I must take my leave," he added sorrowfully.

"She'll want to know what's transpired," I said. "Tell her I had to have them out. So I could be off. To Pistoia."

"To Pistoia?" he asked, frowning.

"She'll know what I mean," I said.

"You cannot go to Pistoia. 'Tis deep into Fiorentini lands and—"

"And we shall not truly go there. Just tell Romana that, all right? For me? Trust me?"

He hesitated. "But you are not leaving now, Gabriella. Right? Not for days, yet. You need to remain still. Allow your skin to heal. Be tended to."

I dragged my eyes open. "I know. Go, Marcello. You and Fortino. Go and see to your guests. Leave me to Lia."

"Are you certain?" he asked, tracing the pad of his thumb over my brows.

"Never more so."

CHAPTER 24

Blessedly, I slept the whole day and through the night, waking only a couple of times when I dared to move. In those instances, my eyes shot open, and I gasped for breath.

Lia was still mad at me, come morning. "You did it so you wouldn't have to face them at the feast. Any of them," Lia said. Her tone was half-jealous, half-accusatory.

I didn't turn over to look at her. I couldn't if I'd wanted to. My flesh was on fire. There was no use arguing. She was mad. Hurt, over something. "What happened?"

I could hear her rustle out from under her covers. "It was awful. Figuring out what to say…what not to say, when everyone's looking at you." She groaned. "We need to get out of here, Gabs. We risk being found out with every hour we're here."

"Did you stick to the rules?" I asked. I closed my eyes, steeling myself for what was to come. I had to move. To pee, if nothing else.

"As best I could," she said. But she didn't sound too sure. We'd agreed to say little about our parents, so we wouldn't have to spin larger lies than necessary. To say little of home at all.

"There was one dude who'd been to Normandy." She paused to sneeze. "He kept asking me about families I might know. Of course, I didn't."

"How'd you get out of that?"

"I started talking about the night Castello Paratore fell, and the men took over from there."

I smiled. Smart of her.

"They're putting on all sorts of games today, in the courtyard. Jousting. Sword fights. The whole knight-gig, you know? Oh, and get this, an archery exhibition too, for which yours truly is to be the star attraction."

"That's great," I said.

Her brow furrowed. "When are we going?" she said.

"One more day, Lia. I think tomorrow, I might be able to move."

"Tomorrow the feast is over. And Marcello and Fortino are totally bringing you to watch the games today, even if you have to be carried in on your bed."

"Seriously?"

"Seriously."

I groaned. She was right, of course. On some level, I had hoped that pulling the stitches, and the subsequent recovery, would keep me out of the mix. "Why can't they just use this excuse? Leave me here?" I shook my head, feeling the straw beneath my cheek crackle.

Did Marcello not see? The less we were together, the better.

"He's not going to let you out of here without him," Lia said.

I closed my eyes, thinking of the pain of saying good-bye to him, as well as the pain of lying to him any longer. There was just no good way out. No simple way out.

I shoved myself upward then, barely stifling my scream. It was animal-like, I admitted to myself. And Lia was immediately beside me.

"That bad?"

"That bad."

She carefully pulled up the edge of the old white shirt I had slept in, and peered at my side. I couldn't bear to look. She shuddered and quickly let the light silk fabric fall. "Better than yesterday, but not good. You are a walking infection waitin' to happen. We gotta go home, Gabs. Fast."

"Maybe tomorrow," I said.

"If these people discover holes in our story, we might go from being the belles of the ball to the bombs. You should see 'em, Gabs. Most of them look at me like I'm some sort of celebrity. But there are some that look at me suspiciously. Like they want to take me down. Like that Romana chick. She has some serious issues."

"I can't ride a horse today, Lia. It already feels like my side is about to rip loose. That'd do it for sure."

"What if I found a wagon? Something you could lie down in?"

"Not today," I said, ending the debate. I lifted my hand to my head. I was sweating—just from the effort of sitting. It was going to take everything in me to squat and go to the bathroom, and she wanted me to travel?

To her credit, she didn't leave me then. Usually, when we got into arguments, she'd run away, go someplace to be alone. But then,

I supposed she thought it worse outside our room's walls than inside them.

Far more dangerous. Far more conflict.

As she thought he might, Marcello appeared after we finished lunch in the privacy of our quarters. He hovered in the doorway, shifting his eyes about the room as if ill at ease. "M'lady, how does the day find you?"

"As well as can be expected," I said, looking away, embarrassed at the memory of my desperation the day before.

"I have brought the physician," he said. I looked back, and he stood sideways to allow a small man to enter. "Dr. Macchione, these are the Ladies Betarrini."

The man nodded, but said nothing, just strode over to me. He peered at me with narrowed eyes as if he couldn't see properly. "May I examine your wound, m'lady?"

Slowly, I lifted my shirt to expose my side, praying there was no infection. My worst fear was that the man would want to put leeches on me, or maggots in the wound to eat away at dying flesh. They did that sometimes. Really. I'd heard all about it from Cook. Totally disgusting.

He lifted his head and looked at Lia. "You stitched her back together, m'lady?"

"I did," Lia said.

"Where did you learn such prowess?"

I looked away from her, not wanting her to see the grin in my eyes. Because the nearest answer was elementary school projects with Grammy. She mumbled something about watching a doctor in our own land do the same, and after a moment's hesitation, he nodded. He stood again, this time moving to the head of the bed to examine my eyes, tongue, and then the beds of my fingernails. Looking for what? Signs of fever, infection, dehydration? Oh, or that body humours thing? I was surprised when he didn't ask for a urine sample. Apparently, they figured out a lot by the odor, appearance—even taste—of a person's urine.

"You are faring far better than I expected," he said at last. "I will leave you a bottle of tonic, which should ease the pain a bit." He bent and pulled a clay bottle from his bag. "Take a mouthful now."

"What is it?"

The little doctor frowned and looked back at Marcello.

"Gabriella, this man is one of the finest physicians in all of Siena," he said, looking as if I was embarrassing him. "He has long tended Romana's own family."

Oh, great. I see what you're saying. If the dude is good enough for ROMANA, then he's certainly more than okay for me, right?

I barely kept myself from rolling my eyes as I reached for the bottle. I took a swig and nearly gagged at the foul, grasslike taste in my mouth, forcing myself to swallow. It burned all the way down my throat. The little doctor went back to his bag and rifled through twenty ton of parchment packets, pulling one out. He carefully unfolded the parchment and took a pinch of the powder. "This may hurt a bit, but it will guard against infection."

"What is that?"

His small eyes narrowed in my direction, as if to say, Who are *you* to keep questioning *me?* No doubt Marcello had been true to his word and summoned only the best from Siena. But we were in the middle of 1342. I had a right to know what the man was putting on me, even if I had just swallowed some unknown tonic.

"Lady Gabriella has some prowess in the healing arts," Marcello interceded.

The doctor sniffed. "It is my own blend of powders, a secret recipe," he said.

I studied him. "All right," I said, bracing myself for the pain.

But when he sprinkled it on my wound, I didn't feel anything. My eyes widened. For the first time since I got injured, I didn't feel anything at all. I was numb from the chest down. It was a little disconcerting. But mostly, it was a relief. I took a deep breath, my first in days.

Gradually, I figured out that it hadn't been what he'd sprinkled on top of me; it had been the tonic.

"Please, Dr. Macchione. I am most curious. What was in that tonic?"

"I cannot tell," he said with a wink. "One doesn't become the finest physician in Siena if one shares all his secrets, right?" He placed his envelope back in his bag and then looked at me. "It is easing your pain?"

"You could say that."

He smiled an eensy smile, just a half second of a tiny upturning of his thin lips. "I shall be within reach, m'lady. You only need summon me. I shall return this evening to administer more medicine to your wound."

"Thank you," I said, watching him scurry past Marcello and out the door.

Marcello looked back at me with a grin. "Fortino and I would be in your debt if you would allow us to bring you out to the games. The people—" He paused to look over his shoulder, as if he could see through the stones—"they shall not rest until they lay eyes upon you. There is much concern over the wounded she-wolf."

"Oh, m'lord, I do not know if I can bear it," I said. Though seeing him here made me want to watch him out in the games. To see him wield a sword one more time. Do his man thing. So I could remember, when I got home. Maybe I could even get Lia to sketch him.

He took a step into the room, lifting a hand as if beseeching me. "We'll carry you in. You'll watch, like Cleopatra, lounging upon her settee."

I lifted a brow. "That would be quite dramatic."

"Evangelia has agreed to give a demonstration of her archery skills," he said, looking to my sister.

"I hardly had a choice," she said, raising her hands.

"Nay," Marcello said with a smile. "Indeed, I believe it will be the most interesting part of the games. Everyone is dying to best her."

I smiled then, too. "I must attend, then. But only if I may wager a small fortune before the event takes place."

His smile grew wider—because I agreed to go? Or because of my dare? "You shall have a difficult time finding takers. Most want to place their hopes on Evangelia's shoulders."

"Except one," she said, meeting his eyes.

"Pay Lord Foraboschi no mind," he said. But I think we both noticed his smile disappear. "He has long been the champion when it comes to archery. He needs to learn how to gracefully abdicate his position when faced with a more skilled challenger."

I flicked my eyes in Lia's direction. She was nervous.

Lord Foraboschi. The creepy, tall guy who hung out with Romana and her entourage. The guy who shot our prisoners while they were tied up. I shuddered involuntarily. But Marcello had looked away, dismissing my concern. "Your days of fear are over. There are only friends among us. Loyal Sienese."

I glanced at Lia again. She clearly didn't agree with him.

"You will attend?" Marcello asked, his eyes on me. It was more of a command than a question. And I felt powerless to say anything but yes.

Light filled his eyes, and he dared to finally cross the room to my side. "I'll send servants in an hour for you. There will be shade, and if you grow weary, simply lift this," he said, pulling a handkerchief from his pocket, "and I'll have you returned to your room immediately." Staring down at me, he rubbed the side of my cheek with the back of his hand.

I nodded, breaking our intense gaze, and then closed my eyes as if falling asleep again.

He started, as if shocked out of his reverie, and turned to go. "The gown?" he whispered to Lia.

"I shall attempt to get it on her," she said. "But I make no promises, m'lord."

He left then, without another word, and I opened my eyes to look at Lia. She was staring at me, chin in hand, shaking her head. She came over to my bed and sat on the edge. "It can't happen," she whispered, looking over my shoulder to the doorway and back. "You realize that, right?"

"Yes," I said, more forlornly than I intended. But I was feeling free, unbound. Maybe it was the medicine. "You'll need to help me remember. Help me memorize Marcello, the kind of man he is. Because I want to find someone like him in our time."

Tears rolled down my cheeks, and I choked, unable to say another word. Maybe the medicine was whacking me out. It was like I had no control over my emotions.

She took my hand and squeezed it. "I'll help you, Gabi. It'll be okay. You're only seventeen. You have your whole life ahead of you." She reached out to stroke my face and tuck a tendril of hair behind my ear. "You'll see. It'll be okay." She rose and pulled my gown from the trunk, shaking it out.

But all I could think of was her hand on my face and how it reminded me of Marcello's touch.

And how I longed for him to touch me again.

CHAPTER 25

The servants came and prepared us like brides on our wedding day, weaving pearls and flowers into our hair. They'd rebound my wound in order to slide the underdress over my shoulders and hips, then the gown on top of it. Blessedly, the pain medicine continued to work. I could wiggle my toes, which kept the panic over paralysis at bay, and I was no longer numb. I wondered if that tonic was a fourteenth-century version of morphine. Whatever it was, I was just glad it was available. *Thank You, thank You, God, that the doctor came.*

Was that the second real prayer I'd ever whispered?

Wouldn't that be an interesting payout, I thought. *I fly through time and come back with some sort of religion.*

It seemed flimsy, a lame second prize to staying with Marcello and living happily ever after, but it was all I had at the moment, and it was something.

Lia was looking at me strangely when the maids stepped away.

"What?"

"Man, Gabi, you are gorgeous."

"That's a good thing, right?"

"Not when there's a chick out there," she said, hooking her thumb over her shoulder, "barely able to keep from clawing your eyes out."

"Never mind about her," I said, laughing under my breath. "Tell me about Lord Foraboschi." She'd said something earlier that had been niggling at me, and I needed to know what was at the heart of it.

She shifted and played with the toe of her tapestry slipper. For the first time that day, I noticed how amazing she looked too. Cinderella would've killed to look like my sister in that moment. "Lia—"

"I couldn't help it." She lifted her big, blue eyes and stared at me.

"What? What'd you do?"

"He was taunting me. Saying that I probably hit the knights in Castello Paratore by accident—that I was aiming in another direction."

"And?"

"I—I started to cry. It was either that or draw my arrow and split his head open, I swear. And then Luca figured out what had upset me and started to get all angry and belted Lord Foraboschi—"

"Oh no," I said with a heavy sigh. "And what did Lord Foraboschi do?"

She rose and paced back and forth. "I think he's a little afraid of Luca. He pretended to go after him, but only when he was really sure that others would stop him." She shook her head. "I don't like the way he looks at me. It's like he knows. Or he's trying to figure me out, figure out how he can bring me down."

"Don't let him get to you," I said.

She hesitated.

"What?" I said.

She licked her lips. "I saw him, earlier. He was whispering in Lord Rossi's ear. He ate lunch beside Romana. He's more than friends with them. He's *close* to them."

I considered that. "Well, it makes sense. He was here with Romana when I first arrived, almost like a guardian or something. Look, until we get out of here, we're going to run into many who feel loyal to the Rossis." I shrugged. "It's only natural, really. They want to see this relationship with Castello Forelli secured, once and for all. Some will want to see Romana to her own, promised happy ending. If I'm in the way, I'm going to be seen as the enemy. And you, as my sister, are one too."

"We should've just gone when—"

"We're here. Let's see it through. Maybe with this pain medicine…maybe there will be an opportunity to escape tonight. With all the comings and goings of the feast, you know."

Her eyes filled with hope. And then fear for me.

"Let's just see," I said, waving down her excitement. "Let's get through the games and see. But Lia, you can't win today." I looked at her, hard. "Let Lord Foraboschi win. It's not worth it, inviting his wrath."

She frowned, struggling with that idea. She was such a weird combination of free-spirited artist and fierce competitor. But only when it came to archery. She'd never let me beat her in archery, even back when we were little and I could really challenge her. Maybe it was the precision thing, like placing just the right stroke with a brush loaded with oil paint. She liked to do that right on the first try too.

"Lia…"

"He really is a pompous, egotistical jerk."

"I agree. There are nicer guys on the planet, but is it worth making this deal more complicated? Don't you think it's already complicated enough, without you taking him on?"

She hesitated.

"Well, think it over," I said, pretty much giving up at that point. "Why risk it? This isn't a historic event anyway, right?"

"Right," she said. But her tone said she still wasn't in agreement with me about throwing the match.

A knock sounded at our door, and then a male servant peeked in. "M'lady," he said. "We're here to escort you to the games."

"Come in," I said, waving him forward. Another came with him.

"Can you walk? Or shall we carry you to your carriage?"

"Let me try and rise," I said, taking hold of each of their arms. But when I came to my feet, my knees crumpled beneath me and I felt a wave of nausea. From the pain? Or was it the medicine?

Luckily, the men had a firm grip on me and carried me on my bed to the hallway, with Lia right behind us. "You okay?" she whispered to me.

"I think so," I said. I lifted my hand to my head. A wave of dizziness was there, then gone.

The little doctor appeared. Why hadn't I noticed him before? "M'lady, are you certain this will not overly tax you?"

I was sitting there, suspended in the air on a bed. It was all I could do not to laugh. "I think not," I managed to say.

"Well then, here is another dose of pain medicine," he said, handing me the bottle.

I gladly took a swig, ignoring the unpleasant taste of grass and fertilizer sailing down my throat. If it would continue to keep that horrendous pain at bay, I was game. I settled back down to a pile of pillows and waved the servants onward, indeed feeling a bit like Cleopatra, lounging upon her settee. All I needed was for them to cover the wood in gold leaf and for a couple of the guys to whip out giant palm branches and fan me.

We went out to the courtyard, and I was a bit shocked at the hundreds of people that lined the edge, all sitting in chairs and beneath tented roofs, shielding themselves from the sun. Marcello smiled and strode over to us, Luca and Fortino at his side, as the servants set me on a platform.

The crowd hushed as Marcello took my hand, bowed and kissed it, then Fortino did the same, still holding it as he turned back toward the courtyard. I caught sight of Lord Forelli, looking befuddled and a little irritated, but with far more color than when I had last seen him. Beside him sat Lord Rossi and Romana. I dared not look to see where Marcello had moved. They all watched my every move.

Fortino turned toward Lia and urged her to his other side, so he could hold both our hands.

"Ladies and gentlemen," called Fortino. "I present at last, the two warriors that turned the tide for Siena, the Ladies Betarrini."

I had expected a cheer, applause, shouting. But what happened next was something I'd never forget.

Every man, woman, and child stood, and as one they bowed or curtsied, as if we were royalty before them. It was deathly quiet, and in the hush, a wave of honor swept over me. I was overwhelmed. I glanced at Lia, who looked like she was feeling the same, lifting a hand to her lips.

Slowly, everyone stood again, and then I saw that they all had flowers in their hands. They paraded past us then, setting their roses and day lilies and daisies at our feet, bowing and nodding with smiles of appreciation. In those precious minutes, I was swept up into the glory of it, all the more glad that we had been there that night, right when Marcello and Luca and the rest needed us most. Maybe we had given them a few more years of health and prosperity, something to lean on in the hard years to come.

When they had finished, the crowd disappeared, back to their seats, but the Nine stood in the center. "Ladies Betarrini," said Lord Rossi. "Siena is forever in your debt. Whatever you need, whenever you need it, ask it of us and it shall be yours."

"Thank you, Lord Rossi," I said. "We did only what your own daughters would have done, had they been in our places. And we would do it again, to serve Siena."

He smiled and raised a goblet in the air. "Well said, m'lady. With that, I declare these games officially begun." And then he rammed the goblet down, and it shattered into a thousand pieces across the cobblestones.

The crowd cheered, and the Nine returned to their seats as the jousting line was erected.

We watched through twelve grueling rounds of jousting, wincing whenever the lance struck a man. Several somersaulted over the backs of their horses, sending the crowd into a riot of laughter and shouts. One jouster's lance broke, but his opponent remained seated. I could barely watch it, knowing that every strike, regardless of the armor, would have to mean broken ribs and, potentially, internal injuries. How many of these men would languish, even die in the coming days?

But then Marcello entered the courtyard on his steed, his golden colors flying. He rode over to Lady Rossi, and she rose and prettily handed him her lace handkerchief, which he took and sniffed in ecstasy, as if inhaling her perfume—much to the delight of the crowd.

Marcello, to his credit, never looked my way, never gave the crowd any cause to wonder if there was competition for his heart. He appeared to ride for her alone. But as he lowered his helmet, I saw his eyes slide over to me for but a half second. I smiled. Too late? Too late to give him encouragement? To ride his best? To know that I understood his predicament? His place?

His eyes were set dead ahead then, studying no one else but his opponent.

"Tell me when it is over," I whispered to Lia, feeling another wave of nausea. The flag came down, the riders urged their horses into a gallop, and I closed my eyes.

The horses' hooves clattered over the cobblestones through the layer of dirt and hay that had been hauled in. I visualized their churning legs, necks outstretched, the clash to come any second—

And then I heard it. Impact. The crowd cheered. I peeked up and took half a breath when I saw Marcello still on his horse. He was looking to Romana, and I looked there too. But she was staring at me, eyes wide and then narrowing in suspicion. Would I ever manage to cover my feelings? Clearly, I was about as subtle as a billboard. I looked over to Lia.

"A cup of water," I croaked, lifting a hand to my head as another bout of dizziness passed through me.

She rose and then hesitated.

I dragged my eyes to look where she did.

Marcello had paused before me, still astride his horse, helmet off, hair blowing about in the breeze. "M'lady, are you ailing?" he asked, his brows furrowed in concern.

"Not now that I know you are victor, m'lord," I said, so quietly that only he would hear.

But then I heard the whispering begin, the medieval version of *telephone*. I knew my words would be passed around the circle of spectators within moments.

Blessedly, the archery round was announced.

"Lift your handkerchief if you are in need of an escape," Marcello said, repeating our earlier agreement, then trotted off to the end of the courtyard.

Lia was there then with my water, and I drank from the pottery goblet, glad to have something to do. I felt the heavy gaze of the crowd, assessing, wondering. Marcello had paid homage to his bride-to-be, but in the end, as victor, it was me he had gone to. I cursed my sick stomach. If only I'd kept calm, had not shifted, I might not have caught his eye....

"Lia, fetch me a bit of bread, would you?" I whispered.

"I'll send some back," she whispered, looking at me meaningfully. "I'm on deck."

I followed her glance to the ring, where ten targets were set up. When Lia rose, the crowd went berserk, cheering, beside themselves to see her in action. Lord Foraboschi rose from Romana's side, bent, whispered something in her ear, then left her. In the gap he left, I spotted the doctor, but when I caught his eye, he moved away, as if not wishing to be seen. I frowned, puzzling over that.

Such an odd little man.

"Do you fear for your sister?" Luca said, sitting beside me. He handed me a plate of bread, cheese, and grapes. "She sent you this."

"You are her servant now?" I asked wryly.

"In every way." He sighed. "The lady has captured my heart. Now she'll capture everyone else's, and I'll have no hope to compete for her. Here, take my hand," he said, reaching for my right. "Mayhap it shall make her terribly jealous."

I smiled. He was so melodramatic. And totally charming. I couldn't believe Lia hadn't fallen for him, too. She usually liked the guys who made her laugh.

It was just as well, I thought with a sigh. Then we'd both be torn. I watched as Marcello took his seat beside Romana again, covering her hand with his. I shoved a piece of bread into my mouth, forcing myself to chew and swallow. The medicine was probably hard on my tummy. If I had taken it in modern times, it'd probably come with the take-it-with-food warning.

The targets were set out, and when Lia reached for an arrow in the quiver on her back, the crowd again went nuts. I smiled as they drew their arrows, pulled, and let them fly at the master's count. All struck within the first two rings of their targets, Lia's dead center. The crowd applauded, and the archers counted out ten more paces, and again let arrows fly. All again were within the first two rings of the center.

I saw Lord Foraboschi lean over and say something to Lia. She paused, and I felt Luca's hand tighten over mine. Then Lord

Foraboschi turned and smirked in our direction. The skin beneath one eye was slightly purple where Luca had decked him.

"Luca, remain where you are," I cautioned, holding on to him. "She'll see this to its best conclusion."

He said nothing, so uncharacteristic of him that I fretted over it. I hoped Lord Foraboschi wouldn't dare to say anything more to Lia. She'd never let him win if he continued to goad her.

The archers walked ten more paces, let arrows fly, and three of them were eliminated, trudging out of the courtyard in defeat.

With seven left, pigeons were released, all painted in colors that matched the archer's arrow tips. They had to find their targets and bring them down. Lia let one arrow fly, and it missed the bird, but she was already taking aim again and, with the second arrow, brought the creature down just before it escaped over the wall.

The crowd exploded in shouts and laughter and excitement again. Only four had managed to come this far. I wondered for a moment if the emotions of killing a bird would slow her down, but with one look at her face, I knew we were sunk. She wasn't going to let Lord Foraboschi win.

I groaned.

"What is it?" Luca asked, leaning toward me. "She's doing as well as we knew she would."

"Nothing. Never mind," I said, shaking my head. I shoved another bite of bread into my mouth, chewed, and swallowed, feeling a pang in my gut and another wave of nausea. What would happen if she was the victor? Would it make Lord Foraboschi more of a lethal threat to us? It was all so dang complicated. His relationship with the Rossis, their relationship with the Forellis…

The games master was calling out the next challenge. Men on the allures above us were carrying hay bales bound to a leather shield. They would appear in random places. The first archer to stick five of them would be declared the victor.

"No," Luca grumbled. "Of all the thoughtless, crass decisions..."

I bit my lip. It was too much like Castello Paratore. Too much like that night. Would Lia again dissolve into tears? The others drew arrows across their bows. Two looked at Lia with concern, as if guessing at what might have given her pause. The games master shouted his count, and arrows began flying. Lord Foraboschi struck one, turned toward Lia and smirked. She tilted her chin in defiance before he turned and fired again, hitting the second. I gripped Luca's hand, hard again.

The crowd hushed, watching the drama play out before them like a silent movie. Lia was staring after Lord Foraboschi, who was aiming at a third moving target, narrowly missing it. Then as if snapping out of her stupor, she suddenly sprang into action, on the move, drawing once, twice, thrice, hitting three targets in quick succession.

Men shouted. Women shrieked. But I knew Lia heard nothing, acting as she had at the castle that fateful night—on instinct. Lord Foraboschi frowned and held a hand out to her, as if complaining about her method, but Lia took her fourth and fifth targets down before he had a chance to bring his hand back to his own bow.

Children ran out and surrounded her, arms up, dancing. The crowd followed, lifting her to their shoulders. Luca laughed and rose, clapping.

When she was turned toward me, her concentrated expression disappeared and an apologetic look replaced it, as if to say, *Sorry! Couldn't help it!*

I sighed and smiled.

After all, a girl's gotta do what a girl's gotta do.

CHAPTER 26

The games went on for another couple of hours, but Evangelia's clear and dramatic victory was really the Big Deal. As things wrapped up with a pretty speech from Fortino, again honoring me and my sister, I tried to beg off, eager to return to my room to try and sleep. *Perhaps with sleep this gut ache will go away....*

But the people wouldn't hear of it. I was carried on my lounge into the Great Hall and deposited in the center of the dais. A goblet of wine was thrust into my hand, and a plate of grapes set beside me. Evangelia hovered nearby but was constantly drawn into conversations and introductions. Romana, to her credit, ventured near and gave me a pretty curtsy.

"No doubt you would've given the swordsmen an apt challenger, just as your sister has done, were you not ailing."

I dismissed her praise. "Evangelia has always been a far better archer than I have ever been at swordplay." I gestured down at my side. "Witness the results of my last challenge."

The doctor was there then, with us. "How is your pain, m'lady?"

He bent and took my wrist in his small hand, feeling for my pulse.

"The medicine seems to be keeping the pain at bay," I said. I noticed then, the beginning tinge of its return. I gestured for him to lean closer. "It is my belly, Doctor. I think the medicine is upsetting my stomach."

He frowned and rose, sniffing as if perturbed by my second-guessing. "Impossible. I've never had a patient who had such a reaction. Have you been eating?"

"Some."

"Clearly, not enough. Do you have pain now?"

"Just a bit," I said, trying to process his reaction. Why was he so defensive? Because I was younger? A woman? Questioning him?

"Take another dose now," he said, handing me the clay flask. "Another at bedtime, and so on." He reached into his bag and pulled out the small packet of powder he'd sprinkled on my wound earlier. "Tonight, before bed, have your sister administer some of this, and sleep with it open, to the air."

I nodded, puzzled. It sounded as if he was leaving. Had he not intended to remain nearby? Promised to be available?

"I must be off. I'm to visit another family not far from here, by nightfall." He gave me a stern look. "You will take your medications as instructed?"

"Yes, Doctor," I said. A part of me was glad. He was weird. He made me nervous. I could take my medicine, with or without him there.

He waited, and I realized he wanted to see me take my next dose in front of him. Obediently, I took a swig, making it look like a bigger mouthful than it was.

Satisfied, he nodded once and moved out through the crowd. By the door, I saw him stop to speak with Lord Foraboschi, receive something and pocket it, then exit through the tall doors. Had it been the Rossis' pull, their demand that set him on to a new patient, leaving me behind?

I shoved the idea out of my mind and lifted my gaze to the room.

My attention was drawn by a woman in a fine tapestry gown, her hair in an elaborate headdress, as she stopped in the center of the room. The crowd took their seats, and wine was passed around. The woman folded her hands, held them slightly away from her body, and began to sing without accompaniment, perfectly on pitch.

Her words were in Latin, but her voice and expression could be understood in any language. She sang of love, loss, victory. She captured the attention of everyone in the room. When her last note rose and rose and rose, a shiver ran down my neck. *If only I could sing like that…*

I wished I could turn and see Marcello, see how this singer affected him, but I could not. Marcello, Fortino, and most of the others were behind me, at the table with the Rossis and the other nobles. To turn and catch his eye then would've been seen by all.

And I was with Lia now. We had to be off, gone from here. Every hour we tarried only brought more angst.

I shifted, glad the small dose of medicine was dulling my pain, but again feeling a rolling wave of nausea come over me. My stomach twisted in a cramp, and I gasped, bringing my hand to my belly. Luckily, everyone at that moment was rising and cheering the singer, unaware of me for but a few seconds. I pulled my legs around and off the lounge, looking madly for Lia. I had to escape the hall—get to my room.

I bent over at the next pang that pulled my stomach in a knot. My heart was racing, faster and harder than I'd ever felt before. My lips parted. Had I not been robbed of breath, I might've screamed.

Cook was beside me in seconds, as was Lia. "M'lady?"

"I am ill," I ground out. "More than just my wound. I must return to my quarters—"

Another pang of pain strangled me.

"M'lady," Marcello said lowly, on my other side.

I looked up at him, desperate, frightened.

"She is ill," Cook said. "We must return her to her quarters."

"On her lounge," he said, waving several servants forward.

"Nay, now," I said, trying to come to my feet again. I was so afraid I was about to vomit, right there, in front of everyone. But then another stomach pain came, rolling through me, making me shudder.

Marcello frowned, bent, and swept me into his arms, careful to keep his hand from the wound at my side. Then he carried me out, the crowd dissolving into whispers behind hands. I couldn't help it. At the next wave of pain, I cried out, wincing and shutting my eyes, hoping it would soon be over.

Luca appeared before us, holding one door, Lia the other. I knew they followed us across the courtyard.

"Where is the physician?" Marcello ground out.

"He left," I said.

"Left? Departed?" He was incredulous.

I nodded.

His handsome face became stormy with anger. “He did not beg my leave.”

“He spoke with Lord Foraboschi. Perhaps he dismissed him. Oh!” I cried.

Marcello was practically running with me now. In short order, I was back in my quarters, in my bed. But I could not stay still. I was writhing in pain.

“It is the medicine,” I said, shaking my head, tears streaming down my cheeks. “I tried to tell the doctor it was helping the pain but making me nauseous.…”

Marcello eyed Cook, and she turned to wave a servant over. When he bent to speak with her, she whispered in his ear, and he was off.

Lia came to my side and took my hand in both of hers. “What can I do?”

“I don’t know,” I said, writhing, embarrassed, but helpless against the pain inside me.

“You have to remain still, Gabi. Your wound—”

“I know,” I said, writhing again, growing rigid, then lax. She was worried I’d rip my tender wound open. I was worried about it too.

But my bigger concern was that something much worse was transpiring inside. Infection? A reaction to the medicine?

Cook and Lia were apparently thinking the same thing. They pushed the men out the door, helped me out of my gown and into my short sleeping gown, then eased me to my side so they could look upon the scar. I glanced down, expecting the wound to be completely opened, oozing with infection. But it looked much as it had this morning, except for a tiny tear in the center, where my movements had pulled it open.

"Maybe it's inside," I said to Lia, then grunted through another wave of pain. They were getting stronger. "An infection. Deep down." But the frantic pace of my heart was scaring me more now. I couldn't get it to calm down. It was pounding so hard I thought that it might look like those old cartoons, with a heart-shaped pillar bouncing in and out of my chest.

The men burst through the door, my medicine flask in hand. Marcello's face was white. "She's been poisoned," Luca said lowly to Lia.

Marcello stared at me for a long moment, and for the first time, other than when he had confessed love for me, I saw a helpless expression upon his face.

"What? Poison? What is it?" I asked.

"Arsenic. Cloaked inside something else, we think," Marcello said. He came and knelt beside my bed, stroking my face. "I shall hunt him down, Gabriella. He shall pay for these crimes—after he tells me who paid him to do such a horrific thing."

He was making me a deathbed promise. Giving me something to cling to as I departed.

"There—" I coughed, winced, and then forced my eyes open again. "There is no antidote?"

His eyes, so wide and brown, grew even more forlorn. He shook his head, looking down in sorrow.

I looked over my shoulder to Lia. There had to be an antidote. I'd taken it too long ago to throw it up. There had to be another option. If only we could Google it…

We had to get out of here. Back to our own time. Immediately. It was the only thing that could save me.

"Lord Marcello, I must speak to you in private," Lia said, reading my mind.

"I am not leaving her," he said, staring at me.

"Then have them leave," I managed to say, my voice ragged.

He studied me, then raised his hand, clearing the room of servants. Cook was last to go, reluctantly closing the door behind her. Luca remained. "He is as close to me as Fortino. Say what you must before us both," Marcello said, pulling his eyes from me for but a second to look Lia in the eye.

She came around the bed and knelt beside me and Marcello. Luca hovered over his shoulder. "What I am about to tell you will be difficult to understand. We do not yet understand it ourselves."

I cried out, wondering if this was what it felt like to have a baby. Labor pains. My insides tearing. Was I already bleeding within? And added to that, was I about to have a full-on heart attack at seventeen?

"Three weeks past we came to you, through the tomb."

"Yes, yes, I know," Marcello said. "We remember it well."

"Nay," she said, reaching out to touch his arm, forcing him to look her in the eye. "We came from another time. The same place, but hundreds of years into the future. We came from that time, to you, here, *through* the tomb. It is some sort of portal."

His eyes grew large and his brow furrowed as he stared at her. "You are witches?" he asked, his tone incredulous. "Practitioners of some dark magic?"

"Nay," she said calmly. "Nothing but two girls who were transported through time—as if we walked through a doorway in error."

He rose, looking frightened and confused. "You speak of madness."

Luca stood beside him, arms folded, no trace of humor in his face.

Lia rose too as I cried out with another pang.

"I must get her home, Marcello. To our own time. She is dying here. You said yourself there is no antidote. But there, in the future, we have antidotes to nearly everything. If I can get her to Radda in Chianti in time…"

I winced, thinking of how far the Etruscan site was from any real sort of medical care, even in our own time. I cried out again, sounding pitiful, even to my own ears. When it was over, I gasped for breath as more tears rolled down my face.

Lia stepped forward and grabbed Marcello's tunic with both hands. "Do you love her? Do you love her as you have professed?" she demanded, all tough, trying to snap him out of his shock.

He stared down at me. I could feel his hot gaze but could not meet it. I was writhing again, shuddering as a wave of pain shook me from the center of my gut outward. The pace was increasing, the time between the pangs diminishing.

"Yes. God help me, I love her," he said angrily.

"Then save her," she said. "*Save* her. Help me get her to the tomb."

CHAPTER 27

Luca went running to the stables for horses. Cook and Fortino appeared in the doorway. "I am taking her to another doctor," Marcello lied, staring into my eyes as he stroked my sweating forehead. I was panting like a pregnant woman trying to bear through constant contractions. At least, like what I'd seen on TV. "She has taken a turn for the worse."

"Let me send a messenger," Fortino said. "Bring the physician here. We shall send our fastest rider."

"Nay," Marcello said. "She will not survive but another day. She has ingested arsenic. We must try and make it to Siena."

Fortino and Cook both brought hands to their mouths.

"Pray that we make it." He rose. "Please, return to the dining hall and spread word that all is well. Keep everyone at peace. And away from us."

"Lady Rossi," I panted.

"Leave Lady Rossi to me," he ground out, pulling aside my covers, and wincing as he saw the widening pool of blood upon the side of my gown. The wound had opened a full two inches, now oozing with each twist of my body.

Yeah, you're doing a number on yourself, I told myself. But I couldn't help it. I again grew rigid, holding my breath against the searing pain. And my heart was seriously going crazy.

"Pull some leggings of some sort over her," he said to Lia.

He turned to the others. "Return to the dining hall and keep everyone inside. Bring forth the jugglers, the singer again. Captivate them. No one must see us as we depart. If somebody wants her dead, I want them to believe they have accomplished their task—so I can hunt them down at my leisure."

We could hear the clatter of horses' hooves from outside, through the open doorways.

Cook bent and kissed my forehead. "God be with you, m'lady. Your return shall be my constant prayer."

"And mine as well," Fortino said, bending to kiss my hand, even as Marcello pulled me up and into his arms.

The two turned and scurried out, shouting at servants in the corridor to follow them, return to the feast. Luca appeared and glanced at Lia. "You need water? Food?"

"We need nothing but to get her home," she said, striding past him. Marcello followed her, holding me hard against him as I grew rigid with another seizure, arching back this time. Outside, he handed me to Luca for a moment, mounted, then reached for me, pulling me into his arms, stretching my legs across the mount, the better to hold me through the ride ahead, I assumed. *No attempt at a sidesaddle this time.*

Distantly, I understood that I'd be dead if I fell off the horse. My sides would split open, and it would be all over.

He shouted at the tower guards, and the massive gates were opened before us. Would it be the last time I ever saw Castello Forelli? I felt a wave of sorrow, wishing I was well, able to take one last look.

He kept a firm grip on me as we tore down the path, the same path we'd taken the night of the attack upon Castello Forelli, and later Castello Paratore. I could tell he was trying to be gentle, easing me forward to duck a branch. But every movement was either an agony to my side or a searing to my gut. And my heartbeat was making me crazy. I literally thought it might stop at any point.

Again and again we came to a stop as the pain overtook me and Marcello struggled to not let me slip to the ground. I concentrated on taking one breath at a time, of surviving just one more breath…

In time, we were crossing the creek, climbing the winding path to the top of the hill. To where I had first met him. Luca and Lia were already there, faster on their own horses. Luca held a torch high, waiting by the tomb's entrance, his brow a mass of confusion and frustration and fear. He handed the torch to Lia and reached for me. I pretty much slumped down into his arms. I hurt too much to even think about being embarrassed. I was crying pretty hard by then.

Marcello dismounted and followed Lia into the tomb's entrance, then turned to accept my body from Luca, dragging me inward. Luca followed behind.

When we reached the center, Marcello looked up at Lia, who stood near the handprints, waiting. "You merely touch those, and you will be gone? Back from whence you came?"

"I hope so," Lia said, "for her sake." Her face was a mask of sorrow and fear. "Let me hold her. I do not think that you should be touching us when our hands are on the prints, lest you leap through time with us."

"Mayhap I should," he said, rising, with me in his arms again.

"Mayhap we both should," Luca said, stepping closer.

"Nay," Lia said. "It might keep us from going. And if you were to come to our time—you would be as lost as we felt here."

I panted, the pain constant, but I could not keep my eyes from Marcello's profile, trying to memorize the line of his nose, the curve of his cheek, the strength of the muscles twitching in his jaw and neck.

This was it. One way or another, I was saying good-bye. Forever.

I could tell I was dying then. Because it didn't hurt.

It was more of a dim assessment. An understanding. Fact.

"Gabriella," he said, looking down into my face. "If all it took was for you to touch the prints to return to your own time, why did you and Evangelia not do that as soon as you could?"

"We had to be together," I said, panting. "It doesn't work with just one of us. And there was…you."

His brows lowered a tiny bit. "You stayed—because of me?"

"Forgive me," I said, shaking my head. "I interfered. Between you and Romana. In so many ways."

"Nay," he said, kissing my forehead tenderly, then my lips, for such a brief moment I wondered if I'd dreamed it. He set me on my feet. Lia wrapped her arm around my waist to hold me up, her fingers from her other hand already on her print.

Marcello lifted my hand in his, kissing the pad of each of my fingers, then looking into my eyes. "You did not interfere, Gabriella. I love you. You have stolen my heart," he said, closing my hand in a fist, covering it with his own. "You hold it now. Do you understand that?"

"I do."

"Then, if you love me, Gabriella," he said, his eyes mad with urgency, "as I love you, return to me."

"You cannot ask that of her—" Lia said.

"Return to me," he continued, ignoring her, never looking away from my face, "and you shall find me waiting."

I wanted to tell him there would be no return.

I wanted to tell him to go to Romana and do what he ought. What was expected of him.

But all I could do was watch as he slipped the palm of my hand to the wall, directly above the print.

I cried out as the muscle at my side stretched and the half-healed wound split further open, just as another wave of pain emanated from my gut.

"Gabi!" Lia cried.

I had dragged my hand to the print, and for the first time in hours, I felt heat and pain from something other than my torso, my pounding heart.

The room was stretching, spinning, yawning wide in that fun-house mirror sort of way.

And in a breath, Marcello and Luca were gone from the room, as if they had never been there at all.

CHAPTER 28

I opened my eyes and stared upward, through the hole in the roof of the tomb, up and up to a blue sky. I felt no pain, and for the first time, wondered if I was dead. If this was the afterlife.

This it, God?

I shifted and felt the grit of sand beneath my head, pebbles digging into my back. *Nope, not heaven.* At least, not as I had imagined it.

"Gabi!" Lia groaned, beside me.

I turned and looked at her. She rolled to her hands and knees, then crawled over to me and pulled me into her arms. "Gabi, Gabi. Are you okay?"

I pulled her closer, assessing my limbs and gut. "I—I think so," I said in wonder. I lifted the side of my short, bloody gown and gazed at my skin—it was perfect, whole.

"Come on, we have to get you to a doctor," she said.

But I held onto her, not moving. "No. I—I don't think so."

"What?"

I moved my hand down my ribs to my waist, to where the gash and sutures and wound had been…and felt nothing but skin and muscle, firm. I shook my head. "I'm fine, Lia. Healed. It's as if it never happened."

We heard voices, a shout. Someone was coming.

"Over to the edge," Lia said in an urgent whisper.

We scuttled over to the side of the tomb, out from view of the passageway. Somebody paused at the entrance, shined his light in our direction and paused as if listening. "*Chi c'è?*" *Who is there?*

I covered my mouth, because I suddenly had the insane urge to giggle. Who was there? *Oh, nobody but two girls who just traveled through time. Don't mind us.*

Lia seized my hand and squeezed it, hearing the man begin to crawl inward. We were going to be in so much trouble. But part of me didn't care. How could I? We'd been through so much. Compared to all of that, what was ahead? A grounding? That was nothing. Nothing!

I scrambled to my feet, hands on hips, determined to meet the guard, not as a cowering victim. But as a…as a…she-warrior.

Lia groaned and then came to her feet beside me just as the guard caught sight of us, shouted in alarm, and stared into our faces.

"*Chi sei? Cosa fai?*" He barked the questions, one after the other. *Who are you? What are you doing?*

"We are Gabriella and Evangelia Betarrini," I calmly returned in Italian. Still looking at my bloody gown. It hadn't all been a dream—

"*Sta male?*" he asked, taking a step closer to me, seeing the blood. He wanted to know if I was hurt!

"I am fine, really. I know it looks bad. We…we just seemed to have become a little lost."

Lia coughed beside me, covering a choking laugh. I laughed then. I couldn't help it. *A little lost* was one vast understatement. Lia dissolved into giggles, then, laughing so hard she was shaking. And I was getting carried along with her. The more angry the guard became, shouting questions at us, the more we laughed, almost-wetting-our-pants kind of laughing.

Another guard arrived, setting us off on another round of laughter as he stared at me in my bloody shirt and Lia in her medieval gown. They probably thought we were in the middle of some weird, ritualistic act.

But then Dr. Manero arrived, all stern and a bit triumphant in finding us there. No doubt he'd use it against Mom. Use us as Exhibit A as to why foreign scholars could not be trusted on Italian soil.

It was only as they were ushering us out that I glimpsed the handprints and instantly sobered. They were pushing me forward, ducking my head and forcing me outward, down the passageway, and I wanted to dig in, push back, refuse to go. They were forcing me away from the path.

The only path back.

Back to Marcello.

The only path back…to love.

... a little more ...

When a delightful concert comes to an end,

the orchestra might offer an encore.

When a fine meal comes to an end,

it's always nice to savor a bit of dessert.

When a great story comes to an end,

we think you may want to linger.

And so, we offer ...

AfterWords—just a little something more after you

have finished a David C Cook novel.

We invite you to stay awhile in the story.

Thanks for reading!

Turn the page for ...

- **Discussion Questions**
- **Interview with the Author**
- **Facebook Fan Site**
- **Acknowledgments**
- **Historical Notes**
- **Bibliography**

DISCUSSION QUESTIONS

Grab your girlfriends and have a discussion at your local coffeehouse about this book! Here are a few to get you started:

1. What was your favorite part of the novel, and why?
2. What part of the novel did you not like? Why?
3. What would be hardest about living in 1342? No showers? No hair products? No forks? No technology? No cars? Using a chamber pot? What would you miss most?
4. Did you relate to Gabi? Why? What is it about her that you see in yourself?
5. If you had been Gabi, would you have fallen for Marcello or Luca? Why?
6. Is it ever okay to steal another girl's guy? Why or why not? Why was it okay for Gabi to do so? Or was it?
7. At first, Gabi thinks she can work things out on her own. Find her own way back to the tomb and through it. She's kind of prideful and stubborn about it, even (sneaking out of the castle, climbing down the wall, taking off on the horse, etc.). How does pride sometimes keep us stuck in a tough situation?
8. Do you think all things, good or bad, happen for a reason? Why or why not?
9. Gabi wonders why God has allowed this to happen to her. If it happened to you, would you think it was God? Or something else?
10. What do you think of the concept of "seizing the day"? Meaning, making the most of what you have, right now, right here? What does living that out do for a person?

11. When Gabi is hovering between life and death, she thinks about what she is living for. What do you live for?
12. If one of your parents died, what is one thing they always say that you'd always remember—that would actually help you deal with life?
13. If you could go back to any time period, when would it be and why? (It may be medieval, like this book.) What would be the toughest part of living in those years for you? What would you miss most?

INTERVIEW WITH THE AUTHOR

Q. You've written contemporary romances, historical women's fiction, general fiction, and more. Why turn to YA fiction now?

A. I'm always drawn to a new challenge. And since I have teen and tween daughters in the house, it's been natural for me to start reading some of their fiction alongside them. I was hooked with the Twilight series and Hunger Games books. I wanted to give them something they could hand to their friends as well as read themselves.

***Q. Have they read* Waterfall?**

A. My eldest has. Olivia and her friends were my very first readers. They set me straight on things that would make other kids roll their eyes. Then I handed it off to more readers in my focus group, and they helped me refine the book further.

Q. Was it hard to write in the medieval time period?

A. To a certain extent. I wrote a medieval series for adults, called The Gifted (*The Begotten, The Betrayed, The Blessed*), that I totally loved writing, so in some ways, it was just going back to what I'd learned for that one. Thankfully, I'd spent a lot of time researching for that, so I didn't have to start over!

Q. Why Italy?

A. Because I'm completely in love with Italy. This is the first year in four that we haven't been back, and I'm in withdrawal.

Q. You got to go for research?

A. Yes! Three times for The Gifted, and once, last fall, for this series. There's just something about the place that is totally romantic, warm, and welcoming. It sucks you in. Don't go. Because then you'll be like me and miss it when you're away too long.

Q. What's next for Gabi and Lia?

A. Mmm, I just wrapped *Cascade* (book 2), and I think it's a really solid second book. The adventure and love story continue, of course. But it's even more dramatic and suspenseful than this one!

RIVER OF TIME SERIES FACEBOOK FAN SITE

Wanna chat with others who've read the book? Ask Lisa a question (or ten)? Interested in winning River of Time-oriented prizes? Follow Lisa as she continues to write about these characters, and check out what's happening with the series by "liking" the River of Time Series on Facebook. Then you'll be the first to know!

ACKNOWLEGMENTS

The quote Gabi remembers, "Courage is not the absence of fear, but the decision that something is more important than that fear," was something I heard in *The Princess Diaries.* The quote was originally written by Ambrose Redmoon (aka James Neil Hollingworth.) I thought it was especially appropriate for Gabi to think about, given all she had to deal with. The other quotes she thinks of, mostly attributed to her mom or dad, are quotes that often come to my mind; I'm uncertain where I first picked them up.

While I worked hard to stay historically accurate, a lot of this series is a figment of my imagination. We visited a medieval castle not far from where I placed Castello Forelli—in that region of Tuscany, they seem to be on every other hill. However, all of my characters, including the Paratores and Forellis, are fictional.

Special thanks to Christine Cantera, writer and blogger at WhyGo France and longtime expat, who helped me with all my Italian and French translations.

MANY THANKS go out to my readers in my focus group, the River of Time Tribe girls, who helped me make this book better (and called me out when I was making my teen characters sound too adult): Olivia B., Cynthia Y., Madison B., Megan D., Mandy H., Megan B., Hannah C., Courtney F., Callie G., Kayla G., Beth H., Cierra J., Ciara K., Keighley K., Emma M., Sarah P., Bridget R., Caitlynn R., Mary Kate B., Kaitlin B., Ellie B., Morgan F., Kirsten G., Joyce H., Diamond J., Kaeli N., Haylee S., Emily B., Courtney B., Hannah C.,

Erin C., Bethany D., Stephanie D., Kassidy K., Lindsay, Shelby L., Hannah M., Jordan M., Dongjoo P., Taylor R., Jillian S., Alysa T., and Rebecca T. Thanks, friends!

HISTORICAL NOTES

While I love the research process and seek to honor the facts in my fiction, medieval historians tend to occasionally disagree on the "facts," forcing authors using their materials to make their best guess as to who might be correct. Add in the fact that there are few resources related to pre-Renaissance, medieval Italian history (translated in English), and I was forced to speculate now and again. Some facts are borrowed from known English history, which is better documented (and more easily read/absorbed by this English speaker). All that said, I did my best to bring you a novel that you could trust as being true to the times and yet not get in the way of the story.

In regard to the Etruscans, my description of the tombs is a fictional combination of a number of different sites and configurations found throughout Italy. Although the artifacts and frescoes inside "my" tombs are like those that archaeologists have excavated—with the exception of the two handprints—no known tumuli like I've described have been found in this portion of Tuscany.

Sidesaddles have been documented in artwork from Grecian and Celtic times but didn't really become popular until Anne of Bohemia (1366–1394) made them her preferred mode of transportation. Later, Catherine de' Medici had her own version, and it developed from there. I added in my own version of the sidesaddle to this series because I couldn't quite imagine the female nobility of Toscana riding astride in their long skirts and thought it fair to utilize such conjecture.

Siena and Florence battled each other for hundreds of years. Lords had their own hilltop castles, the remains of which you can see throughout Tuscany, and were therefore always seeking to extend—or forced to protect—their borders. Politically religious divisions (Guelph and Ghibelline) did not help assuage the upheaval, which did not cease until 1555, when Florence succeeded in conquering Siena once and for all. But my specific battles, of course, are a work of fiction, as are my characters.

I make no claim to be a "historian," but I love history, and my research often gives me new plot turns or aspects of life that enhance my story. What follows is a bibliography—a list of the resources I found most helpful in researching this series and attempting to get my facts right. If you're interested in the medieval era, you might check some of them out. (Frances and Joseph Gies are particularly readable/accessible.) If you actually go that far, be sure to email me through the River of Time series Facebook page—I'll give you a virtual pat on the back, and we can discuss things like trenchers and wiping your face with the tablecloth after dinner.

Lisa T. Bergren

BIBLIOGRAPHY

Alighieri, Dante. *The Divine Comedy.* Illustrations by Sandro Botticelli. Translated by Allen Mandelbaum. New York: Alfred A. Knopf, 1995.

Feo, Giovanni. *The Hilltop Towns of the Fiora Valley.* Pitigliano, Grosseto: Editrice Laurum, 2005.

Gies, Joseph and Frances. *Daily Life in Medieval Times.* New York: Barnes & Noble Books, 1990.

———. *Women in the Middle Ages.* New York: Harper Perennial, 1978.

Hyde, J. K. *Society and Politics in Medieval Italy.* London: Macmillan Press, 1973.

Kleinhenz, Christopher, ed. *Medieval Italy: An Encyclopedia.* New York: Routledge, 2004.

Martinelli, Maurizio and Giulio Paolucci. *Guide to the Places of the Etruscans.* Edited by Claudio Strinati. Florence, Italy: SCALA Group, S.p.A., 2007.

Norris, Herbert. *Medieval Costume and Fashion.* Mineola, NY: Dover Publications, 1998.

Pellegrini, Enrico. *The Etruscans of Pitigliano.* Translated by Patrizia Vittimberga. Pitigliano, Grosseto: Editrice Laurum, 2005.

Strehlow, Dr. Wighard and Dr. Gottfried Hertzka. *Hildegard of Bingen's Medicine.* Santa Fe, NM: Bear & Company, 1987.